A Mother's Sorrow

Margaret Dickinson

A Mother's Sorrow

MACMILLAN

First published 2024 by Macmillan
an imprint of Pan Macmillan
The Smithson, 6 Briset Street, London EC1M 5NR
EU representative: Macmillan Publishers Ireland Ltd, 1st Floor,
The Liffey Trust Centre, 117–126 Sheriff Street Upper,
Dublin 1, D01 YC43
Associated companies throughout the world
www.panmacmillan.com

ISBN 978-1-0350-2458-2

1 3 5 7 9 8 6 4 2

A CIP catalogue record for this book is available from the British Library.

Typeset in Sabon by Palimpsest Book Production Ltd, Falkirk, Stirlingshire
Printed and bound by CPI Group (UK) Ltd, Croydon, CR0 4YY

Visit **www.panmacmillan.com** to read more about all our books
and to buy them. You will also find features, author interviews and
news of any author events, and you can sign up for e-newsletters
so that you're always first to hear about our new releases.

For all my family and friends for their love, encouragement and help throughout the years

One

Sheffield, September 1892

'Get out of this house and don't you dare show your face here ever again.'

Tears streamed down Mary Ellen's cheeks as her father shook his fist in her face. She stood before him, broken and shamed, waiting for a sharp slap, but the blow never came. He had never, in all her seventeen years, struck Mary Ellen. His wife, Edith, and even Flora, his eldest daughter, had felt the back of Patrick Halliday's hand more than once. But Mary Ellen had always been his favourite. Until this moment.

'You can go to him,' he spat. 'Whoever he is, seeing as you won't even tell us who the father of your bastard is.' He paused and added bitterly, 'I would never have thought it of you, Mary Ellen, but when I heard you retching into the chamber pot in your bedroom early one morning, I knew. It was just like your mother was when she was expecting.'

The tears flowed faster as Mary Ellen whispered plaintively, 'Mam . . .?'

But there was no help to be had from Edith. She had been controlled and cowed since the day of her marriage to Patrick. Her parents had known he was hardworking and they'd believed he would care for Edith and whatever family they might have.

'You'd do well to take him,' her mother had said. 'You're not exactly the prettiest girl in the street, now, are you? You might never get another offer.'

In Edith's world, it was all a girl in her position could hope for: to be married and to devote her life to caring for her husband and family. What neither she nor her parents realized then was that Patrick was a quick-tempered bully.

The first time Edith appeared at her old home with a bruise on the side of her face, her mother had been shocked. 'I never would have believed that of him. He's not the man I thought he was.'

An only child, Edith had been born and brought up in a two-up-two-down terraced house, in a street south-west of Sheffield town centre. Her father worked at a local cutlery factory and it had been there that he'd met Patrick Halliday and invited him home to tea.

'He's an enterprising young man,' he'd told his wife and daughter. 'He'll go far. Rumour is that the boss has got his eye on him to be a foreman even though he's only young. He's a hard worker, I'll give him that. Our Edith could do worse.'

And so Edith had accepted Patrick's proposal and they'd settled into the terraced house where he'd been born and had lived on his own since the death of both his parents. It was situated in the next street to where her parents lived but a world away from the life she had known with them. The front door opened from the street directly into a narrow hallway with doors to both the front parlour and the kitchen on the left, while the staircase was directly ahead. The parlour was hardly ever used. It was the best room, with just a few ornaments which had belonged to Patrick's mother in a china cabinet and on the mantelpiece. They were his treasured possessions and Edith's hands shook whenever she dusted them. The kitchen was where the family lived day to day and contained the range where Edith did all the cooking. A small scullery had been built onto the back of the house and, across the backyard, was the privy and a wash house with a copper in one corner.

Although it was a friendly street, with the neighbours watching out for each other through good times and bad, Edith had not been able to make close friends with anyone; Patrick would not allow it. Even the two sisters, Flora and Mary Ellen, had never been allowed to play out in the street, at least not when their father was around. By the time he was due home, they were both washed and dressed in their prettiest dresses or playing quietly together in their bedroom upstairs.

Edith had worked hard all her life to keep her home neat and tidy and as clean as was possible in a town where factory chimneys belched smoke all day long. A hot meal was always on the table for Patrick when he came home after a long day at the cutlery factory. He was the master in the house and no one was ever allowed to forget it. From the day she first crossed the threshold, her days became one long, endless life of drudgery and fear. Everything had to be kept just as his mother had left it when she'd died and everything must be done the way she had done it. The only joy Edith knew were the births of her two daughters. But even in this, Patrick complained. 'You're useless, woman. You can't even give me a son to be proud of.'

Although Patrick demanded his 'rights' almost every night, there were no more children. Patrick took little notice of Flora, their first born, still no doubt hoping that the next one would be a son. But when Mary Ellen was born two years later, he looked down at her and was enchanted. All thoughts of a boy were forgotten in that moment. The baby, even then, reminded him of his mother; the only woman he had ever truly loved and respected. 'She's to be called Mary Ellen,' he'd decreed. 'After my mam. The finest woman who ever drew breath.'

As the two girls had grown, Edith loved them both equally, but Patrick's attention was wholly on Mary Ellen. She was a pretty little girl with golden curls, blue eyes and a sunny smile. Flora promised to be a handsome woman rather than a great beauty. She had even features with a firm jawline, dark brown hair and brown eyes. But there was determination in her face. And it seemed she was going to need all the strength of character she could muster right now.

She moved forward and stood beside her sister. She lifted her chin and faced their father. The years had not been kind to Patrick Halliday. He was thin and already round-shouldered, even though he was only forty-one. His features were sharp, his eyes beady and filled with bitterness. Once, he had been strong and upright, but his muscular strength had wasted through years of being a foreman. He had not needed to do physical labour for some years. He was not well-liked among his work mates and the only people he mixed with outside work and his home were the bar staff at the local pub, which he frequented most nights except Sunday.

'And do you know why she's in the family way?' Flora said bravely.

Patrick's mouth twisted. 'Because she's a dirty little trollop who's let some – some tom cat have his way with her.'

'No, Father, that's not the reason. The truth is, she's never been taught the facts of life. Neither of us have. She wouldn't have known what he was doing. She certainly didn't understand what the result would be. I doubt she even knew she was pregnant until now.'

Patrick's mouth curled. 'Don't try to tell me that. Yer mam must have told you. You did, didn't you, Edith?'

Edith was thin with her brown hair drawn back into an unbecoming bun. It was dull and lifeless, with none of the sheen that had been there in her younger days. There were even flecks of grey already. Her skin was sallow; she only ever went out into the backyard to hang out the washing or to the shops once a week. Her once warm brown eyes were now frightened and wary. As her husband snapped his question at her, Edith dropped her head and turned away and Patrick had his answer. He turned back to Flora. 'So how come you're so clever, miss? Who taught you? Some feller showed you an' all, did he?'

'No, I learned from the girls at school. I only wish I'd told Mary Ellen. I'm sorry now that I didn't.'

'Not half as sorry as she'll be. She's out. She's to pack her things and go. I won't have shame brought to my door. I'll be a laughing stock among the fellers at work. I'll never be able to hold my head up again if they find out. I'm their foreman. I've got to have their respect.'

It was all about him and his reputation, never about his wife and daughters. But Flora stood her ground as she said quietly, 'If she goes, then I go too.'

Still Edith said nothing. She sank into a chair by the range and covered her face with her hands.

'Go, then.' Patrick shook his fist in Flora's face. 'But don't think that *you*'ll be missed, because you won't be.'

Patrick slammed out of the house, the back door shuddering on its hinges.

Mary Ellen broke into fresh sobs and buried her face against her sister's shoulder. 'Oh Flora, don't do that. What will Mam do without you? He'll be so unkind to her.'

Edith lifted her head, her face creased with sorrow. 'You go with her, Flora. I want you to. None of this is your fault. Either of you. I've brought it all on myself. I should never have listened to my parents.' She stood up, moved towards her daughters and put her arms around them. 'You have both brought me the only real love and joy I've ever known. Even my childhood wasn't exactly happy. My parents were strict and never showed me any affection.' She sighed. 'If they ever had any. I was expected to do as I was told, even to the choice of the man I married. How I wish I'd had half your strength, Flora, and stood up to them. But it's all too late now. My life is not going to change, but yours can. So go together and take care of each other, that's all I ask.'

The three women stood together, their arms around one another.

'But are you going to be all right, Mam?' Flora said. 'Like Mary Ellen says, he'll be so cruel to you.'

'As long as I know you're both safe, I can cope. You must write to me if you possibly can. Now, I have a little money I've squirrelled away over the years. You must take it.'

The sisters packed their few belongings into a carpet bag and were gone by the time Patrick came back late that night. Edith had no idea where he'd been, for it was a Sunday evening and the pub was closed. But she didn't dare ask.

As the two young women climbed the hill leading out of the town towards the Derbyshire countryside, Mary Ellen gasped as she struggled to keep up with her sister's long strides. 'What about your Bert? Shouldn't you tell him?'

A lump rose in Flora's throat as she thought of the young man she'd been walking out with for the last three months. Only Mary Ellen knew about the romance; Flora had thought it best to keep it a secret from both her parents. At least, for now. Bert worked in the same factory as their father, but in the purchasing department. He was an office worker and wore a smart suit, a white collar and a neat tie to work. He lived with his widowed mother, Agnes, in a terraced house a few streets away.

'We've got a tiny frontage,' Bert had told her with

a laugh, 'but you can hardly call it a garden. No grass, just paving slabs. Ma likes to grow flowers in pots and in a window box.'

The house was slightly larger than where the Hallidays lived. It had three bedrooms, though the third was scarcely bigger than a box room, and it also boasted a small cellar. Flora had yet to meet Agnes but already she liked the sound of Bert's mother. She was an outgoing, generous woman who only wanted her son to find the right girl and settle down. Since Bert's father had died relatively young after a nasty accident at work, her whole focus had been on her son but she was not a jealous or possessive mother. All she wanted was his happiness and he, in turn, would always take care of her. It was too early in their relationship to talk of marriage, but Flora knew instinctively that Agnes would always be part of their lives if they did marry.

'I'll write to him when we get settled somewhere,' Flora said now to her sister. She didn't voice her concerns to Mary Ellen but she wondered how both Bert and his mother might react to the news that Flora's sister was to have an illegitimate child. Perhaps the blossoming romance would be over before it had hardly begun.

'But where? Where are we going?' Mary Ellen's anxious voice broke into her thoughts.

Flora's footsteps slowed. Taking Abbeydale Road and the Baslow Road, they'd walked for several hours late into the night – or even early morning – Flora didn't know which. They'd reached the edge of the town and now only the open countryside lay before them in the darkness. It was daunting to two young girls who'd only known town life with its rows of houses, any one of which would help them if they knocked on the door. But the open fields and winding roads were alien to them.

'Come on, Mary Ellen. We'll find somewhere to sleep tonight. Thank goodness the weather's still warm. A hayloft will do nicely and then, tomorrow, I'll find work. We'll be all right. I promise. Come on. Best foot forward.'

Two

After dealing them a cruel blow, Fate now seemed to be trying to help. They found a farmer's barn at the edge of a field and snuggled into the hayloft for the night. They left early the following morning before they might be discovered. They'd walked some distance by the time the sun was up and still there was no sign of a village or a small shop. They'd been walking for a couple of hours and already Mary Ellen was tired.

'Oh, do let's rest, Flora. My feet hurt.'

'Just for a while, then.'

They sat down on the grass verge and turned their faces to the warm September sun. Mary Ellen lay down and was soon asleep, but Flora could not rest; she was too worried. Whatever were they to do? Where could they go? She hadn't heard of many places in Derbyshire though she thought that perhaps they'd passed over the border by now. She'd heard of Chesterfield with its crooked spire and of Chatsworth House, where a duke lived, and the plague village, Eyam. And then there was a little town called Bakewell, where the famous Bakewell puddings came from. Maybe . . .? As her thoughts wandered as to where they might aim for, she heard the rattle of a carrier's cart coming towards them from the direction they had come.

'Mary Ellen, wake up.' She shook her sister's shoulder. 'There's a cart coming. Maybe he'll give us a lift.'

Mary Ellen groaned as she roused herself. 'But where to, Flora? Where are we going?'

'Wherever he's going.' Flora stood up and waved to the man sitting on the front of his cart behind the two horses.

'Whoa there, whoa,' he shouted above the noise of the wheels and drew to a halt beside them. He gave them a wide, toothless grin. 'And where might you two pretty maids be off to this fine morning?'

Flora smiled up at him. 'Wherever you're going would be such a help, if you'd be kind enough to give us a lift.' She ran her tongue nervously round her lips and came to a decision. There was no time to discuss it with Mary Ellen before she said, 'We're heading towards Bakewell.'

'I'm going in the right direction, miss, but on'y as far as Baslow. Bakewell's on'y about five or six miles further on though. Will that do you?'

'I'm sure it will. Thank you. Come on, Mary Ellen. Up you get.'

They climbed up, squeezing onto the seat beside the driver. As they travelled, the talkative man pointed out all the landmarks on the way. Flora was grateful; one day she would have to make the return journey home and she wanted to be sure she knew the way. Her first thought at the moment was for Mary Ellen, but if she could get her sister settled somewhere safe,

Flora wanted to go back to make sure her mother was all right. And then there was Bert. She owed him a proper explanation.

'Now, that over there,' the carrier was saying, 'is the parkland of Chatsworth House where the Duke of Devonshire lives. You can't see the house from here but it's a grand place. He owns a lot of the land and properties around these parts. If you're looking for work, you could do worse than find a job on the estate.'

'Thank you. I'll remember that.'

As they drew into the village the carrier pulled up in front of a small shop that looked as if it sold anything and everything.

'This is where I'm making a delivery.'

As the two girls climbed down, Flora said, 'Thank you so much for your kindness.'

'Safe travels to you both,' the carrier said as he tipped his cap in farewell.

Flora and Mary Ellen walked a short distance down the road before Flora said, 'When he's gone, we'll go back to the shop. I can see it sells bread and milk.'

'I'm so hungry and thirsty, Flora.'

'Let's sit on this low wall and we'll be able to see when the carrier leaves.'

It was already well past midday and they'd had nothing to eat since the previous evening when they'd finished the last of the sandwiches their mother had packed for them. When the carrier left, his cart rattling back up the road the way he had come, Flora and Mary Ellen went into the shop. With the little money their mother had given them, Flora bought a bottle of milk.

'I don't reckon I've seen you before.' The jovial shopkeeper smiled. 'I wouldn't have forgotten you. Not from around here, are you?'

Flora hesitated. He looked a kind and friendly man. Tall and rotund with a beaming face for all his customers. He wore a striped apron and a straw hat.

Flora sighed and decided to be truthful. 'No, we're from Sheffield, but we're looking for work. I – I don't suppose you know anyone who might need someone to help with housework or – or something like that. Or if there might be any jobs going on the Chatsworth estate.'

The man glanced from one to the other, biting his lower lip in thought. Flora knew he was assessing them and knew exactly what he was seeing. Two girls – one with a determined set to her face and an angry look, the other sorrowful, her face still showing signs of the tears she had shed. He was a shrewd observer and his next words confirmed it.

'Trouble at home, lass, 'ave yer?'

Flora lifted her head even higher. Wherever their journey would take them, there was no point in lying. 'You could say that, mister, yes.'

The big man sighed. 'Aye well, it happens. 'Specially with lasses.' He was thoughtful for a few moments as if mulling over the problem. 'There's nothing I know of in this village just now. Folks often put cards in my window if they're looking for workers, but there's nothing at the moment. You could try a little further on. Towards Bakewell and mebbe even beyond that. There's farms along the way. They're sometimes glad of a helping hand.' He pulled a face. 'Though perhaps not so much at this time of the year. We're coming into autumn and harvest's just over, so there won't be as much happening on the land as in the spring and summer. Still, it'd be worth a try. Farmers are still threshing, of course, but that's heavy work for lasses.' Flora wasn't sure what he meant but, even though her heart was sinking, she said politely, 'Thank you for your suggestion. It's a help.'

'Look, I'll make you both a cheese sandwich to help you on your way.' He smiled. 'On the house.'

'That's very kind of you.'

He packed up several sandwiches for them that would last them through the day and insisted they take another bottle of milk.

'Good luck,' he said as he stood in the doorway of his shop to wave them off. 'I only wish I could help you more.'

'You've been very kind,' Flora said, shaking his hand. 'Thank you.'

They set off once more and walked and rested through the afternoon. They passed one or two farms, making enquiries at each one to see if they could find work of any kind.

'Oh Flora, what are we going to do? I'm so sorry. This is all my fault. You should go back home. Leave me . . .'

'I'll do nothing of the sort. Now, come on. Let's find somewhere to sleep for the night.'

They were both very tired and already the sun was sinking behind the hills.

'There.' Mary Ellen pointed. 'There's a barn at the edge of that field.'

'It looks a bit tumble-down,' Flora said doubtfully. 'I'm not sure it's safe.'

'Oh Flora, I'm so tired. I could fall asleep on me feet.'

'All right. We'll go and look.'

They stepped inside the opening where a door should have been. The wind whistled through the numerous holes in the walls, but there was one corner that still had a couple of bales of hay stacked against the wall and seemed dry.

'This will do for tonight,' Flora said. 'We can't be far from Bakewell now. Tomorrow, we'll have a good look around there.' She tried to inject optimism into her tone as she added, 'I'm sure we'll find something.'

But Mary Ellen's eyes filled with easy tears. 'I don't think we will, Flora. We should go back to Sheffield. I'll – I'll go into the workhouse.'

'You'll do no such thing,' Flora declared stoutly. 'Not while I've breath in my body.'

Mary Ellen smiled weakly at the fierceness in her sister's tone. 'You're very good to me, Flora. I don't deserve it.'

'Now, we'll have none of that talk. Here, lie down on my coat and we'll put yours on top of us and cuddle up together to keep warm.'

The following day, they passed through Bakewell, pausing to gaze longingly in the window of a bakery at the array of bread, pies and puddings.

'Thanks to that shopkeeper's kindness yesterday,' Flora said, 'we've still got a little money left. Shall we buy something to eat? Maybe they'll give us a drink of water for free.'

'We can only try,' Mary Ellen murmured. She was looking very tired, with dark circles under her eyes. Flora was increasingly worried about her.

They went into the shop. A plump, motherly woman greeted them with a wide smile. 'Now, my dears, what can I get you?'

Flora held out the coins in the palm of her hand. 'Whatever this will buy and could we – beg a drink of water?' She hated using the word beg, but there was no other word for it. To think they were reduced to this.

'Tell you what, I've some bread and cakes left from Saturday. They're still quite all right' – she gave a short laugh – 'but my customers are a fussy lot. They like everything freshly baked. You can have them for a penny.'

The woman fetched two cups of water and then she wrapped up a loaf and four buns and accepted Flora's penny. 'And I've put in a small Bakewell pudding. We're famous for it, you know.'

'You've been very kind,' Flora said. 'Thank you. I don't suppose you know of anyone who might have a job for us, do you?'

The woman glanced shrewdly from one to the other. 'I'm sorry, I don't. But if you take the road towards Rowsley that leads on to Matlock, you might find something there.'

'Thank you.'

They walked on again and after about four miles they came to a little village.

'I can hear trains,' Mary Ellen murmured.

'And I can hear water,' Flora said. 'It might be a river.'

Following the sound, they came to a bridge across which a long lane led further into the countryside. 'Let's follow it,' Flora suggested impulsively. 'I'm sure there'll be a farm up there somewhere. Maybe we can find shelter for tonight and then decide what we're going to do tomorrow.'

'Ought we to stop now, Flora? I don't like the look of those black clouds over there.'

Flora glanced ahead of them and saw dark skies on the horizon. She thought she heard the distant rumble of thunder. 'Come on. Let's get going. I'm sure there'll be somewhere along this lane where we can shelter.'

They walked as quickly as they could up the lane that twisted and turned until they came to a pair of double gates, beyond which stood a mansion, its frontage facing over the dale below with a river running through it.

'Oh my!' Mary Ellen breathed. 'That place looks as if it might have a lot of servants. I wonder . . .'

But at that moment a crack of thunder just above made them jump and they felt the first huge drops of rain.

'We'd better find shelter,' Flora said. 'Come on, we'll go a bit further. I don't like the look of that dog tied up outside the door. Perhaps we can come back here later to ask.'

They hurried on, round a sharp corner, until they came to a farm gate. Ahead were several barns and a farmhouse. The rain was falling heavily now and soon their coats were soaked.

'Quick, Mary Ellen. Into the nearest barn.'

'Is there a dog?'

'I don't think so. Come on, look sharp.'

Ducking their heads against the deluge, they scurried across the yard and into the nearest barn.

'I'm wet through,' Mary Ellen moaned.

'I'm sorry. That was my fault,' Flora said. 'You were right. We should have stopped when you suggested it.'

As her eyes became accustomed to the dimness, Flora looked about her and spotted a ladder leading to what she presumed would be a hayloft. 'Let's go up there. It'll be warmer and drier among the hay and we won't be so easily found, either. And we ought to get out of these wet things. I don't want you catching a chill.'

They both took off their outer garments and snuggled down in the hay, their arms wrapped around each other to keep warm.

As the storm passed, it grew dark outside.

'There doesn't seem to be anyone coming into the barn. Let's stay here for tonight.'

They drank the last of the milk and ate the bread, buns and the pudding the shopkeeper had given them.

'We'll find something tomorrow,' Flora said, injecting more hope into her tone than she was actually feeling. 'Try to get some sleep now.'

Three

Mary Ellen fell asleep but Flora lay awake for some time, staring into the darkness and listening to the creaking and rustling of the old barn. She was physically tired, but her mind was wide awake. She was so worried. Mary Ellen was already looking pale and exhausted and they had only left home two days earlier. If they couldn't find somewhere soon, she feared for her sister's health. Getting a soaking like they'd just had wouldn't do her any good either.

At last, Flora fell into a troubled sleep but as the early morning light filtered through the cracks in the wall, she was startled awake by a cry from her sister.

'Oh – oh, Flora. Something's happening. I have the most awful pain. Aaah . . .'

Flora pushed the straw aside and looked down at her sister's abdomen and then, lower, she saw the stain spreading on her dress. Mary Ellen was bleeding and, by the look of it, quite badly.

Flora scrambled to her feet. 'I'll fetch help.'

'No, Flora, you can't. We'll . . .'

But Flora had gone, climbing as quickly as she could down the ladder, running out of the barn and across the yard to the farmhouse. She ignored the barking dog, chained to its kennel, and banged on the back door. 'Help! Please help me.'

It was opened by a burly farmer. 'Hello, love. What's up?'

'It's my sister. She's bleeding badly.'

The farmer glanced over her shoulder towards the gateway.

'I – I'm sorry, mister. We've been sleeping in your barn.'

The man blinked and then looked down at her, searching her face. 'That's all right. I don't mind. But she's bleeding, you say? Has she hurt herself?'

'I – she – I think it's the baby.' The final words came out in a rush. There would be no hiding the brutal truth now.

'Ah,' he said, as if understanding in that moment what might have brought them to be sleeping rough in his barn. 'I'll get the wife.'

Moments later a plump, motherly woman with her grey hair fastened into a bun at the nape of her neck came to the door, drying her hands on a towel. 'Now then, love. Let's go and have a look at your sister.'

As she stepped across the threshold, another figure appeared behind her. A younger man with broad shoulders, curly brown hair and a smile that crinkled his cheeks and lit up his dark brown eyes. 'What's up, Mam?'

'There's a lass in the barn needs help, Jack. I'll call you if I need you or your dad.'

Flora hurried across the yard at her side. 'I'm sorry if we trespassed, missus, but –'

The woman waved away her protestations. 'Don't

worry about that now. Let's see how we can help you. Where is she?'

'In the hayloft.'

The farmer's wife climbed carefully up the ladder and stepped onto the floor of the loft. She heard Mary Ellen's moans coming from the far corner of the loft and hurried towards her. Blood now soaked the girl's skirt and the hay around her.

'Oh, you poor lass.' The woman dropped to her knees beside her. She lifted Mary Ellen's skirt. 'She's had a miscarriage,' she said softly to Flora. 'We must get help for her at once. Go and tell my husband to send Jack for Mrs Beckett. She's unqualified as a midwife, but she's brought more babbies safely into the world than I can count. She'll tell us what to do for the best. I'm used to birthing lambs, but not babbies.'

Flora scurried back down the ladder and ran across the yard. Banging on the back door again, she shouted, 'Mister, mister, are you there?'

The door was opened again by the farmer. Before he could speak, Flora burst out, 'The missus says to send Jack for Mrs Beckett.'

'Is it coming, then?'

Flora bit her lip. 'The missus says she – she's lost it. There's blood everywhere.'

The man turned and bellowed. 'Jack! Take the pony and trap into the village and fetch Mrs Beckett. Quick as you can. T'lass needs help.'

The young man Flora now knew to be called Jack, pushed past her, thrusting his arms into his jacket as he ran across the yard and disappeared into a stable at the side of the barn. Moments later, he appeared again leading a pony.

'I'll help him,' the farmer muttered and hurried to where Jack was now trying to harness the pony into the shafts of a trap. It seemed an agonizing wait until Jack flapped the reins and drove out of the yard.

The farmer returned to where Flora was still standing. 'If Mrs Beckett's at home, he'll bring her back.'

'I don't know how to thank you, mister,' she said huskily.

'You go back to your sister. See if there's owt you can do.'

Flora nodded and hurried back across the yard. As she put her foot on the bottom rung of the ladder, she heard the farmer's wife call out. 'That you, lass?'

'Yes, missus.'

'Before you come back up, go and ask Mr Clarke for a bucket of hot water. There's a clean one under the sink, tell him. And get him to find you some towels.'

Flora did as she was asked.

'I'll come back with you,' the farmer said, after he'd filled a bucket with hot water from the tap in the kitchen range and found three old, but clean, towels. In the barn, he climbed the ladder carefully and handed the bucket to his wife.

Mary Ellen was crying pitifully. 'Flora! Flora, where are you?'

'I'm here, darling. I'm coming back up in a minute.'

As the farmer stepped back onto the ground, he

22

said, 'Right, lass, up you go. I'll bring Mrs Beckett across as soon as they get back. Let's just pray she's at home. In the meantime, I'll fetch a lantern. It's a bit dark up there to be able to see properly.'

'You're very kind.'

'Aye well, we're not a family who turns its back on someone in trouble. Up you go, lass, and see what you can do.'

'Oh Flora, Flora. I'm so sorry.' Mary Ellen gripped her sister's hand as she knelt beside her while the farmer's wife – whom Flora now knew to be called Mrs Clarke – washed away the blood as best she could and wrapped the tiny mite who had never drawn breath in one of the old towels.

'It's too early for me to tell whether it was a boy or a girl,' Mrs Clarke whispered to Flora. 'Poor little scrap.'

At last, they heard the wheels of the pony and trap rattling into the yard and moments later a voice called out. 'Mrs Clarke? Iris Beckett here. I'm coming up.'

A plump, rosy-cheeked woman of about fifty poked her head through the opening and climbed the last few steps, breathing heavily. 'My word, I'm glad my patients don't normally give birth in such a place. Now then, let's have a look at you.'

Mrs Clarke and Flora moved aside and Mrs Beckett knelt beside Mary Ellen. 'Eee, lass, you've got yourself into a right mess, haven't you?' She was silent for a moment while she gently examined Mary Ellen before saying quietly, 'I'm sorry you've lost the baby, love, but everything's come away cleanly as it should.

23

There's no lasting harm done.' Iris Beckett bit her lip, wanting to ask more questions, but not knowing quite how to phrase them.

As if guessing her dilemma, Mrs Clarke said, 'These two girls will be staying here for a while, Mrs Beckett, at least until this lass is well enough to travel. We'll look after them both.'

'Do you mean here? In the loft?'

'Goodness me, no, Mrs Beckett.' For a moment the farmer's wife sounded affronted at such a thought. 'My husband and son will move her gently into the house. We have plenty of bedrooms and there's only the three of us.'

Iris Beckett beamed at her. 'I'm not surprised. I know you to be a good Christian family. You're certainly not the sort to "pass by on the other side".' She struggled to her feet. 'Then in that case, I'll call again in a day or two to see how she's faring. In the meantime, don't hesitate to send for me if you have any worries.'

'What do we owe you, Mrs Beckett?'

The woman stood a moment looking down at the pale, strained face of her patient. 'I'll do the same as you this time, Mrs Clarke. Me Christian duty. There'll be no charge.'

'Then let me find half a dozen eggs for you.'

'That would be very kind.'

As the two women climbed carefully down the ladder, Flora moved closer to Mary Ellen and took her hand. 'How do you feel, darling?'

'Sore,' her sister whispered. 'How kind they all are. But – but surely they must realize . . .?'

24

'Hush.' Flora patted her hand. 'I'm sure they do, but it sounds as if they're good, churchgoing folk . . .'

Mary Ellen pulled a face. 'But we're not. When they find out, what then?'

Now that the danger for her sister had passed, Flora was able to chuckle as she said, 'Maybe we'll have to be while we stay with them.'

Four

A little while later, Matthew Clarke and his son Jack lowered Mary Ellen down from the loft in a hammock. Then Jack lifted her up into his arms as if she weighed no more than a sack of feathers. He carried her into the house, up the stairs, and laid her gently on the bed his mother had prepared. For a moment he stood looking down at her wan face and his eyes softened. 'We'll look after you,' he said gently, repeating his mother's earlier promise. Then with a nod and a quick smile towards Flora, he left the room.

'You'll be in the bedroom right next door,' Winnie Clarke said to Flora. 'Leave both doors ajar so that if she needs you in the night, then she can call you. And don't be afraid to wake me.' She laughed softly. 'We're used to being up at all times of the night when we're lambing or calving. Now,' she glanced from one to the other. 'Will you tell me your names? I can't go on calling you both "lass".'

'I'm Flora and this is Mary Ellen.' Flora hesitated for a moment and then added, 'Halliday.'

Winnie nodded. 'I'm not going to pry, but I have to ask you one more question. Am I likely to get a policeman knocking on my door? Will anyone have reported you missing?'

The sisters exchanged a glance. Mary Ellen closed her eyes as she whispered weakly, 'You can tell her, Flora. I'm sure she's guessed anyway. And it's only fair we tell these kind people the truth.'

Exhausted by the trauma at home, the long walk and the miscarriage, Mary Ellen fell asleep while Flora explained quietly all that had happened. As she fell silent, Winnie said, 'You poor girls. Matthew and I have a wonderful son, but we were never blessed with a daughter. If we had been, neither of us would ever have turned our back on her whatever she'd done. I'll talk to Matthew and Jack, but I'm sure they'll agree with me that you can both stay here until Mary Ellen is quite well again and then we'll help you decide what you do next.' She glanced down at Mary Ellen's pale face and murmured, more to herself than to Flora, 'Poor lass.'

Then Winnie shook herself and said more strongly, 'While she's sleeping, you come down to the kitchen. I'm sure you're ready for something to eat and drink.'

'But – but it's not morning yet.'

Winnie laughed softly. 'It is in this house. We get up at five-thirty every day – even Sundays, because animals still have to be fed – and it's well past that now. We were just getting up when you knocked on the door.'

What the farmer's wife had said was absolutely true, for when Flora stepped into the kitchen it was to find a warm fire burning in the grate of the range and the two men seated at the scrubbed table eating a hearty breakfast of bacon, eggs, sausage and fried bread.

Matthew waved his fork towards Flora. 'Sit your-self down, lass. The missus will get you summat to eat.'

'It's Flora,' Winnie butted in as she bustled about, breaking eggs into a bowl and setting the frying pan on the hob on the range. 'And her sister's called Mary Ellen.'

Both Matthew and Jack nodded and smiled at her.

Flora smiled tentatively and then glanced around her. She had never seen such a big kitchen. But this was a farm; there would be crops growing, animals grazing on green grass and a wide, open sky.

It was a world away from the life Flora and Mary Ellen knew. To the girl from the back streets of Sheffield, the farmhouse seemed huge.

As both men stood up, ready to start their day's work, Jack glanced down at her. 'I've a long day ahead of me with the threshing but after I've seen to the animals tonight, I'll show you around, if you'd like.'

'Oh, I would. Thank you. I've never seen a farm before.'

For a moment, Jack looked as if he didn't quite believe her so she smiled and added, 'We're townies. We've walked to the outskirts of Sheffield now and again, but we've never been this far into the coun-tryside. To be honest, I don't know exactly where we are.'

'You're in Derbyshire.' Jack smiled. 'Our nearest town is Bakewell or, if you go in the other direction, Matlock.'

Flora nodded. 'Yes, we came through Bakewell

yesterday but we've never been on a farm before. I'd love to look around.'

Jack grinned. 'See you later, then.'

As the two men left, Winnie placed a plate of food in front of her. Flora thought she wouldn't be able to eat a thing, but catching the aroma of eggs, bacon and fried bread, she suddenly found she was ravenously hungry.

Ten minutes later she sat back and sighed. 'That was wonderful. Thank you so much.'

'Keep an eye on your sister and when she's ready we'll give her a little porridge to start with.'

Flora rose from her chair. 'How can I help you?'

Winnie regarded her for a moment. 'Are you any good at ironing?'

Flora hid her smile, remembering the mountains of ironing she'd done at home to help her mother. 'I like to think so,' she said solemnly.

'Right, then. I'll set you up on the table here with my ironing blanket. I have two flat irons on the go at once, heating them here on the range hob. I'll fetch the basket in from the wash house.'

While Winnie fetched the basket, Flora cleared the breakfast table and took the dirty pots to the sink in the scullery. The rest of the morning passed pleasantly enough, though Flora was still desperately worried about her sister. She kept running up the stairs to check on her but Mary Ellen was still sleeping soundly.

'Best thing for her,' Winnie said, as she lowered the clothes airer down from the ceiling for Flora to put the items on as she ironed them.

'While you're doing that, lass, I can get on with

preparing the dinner.' She smiled at Flora's puzzled look. 'I'd better explain. As you already know, farming folk rise early. Breakfast's always at six so we have our main meal of the day at noon, though the menfolk call in for a cuppa about ten o'clock. Then tea is at five and supper at nine. We're always in bed by ten. I don't know what your routine was at home, but that's what we do.'

'A little different,' Flora acknowledged. 'Our household revolved around my father. He works in one of the factories so we always got up fairly early, but our main meal was in the evening when he came home.'

'I suppose our days are organized to accommodate the animals and their needs,' Winnie said thoughtfully, 'but I can see how it would be for you. Do you have a job, Flora?'

'Yes, I'm a buffer girl.'

When Winnie looked mystified, Flora smiled and explained.

'You'll know that Sheffield is renowned for its steel making and engineering and also for its cutlery trade. There are large factories making cutlery – my father works in one of them – but there are also a myriad of little workshops dotted throughout the town.' She smiled fondly. 'They're called "little mesters". They're self-employed craftsmen who make cutlery. Some work alone, some employ one or two workers or apprentices. The buffer women work in the factories but there are one or two enterprising women who have set up their own buffer workshops and take work from the little mesters.'

'But what do buffer girls actually do? I don't think I've ever heard the term before.'

'They polish the cutlery.' Flora laughed. 'I work on spoons and forks mainly. It's a very dirty job and we cover ourselves in brown paper to protect our own clothing as much as possible.' She pulled a face. 'But the grime still gets everywhere so I'm quite used to washing and ironing.'

Winnie nodded towards the garments Flora had already ironed. 'I can tell.' She paused and then asked quietly, 'Will you lose your job by coming here with your sister?'

Flora wrinkled her nose. 'I honestly don't know. The buffer missus in charge of us – I work at the same factory as my father . . .' Silently she added 'and where Bert works too', but she said nothing of her young man to Winnie. She had no idea what was going to happen now that she'd left so suddenly and without a word to him. 'Mrs Shaw is a nice woman,' she went on, speaking of the buffer missus. 'She's strict but always fair.' Despite her present worries, Flora managed a chuckle. 'We're a tough lot to handle. We know how to enjoy ourselves as well as work hard. We sing all day long at our machines and even go out into the town during our dinner break still dressed in our mucky clothes. Folks are used to seeing us, though. We get a lot of smiles and waves, but if anyone dares to cross any one of us, woe betide them. We all stick together. We're a loyal lot.'

'So why didn't you go to one of them to help you?'

'Because my father would have found out where we were and we didn't want to cause trouble for

31

anyone.' She sighed. 'He's a foreman in the factory. He wields quite a bit of power. He could make life very uncomfortable for anyone who crossed him and that would include anyone who helped us.'

'I see,' Winnie murmured. 'It sounds as if Mary Ellen can't go back home, then. Was she a buffer girl too?'

Flora smiled wryly. 'No. Dad didn't want her doing such a dirty job. She reminds him of his mother. He idolized her – his mother, I mean – and so he rather spoiled Mary Ellen. Not that I minded,' she added swiftly. 'I love my sister dearly and would do anything for her.'

'I rather think you've proved that,' Winnie said softly. 'Did she work at all, then?'

'She had a part-time job in the corner shop at the end of our street. I expect that's where she met whoever is the father of her child.'

'She won't tell you?'

Flora shook her head. She could have said so much more – wanted to say more – but despite their kindness, these people were still strangers. She thought about what their daily life at home had been, ruled by one person; the master of the house. She had only told the truth when she'd said that Mary Ellen had been spoiled by their father. Flora was the one who helped with the housework; the cooking, the cleaning, the washing and ironing, even after a long day at work. Worse still, her father took every penny she earned.

Nothing had ever been demanded of Mary Ellen. Patrick had brought home little gifts for her most weeks, even from the time she'd been quite small. Then it had been toys. More recently it had been a box of chocolates; a luxury in their household. Ribbons for her hair or, sometimes, even flowers. There was never anything for Flora, nor even for his wife. He made the difference in his feelings between the womenfolk in his household very obvious. But, strangely perhaps, Flora had never resented this; as she had told Winnie, she loved her sister fiercely and in her own way, Flora had spoiled the golden-haired, blue-eyed, sunny-natured child too. It helped that perhaps Mary Ellen had felt a little guilty. Unbeknown to Patrick, she had always shared the gifts with her sister and helped her mother with the housework where she could.

At ten o'clock, there was a rattle at the back door and Jack and his father came into the wash house. They took off their boots and then padded into the kitchen in their stockinged feet. They sat down at the table for a drink and a pasty.

'Got you working already, has she, lass?' Matthew said.

'I'm glad to be able to help,' Flora said. 'You've all been so kind, it's the least I can do.'

'How's your sister?' Jack asked.

'She's been sleeping all morning.'

'That's a good sign,' Matthew said, nodding sagely.

The two men didn't stay chatting long and were soon gone again until dinner time.

An hour later there was a knock at the door and a cheery voice called out. 'It's only me, Mrs Clarke. I was passing by and thought I'd just pop in to see how the lass is.'

'Come in. Let me make you a drink.'

Mrs Beckett sat at the table and glanced at Flora. 'Now, lass. How's your sister this morning?'

'I keep going up to check on her, but she's still asleep.'

'Best thing she could do,' Mrs Beckett said, echoing Winnie's earlier words. 'But I'd like to take a look at her, just to satisfy myself.' She heaved herself up. 'You lead the way.'

Flora set the iron back on the hob while she led Mrs Beckett up the stairs and opened the bedroom door quietly. As they approached the side of the bed, Mary Ellen stirred and opened her eyes.

'Oh! Oh, Flora. Is something wrong?'

'No, lass,' Mrs Beckett said at once. 'I've just called in on me way past to see how you are. Now let's have a look at you. Any pain anywhere?'

'No, no. Just a bit – sore.'

After a few moments, Mrs Beckett pronounced that all seemed to be well.

'I won't call again unless you send for me, but please don't hesitate if you're worried about anything. Ta-ra, love. I hope you do all right.'

Back in the kitchen, Mrs Beckett told Flora and Winnie, 'She'll likely be a bit low for a while, but that's to be expected. Feed her up a bit and try to get her out of bed as soon as you can. Lying there brooding won't do her any good at all. She's young and strong. It won't hurt her.'

'Thank you, Mrs Beckett,' Winnie said, 'we'll look after her. Now, here's another half a dozen eggs for your trouble.'

'That's very kind of you. Thank you.'

As the back door closed behind the woman, Winnie said, 'I'd best get the dinner on the table. The men will be here any minute.'

'Can I help? I've finished all the ironing you gave me.'

Winnie eyed the freshly pressed laundry on the airer and nodded her approval. She hoisted up the rail until it almost touched the ceiling and then tied the thin ropes around a hook in the wall.

'You can set the table while I mash the potatoes. Everything else is ready.'

Just as she had finished laying four place settings, the back door rattled and Matthew and his son came in.

'How's Mary Ellen?' Jack asked almost before he had got through the door. Flora noticed a swift glance pass between husband and wife at their son's question.

'Mrs Beckett called again this morning and says she's doing well.'

As she brought in a sizzling joint of beef and set tureens of vegetables on the pristine-white tablecloth, Winnie said, 'As soon as she feels a bit better, Mrs Beckett said we shouldn't let her lie in bed too long.'

'I'll show her around the farm when she's well enough,' Jack offered, helping himself to carrots.

Flora saw husband and wife exchange another glance but she couldn't guess what either of them were thinking.

Five

'Right, now where shall we start?' Jack said as both he and Flora stood outside the back door. It was a balmy September evening with the sun dropping behind the hills, casting a red and orange glow over the fields.

'What a marvellous sunset,' Flora murmured. 'We don't see this kind of sky in the town.' She breathed in deeply. 'Or this wonderful fresh air. I never realized it, but there's always a kind of sooty smell on our streets. I suppose it's all the chimneys puthering out smoke.'

'I wouldn't know.' Jack grinned. 'I've lived here all me life and, to be honest, I wouldn't want to live anywhere else. Now, let's start with the farmyard. I'll show you all the barns, the pig sties, the chicken house and the stables. The cows and sheep mostly stay out all year round, though if the weather gets really bad, we bring them into the big barn. You can lose a lot of animals if there's heavy snow and they get caught in drifts. And we often bring sheep indoors when they're lambing, although there is a shepherd's hut out in the fields.' He pulled a face. 'I usually get that job now.'

'What, staying out all night?'

'Got to be done. You can soon lose a lamb and a ewe if they have a difficult birth.' He stopped and his face reddened. 'Oh sorry, that was a bit tactless of me.'

Flora shrugged. 'Don't worry. I'd sooner you were honest.'

He glanced down at her feet and nodded approval when he saw that his mother had had the forethought to lend her some Wellington boots.

Jack showed her around the farmyard, peeking into the various buildings. Flora marvelled at the size of the huge pigs and was unafraid of the two huge shire horses. She rubbed their noses and fed them a carrot under Jack's guidance.

'There don't seem to be many chickens in here,' she commented.

Jack laughed. 'They're out in the field in the daytime, but come dusk they'll find their way here and we lock them up at dark. We don't want Mr Fox around.'

For a moment, Flora looked puzzled.

'Foxes are our enemy. All wild animals kill to eat – that's nature – but the fox kills for sport too. If he got into our chicken house, there'd be several corpses in the morning, but he'd only take one or two away. If he just killed enough to feed himself and his family, we could understand that, but he doesn't. So our hens have to be securely locked up at night.'

Now Flora nodded her understanding. As they returned to the house, Jack said, 'I thought you'd be frightened of some of the animals.'

'No, they're lovely.' She smiled. 'I've only ever seen animals in picture books. It's fascinating.'

'What about your sister? Do you think Mary Ellen will like them?'

'Oh, I think so. She's always wanted a pet – a dog, I think – but where we live is not the place to keep animals.' It was not quite the whole truth; their father wouldn't countenance an animal in the house, not even for Mary Ellen. Flora glanced behind her, her gaze sweeping around the yard and over the fields and hills beyond. She said no more, but she couldn't help thinking what a wonderful place this would be for her sister to live. Because, sadly, she knew that Mary Ellen could never go home again.

'Thank you for showing me around. I'll have something to talk to Mary Ellen about now.'

'Tell her I'll be happy to show her around too when she's well enough.'

After a few days, Mary Ellen, encouraged by Flora, felt able to get up out of bed and sit in a chair. Two days later, she got dressed but still wanted to cling to the safety of the bedroom.

'You really should come downstairs now,' Flora tried to persuade her. 'It'll look ungrateful if you don't make the effort. It's been a week now and Mrs Beckett said you should get some gentle exercise. You won't get stronger hiding away up here.'

Mary Ellen shrank back into the chair. 'But we'll have to leave then, won't we? Where will we go?'

'They seem very kind people, Mary Ellen. I don't think they'll make us leave before we're ready. And as for where we'll go, well, perhaps it'd be best if I try to find some work and somewhere for us to live first.

Then I'll come back for you. That's if they wouldn't mind you staying here. You certainly won't be able to walk far for several days yet. Weeks, probably.'

Tears sprang to Mary Ellen's eyes. 'I – I can't ever go home, can I?'

Flora didn't know how to answer her, because the truth was no, she couldn't. Gently, she said, 'Are you going to tell me who it was?'

Mary Ellen shook her head violently. 'No, I won't, so don't ask me. Don't ever ask me again.'

'Oh, darling Mary Ellen, don't upset yourself. I promise I won't ask any more. You must put it all behind you, get better and move on with your life.'

Mary Ellen bit her lip. 'You ought to go home. There's your Bert. Whatever must he be thinking? Have you written to him?'

'No. I don't like to. I'm not sure if his mother knows anything about me.' There was a silence between the two sisters until Mary Ellen pulled herself up out of the chair and said, 'Yes, you're right. I must come downstairs and start to get myself stronger.'

As they stepped into the kitchen, Winnie smiled a welcome. 'It's good to see you up and about. Now, come and sit by the range. You can shell some peas for me.'

'What would you like me to do, Mrs Clarke?' Flora asked.

'You can take this basket and go and collect eggs from the hen house. And make sure you have a look in the long grass on the outside. Little rascals often lay their eggs there. That's if the rats haven't stolen them first.'

The sisters glanced at each other and then looked at Winnie.

'Rats? Stealing eggs?' Flora said. 'How do they do that?'

Winnie laughed and paused to explain, her busy hands unusually idle for a brief moment. 'They're ingenious creatures. One rat will lie on its back holding an egg on its stomach and another will pull it away by its tail. I don't know how they break the egg – I've not seen that happening.'

'You've actually seen them doing that?' Mary Ellen was wide-eyed.

Winnie laughed. 'Oh yes, but I have to admit they're the only animal I really don't like. I hate 'em, in fact, even though they're all God's creatures. I've even got a sneaking admiration for Mr Fox. They're beautiful to look at even though they're the bane of a farmer's life.'

Outside in the September sunshine, Flora breathed in deeply. Although the air was filled with farmyard smells, she loved it; it was so very different to the town. She wandered around to the hen house and stepped into the gloom of the windowless building.

'Hello, there.'

'Oh! Jack. You made me jump. I didn't know there was anyone in here.'

He chuckled. 'Just mucking the place out. Come for the eggs, have you?'

'Yes.' She glanced around her. 'But where do I look?'

'The nesting boxes down the sides. And don't forget to look outside.'

'Yes. Your mam told me that.'

'How's Mary Ellen?'

'Getting better. She's come downstairs.'

Jack's face seemed to light up. 'Oh, that's wonderful. I'll pop in to see her when I've finished here before I go back out to the fields.'

Flora nodded. She did not state the obvious; that he would see Mary Ellen at dinner time. In the event, however, it wasn't until just before dinner time that Jack came in. He padded into the kitchen.

'I'll stay for me dinner now I'm here. I'll be up the hill this afternoon.' He sat down in the chair opposite Mary Ellen and gazed at her. 'How are you feeling?'

'Better, thank you, Jack. You've all been so kind to us, but me an' Flora ought to be moving on soon.'

As she watched them both, there was no doubt in Flora's mind that Jack's eyes clouded at Mary Ellen's words. 'There's no rush. You – you must make sure you're quite fit. Are you planning to go back home?'

Mary Ellen dropped her gaze. 'No,' she whispered. 'I – I can't go back, though . . .' she looked up again to meet his eyes – 'Flora ought to. There's her young man to think of. She left without telling him.'

'Ah, I see.' He didn't really, though he could perhaps make a shrewd guess at what might have gone on. Then his face brightened. 'Perhaps you could stay here while she makes a trip home to see him and explain. There's certainly no need for you to leave yet.'

'But what will your mam and dad say?'

Jack's grin broadened. 'You leave them to me. I'll sort it out.'

41

Six

The following day, after the menfolk had finished their dinner and gone back outside and Flora had helped Winnie to wash up and put away all the pots and pans, the three women sat beside the range for a brief rest.

'Now girls, I want to talk to you both,' Winnie began. Flora and Mary Ellen exchanged a nervous glance, but Winnie carried on as if she hadn't noticed. 'Jack had a word with me and his father last night after you'd both gone up. We're quite happy for you both to stay here for as long as you want, but he tells me that he thinks you, Flora, want to go home as you have a young man back in Sheffield. Is that right?'

Before Flora could speak, Mary Ellen said, 'Yes, it is, Mrs Clarke, and I don't want her to lose him on account of me.'

Winnie glanced between the two of them, a slight frown on her face. 'But your parents will have told him what's happened, surely? He'll know that Flora will be coming back sometime.' She paused before adding, uncertainly, 'Won't he?'

Mary Ellen twisted her fingers together as she said haltingly, 'My father threw me out when – when he found out I'd got myself in trouble.'

Winnie gave a tut of exasperation. 'Oh, that silly phrase. It does so annoy me. No girl "gets herself into trouble". There's always another party involved.'

'I had to leave straightaway,' Mary Ellen went on. 'And Flora came with me.'

'Quite right,' Winnie said firmly and then added, 'Now, I haven't wanted to pry and I still don't, but I've just one question, love, and then I'll ask you no more. Won't the young man concerned marry you?'

Tears spilled down Mary Ellen's cheeks as she shook her head and said huskily, 'No, there's no chance of that.'

The other two women waited, but Mary Ellen would say no more. After a few moments' silence, Flora said quietly, 'Our parents don't know about Bert, so he won't have been told anything.'

Winnie pursed her lips but all she said was, 'Then I think you should go back home, Flora, even if only for a visit, and explain everything to your young man. And what about your job?'

Flora nodded. 'I'll go and see Mrs Shaw. See how things stand.' She bit her lip, hesitating to add, 'I might not even have a job any more.'

Winnie turned back to Mary Ellen. 'Flora told me that you had a little job in the corner shop at the end of your street?'

Mary Ellen dropped her gaze and whispered, 'Yes. But I wouldn't go back there even if I could go home.'

'So will your employers know what's happened?' Winnie's question included both girls.

The sisters exchanged a glance and Flora said, 'Not unless Mam has told them.'

43

'Which she won't have,' Mary Ellen said. 'And neither will Dad.'

'Then I really think you should go back and straighten everything out, Flora. Mary Ellen can stay here with us. As she gets stronger, she can help me about the house.' She smiled. 'It's rather nice to have another woman for company.'

Winnie said no more but she was thinking back to the conversation she had had with her son the previous evening.

'Look, Mam, I've taken a liking to Mary Ellen. And before you say anything, I do realize that she's perhaps not the sort of girl you would have chosen for me with her past, but I reckon the poor lass has been the victim in all this. Maybe I'll find out the truth one day but, in the meantime, I'd like her to stay here.'

Winnie had stared at her son for a moment but then she'd smiled. 'Jack, we're a Christian family and always try to practise our beliefs. We'll not turn our back on a lass in trouble. Your father and I have always adopted the phrase "There but for the grace of God go I". And to be honest with you, son, that could well have been me if your father had not been the good man that he is.'

Jack stared at her and his mouth dropped open. 'Mam, what are you saying?'

Winnie chuckled. 'I think you know full well what I'm saying. If you check the date of our marriage and your birthday, you'll see that there is barely six months between the two dates. But, like I say, your father's a good man. One of the best.'

'But – I mean – was it what you call a shotgun wedding? Did your father go after him?'

'No, nothing like that. Our wedding date was all planned. We just had a bit of fun before, that's all.'

'Did anyone guess?'

'No one ever said anything, but I think there were a few raised eyebrows and a bit of counting the months on their fingers when you arrived.' She laughed again.

But Jack was still very serious. 'It doesn't sound as if it was that way for Mary Ellen.'

Winnie's smile faded. 'No, lad, it doesn't. Maybe one day she'll tell you.'

'I shan't press her.' There was silence between them until Jack patted his mother's hand and said simply, 'Thanks, Mam.'

Two weeks and a day after their father had told Mary Ellen to leave, Flora left Dale Farm walking back the way they had come. She planned to sleep again in the barns where they'd previously sheltered and hitch a lift whenever she could from local farmers or a carrier's cart. When she reached Baslow, she called in to the village shop and noticed for the first time the name 'Marshall's' above the door.

'Hello, lass. You're back again. How's things?' The rotund and smiling shopkeeper greeted her and then glanced behind her. 'Where's your sister? Is she all right?'

'Yes – and no.'

'You sit down on that barrel there and tell me all about it. I'll make us a cuppa. I was just about to have one. There's not a lot doing at the moment.'

Minutes later, the shopkeeper said, 'Now then, lass. What's to do?'

Flora took a deep breath. 'You probably guessed that one of us was in trouble. It was my sister. After we left you, we walked and walked and sheltered in farmers' barns along the way. Then on the night after we'd passed through Bakewell, she got the most dreadful pains and – well, to cut a long story short, she lost the baby.'

For a moment, the man looked shocked and anxious. It was obvious that he feared there was worse to come.

'The farmer and his wife were so kind – just like you . . .'

He waved away her compliment and Flora continued with her tale. 'They took us in and have been looking after us both. They're still caring for Mary Ellen but we all thought I should go back home – at least for a visit.'

'Can I ask? Was it Dale Farm?'

Flora's eyes widened. She was surprised he should know of the exact farm; it was several miles away. 'Why – yes, yes, it was. How . . .?'

He chortled at the look on her face. 'Round these parts, lass, not only do we know each other, but a lot of us are related. Sometimes quite closely, others more distantly. Winnie Clarke is my cousin on my mother's side. So it's not really the coincidence it might sound.' He stuck out his hand. 'My name's Percy Marshall. Mind you, you might have guessed my surname, seein' as how the name's over the shop door. I'm pleased to meet you properly. So,' he went on when they had shaken hands, 'where is she now? Still at Winnie's?'

Flora nodded. 'Yes. They said she could stay there at least until I've been home. I – we – don't think she'll ever be welcome at home again, you see.'

'But you're going back to find out? Is that it?'

'Not really. I think we both know the answer. It's just that I have a job and I left without telling them why and – and I also have a young man I'm walking out with, although,' she added quickly, 'my parents don't know anything about him.'

'Mmm,' Percy Marshall said thoughtfully, 'sounds like you've got a few problems. Mebbe going back will help you sort them out.'

Flora nodded but her expression was doubtful. She didn't hold out much hope.

'Oh, so you've come crawling back, have you? Well, I hope you haven't brought *her* with you.'

It had taken Flora two days to get home, arriving just after her father had got in from work. Now she faced him squarely, her strong chin jutting forward. 'No, I haven't, Dad. I've come back to see that Mam is all right and to see if I still have a job.'

Patrick glared at her, his eyes sparkling with anger and resentment. 'Then you'd best get along to work and ask. Gossip has been rife since you upped and left without a word.' He turned away but flung the words back at her over his shoulder, 'And don't think I don't know about you and Bert Weston. You'll not see him again if you know what's good for you – and for him.' Then he slammed out of the house on his way to the nearest pub.

'Oh Flora,' Edith wailed, wringing her hands. 'Not you an' all bringing trouble to our door.'

'Mam,' Flora put her arms around her mother, 'Bert and I are just walking out, that's all. I don't even know if he feels the same way about me.'

Edith looked up into her daughter's face. 'You – you mean, you're in love with him?'

'Yes, I am,' Flora said firmly. She'd only realized just how much Bert meant to her since she'd left home. He was so kind and caring and had a wonderful sense of humour. But now, she wasn't sure whether he would want to see her again. Her sudden disappearance without a word must have hurt and bewildered him.

'Oh Flora, do be careful. Marriage isn't all it's cracked up to be.'

'I can see that, Mam,' Flora said wryly. 'You deserve better than the way Dad treats you.'

'I was too weak and cowardly to stand up to my parents and what they wanted me to do – what they *told* me to do. And now I'm too cowardly to stand up to your father. It's my own fault, Flora. But I fear for you and for Mary Ellen. Tell me how she is. Please.'

Sitting huddled in front of the range and, holding her mother's hands, Flora told her everything that had happened since they had left home.

'Poor Mary Ellen,' Edith whispered. 'I should have been with her. I . . .'

'Don't blame yourself for that, Mam. There was nothing you could have done.'

'But I should have told her – both of you – what could happen if you let a man – near you.' Edith was skirting round the facts of life that were so brutal in her experience. She hadn't wanted that for her daughters and so, by keeping them in ignorance, she had thought she could shield them. Now she realized that the opposite was the truth. Innocence was no protection.

Flora was moved by her mother's piteous expression. She squeezed Edith's hands. 'Don't blame yourself, Mam. I only wish I'd told her. I found out when I was still at school and I suppose I took it for granted that Mary Ellen had learned the same way. It seems you and me were both wrong.'

'Did she – did she tell you who it was?'

'No, she won't tell anyone. All she'll say is that there is no chance that he will marry her.'

'Do you think he's already married, then?'

Flora sighed. 'I wondered that, but I really don't know. We'll probably never know. You'd think it's probably someone around here. Someone she's met while working at the corner shop.' She sighed. 'And that's another thing I'll have to do. I'll have to go and tell Mr Turner that she won't be coming back to work for him.'

'I haven't dared go down to his shop. I thought he might ask me awkward questions.'

Flora patted her hands and then stood up. She yawned. 'I'll see to it all tomorrow but I'm off to bed. At least Dad hasn't told me to leave.'

'No. Not yet. But he might if you go on seeing Bert Weston.'

Flora's mouth tightened. There was no way she was going to stop seeing Bert unless the young man himself no longer wanted to walk out with her. By tomorrow she would have the answer.

Seven

Flora rose early the next morning and walked to the factory where she worked.

'Hello, stranger. Where've you been for the last two weeks?' Flora's friend, Evelyn Bonsor, greeted her with a smile. 'Mrs Shaw has been doing her nut. You've only just come back in time. She was talking about setting someone else on to replace you.'

Flora pulled a face. 'I'd better go and find her and explain.'

'And then you'd better tell me . . .' Evelyn pointed a finger at her own chest, ''cos me and the other girls have been doing extra to cover for you so she won't sack you.'

'Oh, that's so kind of you.' For the first time since their troubles had begun, tears filled Flora's eyes.

'Hey,' Evelyn touched her arm, 'don't take on, m'love. Go and see her now. Get it over with, but we're all behind you. I don't reckon she dare sack you.' She laughed loudly. 'We'd all walk out on strike if she did.' The buffer girls were known as strong-minded women. Some of them could be a little loud and raucous at times – they liked to have fun – but they were a band of women with a collective heart of gold and stood no nonsense from anyone.

Flora smiled weakly as she said softly, 'I'll tell you about it at dinner break, if we can find somewhere quiet. I don't want everyone knowing. But first, I'd better go and face the music.'

Evelyn Bonsor had been Flora's friend ever since she'd arrived at the factory to begin work. Four years older than Flora, she was now married with a one-year-old little boy, Max, whom her mother looked after during the daytime so that Evelyn could continue to work. Divested of her bulky buffer girl's clothing, Evelyn was tall and slim with brown curly hair, a wide smile and mischievous eyes. She was very happily married to Howard Bonsor and lived two streets away from the Hallidays, coincidentally just opposite where Bert Weston lived with his mother. Evelyn knew all about Flora's romance with Bert and had assured her, 'When he feels able to take you home to meet his ma, you'll love her. She's a lovely woman.'

But now all she said was, 'Off you go, then, and find the missus.'

Mabel Shaw was a big woman in every sense of the word. She was tall and although a little over-weight, she carried it well. She was sharp and missed nothing that went on among the girls over whom she had charge. But she was at a loss to understand why one of her best workers had suddenly not turned up to work. She had sought out Patrick Halliday, but the man had been sullen and uncommunicative to the point of rudeness.

'You mind yer own business, yer nosey old biddy, and let me mind mine,' was all he had said.

'It is my business when your daughter doesn't come

into work without sending a word of explanation,' Mabel countered, but Patrick had turned his back on her. With a sigh, Mabel had turned away. She'd wondered whether to visit their home – or to ask Evelyn to go – but she'd heard the rumours that all was not what it perhaps should be in the family home.

But now the girl stood before her. Mabel folded her arms across her ample bosom and waited, fixing Flora with her sternest glare.

'I'm so sorry, missus. We've had trouble at home.'

Mabel sniffed. 'You're not going to tell me you're in the club, are you?'

Flora shook her head. 'No, but my younger sister was and Dad threw her out. So I went with her.' She went on to tell Mabel all that had happened but ended by saying, 'Please keep this to yourself, missus. I don't want my sister gossiped about.'

Mabel nodded. 'I can understand that. No one'll hear it from me, lass.' She was thoughtful for a moment before saying, 'I expect you'll want time off to go back to see her. Will she be coming back here once she's quite well again?'

'I really don't know yet. I'd have to find somewhere for her to live and some work for her to do. She won't be able to come home and I don't know if Mr Turner would have her back to work at the shop. Besides . . .' she bit her lip – 'it's a bit close to home.'

Mabel stared at her. 'D'you mean Jim Turner that runs the offy at the end of your street? Is that where she worked?'

'Yes.'

Mabel's lip curled. 'Well, if you ask me, you need

look no further for the father of her child. He's always been known as a lecherous old devil with young girls. I'm surprised your father ever let her work there if he was so protective of her.' She sniffed. 'But then fellers stick together, don't they? I expect Jim Turner let your father run up a tab for his booze, so he wouldn't want to say owt.'

Flora was shocked. She'd always known Jim Turner was friendly, perhaps too friendly sometimes, but she'd never seen any harm in him. Now, she wondered.

'Anyway,' Mabel was saying, 'get to your work now but let me know before you take off again, lass. There's a good girl.'

Flora waited near the factory gate as the menfolk streamed out at the end of their shift. Usually, the office workers left around the same time too. She scanned the faces trying to see Bert, but she didn't spot him until he was standing beside her.

'Flora,' he said in his soft, deep voice and she turned to look into his face – a face that was filled with sadness and anxiety. Bert was a little taller than she was, with broad shoulders, sandy-coloured hair and the kindest hazel eyes that she had ever seen. But now those eyes were wary, a huge question in them.

'Oh Bert,' she breathed, 'I'm so sorry I went away without telling you. It all happened so suddenly. I couldn't get word to you.'

'What happened?' His voice was tight. He couldn't hide his hurt and anger.

'It was . . .' she began and then stopped. His workmates were still walking past them, nodding and smiling and throwing out the odd teasing remark.

'Don't let Patrick Halliday catch you, lad. He'll have yer guts for garters.'

'We can't stay here, Bert. Walk with me and I'll explain everything.'

'It'd better be good,' he muttered, but fell into step beside her.

As she repeated her story, she saw the anger fall away from his face, but the hurt remained. Though now it was for a different reason.

'Oh Flora,' he said sadly, 'why didn't you come to me? I'd have helped you. I'd have helped you both.'

'I – I didn't like to. Whatever would your mother have thought?'

'She wouldn't have thought anything, Flora. She knows all about you. I don't have to keep secrets from my mother.' He was an only child and Flora was surprised that he'd told his mother about his tentative romance. As if reading her mind, Bert said, 'My mother's perhaps not what you would expect. She's not possessive like you might think she'd be with an only child and being a widow too. All she wants is for me to be happy. And if you're the one to make me happy – and you are, Flora – she'll welcome you with open arms.'

'Oh Bert . . .' Since that awful day when Patrick had banished Mary Ellen from their home, Flora had been the strong one, but now, at Bert's kind words, her resolve crumbled. Tears flooded down her face. 'I'm so sorry I went off without a word. I just had to look after Mary Ellen.'

'Of course you did. I understand now. Come here,' he said tenderly and folded her into his strong, comforting arms. 'We'll work things out, I promise.'

Her voice muffled against his coat, Flora said, 'But your mother won't be so willing to accept me when she hears about Mary Ellen.'

'There's only one way to find out. You must come and meet her. And there's no time like the present.'

Flora looked up into his eyes. 'Oh, I couldn't come looking like this. I must go home and wash and change first.'

Bert chuckled – a deep, comforting sound. 'You do look a bit like a chimney sweep. So go home, have your tea and come round afterwards. Aw reet?' he added in his broad accent. He was a Sheffielder, born and bred, and proud of it.

A quiver of nerves shot through her, but she nodded. 'See you in about an hour, then. It might be a bit longer. I'll have to wait for me dad to have his tea and then go to the pub.'

He kissed her forehead and squeezed her before loosening his embrace. 'See you later.' He walked away from her down the street, whistling cheerfully. He had been so unhappy these last two weeks, not knowing why Flora had left so suddenly without a word. But now it all made sense. He would support her in any way he could but he didn't intend to let her get away again.

Eight

As soon as he got through the back door of his home, Bert said, 'Ma, we've got a visitor coming tonight.'

Startled, Agnes looked up from where she was placing knives, forks and spoons on the table for their tea. Then she smiled. 'That'll be nice, son. Who is it?'

'Flora. The girl I've been telling you about.'

Agnes paused. 'Oh, it's all still on, then? You've been looking so miserable the last couple of weeks or more, I thought it must be all off.'

'Aye,' Bert said wryly, 'an' I thought so too. She went away without telling me owt, but it seems she's had trouble at home. Her sister, Mary Ellen, was in the family way and their father threw her out and so Flora went with her. It all happened very suddenly.'

Slowly, Agnes resumed laying out the cutlery. 'I know it's a shame and disgrace an' all that, but you don't turn your back on your daughter like that. What about the mother?'

Bert shrugged. 'I don't know much about her but it sounds as if she's completely under the old man's thumb. He works at our place, but I only know him by sight.'

Agnes sighed. 'That's the way in many households. Master of the house and all that. Thankfully, it never was that way in ours.' She looked up sharply at her son. 'And I trust it won't be in yours when you decide to settle down. Your dad was a good man. A kind and thoughtful husband and a wonderful father. You're very like him. At least, I hope you are.'

'I try to be, Mam,' Bert said solemnly.

'So is Flora "the one"?'

'She is for me. I just hope she feels the same way.'

Agnes needn't have worried; the moment Flora stepped through the door, the two women took an instant liking to each other. Agnes, small and slim but with boundless energy, held out both her hands in welcome.

'I am so pleased to meet you, Flora. Come and sit down by the fire. Autumn's getting a bit chilly now, isn't it? Can I take your coat?'

'Thank you, Mrs Weston,' Flora said nervously, but as the woman chattered on, Flora's unease fell away. Bert's mother was so warm and friendly. When she said, 'Bert has told me about the bit of trouble you've had at home over your sister. Poor lass. How is she?' the last shred of Flora's doubts about meeting Bert's mother disappeared.

'She was recovering well when I left her but, of course, I haven't heard anything since.'

'I expect you'll want to go back and see her as soon as you can.'

'I do. Mrs Shaw – the buffer missus – has been really understanding. She's said she'll give me some time off.'

'Has your sister anywhere to go? Permanently, I mean.'

'That's what's worrying me. The people who took us in were so very kind, but we can't expect her to be able to stay there for ever.'

'And there's really no chance of her being able to come home?'

Flora shook her head. 'None.'

'I tell you what,' Bert said suddenly. 'Why don't I take you to see her?'

Flora smiled. 'I'd like that but it's a long way. It took us the best part of three days to get there and that was with the help of a lift on a carrier's cart. And almost the same time for me to walk back, although I was a bit quicker on my own. And I hitched a couple of lifts along the way.'

But Bert was smiling. 'I know where I can borrow a pony and trap. That wouldn't take nearly as long. I reckon we could do it in a day, if we set off early. How about it, Flora?'

'That would be wonderful.'

'Would your mother like to come too?' Bert asked.

Flora's face fell as she shook her head. 'Best not. Dad would take it out on her afterwards.'

There was silence in the room, each one with their own thoughts about what Flora had just said.

After Flora left, Agnes said, 'Well, son, you've found a nice lass there. I like her and as far as I'm concerned you can get married and she can come and live here. You can have my front parlour, which hardly ever gets used, as your own sitting room and we'll get a double bed for your bedroom.'

'You've got it all worked out, haven't you?'

Agnes laughed. 'I've been thinking about it for years, ready for the time when you met a nice girl. Not that I'm trying to rush you into it, mind. I want you to be sure. Both of you.'

Bert put his arms around his mother and, taller than her by a good six inches, he kissed the top of her head.

The following evening on her way home from work, Flora called in at the corner shop where her sister had worked part-time. When he saw who it was, Jim Turner's eyes were suddenly wary and colour flooded his face. They stood staring at one another for a long moment, before he cleared his throat and asked, 'Can I help you, Miss Flora?'

'I don't think so, Mr Turner.' She wanted to add, 'I think you've done more than enough already', but she knew she could make no accusations. If what Mrs Shaw had said was true, this was the man who had taken advantage of her young, naive sister, but she had no proof while Mary Ellen remained silent.

Flora took a deep breath. 'I've come to tell you that Mary Ellen will not be coming back to work here.'

Was it relief she saw flit across the man's face? She couldn't be sure. Again, he cleared his throat and avoided looking directly at her as he said, 'I'm sorry to hear that. She was – er – very well-liked by all my customers. Especially by the gentlemen. They like to be served by a pretty girl.'

Flora's eyes narrowed. Had he guessed that Mary

Ellen was in trouble and he was trying to make out that one of his customers was to blame? A sudden spark of devilment made Flora say, carefully, 'It would seem, Mr Turner, that one of your customers was not so much of a "gentleman" after all. I shall be making enquiries around the neighbourhood to find out which of them did not – *respect* Mary Ellen as he should have done.'

Jim Turner's colour deepened, his eyes bulged and a vein throbbed purple in his temple. For a moment, Flora wondered if she had pushed matters too far and he was going to have a seizure, but at that moment, the door-bell clanged as a customer entered the shop.

Having said all she wanted to say, Flora gave him a brief nod and left the shop.

'That'll give him summat to think on,' she muttered to herself as she marched back towards her home, smarting with anger at every step. There was nothing more she could do. Nothing could ever put matters right, but she hoped she had given the man many a sleepless night.

The proposed trip to the countryside took place on the second Sunday in October just over two weeks after Flora had returned home.

'So where exactly is this farm?' Bert asked as they took the road up the hill towards the Derbyshire countryside.

'I'm not sure of all the names of the villages we passed through, but I do know the carrier took us to Baslow and then we walked to Bakewell and, further on, into a little village. We crossed a bridge where two rivers meet and just kept walking. The farm was up a long lane right in the middle of nowhere, really. But it was what we were looking for. We didn't want to stop anywhere that was busy.'

'But you can remember the way?'

'Oh yes.' She laughed. 'I didn't even get lost when I came back on my own.'

'You must have a very good sense of direction.'

After a very early start, they arrived at Dale Farm in the middle of the morning. To Flora's surprise, the yard was silent and there was no reply when she knocked on the back door.

'Where can they all be?' she murmured and then a smile curved her mouth as she realized. 'Oh, I was forgetting. It's Sunday. They'll be at church.'

Bert raised his eyebrows. 'Church? Your Mary Ellen?'

Flora chuckled. 'Well, yes. She'd have to go with them if they'd wanted her to. It's the least she could do.'

They waited for just over an hour before they heard the clip-clopping of hooves and the rattle of wheels as a horse and trap turned into the yard.

'Oh Flora! Flora!' Catching sight of her sister, Mary Ellen stood up and would have overbalanced if Jack had not caught her to steady her. Once both were safely on the ground, the sisters ran into each other's arms.

'Mary Ellen. How are you?' Flora stood back a little. 'You look wonderful. So much better.'

There was a pink tinge to Mary Ellen's cheeks and

her eyes were sparkling. 'Mr and Mrs Clarke have been so wonderfully kind and – and Jack too. We've just been to church. Flora, I never knew how comforting church services could be.'

Introductions were made all round and, as Bert and Jack shook hands and eyed each other, Flora could sense that they liked what they saw because both of them grinned.

'We can let your horse out of the shafts for a bit, Bert, turn him loose in the field to graze. I expect you'll be staying a while.' Jack laughed. 'You mustn't miss me mam's Sunday roast.'

'We don't want to impose, but I thought it better if I brought Flora back to see Mary Ellen. It's a long way for her to walk. I think it must be twenty miles or so.'

Winnie Clarke ushered everyone into her warm kitchen. The menfolk sat by the range while the women prepared the meal together under Winnie's instructions, although Flora noticed that Mary Ellen seemed to know just what to do.

'Dinner's ready,' Winnie called out.

They sat around the large kitchen table. While they ate, the talk remained general but once they had all had finished, the conversation turned to what was uppermost in everyone's mind. Winnie came straight to the point, as was her way.

'We've all taken to Mary Ellen.' She smiled. 'Especially Jack. Now, they're not rushing into anything, but we'd like Mary Ellen to stay with us and see how things go. I know it's all happened rather quickly, but is that all right with you, Flora?'

'Oh Mrs Clarke, you don't know what a relief that is. I've been so worried as to what was going to happen to Mary Ellen.' She touched her sister's hand. 'But I can see how happy she is. Thank you – all of you.'

'She's even taken to the farming life,' Jack said, grinning. 'You should see her milking cows. It's as if she's been doing it all her life.'

'Things have moved on a bit for us, too,' Bert said. 'I was very hurt when Flora just upped and left without a word. But I understand why now.'

'I'm so sorry, Bert,' Mary Ellen whispered. 'It was all my fault.'

'Don't worry, Mary Ellen. It's probably brought matters to a head. Flora's now met my ma and they get on really well. So we're going to see how things go too.'

'It sounds as if things are working out very nicely for both of you,' Winnie said happily.

'There's just one problem,' Flora said and glanced at Mary Ellen, who looked up at her with fearful eyes and whispered huskily, 'Dad.'

Nine

Over the coming weeks, the sisters wrote regularly to one another, Mary Ellen sending her letters to Bert's home. Christmas passed but it was not a time of celebration in the Halliday household. Edith had sunk into lethargy that not even Patrick's harsh words, or even slaps, could dispel. He spent more and more time – and money – at the pub, coming home most nights the worse for drink and in a foul mood. Home life for Flora was miserable. Only her friends at work and Bert and his mother kept her going.

'Would you like me to visit your mother?' Agnes Weston offered at the beginning of February. 'Perhaps I can help.'

'It's kind of you,' Flora said. 'Let me talk to her and I'll see what she says.'

The following evening after Patrick had left to go to the pub, Flora built up the fire in the range with the meagre bit of coal they had left and mother and daughter sat together.

'Coal man comes tomorrow,' Edith said absently.

'Mam, listen to me for a minute. You know I've met Bert's mother now, don't you? Well, she's offered to come round to see you . . .'

Edith's eyes widened and the colour drained from her face.

'I don't think that's a good idea. The place is such a mess and besides, your father . . .'

'Well, you could go to her house, then. You go out shopping, usually on a Thursday, don't you? You could call in to see her then.'

'But what if he found out? He's never allowed me to have friends, not even with the neighbours. He even stopped me going to see my parents so often when we were first married. Oh Flora, I don't know if I dare.'

'Mrs Weston understands the problem. Just call and see her. She's only two streets away. It wouldn't matter if she wasn't in.'

It took a week for Edith to pluck up the courage to make a detour on her way home from shopping and knock tentatively on the door of the address Flora had given her. When it opened the two women stood staring at each other for a moment. Edith couldn't find her voice so it was Agnes who spoke first. 'You must be Flora's mam. She has your eyes. Do come in. You're very welcome. Put your shopping down there and let me take your coat. Chilly today, isn't it? Still, we'll soon be into spring . . .' On and on Agnes chattered, trying to put her nervous guest at ease. As they sat together, Agnes scrabbled around in her mind for something else to talk about. Her glance rested on a newspaper that Bert had left lying on a shelf beside his chair near the range.

'Do you read the papers, Edith?'

'Not – not very often. Patrick sometimes brings one home from the pub. Why?'

'There was something very interesting in Monday's edition. I think it's the one Bert has left here . . .' She jumped up and retrieved the paper from the shelf, turning the pages until she found the piece she wanted.

'The mayor has received a telegram telling him that Her Majesty "has been graciously pleased to confer upon Sheffield the status and dignity of a city". Now what do you think to that, Edith? We live in a city now. Fancy that, eh?'

Edith tried to smile. She couldn't quite see how it would benefit the ordinary working-class people, yet Agnes seemed delighted and excited by the news. As if answering Edith's unspoken question, Agnes said, 'Of course, I don't suppose it'll make any difference to the likes of us, but it's a matter of pride, isn't it?'

'I – suppose so,' Edith said, trying to drum up some enthusiasm but failing.

Laying aside the paper, Agnes sighed inwardly. She sat down again and brought the conversation back to their own family. 'Have you met my Bert yet?'

Edith shook her head. 'I – we – daren't let him come to the house. My husband knows about him but he's told Flora to stop seeing him.' With a tremulous half-smile, she added, 'She won't, of course.'

'They're not rushing into anything,' Agnes said, 'but I think they'll want to get married before long. I've said they can come and live here.'

Edith's face was bleak as she realized she was going to lose her other daughter too. The girls had been her life; the only reason she had forced herself to keep living through a miserable existence. As if reading her mind, Agnes said gently, 'She'll only be a couple of streets away and you can visit any time you want to.'

Edith tried to smile weakly. 'You're very kind. But he'll never allow it and Flora will only be twenty next month. He'll never give his consent.'

'A year's not too long to wait.' Agnes laughed. 'It might seem it to them, though it will soon go. But it might be possible for you to sign for them. We'd have to find out if one parent can give permission.'

'I couldn't do that. Patrick would kill me.'

Agnes was startled to hear the seriousness in Edith's tone. 'Oh well, they'll just have to wait then. Perhaps it won't be such a bad thing anyway. At least they won't have been too hasty.'

'Not like I was,' Edith murmured. 'Patrick was so different before we married. It must have been an act because the moment he got the ring on my finger, he changed. It'd all been show.'

'Didn't your parents see through him?'

Edith shrugged listlessly. 'I don't think so, but they were so keen to get me married off, I don't think they'd have bothered if they had.'

'I'm sorry to hear that.'

By the time Edith reluctantly got to her feet and picked up her shopping, the two women were on first name terms.

'You come here whenever you like, Edith.' Agnes guessed that Edith had few friends, if any. 'And your secrets are all safe with me. I might be chatty, but I'm not a gossip.'

Edith had gleaned as much; not one word had

passed Agnes's lips about her neighbours unless it was to say something nice.

'That's very kind of you,' Edith said. 'I'm only sorry that I can't invite you back to my house, but . . .'

'Please don't give that another thought,' Agnes said, as she helped Edith put her coat on.

'Thursday's my shopping day,' Edith said.

'Friday's mine, so that works out nicely. You come here after you've done your shopping on a Thursday morning.'

'Flora goes to the market after she finishes work on a Saturday. There's often some good bargains then.'

'Yes, you're right. Bert goes for me too.'

'I wonder if that's how they met. Flora hasn't said.'

'I think they met at work. Bert works for Rowleys too. He's in the offices.' There was a note of pride in her tone. It was a 'step up' for a young man to have an office job.

Edith looked fearful. 'Perhaps that's how Patrick got to know about them seeing each other.'

Agnes smiled and patted Edith's shoulder, more sorry for the poor, defeated woman than she could put into words.

'See you next week, then.'

'I'll look forward to it,' Edith said with a smile.

As Agnes closed the door behind her departing guest, she realized that that had been the first time she had seen Edith smile properly.

'I went to visit Bert's mam today,' Edith told Flora as soon as the back door had closed behind Patrick on his way to the pub.

'I'm so glad.'

'She's a lovely woman. She made me so welcome. If her son is anything like her, you'll be all right with him.'

'Yes, Mam. I will. I know I will. He's going to pop in a bit later to meet you.'

'Oh no, he mustn't. He can't.'

'Dad won't know. Bert's going to the pub for a pint and then, when he knows Dad's safely there, he'll leave and come here. He won't stay long.'

Edith chewed her lip nervously. 'I want to meet him – of course I do – but if your dad finds out . . .'

'He won't.'

Edith sat twisting her fingers nervously and when Bert arrived about half an hour after Patrick had left, she was like the proverbial cat dancing on hot bricks.

'I'm pleased to meet you, Bert. I met your mother today and we got on very well.'

Bert held Edith's hand in his warm grasp. 'Yes, she told me when I got home from work. She says you're to go round to see her any time you like.'

'We've arranged that I shall go on a Thursday morning after I've done my . . .' Edith stopped short as a rattle sounded at the back door. Bert felt her hand tremble as she whispered, 'Oh no!'

Edith dragged her hand away from Bert as if his touch was now burning her. Patrick came into the kitchen with a smile that was more like a baring of his teeth than an expression of pleasure or welcome.

'Ah, I thought as much. I've been watching you, Bert Weston. I saw you leave the pub soon after I got there and I wondered if this is where you were headed when you thought I was safely out of the way. Now, you can tek yourself off and I don't want to see you here again or hear that you're still hanging around Flora. We've had enough trouble in this house with her whore of a sister.'

'I mean no harm to Flora, Mr Halliday. We're walking out together and . . .'

'You're doing no such thing.' He grabbed Flora's arm in a painful grasp and pushed her towards the door leading to the staircase. 'Get up to your room and stay there until I say you can come down. And you . . .' He jabbed his finger into Bert's chest. 'Do as I say and get out.'

'Please go, Bert,' Edith whispered, but both Bert and Flora stood their ground. They faced the angry man together.

'We're walking out together . . .' Flora began and Bert ended the sentence by saying, 'And we're going to get married.'

Patrick's face twisted into a sneer. 'She's under twenty-one. You can't marry without my permission.'

'Then we'll wait until she's of age,' Bert said calmly. Bert was tall and broad-shouldered. If it came to a physical fight, there was no doubt which one of them would come out on top. It wasn't Patrick Halliday and he had the sense to know it. But he could still act threateningly. He thrust his face close to Bert. 'Then you'd better watch yerself on dark nights, young feller, 'cos I've got mates and if I ask 'em, they'd give you a good hiding. So, if you want to keep your pretty face, I'd think again if I was you.'

With that, Patrick turned, left the room and seconds later they heard the back door slam again.

'Oh Bert,' Edith said, tears now running down her face. 'Don't put yourself in danger.'

'Don't you worry, Mrs Halliday. I can look after myself. I go to the local boxing club twice a week. Just to train, mind you. I don't get involved in any bouts. And what he seems to forget is that I've got mates too and we're all twenty years younger than him and his cronies. Besides, I'm not sure who these mates are he's referring to. As far as I know, no one at work likes him. Sorry, Mrs Halliday. It wasn't very nice of me to say that.'

'Don't apologize, Bert. I can imagine it's true.'

'I don't want any of you getting into a fight,' Flora said. Although she held back the tears, her voice wobbled.

Bert squeezed her hand. 'I'll sort it out, but I'm not giving you up, Flora, love. Not for him or anyone else.' He gave her a peck on the cheek as if to seal his promise. 'I'll be off now.' He took Edith's hand gently. 'You'll be all right, both of you, won't you?'

She nodded but he could see the fear in her eyes. Tonight had probably earned her a slap or two when Patrick came home later.

'I'll see you out,' Flora murmured and followed him out of the room to the back door where they exchanged a proper kiss. 'Take care, darling,' he whispered before turning away and disappearing into the darkness.

Ten

Bert headed to the street where he lived but he did not go into his own home. He marched along, determination in every step and indignation driving him on. Instead, he went to see his friend, Howard Bonsor, who lived on the opposite side of the same street a little further up. Howard was the husband of Flora's friend, Evelyn. Knowing they had a little boy, Max, who might now be asleep, Bert knocked gently on the door. It took another knock before Howard opened the door. 'Ey up, pal. Come on in.'

'A' you sure? It's getting a bit late, but I just wanted a quick word.'

'It's fine. Another hour, though, and I'd have been in me bed.' Howard grinned. 'Come in and have a beer. Missus has already gone up. Little 'un's a bit fretful. She reckons he's teething. So there's just the two of us.'

They sat together in front of the dying fire while Bert explained the situation he found himself in. 'I really love Flora and want to marry her but I don't want to cause more trouble for her or her mam. Mrs Halliday's a poor little thing, frightened of life itself, though I'm guessing it's mainly him she's afraid of. I reckon he's a might too handy with his fists.'

'I reckon we should let him know how he stands with us sooner rather than later,' Howard said. 'We'll go and face him in the pub right now. You reckon that's where he'll be?'

Bert nodded.

'Reet. I'll just let Evelyn know where I've gone . . .' He grinned. 'But not exactly why.'

Twenty minutes later the two young men walked into the local pub.

'Have you seen Patrick Halliday?' Bert asked the landlord who was, as usual, serving behind the bar.

'Aye, he was in earlier but he left – oh, now let me think – must be over a couple of hours ago now. Not been back since.'

Bert frowned. 'Really?'

An old man sitting at the bar laughed juicily. 'I reckon I can tell you where he'll be.'

Bert and Howard turned to look at him. The old man tapped his finger on the side of his nose. 'He'll have gone round to see his fancy piece.'

'His – *what?*' Bert spluttered.

The man laughed even louder and turned to the landlord. 'Ain't that right, Alf?' Without giving the man behind the bar time to answer he went on. 'She's t'barmaid here but Alf lets her go early if it's not busy. It's been goin' on a while. That's why Halliday spends such a lot of time here.' He laughed again and winked. ''T'ain't because he's so fond of Alf's beer, it's because he's fonder of his barmaid. He spends every night here when she's working and when she ain't, he's round at her place.' He laughed so hard at his own joke that he ended up with a fit of coughing.

'Is this right, Alf?' Bert asked.

'Aye, it is. I don't reckon it's a secret as they carry on in front of the whole bar . . .' He waved his hand to encompass the entire room. 'Everybody knows.'

'Everyone except his wife and daughter,' Bert murmured. He was silent for a moment before asking quietly, 'I know her name's Lily, but where does she live, Alf?'

'Now, Bert, I don't want no trouble. I don't want you going round there.'

'I won't. *We* won't. I give you my word. I'd just like to know, that's all.'

'Sorry, Bert. I never give out the personal details of my staff.'

As they left the pub, Howard said, 'You weren't going there, were you?'

'No, but I just want me facts right when I tell Flora. Never mind, we'll find out another way.'

'The dirty devil,' Flora exclaimed indignantly when Bert told her the following evening as they walked home together after work. 'All that fuss he made about poor Mary Ellen and he's making a whore out of some poor girl.'

'She's not a girl. She's an older woman.' He laughed. 'Well, older in the way that she must be in her early forties.'

'You know her?'

'Oh yes. I've seen her lots of times. Don't forget

that pub is my local too. You ask Evelyn about Lily Parker. She'll fill you in.'

'I most certainly will. Thanks, Bert.'

Flora decided not to say anything to her mother until she'd found out more. The following day she cornered Evelyn during their brief dinner break.

'What can you tell me about Lily Parker, the barmaid at our local?'

Evelyn wrinkled her brow trying to decide what to say to be fair to the woman. 'She's never been married but she's had – now how shall I put it – a lot of men friends.'

'Is she a whore?'

Jokingly, Evelyn accentuated her Sheffield accent for a moment. 'Ee, tha can be reet blunt when tha wants, Flora Halliday.' Then she smiled and went on, 'Not exactly. She just likes men and the company of men. I suppose working in a pub doesn't help. She *has* to be friendly to the customers as part of her job and I suppose it just develops from there.'

'And is there more than one at once?'

'Not that I know. Just that she has a string of 'em.' Evelyn paused and then asked, 'Why do you want to know?'

So Flora told her.

'What are you going to do about it?' Evelyn asked.

Flora was thoughtful. 'Nothing straightaway. I need to think it through first and probably talk to my mam. I don't know what she'll want to do.'

Flora was rather afraid her mother would want to ignore it. If Patrick were to leave her, she would have no means of earning her own living. Flora wasn't even sure her mother had had a job before she'd married Patrick – she knew very little about Edith's early life – but she certainly hadn't worked outside the home since and even though she was only in her early forties, work for her would not be easy to find. Perhaps Edith would think that 'the devil she knew' was better than having a complete upheaval in her life.

Evelyn sniffed. 'Well, I know what I'd do if I found out that my Howard had been playing away.' But then in a softer tone she said, 'Though I have to realize that not all women are as lucky as I am. I've always got me mam who'd support me. It must be hard if it happens when you're older.'

Flora sighed. 'Her life with him isn't very good, but it's the only one she knows, so I don't know how she's going to react.'

'Bert,' Flora asked the following evening, 'do you think you could take me to see Mary Ellen again? I ought to tell her about Dad.'

'Have you spoken to your mam yet?'

Flora shook her head. 'That's what I want to talk to Mary Ellen about. I'm really not sure what I ought to do and I want her opinion.'

'Right, I'll see my mate and we'll go on Sunday again. Wrap up warm. It'll be cold travelling in the trap and the roads will be muddy. It might take us a bit longer than last time.'

They arrived at Dale Farm just after the Clarke family had returned from attending church. Mary Ellen flew into Flora's arms, her face shining with joy. 'Oh, it's so wonderful to see you. I've so much to tell you.'

Flora glanced worriedly at Bert. She didn't want to spoil her sister's obvious happiness but she needed to tell her what had been happening at home. They were made so welcome again, though Flora didn't want to divulge the real reason for her visit until she could speak to Mary Ellen alone. After dinner and helping Winnie to clear away and wash up while the menfolk lingered near the fire, Mary Ellen linked her arm through Flora's. 'Put your coat on, I want to show you around the farmyard. It's lambing time and we've got two sweet little lambs in the barn that I'm helping to rear by hand.'

'Why?'

'The mothers can't feed them so we do. Mrs Clarke has shown me how to do it. But I've something else to tell you, Flora.' Her smiling face turned a little pink as she said shyly, 'Jack has asked me to marry him.'

Flora's mouth dropped open. 'Oh Mary Ellen. That's wonderful, but – but are you sure? I mean it's a bit sudden, isn't it? And –'

'I know exactly what you're thinking. Is *he* sure? And what about his parents? Do they approve?'

'Well – yes. I'm sorry, but that is what I was thinking.'

'We all sat down and had a good chat about it. I'm willing – more than willing – to accept their way of life. I already love the farm.'

'What about their churchgoing?'

'I find it a great comfort. We've not been brought

up to go to church, have we, so I didn't know what I was missing. But it's wonderful. It's only a small community here.' She laughed. 'It's rather like our street – everyone knows everyone else's business – but instead it's a whole village.'

'And do they know about you?'

'Oh yes. I had a long heart-to-heart with the vicar. He's a lovely, understanding man. Forgiving too. He's accepted me into his congregation and, of course, everyone in the village follows his lead.'

'But you're underage. You need parental consent to get married.' As do I, Flora was thinking.

'Oh, we're not rushing into getting married. We both need time to get to know each other and – and to be *really* sure.' Mary Ellen hesitated and then, with tears in her eyes, said in a rush, 'I am so very sorry about what happened but it really wasn't my fault.'

Flora waited but Mary Ellen said no more.

'I have something to tell you.'

'Oh,' Mary Ellen's eyes sparkled, 'about you and Bert?'

'Well, yes, that's all going really well. We're planning to get married too, but, like you, not straightaway. No, it's something we've heard about Dad.'

Mary Ellen frowned as the ugly scene with her father replayed in her mind. 'Go on,' she muttered.

'He's got a fancy woman.'

Mary Ellen's mouth dropped open and she stared at her sister. 'Bert and his friend heard it in the pub. It's the barmaid there.'

'And he had the gall to –' Mary Ellen began but then shrugged philosophically. 'Oh well. It's different for him. He's a man.' She sighed heavily. 'What about poor Mam?'

'I haven't told her yet. That's why I've come to see you. I wanted to know what you thought I should do.'

Mary Ellen wrinkled her brow. 'Difficult, isn't it? I mean, if he leaves her, how will she live? Especially after you're married. Did she ever have a job? Before they were married, I mean?'

'I've no idea but, even if she had, that's over twenty years ago. Who'd employ her now? And would she be able to stay in the house? It's rented in his name.'

'What do other women do when their husbands leave them? We know it happens.'

Flora shrugged. 'I've really no idea. Some go home to their families, I suppose.'

'Mam can't do that. Both her parents are dead and she was an only child. I don't think she's got anyone she can turn to.'

'Except us,' Flora murmured.

Mary Ellen didn't answer, but then Flora asked her a direct question. 'Do you think I should tell her what we've heard?'

Now, Mary Ellen didn't hesitate. 'Yes, I do. It's not fair not to, because now she can make up her mind what she wants to do and, even if she doesn't want to *do* anything, at least she'll be prepared if he walks out on her.'

'That's what I'll do, then. And now we'd better go back in. Bert will be wanting to set off home soon.'

Eleven

'What does Mary Ellen think?' Bert said as he manoeuvred the trap out of the farmyard gate and took the road towards the city. The roads were muddy from recent rain and Bert had to be careful to keep the wheels of the trap out of the deep puddles at the side of the roadway.

'That I should tell Mam what we've heard. At least she'll be prepared.'

'I think Mary Ellen's right. If he does leave, it won't be such a shock.'

'I'll tell her tomorrow night. Dad will be at home tonight, it being Sunday.'

When Flora entered her home, her father didn't speak to her and Edith was too afraid of him to ask about Mary Ellen in his hearing, so it wasn't until the following evening when Patrick had gone out that mother and daughter were able to speak freely.

'She's looking really well again and Jack has asked her to marry him.'

Edith gaped at her. 'Really? What about his parents? I know they've been amazingly kind, but surely they can't want their son to *marry* her?'

'The Clarkes are a good, churchgoing family, Mam,

and they practise their faith.' She went on to tell her mother everything that Mary Ellen had said.

'Well, I never,' Edith murmured and a small smile, that was rarely seen, curved her mouth. 'I'm so happy for her. Perhaps one day,' she added wistfully, 'I'll get to meet this wonderful family.'

'Bert would take us –' Flora began, but Edith shook her head and the fear was back in her eyes. 'Oh, I couldn't, your father . . .'

'Mam, there's something I have to tell you about Dad.' Flora took a deep breath. 'He's seeing another woman.'

Edith stared at her for a long moment and then a smile spread across her face and she began to laugh. For a few seconds, Flora thought her mother was hysterical but no, her laughter was genuine. It was a sound that had not often been heard in this house. Edith wiped her eyes. 'Oh Flora, my darling daughter, that's the best news I've had in years. No wonder he hasn't troubled me in a long time. You know what I mean. That explains it.'

Flora sat staring at her mother. This was not the reaction she had expected and yet, it was a lot better than she could have hoped for.

Edith wiped the tears of laughter from her eyes as she said, 'Do you know who it is?'

'Her name's Lily Parker and she's the barmaid at the pub he goes to.'

Edith nodded. She was still smiling; it seemed as if now she couldn't stop.

Flora hesitated to introduce a note of cold reality into the conversation when her mother seemed to be taking the news so well, but she felt she had to ask. 'If he went to live with her, what would you do?'

'I really don't know and to be honest, I don't care. All I know is that I would be a lot happier even if I ended up in the workhouse.'

'Oh Mam, I'd never let that happen.'

Edith took Flora's hand and kissed it. 'I know you wouldn't.'

'Are you going to face him about it?'

Edith frowned. 'No, let's wait and see what happens.'

'If he did go, I don't know if you'd be able to keep the house. The rent book's in his name, isn't it?'

'I'd have to talk to the rent man. Contrary to popular belief about rent collectors, ours is a nice old boy. Mr Tomlinson. I've always got on well with him.'

'That's because you always pay on time. He's never had any trouble with us.'

'That's true, I suppose, but I'm sure he'd give me good advice and help if he could.'

'Would he turn a blind eye? You know, as long as the rent was paid on time?'

Edith shook her head. 'I doubt he'd be able to. And even if I didn't tell him myself, he'd certainly get to hear about it. Something like that wouldn't stay secret for long around these parts, now, would it?'

'No,' Flora said shortly. 'It wouldn't. It seems a lot of folk know already.'

There was silence between them until Flora asked hesitantly, 'Mam, did you have a job before you got married?'

Edith smiled wistfully. 'Yes, I was learning to be a dressmaker. I worked for a lovely lady called Miss Kendall. She'd never married. I believe she'd been engaged, but her fiancé had died of tuberculosis.' Her smile faded. 'But of course all that stopped when I married Patrick. I wasn't allowed to go out to work. He wouldn't even let me have a sewing machine at home to make clothes for you and Mary Ellen in case I started doing little jobs for other people. It was silly, really, because I could have earned a little bit of money. But he didn't want me to have a shred of independence.'

'Where is Miss Kendall now? Is she still alive? I mean, what sort of age was she when you knew her?'

'Well, I hope she's still around. I think she's about ten years older than me so she'd be in her early fifties now.'

'Maybe,' Flora said slowly, 'it'd be worth finding out if she's still in business.'

Mother and daughter regarded each other solemnly. Then Edith sighed. 'I know what you're thinking, but it's a long time since I did any sewing. I've probably lost my touch by now.'

'You'd soon pick it up again,' Flora said with a confidence that she was not feeling. It was more a hope. 'Let me see if I can find out anything. Where did she used to live?'

'When I knew her, she lived on Abbeydale Road. It wasn't exactly a shop, but she used to display one or two dresses in her front bay window and had her name – Miss P. Kendall, dressmaker – over her front door.'

'That's not far away. I wonder if she's still there,' Flora murmured. 'It'd be nice to know.'

On the following Sunday, dressed in the only coat she possessed, Flora walked the distance from her own home to the street where her mother had said Miss Kendall, the dressmaker, had once lived. It wasn't actually necessary yet for her to find her mother's former employer, but Flora was intrigued. She liked to be forewarned and forearmed of any trouble that might arise. And she was sure that at some time, probably in the not-too-distant future, there would be trouble in the Halliday household. As if we haven't had enough recently, she thought, but then silently gave thanks for the kindness of strangers. All being well, Mary Ellen would be safe and cared for from now on.

As she neared the number Edith had given her, Flora found she was holding her breath, but her heart skipped a beat when she saw that the front window was still dressed out with women's clothes. She glanced up to read the sign above the door: MISS P. KENDALL, DRESSMAKER. Just like her mother had said, even after all this time. The window showed a 'closed' sign, which was to be expected, it being Sunday. Flora took in the fashions displayed in the window. Everything was beautifully made. Flora felt a pang of pity for her mother. If Edith had been clever enough to make lovely clothes like this, what a terrible shame it was that she had not been allowed to carry on. What a dreadful waste of a wonderful skill. She was about to turn away when she heard the click-clack of heels on the pavement and looked round to see a smartly dressed woman walking towards her. She wore a close-fitting coat with a fur collar and a hat on her elegantly coiffured head. As she drew nearer, Flora could see that she had flawless skin and her blue eyes were sharp. This woman, Flora thought, didn't miss a thing. Her brisk walk slowed until she came to a stop in front of Flora.

'I'm sorry, but I am closed today,' she said. 'Was there anything particular you wanted?'

'Good morning, ma'am,' Flora said politely. 'Are you Miss Kendall?'

The woman smiled and her face seemed to light up. 'I am indeed. And who might you be?'

'My name is Flora Halliday.'

For a moment Miss Kendall frowned and then, as if the name meant something to her, a look of sadness crossed her features. 'The only Halliday I knew was poor Edith Furniss, who married a man called Halliday.'

'I'm her daughter,' Flora whispered, shocked that the term 'poor' should be applied to her mother.

Miss Kendall was peeling off her gloves and fishing in her reticule for her door key. 'Come in, my dear. I'll make us a cup of tea. Come through,' she added as she led the way down a short passage, passing the front room and going into a room that had obviously been turned into a workroom, although it was still a kitchen, for a range stood along one wall. A sewing machine, which was obviously used every day, stood in one corner. One wall of the room had been shelved to hold bolts of cloth and all the other equipment a dressmaker would use. Flora was fascinated.

'Your mother used to work here,' Miss Kendall said softly. She nodded towards the far corner of the room. 'That's the machine she used over there. I hadn't the heart to get rid of it when she left, and besides, it's nice to have a spare one. Please sit down,' she invited as she took off her coat and began to set the kettle on the hob and place cups and saucers onto the table.

'Now,' she said at last, 'how is your mother?'

Flora hesitated. This was the difficult part. She cleared her throat. 'She's well enough but I have to be honest with you, Miss Kendall. She has not been happy in her marriage, I'm sorry to say.'

'And I am sorry to hear that, but I too must be honest. I met her husband once when I called to see her just after her marriage to ask if she would be willing to do some work for me in her own home. Your father more or less threw me out.'

Flora nodded. 'Yes. He would have done. He controls her completely.'

There was a silence but Flora did not continue.

'So,' Miss Kendall asked gently, 'why have you come to see me?' She smiled. 'Are you wanting to take up dressmaking?'

Flora shook her head. 'I might well have done if I'd known about it sooner. But I didn't know until this week that that is what my mother had done before her marriage.' Her voice was flat with disappointment as she realized her lost opportunity. 'I just did what my father demanded and got a job as a buffer girl where he works.'

Another long silence ensued before Miss Kendall prompted, 'So why are you here?' She smiled again. 'Apart, perhaps, from curiosity.'

Flora took a deep breath. Miss Kendall was, like Edith had said, a lovely lady. Flora was sure she could trust her. 'We've had some family trouble just recently. I have a younger sister, Mary Ellen. She was always my father's favourite. Not that I minded,' she added swiftly. 'We all loved Mary Ellen dearly, but she – she got into trouble recently and my father threw her out of the house.' She recounted the sorry tale briefly, ending, 'But now we've found out that my father has – has a lady friend. We're not sure what he's going to do and – and . . .' She faltered but the kindly woman took up her words. 'You're not sure what will happen to your mother if he were to leave her.'

Flora nodded. The woman was silent for several moments before saying slowly, 'Edith was an excellent dressmaker and I'm sure she could soon pick it up again even after twenty years or so. I could put plenty of work her way – that wouldn't be a problem – but I don't think I could find accommodation for her . . .'

'Oh no. We wouldn't expect that. But just to know that perhaps she could earn some money would be wonderful.'

'Has she her own sewing machine?'

Flora shook her head. 'He – he wouldn't let her have one.'

Miss Kendall pursed her lips but made no comment. Instead, she said, 'Not to worry. I'll get that one' – she nodded to the spare machine in the corner – 'spruced up and ready for use.'

Tears filled Flora's eyes and her voice was husky as she said, 'That is so kind of you.'

'Don't mention it,' Miss Kendall said, 'I have an ulterior motive. I could do with some help. Sometimes I have to turn work away because I can't cope with it and I don't like doing that. One loses valuable customers that way if you can't do what they want when they want it.'

But Flora guessed that her offer was more out of kindness than necessity. Just like the Clarkes. How kind some people were. She stood up and held out her hand. 'Thank you for your time and your offer. It's been lovely to meet you.'

'Tell your mother if she'd like to come and see me sometime, I'd be delighted to see her again.'

'I'm sure she'd love to see you too, but I don't know . . .' Flora's voice trailed away uncertainly.

Miss Kendall guessed that it was a matter of if Edith would dare to come to see her. If her husband were to find out . . .

'And where, might I ask, have you been?' Patrick accosted Flora as she stepped through the back door.

'Just out for a walk,' Flora answered blithely.

'With *him*, I suppose.' Patrick raised his hand as if to strike her, but Flora, even though her heart began to hammer in her chest, stepped towards him instead of cowering away. She thrust her face close to his. 'Don't even think about it. You and your so-called mates would be no match for Bert and his pals, so I wouldn't threaten me or my mam again if I was you.'

'That namby-pamby lot? They're just a lot of

soft-handed penpushers.' Patrick sneered. 'We'll take 'em on any day of the week.' But she noticed that his arm dropped away and he made no further move to strike her. He turned away and slammed out of the back door. Flora took a deep breath, trying to still her racing heart, and stepped into the kitchen. Edith sat in her chair near the range and when she turned to look up at Flora, her daughter saw that there was a fresh bruise down the side of her face and a cut on her lip.

'Oh Mam,' Flora whispered. 'This can't go on.'

Edith shrugged. 'It was my fault, I – I cheeked him.'

'What on earth do you mean? You're his *wife*. You shouldn't be getting a slap for answering him back like a child would.'

'I made a mistake, Flora.'

'What was it about? Not – about *her*?'

Edith shook her head and then winced as if pain shot through her. 'No, I wouldn't bring that up. I think he'd kill me if I did. No, he complained about the dinner and I told him to cook it himself if he wasn't satisfied. I shouldn't have said it, Flora. It was stupid of me.'

'So, what are we going to do?'

Edith shook her head sorrowfully. 'What can we do?'

Twelve

A week passed without anything more being said but on the following Sunday evening, a day when Patrick did not normally go out, he left the house.

'He'll have gone to see her,' Flora said. 'I'm going to follow him.'

'Oh Flora, do be careful. If he sees you . . .'

'He won't.'

She left a few moments after her father and caught sight of him walking down the street. Even if he turned round, she told herself, he would not recognize her through the dusk.

At the end of their street, she saw him turn to the right and she quickened her pace until she reached the corner. She saw him a little way ahead, now crossing over the road and then turning to the left. Again, she hurried after him. Arriving at the next corner she spotted his shadowy figure. She was about to set off again but then she hesitated as she saw him stop in front of a house and raise his hand to knock on the door. After a moment, light flooded into the street as someone opened the door and she saw Patrick step inside. She stood for a few moments, biting her lip in indecision. She wanted to go right to the house and memorize the number, but she was afraid he might come out again and catch her in the act. She walked hesitantly a little way down the street, counting the numbers as she went. Stopping a short distance from the house, she counted the numbers ahead and estimated he had entered number twelve. Not wanting to take any further risk of being seen, she turned and hurried back towards her home to tell her mother what she had seen.

'I shall go and see her tomorrow.'

Now real fear was in Edith's eyes. 'Flora, please don't. It's dangerous. If he finds out . . .'

Flora shrugged. 'It might be for the best all round if he did.'

Edith shuddered as if already feeling the expected blows. Flora regarded her mother steadily. 'You know what I told you about what Miss Kendall said. Have you been to see her?'

Edith shook her head. 'I'd like to but . . .'

'Just go, Mam. You might feel a lot better if you talk to her. I know she'd like to see you because she said so and she more or less said she'd have work for you.'

'I do so wish I had more courage.'

'If you go in the morning, he'll never know. And have you called in on Bert's mam any more?'

Edith nodded. 'Yes, I called last week. She made me very welcome.'

'And so will Miss Kendall. I'm sure of it.'

Edith took a deep breath. 'Yes, you're right. I'll go this week. It'll have to be on my regular shopping day so that he doesn't hear I've been out on any other day.'

Flora sighed but said no more. What a dreadful way for any woman to have to live. She was certainly not going to kow-tow to Bert after they were married, but then Bert was a very different personality to her brutal father.

The following morning, Flora approached the buffer missus. 'Mrs Shaw, may I please take an extended dinner break today? I will make up the time later in the week, I promise. I have an urgent errand to do on behalf of my mother that can only be done in the daytime.'

Mabel Shaw regarded her thoughtfully. Flora was a hard worker, excellent at her job and always reliable. She never shirked helping out if they were short staffed by doing extra hours.

Mabel kept her voice low as she said, 'Just so long as you don't broadcast the fact. I don't want everyone thinking they can take time off during the day.'

'No, I won't,' Flora promised.

'Very well, then. I can spare you an extra hour.'

So, when everyone broke off for their dinner break, Flora hurriedly divested herself of her grubby clothes, sluiced the grime from her face and set off at a brisk walk towards the street where she had seen her father enter the house. Luckily, it was not too far from the factory so after fifteen minutes she was turning into the street. Without hesitation, she knocked on the door and waited, tapping her foot impatiently, until it opened.

The woman standing there was wearing a low-cut blouse which showed the cleavage of her generous bosom. She wore face powder and rouge and her hair was an unusual red-orange colour.

'Are you Lily Parker?' Flora said without preamble.

'An' who wants to know, might I ask?' the woman said, putting one hand on her hip and regarding her visitor with steely blue eyes.

'Flora Halliday.'

Now Lily looked her up and down. 'Oh, so you're his daughter, are you?'

Flora was quite impressed by the woman's honesty. She made no pretence at trying to hide her relationship with Patrick. 'I suppose your mother's sent you to beg me to give him up. Is that it?'

Now Flora smiled widely. 'On the contrary, you can have him as far as we're concerned. In fact, I'll help him pack and bring his stuff round here.'

Lily gaped. 'Well, I never. I've not had that response before.' She regarded Flora through narrowed eyes. 'Where's the catch?'

'No catch, I promise.'

'But it'll shame his wife. Him leaving her. She'll be gossiped about for months. Years, even.'

Flora shrugged as if that would be of no importance. Indeed, it would not. Whatever tongues said could not hurt Edith as much as Patrick's brutality over the years had done. But about that, Flora kept silent. She didn't want the woman to have any reason for second thoughts. At the moment Flora suspected that everything in Lily's garden was rosy and she didn't want to give her any reason to doubt that it might not always be so.

Lily was still frowning as if weighing up the odds.

Then she gave a quick nod. 'I'll talk to him tonight. See if he wants to move in with me.'

'You do that.' As Flora turned away to leave, Lily said, 'Life's full of surprises, isn't it? I never expected something like this to happen. Mind you, I do know they don't get on. He ses your mother's a right shrew. Very demanding and not very willing in the bedroom either. He'll be all right with me. I'll make him happy.'

Flora managed to stifle the laughter that bubbled up inside her. What lies her father must have spun. Perhaps he would be different with Lily. She hoped so. She wouldn't wish her father's brutality on any other woman but her concern had to be for her mother. Edith would be so much better off without him, and Bert had already promised that they would make sure Flora's mother was cared for whatever happened.

That evening, as soon as Patrick had left the house, Edith whispered, 'Did you see her?' Flora went on to describe Lily Parker, ending, 'It sounds as if she wants him to go and live with her.'

Edith's mouth dropped open and she stared at Flora as she said slowly, 'She can't know what he's really like.'

'I don't expect she does.'

'He'll be acting like he did when we were first courting. He'll have taken her in, just like he took me in – and my parents. They thought butter wouldn't melt. He was charming and attentive . . .' Her voice trailed away as she remembered better times and realized how easily she had been duped.

'I've got a feeling, Mam, that she will know just

how to deal with him. You were so young and under your parents' influence still. She's an older woman – about the same age as Dad, I would guess – who's had quite a bit of experience with men, if what's said about her is true. I reckon she'll be able to hold her own.'

Edith sighed. 'I hope so for her sake. I wouldn't wish the life I have with him on my worst enemy.' She paused and then added, 'So what happens now?'

'We wait and see.'

Life carried on as usual and yet, it wasn't quite as normal. Patrick was hardly ever at home and when he was, he was not as nasty tempered. And then one evening in April after he'd eaten his tea, he stood up and faced both Edith and Flora.

'I'm leaving,' he said bluntly.

If he had expected shock or protestations, he was disappointed. Edith sat quite still with her eyes down-cast. It was Flora who looked up and said, 'That's the best news we've had recently.' She smiled sweetly at him. 'Would you like me to help you pack and carry your belongings round to Lily's?'

Now it was Patrick's mouth that dropped open. 'You – you know?'

'Oh yes,' Flora said airily. 'We've known for a while. It seems she would like you to move in, so I think it's the best solution for everyone.'

His glance slid towards Edith. 'But how will you manage?'

Edith opened her mouth but it was Flora who said, 'Don't you concern yourself about Mam. I'll look after her.'

'They might not let you keep the house. It's my name on the rent book.'

'Of course it is, but we'll work something out. Now, you just pack your things and get out of this house.'

Her words were an echo of what he had said to Mary Ellen and all three of them were aware of it.

Patrick was gone within an hour. Flora rummaged in the kitchen cupboard and found half a bottle of port left over from Christmas and mother and daughter sat quietly by the range and toasted each other.

'Oh Flora, I can't tell you how relieved and happy I am. I never thought to hear myself say it but I don't care what happens to me. Even the workhouse would be better than the life I've had with him. You and Mary Ellen have given me the only happiness I've known in the last twenty years.'

'Don't you worry about that, Mam. You'll not end up in a workhouse while there's still breath in my body, I promise you.'

She poured another glass of port for them both.

'You'll have me tipsy,' Edith chuckled. It was a lovely sound to hear; one that had rarely been heard in this house.

As they lingered by the fire, Flora said, 'Have you been to see Miss Kendall?'

'No, but I will.' She paused as she thought about the new freedom she now had. It was a heady feeling as she added softly, 'I can go where I like now, can't I? Whenever I like. Do what I like.'

A lump rose in Flora's throat as she said softly, 'You can, Mam. Indeed, you can.'

They smiled at each other and then Flora got up. 'And now I'm going to write a long letter to Mary Ellen and tell her everything that's happened and that she can send her replies here now.'

Edith looked up. 'Tell her – tell her she can come home if – if she wants.'

Gently, Flora said, 'I'll tell her what you've said, Mam, but don't get your hopes up. I don't think she'll want to. She's happy there. Very happy.'

Edith nodded. 'Well, that's all I want for her. All I want for both of you.'

Mary Ellen's reply, addressed to her mother for the first time since she'd left home, came by return of post. As Flora had predicted, she did not want to leave the home she had found with the Clarkes, nor the man who loved her and whom she now loved devotedly in return.

Mrs Clarke says you're very welcome to visit any time, Flora and Bert can bring you. She says you can stay for a week if you want.

Tears filled Edith's eyes, though now they were not tears of sadness; she was touched at how kind they were.

'Have you been to see Miss Kendall and called again on Bert's mam?'

Edith shook her head. 'Not yet, but I will. I promise I will.'

Edith fulfilled her promise that very week when she went to do her Thursday shopping. Agnes Weston opened the door with a beaming smile. 'Come in, come in, my dear. It's so good to see you.'

As they sat down together, Edith said hesitantly, 'I expect you've heard that my husband has left.'

'Best thing that could have happened. Don't feel bad about it.' Agnes leaned closer. 'You don't, do you?'

'Heavens, no,' Edith said with a smile. 'It's just all the gossip there'll be. I don't mind for myself, but it reflects on Flora, doesn't it?'

Agnes wrinkled her forehead thoughtfully. 'Not really. Flora is a strong-minded, sensible girl. I think her only concern was how you were being treated. Have you got any plans? Will you be able to stay in the house?'

Edith sighed. 'I don't know yet. The rent man is due to call tomorrow. I'll have a chat with him. It's no good trying to hide what's happened. He'll hear soon enough from the neighbours.' She smiled as she added, 'Most probably before he even reaches my door!'

'Don't worry. We'll soon think of something if you have to leave. See what your rent man says tomorrow and we'll take it from there.'

Thirteen

The following morning as the time approached when the rent man usually called, Edith was nervous. She'd never felt uneasy before; Mr Tomlinson was a nice man, though she realized he might not have been so friendly if she'd ever fallen into arrears with her rent. But the money had always been sitting on the kitchen table waiting for him, as it was today. Beside it, she placed a tankard of beer. Edith always fetched a jug of beer from the corner shop on rent days. She knew it was what he liked but often thought that if he got such a drink at every house he visited, at the end of the day he must have been, quite literally, rolling home.

'Nah then, missus,' Wilf Tomlinson greeted her when she opened the front door to him and invited him to step inside. Wiping his feet and taking off his smart bowler hat, he followed her down the short passage into the kitchen where he sat down at the table without waiting for her invitation. His eyes sparkled when he saw the beer. 'That's very kind of you, Mrs Halliday. I don't mind if I do. You're me last call this morning so I won't be breathing beer fumes over the tenants.'

Edith smiled and nodded and sat down opposite

him. Although her heart was beating a little faster than normal, she felt surprisingly stronger than she had done for years.

'Mr Tomlinson, if you haven't already heard, I am sure you will do so before very long. My husband has left me to go and live with the barmaid from our local pub. So I need to ask you if the tenancy of this house can be transferred to me in those circumstances?'

Wilf stroked his chin thoughtfully. 'Well now, we'll have to give this some careful thought. I'll have to talk to my superiors, of course, but it should be possible, that is if you think you can always meet the rent.'

'Of course,' Edith murmured. 'That goes without saying.'

'Do your daughters still live with you?'

'Just the one now, Mr Tomlinson.' Edith forbore to say that Flora might be getting married in the not-too-distant future. No need to complicate matters, she thought.

'And she's working?'

'Yes, she's a buffer girl at Rowleys.'

'Very well. I'll see what I can do. I'll put in a good word for you. Your rent's always paid on time.' He reached out for the money lying on the table and put it into the leather satchel he carried. 'Thank you for the beer, missus,' he added as he got up. 'I'll see you in a month's time if not before.' He picked up his hat. 'Ta'ra for now.'

After Mr Tomlinson had left, Edith sat lost in thought for a few moments then, suddenly galvanized, she jumped up and reached for her hat and coat. Locking the door behind her, she set off down the street before she could change her mind, but when she turned into Abbeydale Road, her steps faltered a little. She took a deep breath and made herself walk on. She looked about her; the street had altered very little since the last time she had been here over twenty years ago. Then she had been full of hope, looking forward to her wedding day and excited at the thought of becoming a wife and mother. Such a lot had changed in her life since then. And now she was standing in front of the house where she had once worked as a seamstress in the back room. How she had loved the work.

The door opened, making her jump, and she turned to see Miss Kendall smiling at her.

'Edith, my dear. How lovely to see you. Do come in.'

Although she kept the smile on her face, Miss Kendall was shocked by the change in the girl she had once known so well. Edith was much thinner and stooped a little even though she could only be in her early forties. There was anxiety and, yes, fear in her eyes. She looked cowed, Miss Kendall thought. But then, if what Flora had told her was true, and she had no cause to doubt it, there was good reason.

Miss Kendall gestured again for Edith to step inside and Edith followed her to the back room.

Edith stood, looking round. 'Oh,' she breathed as a smile lit up her face. Now, there was a glimpse of the girl Miss Kendall remembered. 'Nothing's changed at all. Everything's just as I remember.'

Miss Kendall laughed. 'I'm not sure that's a compliment to me to think that I haven't changed anything in twenty years.'

'Why change anything if it doesn't need it? Oh look! Just look! You've still got the sewing machine I used.'

'I have, Edith,' Miss Kendall said softly. 'It's still sitting there just waiting for you to come back if you'd like to.'

Edith turned to look into Miss Kendall's eyes and her own eyes filled with tears. 'Do you mean it? Could I really come back and work for you? I – I might be a bit rusty.'

Miss Kendall shrugged. 'You'd soon get it back, Edith. You were a very good seamstress. I was so sorry when you left. I tried two other girls but compared to you, quite frankly, they were rubbish.'

Edith felt the colour rise in her face at the compliment. She had become unused to receiving – and accepting – praise of any kind.

'So what do you say? Will you come back and work with me?'

'I would love to, but are you really sure? Patrick – my husband – has left me now, so there'll be gossip. I wouldn't want it to reflect badly on you.'

'It won't. There has been all sorts of gossip and theories about me over the years. Why have I never married? Why do I live alone? Have I got a man friend?' She smiled widely. 'But I just ignore it all and get on with my life. But if you're not comfortable seeing clients, I can do all that in the front room.'

It seemed to Edith that Miss Kendall was not going

to let anything stand in the way of their old relationship being rekindled. And this was endorsed as she
added with a sigh, 'I need you, Edith, as much as you
need me. I've got more work coming in than I can
handle.' She laughed. 'My only question is, when can
you start?'

'Mam,' Flora said, coming in by the back door, 'we've
got a present for you. Come in, Bert.'

Bert appeared carrying a heavy box. 'Evenin', Mrs
Halliday.'

'Put it on the table, please, Bert,' Flora instructed.

'Whatever . . .?' Edith began and then she guessed.
'Oh Flora, you shouldn't have spent your hard-earned
money on me.'

'Bert found it. It's only second-hand but his mate
has cleaned it up and it works a treat. Do open it,
Mam.'

Flora was more excited than her mother and Bert
was grinning like the proverbial Cheshire cat.

It had been three days since Edith had told Flora
that she'd been to see Miss Kendall and that she was
to start working for her the following week. 'I'm just
so afraid my work won't be up to her high standards.
It's been so long . . .'

When Flora had told Bert what had happened, he'd
said at once that he would look out for a second-
hand machine so that Edith could do some work at
home and practise her skills to bring them back up
to what they'd once been. It hadn't taken long to find
one and now, he lifted the machine out of the box
and set it on the table.

'Oh Bert. It's grand. It's a Singer – just like the one I used at Miss Kendall's. In fact, she's still kept the very same machine. I saw it when I visited her. This is perfect. Thank you – both of you. But I'll pay you back as soon as I start earning.'

'No need,' Bert said. 'Please let us give you this to set you on your way.'

'And I plan to go to the market on Saturday and set you up with some cottons and materials,' Flora said. Then, as an afterthought, she added, 'Perhaps you'd like to come with me?' Even she wasn't yet used to the fact that Edith now had greater freedom.

'Oh, that would be lovely.'

They found some grand bargains and carried their purchases back home in triumph. 'Oh Flora, I can't wait to get started.'

'You've got all day tomorrow to practise before you start at Miss Kendall's on Monday.'

'I shall start tonight.'

Flora smiled. She couldn't ever remember seeing her mother so happy.

Edith sewed far into the night and all the following day, pausing only to eat, though she didn't work so late on the Sunday night; she didn't want to be too tired on her first day back at work. She set off on the Monday morning, dressed in the best clothes she possessed and full of eager anticipation. She was a little nervous when she knocked on the door but Miss Kendall made her feel so welcome and set her to work at once.

'I'm giving you something fairly simple, Edith, to

begin with. Not because I am questioning your ability, but because I think you will be happier.'

'You're quite right, Miss Kendall. Thank you.'

They worked side by side all day, with Miss Kendall only leaving the back room to answer each knock at the front door. When, at six o'clock, Edith left, she was tired but elated. She felt as if she were walking two feet above the pavement. She quickened her footsteps; she wanted to be home before Flora and to have the tea waiting for her on the table. She stepped in the back door and hurried into the kitchen – but she stopped short and gasped as she looked around the room with horrified eyes. Everything was in chaos; everything that could be broken had been smashed to smithereens. All her crockery, glassware, even her three precious china figurines from the mantelpiece – the only mementos she had from her parents' home – lay shattered on the floor. Her gaze went to the tea caddy, which usually stood on the corner of the shelf and held her housekeeping money. It lay open and empty on the floor. And worst of all, in Edith's eyes, her lovely sewing machine had gone. Slowly, she went from room to room taking in all the destruction. It was the same in the front room and upstairs. Both bedrooms – hers and Flora's – had been ransacked. All their clothes had been dragged from the wardrobes and chests of drawers and torn to shreds.

This was more than just a burglary, she thought. This was vicious, vindictive vandalism.

She was still sitting on her bed when she heard the

back door open and Flora's cheerful voice call out. 'Hello. You home, Mam?' And then there was a sudden silence and she knew Flora had stepped into the kitchen and seen the wanton destruction. She heard her daughter cry out with sudden fear in her voice. 'Mam! Mam! Where are you?'

'I'm here, Flora. Up here,' she managed to call, though her voice was unsteady. Flora's footsteps pounded on the stairs and then she rushed into the room. She was breathing heavily and only calmed a little when she saw her mother was unhurt. Flora sank down onto the bed beside Edith and gazed around. 'Is – is my room the same?' she asked huskily.

Edith couldn't speak so she just nodded.

'Who – who would do such a thing? We've hardly anything worth pinching.'

Edith had already had a few moments to think. 'I don't think robbery was the motive. I think it's someone who wants to hurt us – me. My sewing machine has gone.'

'But that's to be expected. It's probably the most valuable thing we had in the house, but why all this?' Flora gestured around them at the clothing lying in tatters on the floor.

'It's – it's revenge.'

'Revenge? Whatever for?'

'He – he wants to see me completely destroyed.'

'Mam – what are you talking about?'

'Flora – there was no break-in. Someone – the person who's done this – had a key.'

Flora gaped at her. 'Oh Mam!' she whispered. 'You don't think Dad's done this?'

Edith shrugged. 'Who else has a key except you and me?'

They sat in silence until at last Flora heaved herself up. 'Let's go and find something to eat – if we can.'

They made a meal out of bread and cheese; neither of them felt much like eating and certainly they didn't want to go to the trouble of cooking. Together, they began to clear up the mess. In the front room, the small china cabinet had been pushed over.

'Help me lift it, Flora. I expect everything in it will be smashed to pieces.'

Together they righted the piece of furniture and then Edith stared at the floor in surprise. There were no pieces of broken china or glass there.

'Well, that proves it,' she said grimly.

'Proves what, Mam? I don't understand.'

'All his precious bits and pieces that were his mother's have gone. He wouldn't have wanted them destroyed. Your dad's done this, I'm sure of it now.'

Fourteen

About an hour later, there was a knock at the door and Flora opened it to find Bert on the doorstep.

'Hello, love,' he began, but his smile faded when he saw the distress on her face. 'What's up?'

She held the door wider open. 'Come in and see for yourself.'

It took Bert a few moments to take it all in and to realize what had happened. 'Who . . .?' he began but Flora said in a flat voice, 'There was no break-in. Someone had a key.'

He stared at her for a few moments and then his face darkened with anger. 'Well, we know who that is, then, don't we? Right,' he said through gritted teeth. 'You leave this to me.'

'Are you going to the police?'

Bert gave a wry laugh. 'No, this is best dealt with by me and a few of my mates. Don't you worry any more, love.'

'Oh Bert, don't . . .' Edith began fearfully but the young man put his arm about her shoulders.

'You're not to worry yourself any more, Mrs Halliday. I'll take care of it.'

She turned frightened eyes towards her daughter.

'Oh Flora, stop him. I don't want him getting hurt on my account.'

Flora smiled grimly. 'I wouldn't want to stop him, Mam, even if I could. Bert knows what he's doing.' She glanced at the man she loved. 'Just be careful, love. That's all.'

Lily opened the door.

'Well, well, well, if it isn't the handsome Mr Weston. And to what do I owe *this* pleasure?'

Bert grinned – his quarrel was not with Lily – but in answer to her question he stuck his sturdy booted foot in the door so that she could not close it again.

'Good evening, Lily,' he said smoothly, as Howard Bonsor appeared at his side.

'Hello, Lily love.' Howard too gave her a beaming smile. 'We'd like a word with your house guest if it's convenient.'

Lily frowned. 'Now, boys, I don't want no trouble.'

'No trouble, I promise you, Lily, unless Mr Halliday decides to make some. It's really up to him.'

'He's not going back to her, if that's what you think.'

'We don't want him to,' Bert said shortly. 'We're all happy for him to stay exactly where he is, but you see there's been trouble at his old house and a particular item has gone missing. We think he might know something about it.'

Lily wriggled her plump shoulders. 'Whatever he's taken – and I'm not saying he has, mind – it's his to take.'

'Not in this case, because it's something I've just

bought for Mrs Halliday. And I've got the receipt to prove it if it – er – becomes necessary. So why don't you open the door, Lily love? Let's keep it friendly, shall we?'

He pushed the door firmly and Lily stepped back. 'Oh, get it over with, then.' She raised her voice. 'Patrick, there are two *gentlemen* to see you.'

They stepped into Lily's sitting room to see Patrick Halliday sitting with his feet up near a glowing fire in the range. Bert glanced around and saw the sewing machine, sitting on the table.

'Evenin', Mr Halliday. I have reason to believe,' Bert said, 'that you have paid a visit to your old home today.'

'Nah, wasn't me.'

'So why is the sewing machine I've just bought for Mrs Halliday sitting here on Lily's table?'

'Must be a different one. That's Lily's.'

'Really? Now, Howard, will you do me a little favour? Before I look too closely at the machine, will you tell me if, on the name Singer printed on the side, most of the "r" has been rubbed away?'

Howard looked closely at the machine. 'Yes, it has.'

Bert stared fixedly at Patrick, who glanced away. 'Oh, tek it, then,' he muttered morosely.

'And what about all the damage you did? Not a plate nor a cup and saucer remains whole. You've ripped their clothes to shreds and you've taken money. I think we'll have that back too.'

Patrick glared up at Bert but at the same moment, Lily gasped, 'He's done *what*?'

Bert recounted all the damage that had been done

in the Halliday house. 'But strangely,' he added pointedly, 'all the china and glass from the cabinet in the front room that was once his mother's has all disappeared. Not that Mrs Halliday wants it back. You're welcome to it.'

'That sounds like a burglar. Patrick wouldn't do all that,' Lily tried to dispute the allegation, but, even to her own ears, her protestations sounded weak.

But Bert was still smiling grimly. 'Ah, but you see, Lily, he omitted to stage a break-in to make it *look* like a burglary. Whoever did all that had a key and the only person who still has one other than Mrs Halliday and Flora is Mr Halliday. But,' he went on, turning back to Patrick, 'we will take the sewing machine and the money you took. And we'll have your key so there'll be no more uninvited visits.'

When Patrick made no move, Bert pretended to sigh heavily with regret. 'Then I think it's time to call the police, Howard, don't you?'

'No, no, don't do that,' Lily cried before Howard could either answer or make a move. 'Give them the key, Patrick, and the money.' She moved towards the sideboard and opened a drawer. 'Here,' she said, pushing a bag of coins towards Bert. 'Take this an' all and tell his wife I'm sorry. I knew he was going round there, but I thought it was only to collect some more of his belongings. I – I never thought he'd do owt like that.'

'Now, just hang on a minute, Lil,' Patrick began. 'That money's rightfully mine. It came out of my wages . . .'

'No, you look here, Patrick Halliday. If you want to stay here in *my* house, you'll do what *I* say.'

When Bert had everything he'd come for, including the sewing machine, he turned to leave with a parting shot towards Patrick. 'Don't go near your old home again if you know what's good for you.'

Patrick's lip curled. 'She'll not be there long. It's my name on the rent book. They'll throw her out.'

'We'll see,' was all Bert said calmly. 'But whatever happens, I'll be watching out for her and Flora.'

'We all will,' Howard added grimly. 'And their neighbours too because I'll make sure they all hear about this. I promise you.'

Out in the street again, Howard chuckled. 'Looks like he's met his match with Lil.'

'I hope so – for her sake,' Bert said.

Bert and Howard returned to the Hallidays' house where Bert set the sewing machine triumphantly on the table.

Howard glanced around at the devastation, which wasn't quite as bad now as it had been for Edith and Flora had already cleared up some of the mess.

'My God! Did he do all this?' Howard said. 'We should have given the bastard a good thumping.'

'I was very tempted but, for once in my life,' Bert said, 'my head ruled my heart. I didn't want to give him any cause for complaint against us.'

'Well, we can always catch him one dark night . . .'

'No, no, please don't, boys,' Edith pleaded. 'I'm more grateful than I can tell you for what you've done tonight, but, please, let it be now.'

113

'Mam's right,' Flora put in. 'We don't want any more trouble especially as we've had some better news while you've been out. The rent man called. He was appalled by all this' – she gestured towards the wreckage – 'but he told us he's able to grant Mam the tenancy in her own name and he also suggested getting the locks changed so that we know there are no more keys floating about.'

'Now, that is good news and about the locks an' all.'

'I could do that for you, Mrs Halliday,' Howard said. 'If you'd like me to. The sooner that's done the better, I reckon.'

'That's very kind of you, Mr Bonsor . . .'

'Oh, please call me Howard.'

Edith smiled. 'Then thank you, Howard. I would be very grateful.'

Bert fished the money and the key out of his pocket.

'Oh, thank goodness you've got the money back,' Edith said, tears filling her eyes. 'It's the first time ever I've not had the rent money waiting for him.'

'Mr Tomlinson was very understanding,' Flora said. 'He said he'd call back next week and she could pay whatever she could manage to scrape together.'

Edith was busily counting the money. 'It's all here. Oh, thank you, both of you. I'm so grateful.'

The following morning, Edith was feeling much better, though the moment she arrived at Miss Kendall's home, her new employer remarked, 'You look very tired about the eyes, Edith. I hope you haven't been sewing far into the night. There's no need. You're

114

already doing very well. Better than I could have expected.'

Edith shook her head and explained swiftly what had happened the previous day. 'Oh, my word!' Miss Kendall exclaimed. 'Did you call the police?'

Edith shook her head. 'No, Flora's young man and one of his friends sorted it out. I don't think there'll be any more trouble.'

'Well, if there is, there's always a bed here for you. I have a spare bedroom.'

'That's very kind of you.'

'Oh, and by the way, perhaps in the confines of these four walls you can call me by my Christian name – or rather, the nickname my family uses.'

Edith waited, but Miss Kendall still seemed rather shy of divulging her name. Edith had never known her other than as 'Miss Kendall'.

Colour rose in the woman's cheeks as she said, 'My name is Persephone but my family call me Seffie. When my younger sister started to talk, she couldn't say the full name and called me Seffie and it stuck.' She pulled a face. 'I don't like the name Persephone anyway. It was far too grand for where we lived. I used to get teased mercilessly at school.'

'I can't say I've ever heard it before, but I think it's rather nice.'

'Well, like I say, it's Seffie, but just when we're alone. Please, not in front of customers – or anyone else, for that matter. Anyway, if you're sure you're feeling up to it, let's get started. I've taken on two more pieces of work so there's quite a bit to be getting on with.'

*

When Edith arrived home that evening, she found Flora already there. On the table were two sets of crockery to replace the broken items.

'Bert's mam has sent these round to tide us over. And by the way, Bert has offered to take us both to see Mary Ellen on Sunday.'

'Oh, that would be lovely,' Edith said and tears sprang to her eyes. 'Everyone is being so kind. I must call and see Mrs Weston again. Does she know I've got a job now?'

'Yes, Bert has told her everything. She sent a message that she'd love to see you when you feel up to it.'

'Please tell her I'll call on Saturday afternoon. Miss Kendall insists we only work the mornings on Saturdays.'

'She sounds like the perfect employer.'

'She is. We're getting along very nicely together,' Edith said happily. And now she had something else to look forward to; a visit to Mrs Weston's and even more exciting, a trip into the countryside to see Mary Ellen and the family who had been so kind to her. The shock and distress of finding the chaos in her home began to fade just a little.

'Oh Mam!' Mary Ellen exclaimed as Edith climbed down from the pony and trap as it came to a halt in the farmyard. At once, she was enveloped in a bear hug by her younger daughter. 'You look wonderful. Flora has told me everything that's happened in her letters.' She stood back and held her mother at arm's length. 'But I have to admit I didn't think you'd be looking so much – *better.*'

Introductions were made all round and the Clarke family welcomed Edith into their home.

After they'd eaten Sunday dinner, Edith helped clear away and in Winnie's farmhouse kitchen, she said, 'I can't begin to thank you enough for your kindness to Mary Ellen. I feel so ashamed that I didn't stand up to Patrick and –'

Winnie patted Edith's hand. 'Don't blame yourself, my dear. Mary Ellen has explained everything to us. I just hope you don't mind us knowing.'

'Heavens, no!' Edith said without stopping to think. Then she wondered if the use of the word 'Heavens' was blasphemous in their eyes. Still, it was said now and she couldn't unsay it. That was the thing about speaking without thinking first; you could never unsay words that had passed your lips.

But Winnie was still smiling at her. 'And I want to know if you're happy about the growing romance between Mary Ellen and Jack?'

'Oh, of course, but I can't help feeling a little surprised that – that he's willing to marry her in – in the circumstances. You're a very forgiving and under-standing family.'

Winnie shrugged. 'It's our faith,' she said simply as if that explained everything. 'Now come along and sit by the fire. It's still a little chilly for May, isn't it?'

It was so easy to talk to Winnie that Edith found she could unburden herself to her in a way she had never been able to with anyone else. Not even with Agnes Weston or Seffie, even though she was now good friends with both of them. But there was some-thing about Winnie's calm sympathy that encouraged the sharing of long-buried secrets. Edith found herself telling Winnie about her early life, her disastrous marriage, and she shed tears when she admitted how she felt she had let Mary Ellen down so disastrously.

Winnie patted her hand gently. 'But things are better for you now, aren't they? And I promise you, you need feel no more guilt about Mary Ellen. Jack loves her dearly and we will take care of her. The whole community have taken her to their hearts.'

'You're such good people. I wish –' Edith bit her lip.

'Mary Ellen has taken to our churchgoing way of life of her own accord. We didn't force her to accept it, but she finds it gives her great comfort.'

Edith nodded. 'Perhaps I should try it. Seffie goes to church sometimes. Maybe . . .'

Winne patted her hand again. 'No harm in trying, Edith, my dear.'

They left the farm in the afternoon arriving back in the city at dusk.

'I'll just see you both safely inside,' Bert said, still a little anxious how they might find things, though he did not voice his fears aloud. But all was as they had left it. Bert didn't stay long. 'I must get the pony and trap back to my mate. I'll see you tomorrow evening after work, Flora. Goodnight, Mrs Halliday.'

'Goodnight, Bert. And thank you so much.'

Bert smiled and nodded and then he was gone.

They settled into a happy new routine. Edith was well established in her employment with Seffie. Flora and Bert grew ever closer and Mary Ellen was ecstatically happy in the countryside. She found she had a love for and an affinity with animals and, though she helped her future mother-in-law in the house, she was at her happiest outside helping on the farm. And in each season that first year she found joy in everything; haymaking, harvesting, threshing, ploughing and planting. And, of course, caring for the animals. The only sadness caused was when the animals were sent to market. She closed her mind to what would happen to them after that.

In the city on Christmas Eve, Bert said, 'Flora Halliday, will you marry me?'

Pink with pleasure, Flora said, 'Oh, yes, Bert, yes.'

'I thought we could get married on your twenty-first birthday in March. How would you feel about that?'

'Perfect.' Then her face fell. 'There's only one problem.'

Bert blinked. 'Is there? I can't think of anything.'

'Who's going to give me away?'

'Ah, of course. You won't want to ask your father, I take it.'

'Not in a million years, Bert.'

'Have you no male relatives? Uncles? Cousins?'

Flora shook her head. 'There's no one. Mam and Dad were only children.' She paused and then added, 'I wonder if Howard . . .'

'I was planning to ask him to be my best man, but if –'

'No, no, he must do that. He's your best mate.'

They were both thoughtful for a few moments before Bert said, 'What about Mr Clarke or even

Jack? I mean we'll be asking them to the wedding and Mary Ellen will be your bridesmaid, won't she?'

Flora looked up and smiled. 'What a lovely idea. I'll ask Mam what she thinks and, if she agrees, I'll write to Mary Ellen.'

Fifteen

The months between Bert's proposal and their wedding day seemed to fly and by 3 March 1894 – Flora's twenty-first birthday – everything was ready. The church was booked, the bridal gown made by Edith and Seffie, together with a bridesmaid's dress for Mary Ellen and a wedding breakfast to be held at Agnes Weston's home.

'My front room will be plenty big enough,' she'd told Flora. 'There won't be that many guests unless, of course, you'd prefer to have it in your local pub?'

Flora and Bert had glanced at each other. 'I think not,' Flora said. 'Here will be lovely. We'll help you get everything ready and I'm sure Mam will help too.'

The two mothers worked well together. Edith deferred to Agnes's ideas; after all it was her home that was being disrupted.

'Mary Ellen and Jack are going to stay with me two nights,' Edith said, 'though Mr and Mrs Clarke can only come for the day itself. They must go back to the farm the same evening. There are all the animals to see to.'

'Of course. It must be a good life on a farm, but very hard work,' Agnes said.

Edith nodded. 'It is, but Mary Ellen loves it.'

'I'm pleased for her. You wouldn't have thought a city girl would have taken to it so well.'

'No, and of the two sisters, I would have said Flora was the most likely to take to that way of life. She was the strong one. Mary Ellen was always so pretty and delicate.'

'Have you enough room to sleep them all?' Agnes asked.

'Mary Ellen will sleep with Flora and Jack will sleep on the couch in the parlour. It's all arranged and, of course, on their wedding night, Flora will be here with you.'

The two mothers glanced at each other; one with happy memories, the other with recollections she would rather not think about.

'Not exactly *with* me,' Agnes said. 'I've arranged to spend a few nights with a friend who lives in the next street. I want to give them a little time on their own and they'll want to get the front room turned into their own sitting room. We've decided that we'll eat together in the kitchen, but they'll always have the other room to go to, to be on their own. I never use it anyway so very little will change for me. Flora tells me she intends to carry on at work, at least for the time being.'

Edith nodded. 'Are you happy about that?'

'Perfectly. It's the sensible thing to do. They need to save to be able to furnish their own place in time. And if little ones come along . . .'

The two women exchanged another glance and smiled. It was another happy thought.

*

The wedding was a quiet affair and yet it was in keeping with the kind of weddings a buffer girl and an office worker had. Flora was nervous on the morning of the wedding.

'I don't know what you're worried about,' Mary Ellen teased her. 'It's not as if you're afraid Bert's going to do a last-minute runner.' She paused and then added, 'Are you?'

'Heavens, no!' Flora laughed shakily.

'So what is it?'

'I'm just afraid Dad might turn up and cause trouble.'

Mary Ellen frowned before saying thoughtfully, 'I don't think he'll do that. What does worry me is when Mam is left here on her own. Is she going to be all right?'

'Well, I suppose we could live with her, but it's been arranged for a long time – even from before Dad left – that we should live with Mrs Weston.'

Mary Ellen nodded. 'Whatever you do, one of them's going to be left on her own.'

'I know. It is a bit of a worry, to be honest, but we've had all the locks changed and, since he's left, Mam's started to get friendlier with the neighbours.'

'That's good. He would never let her have friends before, would he?'

'And she's always got Miss Kendall to go to.'

'Is Miss Kendall coming to the wedding?'

'Oh yes. We couldn't possibly leave her out.'

The sisters stood and looked at each other. 'Oh Flora,' Mary Ellen whispered. 'You look absolutely beautiful.'

'You don't look so bad yourself.'

'It's time I was leaving to get to the church with Mam. It's a ten-minute walk. Thank goodness it's not raining. You were taking a bit of a risk getting married in March.'

Flora grinned happily. 'Couldn't wait any longer.'

'Right. I'm off. There'll only be Mr Clarke waiting for you downstairs. He's like a dog with two tails at being asked to give you away.'

'He's a lovely man.'

'They're a lovely family, Flora. I've been so lucky to find them after . . .'

'Now then, no unhappy thoughts today. Off you go. Wait for me in the porch, won't you?'

'Of course. I know what I have to do.'

She leaned forward and gently kissed Flora's cheek. 'Enjoy your day, my darling sister, and be happy for the rest of your life. No one deserves it more than you.'

Mary Ellen's sweet words brought tears to Flora's eyes, but she blinked furiously to hold them back. It wouldn't do to turn up at the altar with red and swollen eyes.

The wedding service went smoothly and, as the party walked back to Agnes Weston's house, folk came out of their houses to clap and cheer the happy couple on their way. It was a tight squeeze in Agnes's front room, but the guests mingled freely, finding themselves a place to sit.

'My word, you've been busy preparing this wonderful spread,' Winnie Clarke said.

'Edith came round early this morning to help.'

Agnes glanced at the woman who was now more or less related to her through the marriage of their children.

'I've enjoyed helping,' Edith said. 'I think there's going to be enough.'

'I'm sure there's plenty,' Winnie said, glancing at the table so laden with food that there scarcely seemed to be an inch of white tablecloth visible. 'Though you'll have to watch my husband and son don't take more than their fair share. They've both got an appetite like one of our shire horses. Now, let me help you. I'll go and ask that nice-looking lady in the corner what she'd like. She's looking a bit left out and we can't have that.'

'That's Miss Kendall,' Edith said. 'It's the lady I work for and she helped me make the dresses for Flora and Mary Ellen.'

Winnie stared at Edith in amazement. 'You *made* their dresses?'

'Well, yes. I was a dressmaker before I married. I worked for Miss Kendall then and she's been kind enough to take me back since . . .'

'I'm sure she's lovely, but if you can sew like that, Edith, she's taken you on your own merit.' Winnie's smile broadened. 'I certainly know where to come to get my new outfit at Easter.'

Edith looked puzzled until Winnie explained. 'I always have a new outfit at Easter each year. It's the only time I buy new clothes and it's a tradition among all the women in our church.' She laughed. 'We don't just have an Easter bonnet; we have the full works.'

'But Easter is less than three weeks away.'

Winnie loaded a plate with sandwiches and sausage rolls. 'Then I'd better go and talk nicely to Miss Kendall, hadn't I?'

Edith stared opened-mouthed after her as Winnie weaved her way across the room to sit beside the dressmaker. Within two minutes the two women were deep in conversation.

'It's all arranged,' Winnie told Edith happily a little later. 'You and Miss Kendall are to come out to the village and stay a night or two with us on the farm to take measurements.'

'Measurements?'

'For new outfits.'

'But – but we could take your measurements today.'

Winnie laughed. 'Yes, but not those of half the village.'

Edith stared at her. 'Half the . . .?'

'You just wait and see. When I go back and tell all my friends, they'll be queueing up to have you make them new outfits for Easter.'

'We couldn't possibly do that many by Easter.'

Winnie shrugged. 'Well, as many as you can, then, because I'm sure some ladies will be prepared to wait. I bet most of them have never had an outfit made especially for them. I certainly haven't.'

'And – and Miss Kendall has agreed to this.'

'Oh yes, it's all arranged. Jack will come to fetch you early on Tuesday morning and bring you back late afternoon on Thursday. So get your bags packed, Edith. You're coming for a little holiday!'

Edith smiled weakly. It would be lovely to spend time at the farm with Mary Ellen and the Clarke family, but the amount of work there would be to do didn't sound like much of a holiday. Still, she told herself, she wasn't really sure what a holiday should be anyway; she'd never had one.

While Agnes took herself off to stay a few nights with her friend and the newlyweds settled into their new roles as man and wife, Edith packed a small suitcase and set off early on the Tuesday morning. As she turned the corner into the street where Seffie lived, she saw the pony and trap already standing in front of the house. She quickened her step, fearing she had kept them waiting but, as she drew near, she could see Jack knocking on the door, which opened and Seffie appeared, already dressed in her hat and coat.

'Ah, there you are, Edith. Perfect timing. Good morning, Jack, do come in. Would you like a drink?'

'No, I'm fine, thank you, Miss Kendall.'

'I'm afraid I've two suitcases.' Seffie laughed. 'I look as if I'm coming for a month, but the larger one contains fabric samples and patterns.'

'No problem, Miss Kendall,' the young man said, picking up her cases with ease. As he turned towards the trap, he greeted Edith. 'Good morning, Mrs Halliday. All set?'

Having stowed their cases in the back, Jack helped the two women into the trap and they set off, the wheels rattling loudly in the stillness of the morning air. As they left the city streets far behind, Seffie looked about her. 'What beautiful countryside. It's many years since I took a trip out here. I'd forgotten just how magnificent Derbyshire is.'

Edith was silent; the only time she'd been this far outside the city had been a few weeks earlier when Bert and Flora had taken her to the farm.

'It is beautiful,' she murmured. 'So peaceful.'

They were treated like visiting royalty by the Clarke family.

'No, no, you're not to help with the washing-up,' Winnie insisted. 'Mary Ellen and I can do all that. You're going to have plenty of work over the next two days. I've rounded up at least ten ladies to come to have their measurements taken.'

'Oh dear,' Seffie said worriedly. 'I don't think we'll be able to get eleven outfits ready for Easter.'

'No matter,' Winnie said. 'They all understand. They don't mind waiting because they're all so thrilled to have something made especially for them.'

Seffie relaxed. 'That's all right, then. We'll do our best, of course, but I must mind I don't neglect any of my regular customers.'

'You can put me at the bottom of the list,' Winnie added. 'I really don't mind. I shall have my new Easter bonnet anyway. You don't do hats, do you? We have a lady in the village who always makes hats for all of us.'

'No, we don't. And I wouldn't want to take her business anyway. Is that all she does?'

'Yes. She's very clever with hats, but useless at making garments. She says so herself.'

Over the next two days, Seffie and Edith never seemed to have a moment to themselves except to eat and to sleep. There was a steady flow of visitors to the farm to see them. By the end of the afternoon on Thursday they had fifteen orders. Word had spread and more had been added to the list.

'Have we seen everyone?' Seffie asked Winnie. 'I know Jack's ready to take us home, but I wouldn't want to miss someone.'

'No, Iris Beckett was the last one. Now, I've packed a hamper for each of you to take home. You're going to be so busy you won't have time for shopping and cooking. Just one thing I want to ask. Will you need to come again to give the ladies their fittings?'

'It would be best,' Seffie agreed.

Winnie beamed. 'Just you let me know when and I'll sort it all out this end so they all know. Mary Ellen's got the list of everyone who came. We've loved having you here – both of you. I only wish we'd had more time to chat. Maybe in the summer you could both come for a proper holiday. Mary Ellen could take you for little trips out into the countryside. She's learning how to drive the pony and trap.' Winnie's beam of pride couldn't have been wider if Mary Ellen had been her own daughter.

'What lovely people they are, Edith,' Seffie said as they stood at the door of her home to wave Jack off.

'They are. Mary Ellen has been very fortunate to find them.'

'She can put all that sadness behind her now and look forward to what I think – what I hope – is going to be a very happy future for her. Now, Edith, let's go inside and make a cup of tea because I have a proposition to put to you.'

When they were seated either side of the kitchen range, Seffie said, 'Why don't you stay here for the next few weeks? My spare room is always kept ready even though, to be honest, I rarely have visitors. It would be so much easier than you having to go home each night, cook for yourself and so on. You haven't even got Flora at home to worry about now, have you? We can pool these wonderful hampers Mrs Clarke has given us. We can work, eat and sleep without interruption. What do you say?'

Edith smiled. 'If you're sure, I think it's a wonderful idea. I must go home on rent days, though, but it would save me a lot of time going backwards and forwards and Flora's taken her belongings to Mrs Weston's now.'

Seffie chuckled. 'She's Mrs Weston too now, don't forget. Bring whatever you want from home, Edith. We can wash and iron on Mondays and Tuesdays between us and still keep the sewing going.'

The two women, who were fast becoming firm friends, smiled, looking forward to the next couple of weeks. And just before Easter, there would be another trip to the countryside to fit the garments they had made.

There was so much to look forward to, Edith thought. After all the years of hardship, even from as far back as her childhood, she couldn't believe how lucky she was now.

Sixteen

They worked very well together and their friendship deepened. Although Seffie was older, Edith enjoyed the company of another woman. She'd brought all the clothes she still possessed with her; there weren't many since Patrick's destructive visit and Seffie promised that as soon as their outstanding orders were fulfilled, Edith could make herself some new clothes.

They had arranged with Winnie that they should visit on the weekend before Easter for the fittings and then deliver the finished garments – at least as many as were ready – on Easter Saturday.

Mrs Clarke says, Mary Ellen had written, *you're both very welcome to stay for a night or two if you would like to. Though I should tell you, the family will expect you to attend church with us on Easter Sunday.*

'That's most kind of them,' Seffie said when Edith read out the invitation from her daughter's letter. 'I must admit I'm not a regular churchgoer,' she went on. 'But I do attend now and again.'

Edith said nothing; neither her parents nor Patrick had ever encouraged her to go to church, though she had to admit that since Mary Ellen had said how much comfort she gained from the services and belonging to the community, she was intrigued. She would never forget how these good people had been so kind and forgiving towards Mary Ellen. They could have shunned her and sent her away in shame. Instead, they had opened their arms to her and accepted her, faults and all. And she remembered her conversation with Winnie Clarke too. Maybe she really ought to give it a try.

'Shall we accept, then?' she asked and Seffie nodded. 'I think we'll both have earned a little break by then.'

Two evenings before they were due to make their proposed visit to the farm, there was a knock at the door.

'Could you see who that is, Edith dear? I'm just in the middle of a particularly difficult pleat.'

When Edith opened the door, she was shocked to see both Flora and Bert standing there. Bert looked solemn and Flora had tears running down her face.

'Oh, my dears.' Edith reached out a trembling hand. 'Come in. Whatever's the matter?'

Once inside, Bert explained swiftly. 'It's your house, Mrs Halliday. There was a fire last night.'

'Everything's gone, Mam,' Flora blurted out. 'Everything.'

'It was lucky it didn't spread to your neighbours or the whole street might have gone up. The firemen did an amazing job but they couldn't save anything of yours.'

'But – but everything was fine when I visited at the weekend. Oh dear, oh dear. But do come in. We must tell Seffie.'

As they repeated everything to the dressmaker, Bert added, 'Mam says you must come and stay with us until we can find somewhere else for you . . .'

'No need,' Seffie said swiftly. 'She can go on living here. At least, if that's what you'd like, Edith?'

Edith sat down on the nearest chair as shock hit her suddenly. 'Yes, yes, at least for a while,' she said weakly. 'If – if that's all right . . .'

Seffie took one look at her and said, 'Put her head between her knees, Flora. I think she's going to faint. I'll make some hot, sweet tea.'

When Edith had recovered a little and they were all sitting together drinking tea, Seffie asked, 'Have you any idea how it happened?'

'Everything was all right when I went round four days ago,' Edith murmured again.

Flora and Bert glanced at each other. 'The superintendent thought it had been started deliberately,' Bert said gently. 'There was a strong smell of paraffin on the hearth rug and he says that's where the fire started.'

Edith stared at her son-in-law. 'But who would . . .?' she began and then stopped. 'Oh no!' she breathed. 'He wouldn't do that, would he?'

Bert's expression was grim as he said, 'The fire officer informed the police and we were questioned. We told them about the destruction caused a while back, how there was no break-in and how we found your sewing machine at Lily Parker's house. We didn't exactly point the finger. We just told them the truth.'

Edith closed her eyes and groaned. 'He'll come after me.'

'He doesn't know you're here, does he?' Seffie said.

Edith shuddered. 'If he doesn't, he'll make it his business to find out soon enough.'

The next couple of days were worrying for all of them, but only Edith felt real terror. She scarcely slept. She was relieved when the day came for them to go to Dale Farm and yet she was anxious that something might now happen to Seffie's property. Seffie said very little on the matter to Edith though she was worried. She asked her neighbours to keep an eye on her home but on the night before Jack was due to pick them up, Bert arrived to see them.

'He's in custody,' he said at once. 'The police went round to Lily Parker's house. They found a can of paraffin in her wash house and there were traces of paraffin found on his working clothes and he was carrying a box of matches. He's been arrested, but not charged yet.'

Edith sat down suddenly as her legs gave way beneath her. 'What about – what about Lily Parker?'

Bert shrugged. 'I haven't heard what her reaction has been but if he goes to prison, I doubt she'll wait for him. Lily doesn't like to be without a man friend for very long.'

For a few moments, no one spoke but then Bert said gently, 'Mrs Halliday, Flora and me have been round to your house. There's nothing to salvage, I'm afraid.'

Edith nodded sadly. 'There wasn't much left worth keeping anyway, except the sewing machine you bought me. Not after – not after . . .'

'That's been burned, I'm afraid. I'm so sorry.'

'Don't worry,' Seffie said, feeling better now that the man was in gaol at least for a few days. 'Your home is here now, Edith.' She glanced at Bert. 'I'll make sure she has everything she needs. You probably already know that we're going on a short visit to Dale Farm early tomorrow morning. We'll be back on Monday evening but then we're going there again over the Easter weekend.'

Bert smiled. 'Yes. Flora's told me all about it.'

The two weekends spent at the farm were busy, yet no work – except feeding the farm animals – was done on the Sundays. After the church service on Easter Sunday the congregation paraded through the village to celebrate the day and to show off their new finery which, this year, was not only a new hat!

'Everyone's so delighted with their outfits. Even those you didn't manage to get finished are still looking forward to you bringing them. When do you think you'll be wanting to visit again?'

Seffie wrinkled her forehead. 'About three weeks, Mrs Clarke, we'll write and let you know definitely. Will that be all right?'

'Of course. You're welcome to stay a bit longer if you want.'

Seffie and Edith glanced at each other. 'That's kind of you, but we don't want to stay away from home for too long at the moment,' Seffie said.

They had, of course, told Mary Ellen and the Clarke family everything that had happened. Winnie Clarke nodded her understanding. 'You're welcome to come here any time you want to. Both of you. We love having you and it's good for Mary Ellen and her mother to see each other.'

Once they were safely back at Seffie's home, they found everything was just as they had left it, but there was news about Patrick. Both Bert and Flora arrived during the evening on the day following their return.

'He's been charged with arson and also with criminal damage and theft for the previous occasion. His trial won't be for a while but he's not been granted bail.' Bert smiled. 'So you can both sleep easy in your beds.'

Flora hugged her mother and then turned to Seffie. 'I can't thank you enough for taking her in.'

Seffie smiled. 'While I wouldn't have wished for such a dreadful thing to happen, I have to say I'm delighted to have her here. We get on so well both living and working together. And it's thanks to your family that I am now getting out and about into the countryside. Living alone, one tends to get a little insular and forgets to make the effort to go out and make friends.'

'You're a fine-looking woman, Miss Kendall, if you don't mind me saying so,' Bert said. 'Why have you never married?'

'Bert!' Flora was shocked. 'Don't ask such personal questions.'

But Seffie only laughed. 'It's all right, Flora. I don't mind being asked though my answer is a little sad, I'm afraid. I had a fiancé once when I was twenty but he died of consumption and I've never since met anyone I could love like I loved him.' There was silence in the room until Bert said, a little shamefaced, 'I'm sorry I asked you. I didn't mean to revive painful memories for you, Miss Kendall.'

'It's all right, Bert, honestly. And why don't you and Flora call me Seffie, like your mother does? It's a nickname but I don't like my proper name and it's a mouthful anyway.'

Bert opened his mouth to ask what it was but before he could say a word, Flora said, 'Don't even think about it, Bert Weston.' They all laughed together.

After the young couple had left, Seffie said seriously, 'You are happy about coming to live here, aren't you, Edith? I wouldn't want you to feel you were being pushed into it because of what's happened. I mean, we could . . .'

'Seffie, you might not believe me, but I don't know the last time I felt so happy about anything. Probably only when my daughters were born.'

Seffie beamed. 'That's wonderful. We'll get along very well together, I'm sure. And now, we'd better get to work. We've still got a lot to do before we can go back to Dale Farm.'

Seventeen

The weeks passed and everyone welcomed July's warm days, although the buffer girls sometimes found the hot weather unbearable for there was no way they could shed their protective layers.

Word filtered back that Lily Parker intended to stand by Patrick. Bert chuckled at the news. 'I reckon she's realized she's getting a bit long in the tooth to get another feller. Better the devil she knows, eh?'

'Just so long as he never tries to come back to Mam,' Flora said. 'Has there been any news of his trial?'

'It's in two weeks' time. I heard yesterday. I've got to go as a witness for the prosecution.'

'Why? You didn't see anything.'

'They're charging him with the criminal damage and theft and I've got to tell the story of the sewing machine.'

'Ah, yes. I was forgetting about that.' Flora paused and then asked, 'How long d'you think he'll get?'

Bert wrinkled his forehead. 'Difficult to say really. I should think at least six months' prison for the damage and theft. Who's to know for the arson. It's a very serious offence. I mean, he couldn't have known for certain whether or not your mam was still in the house. And he certainly put the neighbours in danger. It was only because of the firemen that their houses didn't catch light as well. Anyway, I'd better be off. See you tonight.' He gave her a long hard kiss and then left the front room they now shared as their sitting room. Passing through the kitchen, he gave his mother a peck on the cheek.

Flora followed him. 'I'd best be off, an' all. Evelyn will be waiting for me.'

Now that they lived just across the road from each other, the two young women walked to and from work together.

'Ta-ra, love,' Agnes said. 'See you later.'

Flora crossed the road just as Evelyn emerged from her own home two doors up on the opposite side. When Evelyn caught up with her, Flora said, 'Are you all right? You look a bit peaky. Is the hot weather getting to you?'

'I've been sick first thing in the morning for a few weeks now, Flora. I must be in the club again. I reckon I'm about three months gone.'

Flora stopped walking and stared at her friend. 'Is – is that a sign, then?'

'Oh yes, didn't you know? It's usually the first sign you get, other than missing your you-know-what. Why? Do you think you could be expecting too, then?'

'I – it's possible, now you've told me that. I was sick yesterday morning and again today. I thought it must have been something I'd eaten, but . . . perhaps not.'

'Are you pleased?'

Flora laughed nervously. 'I think so. It just takes a bit of getting used to, that's all.'

'What will Bert say?'

Flora smiled at the thought of her husband. 'He'll be thrilled. He can't wait for us to start a family.'

'Aw, that's nice.'

'What about Howard?'

Evelyn laughed aloud. 'He's over the moon. He saw me throwing up so he guessed almost before I did. He's always said he wants a barrowload of kids. I reckon he's on his way to getting it. Only thing is,' she went a little more seriously now. 'I might have to give up work. Two little 'uns might be a bit much for my mam to cope with. She's not as well as she used to be.'

'I think Bert would like me to stay at home too when we start a family.'

'It'll be nice to be able to help each other,' Evelyn murmured. 'They'll both be more or less the same age and grow up together and little Max will watch over them both. I know he's only just three, but he's such a kind little chap already. He's always trying to help his grandma.'

Flora knew that while Evelyn went to work, Max spent every day with his maternal grandmother, who lived in the next street. She'd met Evelyn's mother a few times but hadn't got to know her well. The woman seemed very reserved, shy almost, totally unlike her ebullient, out-going daughter.

Flora linked her arm with Evelyn's. 'Now we've both got something good to look forward to. My mam's nicely settled with Miss Kendall. Dad's safely in prison and likely to be for a while and we've got the two best husbands in the world. How good is that?'

'Have you heard when the trial is to be?'

'Two weeks' time. Bert has to go to give evidence.'

No one in Patrick's family, apart from Bert, who was obliged to be there, attended the trial but they eagerly awaited news when he arrived home.

'It didn't take the jury long to decide. He was found guilty on all charges,' Bert said as he sat in Seffie's kitchen. He and Flora had walked the mile or so between their homes to tell Edith what had happened. 'He got two years penal servitude.'

There was silence for several moments before Flora said shyly, 'I've got a bit of good news for a change. I'm fairly sure I'm going to have a baby.'

Over the two weeks since she'd talked to Evelyn, the sickness had occurred every morning and there were other signs too which Evelyn had told her about.

Edith dabbed at her eyes with a handkerchief. She had shed no tears over the news about her husband, but now she wept with joy at the happy news.

The two young women compared notes about their pregnancies.

'When are you due?' Flora asked Evelyn. 'You look much bigger than me.'

'I've worked it out to January or February.'

'I think I'm March. About a year after we were married.'

As summer gave way to autumn and the weather

141

became colder, Evelyn found the walk to work harder. 'I'm starting to waddle and Mrs Shaw is concerned about me standing all day,' she told Flora. 'My ankles are beginning to swell. Howard says I should give up work now. How are you feeling, me love?'

'Fit as a flea. It doesn't seem to be bothering me, but then I'm not the size you are.'

Evelyn pulled a face. 'I'm like a house side, aren't I?'

'If Howard is keen for you to give up work, then I think you should listen to him. You don't want to end up in hospital.'

Evelyn pulled a face. 'No, I don't. It's even beginning to worry little Max. The minute I get home at night he takes my hand and leads me to a chair, fetches my slippers and helps his grandma get the tea ready for us. And he's not four till April.'

'He's a grand little chap.'

As they arrived at the gates into the factory, Evelyn made her decision. 'I think you're all right. I'll speak to Mrs Shaw today.'

Evelyn left two weeks later and all those who cared about her were relieved, especially her little son. He loved having his mam at home and followed her everywhere.

Agnes laughed to see it. 'Howard was always a good little lad, but I've never seen anything like Max. He'll make some lucky girl a wonderful husband some day.'

Evelyn laughed. 'Give him a chance, Mrs Weston. Let's get him to school first.'

Flora called to see her friend most evenings after work. On a visit just before Christmas, Evelyn was sitting by the range her hand on her very large stomach looking a little shocked.

'What is it? What's the matter, cos I can see there's something?' Flora said at once, sinking into the chair on the opposite side of the hearth.

Evelyn met her anxious gaze, but then she smiled. 'It's twins.'

Flora's mouth dropped open. 'Oh my!' was all she could say. 'No wonder you're so big,' she added, when she'd recovered from the surprise.

'At least I've done the right thing in giving up work. I can't expect my mam to manage three little ones.'

Flora shook her head. 'No, it wouldn't be fair.' She laughed. 'You'll probably be very glad she's around to help anyway. Is she – I mean – is she pleased?'

'Oh yes. Tickled pink. She says she always wanted more children. She lost one – a little girl – two years after having me so she's hoping that at least one of them is a girl.'

'It'd be nice to have one of each, wouldn't it?'

'How are you feeling? Everything all right?'

'Absolutely fine,' Flora said happily. 'I'll admit to you now that I was a bit worried in the first few months. Having watched Mary Ellen lose her baby, well, you know . . .' She paused and then asked quietly, 'What's it like? Giving birth?'

'I'm one of the lucky ones. Max came very quickly – especially for a first – and just popped out. There is a bit of pain – no denying that – but you soon forget it once your baby is in your arms. There's nowt to it, m'love. Nowt to it at all.'

*

Evelyn was quite right in her prediction for herself. She gave birth to twins – a boy and a girl – quite easily and swiftly in the front bedroom of her home with only the local handywoman and her own mother to help.

'How lovely,' Flora said, as she looked at the two tiny babies in the wooden rocking cradles, which Howard had made. 'One of each. How clever you are, Evelyn. What are you going to call them?'

'Lee for the little boy and Jessie for the girl.'

'What does Max think of his brother and sister?'

Evelyn smiled. 'He's absolutely adorable with them. So protective. He's amazing for such a young child.'

As if to confirm what Evelyn had said, Jessie began to whimper and a minute later Lee set up a louder howl. The bedroom door opened and Max trotted in. He went straight to the cribs and began to rock them, one in each hand.

Evelyn laughed aloud. 'See what I mean? Isn't he a little love?' She held out her arms. 'Perhaps you'd pass Lee to me, Flora. I expect they're both getting hungry but he makes the most noise.'

With the baby boy suckling happily and Jessie quietening under her elder brother's ministering hand, Flora crept away.

Flora was not so lucky with the birth of her daughter. She had a long and difficult labour. Agnes grew anxious and sent word for Edith to come to be with her daughter. The 'handywoman' employed as an unqualified midwife was very experienced and known to and trusted by both Agnes and Edith, but even she, after Flora had suffered long hours of pain until she was exhausted, said, 'I think we should call a doctor.'

The child was born in the early hours of the second day of Flora's labour.

'It's a girl,' the doctor pronounced, 'and despite the poor mother's travail, she is hale and hearty. Just listen to her exercising her lungs. Have you a name for her, Mrs Weston?'

'Nancy,' Flora said weakly. 'She's to be called Nancy.'

It took three weeks before Flora felt strong enough to come downstairs though she roused herself enough during those weeks to keep her baby girl fed. At other times, Agnes or Edith, when she could visit, looked after their granddaughter.

'She's a pretty little thing,' Agnes said. 'Blond hair and blue eyes.'

'She's very like her Aunty Mary Ellen,' Edith said. Evelyn, fully recovered now from the birth of her babies, came over every day to give support and advice to her friend.

'There'll be no more babies for us,' Bert declared as he picked up his daughter and rocked her in his strong arms. 'I'll see to that. I'm not having my Flora go through all that again. We could have lost her. Nancy's perfect. We'll be happy with just her.'

Agnes smiled. 'Well, you'll not be short of playmates for her if Evelyn keeps on dropping them out like she is doing.'

Edith smiled and dropped a kiss on her granddaughter's downy head before leaving to return home to Seffie. When she arrived, there was a letter waiting for her from Mary Ellen telling her that she and Jack were planning to be married two days after Mary Ellen's twenty-first birthday in April the following year.

Edith felt her happiness was complete.

Eighteen

It was a pretty country wedding that took place in April 1896 in the village church where the Clarke family worshipped. Although she was just over one year old, Nancy was still too young to carry out the duties of a proper bridesmaid. However, her grandma Edith made her a pretty pink dress to match those that she and Seffie had made for the two little girls who were the official bridesmaids for Mary Ellen. They had also made the bridal gown.

'Can't you be my matron of honour?' Mary Ellen had asked her sister but Flora had shaken her head. 'I'd really rather not. I'd feel a bit out of place beside the two little girls you've chosen. They're so sweet and pretty. But I promise I'll be close by if you need me.'

'They're Mrs Beckett's granddaughters. She brought them into the world and she's so proud of them. They're eight and nine – old enough to behave sensibly.'

'It was kind of you to invite Evelyn and Howard and their family, but Evelyn says it's a long way to bring three children just for a day. Max would be fine, but the twins – especially Lee – take some managing, I don't mind telling you. He's a lovely little boy – a handsome little chap with his fair hair and bright blue eyes – but he's a handful. So it'll just be us and Bert's ma who'll be coming.'

'There's plenty of room in the farmhouse for you all to stay. I'm so looking forward to you being there on the morning to help me. I'm sure I shall be nervous.'

It was a fine day and the whole village turned out to see the wedding of the year in their small community. They clapped when the happy couple emerged into the spring sunshine and threw confetti, flower petals and rice.

At the wedding breakfast, the farmhouse rang with laughter until late into the night. There would be little sleep for Matthew and Winnie that night for they had said they would feed the animals early the next morning. Although the young couple were not going away on honeymoon, Winnie wanted them to feel that they had a few hours to themselves. She had reorganized the bedrooms so that Jack and Mary Ellen had a room of their own at the far end of the farmhouse and she had turned the bedroom next to it into a small sitting room.

'Just so you have somewhere to go to be on your own now and again,' she'd said.

'You're so thoughtful,' Mary Ellen had murmured in thanks.

Winnie had laughed. 'Well, I'm not too old to remember what it's like to be newlyweds. We love to be together as a family, but you and Jack need some time on your own too.'

As the family from the city returned home the following afternoon, they were all reflecting on what a happy wedding day it had been; one that, only a few years ago, they could not have imagined ever happening for Mary Ellen.

Howard Bonsor and Bert Weston had been friends ever since their schooldays and they had started attending the home games of Sheffield United Football Club after its formation in 1889. It was a practice that had not ceased even after their marriages.

'They work hard enough all week,' Evelyn said soon after Flora had married Bert and had come to live in the same street. 'And my Howard is always willing to help with Max. He deserves a Saturday afternoon off when his team is playing at home.' She had grinned mischievously as she'd added, 'And now you and me can have an afternoon off, an' all. We can have a good old natter together.'

'What about little Max? Does he go with his dad?'

'Not yet, but Howard plans on taking him when he's a bit older.'

As the summer after Mary Ellen's wedding turned towards autumn and the football season began, Howard said to Bert, 'Do you mind if I bring Max to the game on Saturday?'

'Of course not.' He chuckled. 'It's high time he learned where his loyalties lie. How's he getting on at school? He started just after Easter, didn't he?'

Howard laughed. 'Very well, it seems. His teacher says he's quite bright but his overriding quality is his kindness and thoughtfulness for others. He sorts out playground fights without a teacher having to get involved and when they started back this week, even the headmaster noticed how he shepherded all the new kids together and took them on a tour of the school, showing them where everything was so they didn't feel overwhelmed by being away from home for the first time.'

'Unusual in a young boy, isn't it? But he's like that at home, isn't he?'

'Yes, always has been, so I think he deserves a treat and I reckon a visit to the football might be the very thing.'

And so it became a regular Saturday afternoon outing for the three of them, every two weeks when 'their' team was playing at their home ground in Bramall Lane.

As the New Year of 1897 dawned, there was great excitement throughout the city.

'Have you heard?' Flora asked as she entered the Bonsor house by the back door carrying Nancy on her hip. She set her down on the floor and the little girl toddled to the corner of the room where Howard had built a wooden playpen to keep the twins safe while Evelyn was busy. Evelyn picked her up and set her inside the pen. At once, Lee pushed Nancy and she fell backwards banging her head on the wooden rails. She began to wail. Evelyn bent down and rubbed the child's head. 'There, there, m'love. Lee, just behave yourself.' As Nancy's cries lessened, Evelyn stood up and eased her back with a grimace. 'I know it sounds mean, but how I wish Max didn't have to go to school. He keeps 'em all in order when he's here.'

Flora regarded her friend with her head on one side. 'You're pregnant again, aren't you?'

Evelyn smiled and turned a little pink. 'Yes. About three months gone, I think.'

'So Howard's well on his way to getting that barrowload of kids he wanted.'

Evelyn laughed. 'Just so long as it's not twins again, and I hope it's a girl. Jessie's a placid little thing, but Lee . . .' She shook her head as if in despair, but she was smiling fondly. 'He got out of the backyard the other day and was off down the road like a whippet.'

'He's a grand little lad,' Flora said. 'He's got spirit, Evelyn, and youngsters need that these days.'

'I know.' Evelyn paused and then asked, 'What were you going to tell me when you came in? We got side-tracked.' She glanced towards the playpen but the three children were playing together now quite happily. 'Sit down, Flora, and I'll make us a drink.'

'You know it's the Queen's diamond jubilee in June, don't you? So as part of the celebrations, she's coming to Sheffield in May to open the new Town Hall.'

'Never! Is she really? We'll have to go and see if we can catch sight of her. What fun. I've never seen a member of the Royal Family. Have you?'

'No and neither has Gran. She's getting very excited.' Since Nancy's birth, Agnes had become known as 'Gran' and Edith was referred to as 'Grandma'.

'And,' Evelyn went on, 'we'll have to have a party to celebrate the jubilee in June.'

Flora laughed aloud and pointed towards Evelyn's stomach. 'I rather think you might be having a party of your own around that date.'

'You might well be right, but if it's a girl, we'll call her Victoria.'

'And if it's a boy?'

'It won't be,' Evelyn said firmly.

On 21 May 1897, crowds lined the streets on the route the Queen's carriage would take to reach the Town Hall. Agnes, Flora and Nancy got a good place right outside the building.

'Isn't it magnificent,' Agnes murmured, her gaze roaming over the stonework and the fine carvings depicting the industries of the city.

'It is,' Flora said. 'Just stand down a minute, Nancy darling. You're such a big girl now. You're heavy for Mummy.'

'I can't see the Queen now,' Nancy pouted.

'I'll lift you up again when she comes, I promise.'

A man standing in front of them turned. 'I'll carry her, missus, if tha'll let me.' He grinned. 'I won't run off with 'er.' He gestured towards the woman standing next to him. 'My missus wouldn't let me.'

The woman too now turned and smiled at Flora. 'She's safe enough with my Joe, love.'

'That's kind of you. I'm very grateful. Her name's Nancy.'

'Think nowt of it.' Joe lifted Nancy into his arms and began talking to her and pointing out things of interest. 'See all them pretty flowers and the flags flying? That's to say "Welcome" to the Queen.'

'Evelyn said Howard will bring Max a little later when he can leave work and Max will be home from school,' Flora said to Agnes, 'but Evelyn's too big to walk all this way and then to stand among the crowds.'

Agnes chuckled. 'And the twins wouldn't be interested. At least Lee wouldn't be.'

'I wanted Nancy to see it all though. I know she's only just two but I'm sure she'll remember some of it.'

Just before four o'clock, finely dressed men and women began to take their places on either side of the main doors to the building. Soldiers took up their positions lining the route and bands began to play. There was plenty to see and Joe pointed out everything to Nancy while Flora, Agnes and Joe's wife, who, they found out, was called Bella, chatted amiably. The time passed quickly until just before five o'clock when there was the sound of a gun being fired.

'Don't be frightened, little 'un,' Joe said at once. 'It's to say the Queen's train is arriving. There'll likely be more shots. It's called a gun salute. It shouldn't be long now before she gets here.'

Just as Joe finished speaking, they heard a shout, 'Aunty Flora! Aunty Flora! We're here.' And they turned to see Bert, Howard and Max weaving their way through the crowd to join them.

'Have we missed anything?'

'Not really,' Flora said. 'Just the dignitaries and the soldiers taking their places. By the way, this is Joe and his wife, Bella. Joe's kindly lifted Nancy up so she can see.'

'Good to meet you, Joe,' Bert said, offering his hand. 'I'm Bert, Nancy's dad, so I can relieve you now, but it was very kind of you to help out. We wanted Nancy to see this day.'

'It's been a pleasure,' Joe said, as he handed Nancy

over and Bert perched her on his shoulders. 'She's such a good little lass.'

Bert introduced Howard and Max and the new-found friends still stood together to watch the proceedings.

'Come and stand in front of us, lad,' Joe said to Max. 'You'll be able to see a bit better. How old are you?'

'Six, mister.'

'You're a big lad for six. Can you see now?'

'Yes, thanks, mister.'

They heard the sound of cheering growing louder, coming towards them like a tidal wave.

'That'll be her coming,' Joe said and before many more minutes had passed, they saw the open-topped carriage draw up in front of the Town Hall. Speeches of welcome were made but the Queen did not alight from the vehicle.

'They say she has heart trouble and mustn't exert herself,' Joe said. 'I've been hearing all the gossip about the arrangements because I've helped to build it. I'm a stone mason.'

'Are you really?' Bert said, a little in awe. 'Have you done some of those magnificent carvings?'

'Aye, I have, and on the inside too. You must take a look one day. It is a magnificent building, even if I say so myself.'

'So perhaps you can fill us in on what's happening, then,' Howard said. 'Isn't she getting out of her carriage?'

'No,' Joe said. 'She's going to touch a gold key and then the doors will open as if by magic.' He laughed as he added, 'But all that does is put a light on inside and three burly builders will open the huge main door. It's just a bit of theatre that'll please the crowd.'

Moments later, when the doors swung open, a huge roar went up among the crowd and they watched as several people were then presented to Her Majesty before the trumpets sounded, the National Anthem was played and the carriage moved off.

'Where's she going now?' Agnes asked. She'd been very quiet during all the proceedings and had been fascinated by it all.

'There's going to be a procession through the streets and then I believe she's travelling to Preston. After that she'll go to Scotland and finish up in Balmoral late tonight.'

'For a well-earned rest, I hope,' Agnes said. 'I know she's well-looked after, but she's an old lady now, none-the-less.'

'You're right,' Joe said. 'She's seventy-eight in three days' time.'

'Then all I can say is "God Bless Her" and thank her for coming to our city.'

Joe nodded. 'It's the first time a reigning monarch has been here. It's been a great day and I'm glad I've seen it.'

'So are we,' Howard said. 'I'm just so sorry my Evelyn couldn't be here. She'd have loved it all.'

'I'm sorry to hear that,' Bella said. 'She's not ill, is she?'

'No, she's fine, but she's expecting a baby in about a month's time. These crowds would have been a bit much.'

'Then we send her our very best wishes for a safe delivery,' Joe said. He held out his hand. 'It's been good to meet you all, especially my little friend Nancy.' Joe tickled her cheek and Nancy smiled. 'She's going to be a real heartbreaker when she grows up. You'll have all the boys chasing her.'

'Well, they'll have to get past me first,' Bert laughed.

Nineteen

On Sunday, 20 June 1897, the day that the Queen celebrated her diamond jubilee, sixty years after she had come the throne as a young girl of eighteen, Evelyn gave birth to her fourth child.

When she saw the local handywoman leaving her friend's house late in the afternoon, Flora knew that the baby had arrived. Leaving Nancy with Agnes, she hurried across the street. Evelyn's mother opened the door with a smile. Because Evelyn did not go out to work now, her mother no longer looked after the children regularly, but she was always on hand to help out if needed.

'Is she all right?' Flora asked at once. 'Is it a girl?'

'Mother and baby are both fine, but no, it's another boy. They're calling him Victor in honour of the Queen.'

'Can I see them?'

'Of course. Go on up. You know which is her room, don't you?'

Flora climbed the stairs and opened the bedroom door. Max was sitting on his mother's bed, watching her cradling the new arrival. He looked up as Flora entered.

'It's another boy, Aunty Flora. His name's Victor.'

'I know. Your grandma's just told me. So, Evelyn . . .' she smiled at her friend, who was looking rosy-cheeked from her labour but supremely happy – 'not a little girl this time.'

Evelyn laughed. 'No, but I really don't mind as long as he's healthy and he seems perfect. And besides, Max will keep him in line, won't you, Max?'

The six-year-old, who seemed far older than his tender years, nodded. 'I'll do my best, Mam, but I do hope he's not going to be a naughty boy like Lee.'

Evelyn laughed. 'It'll be a while before he can get into mischief, but just remember, Max, that whatever Lee does, we don't blame you. We know what a little rascal he is. Now off you go and play with Lee and Jessie.'

'They can all come over to our house if it'd give you a bit of peace and quiet,' Flora offered.

'That's good of you, Flora, but they'll be fine with Max and Howard's at home too. Now, tell me what plans you have for Tuesday?'

Tuesday, 22 June had been declared a bank holiday and was to be the official day on which the Queen's accession to the throne sixty years earlier would be celebrated.

'Several of our neighbours have suggested we should join forces and have a party out in the street, if the weather's fine,' Flora told Evelyn. 'We all know each other and the children play together anyway.'

'That's a very good idea. I wish I could join in.'

'Howard can put a chair near the window for you and you can watch from there. It's lucky your bedroom's at the front and overlooks the street. It

158

wouldn't be wise to come outside, Evelyn, not so soon after giving birth.'

Evelyn grimaced. 'I know but I'll do as you say and watch from up here.'

Tuesday dawned sunny and warm.

'I hope it's as nice as this in London for the Queen's procession,' Flora remarked as she and Bert carried a table out into the street and then fetched chairs to go around it.

'I hope so. There's to be a service of thanksgiving at St Paul's, it said in the paper, but they're holding it outside as the poor old queen is too lame to climb the steps.'

'I expect the streets will be lined with people like they were when she came to Sheffield last month.'

'That was a great day, wasn't it?' Bert said. 'But today will be just as good. Celebrating with our friends and neighbours. Now, I'm going to help Mr Hopkins bring his piano out into the street. He's promised to play for us, so there'll be singing and dancing before the day's over, I guarantee.'

Flora glanced up at Evelyn's bedroom window. 'How I wish Evelyn could join in.'

Throughout the day, Flora did not forget her friend. She ran up and down the stairs to Evelyn's bedroom with sandwiches and cake and even trifle. Everyone in the street had contributed food and drink.

'It's a grand party. I've never heard of this being done before, Flora,' Evelyn said, as she watched from her window and licked cream from her fingers. 'It's such a good idea to celebrate a national event. I wonder if we'll start a trend. Everyone will remember today, even the kids as they grow older will still talk about it. A street party, that's what it ought to be called. We'll have to do it again in a couple of years' time at the turn of the century.'

Flora laughed. 'I'll spread the word.'

Evelyn was right; the party in their street was remembered and talked about in the weeks and months to come and Evelyn's idea to celebrate on New Year's Eve 1899 began to take shape.

'I'm not sure we should be making merry when our army lads are at war in South Africa,' Bert said seriously when what came to be known as the Second Boer War began in the October.

'The best thing we can do is to carry on as normal,' Flora and Evelyn agreed. The menfolk followed their lead. 'Besides,' Flora added, 'we don't want to disappoint the children. They're counting on having a party, even if it is on the thirty-first of December instead of on a warm June day.'

All thoughts of a faraway war were put aside and the neighbours concentrated on giving their families another day to remember.

As the years passed and the children grew, Nancy Weston became part of the Bonsor family. With no brothers or sisters of her own, she trotted across the road every day to join in the boisterous games of the growing family. It had grown by two more boys; Warren in 1898 and Stanley in 1900, when Evelyn declared to Flora, 'I've told Howard that's enough now though I reckon he was trying to produce a football team to rival Sheffield United. We've been lucky, though, Flora. I know that. We've got six healthy kids and that's enough. The house is bulging at the seams, even though Howard has made a bedroom in the cellar for Max and Lee and built a room in the loft too.'

The two women's friendship grew stronger through the years. They crossed the road almost every morning for 'elevenses' together, with Agnes joining them whenever Evelyn came to Flora's home.

'You're welcome to come across with Flora, you know, Mrs Weston,' Evelyn told her, but Agnes merely smiled and shook her head. 'That's kind of you, love, but you two need time together to have a good old gossip without me there. But I appreciate your kind thought and I'm glad to join you when you come here.'

And so, the two families became almost one with Edith popping in now and again. She was still living happily with Seffie and loving her working life. Of Patrick, there was little news. They'd heard when he was released from prison but, to their relief, he made no attempt to visit them, not even to see his grand-daughter.

'We're better off without him,' Bert declared. 'I never thought I'd see your poor mam so happy. I'm glad for her and we don't want him turning up and ruining it.'

Flora and Mary Ellen wrote every week to each other and, twice a year, Flora, Bert, Nancy and Edith made a trip to the countryside to visit the Clarke

family. But there was no sign of a child for Mary
Ellen and Jack. Though neither of them liked
to mention it, both Edith and Flora worried about
her.

Lee Bonsor was still a little rascal. 'He's a loveable
rogue,' Evelyn said fondly while Howard muttered,
'I could think of a very different name for him. He
teases Jessie and Nancy unmercifully at times.'

'It's only in fun. He's not a bully and Max watches
out for them. Besides, Nancy's quite capable of
sticking up for herself. She gave him a bloody nose
last week when he pulled her pigtails.'

Howard grinned. 'Good for her. I only wish Jessie
had a bit more spirit and would stand up for herself.'

'She's a gentle little soul but she's got plenty of
brothers, and Nancy too, to stick up for her.'

'Max is a good lad. He looks out for all of them.'
Howard chuckled. 'He's rather like a shepherd tending
his sheep.'

'He's kind and caring. He takes after you and with
his colouring too – brown hair and soft dark eyes,'
Evelyn said. 'It's Lee with his fair hair and blue eyes
and that wicked smile who's going to cause us problems and goodness knows what the other three lads
will turn out like.'

'Only time will tell, love.'

'Hello, Max,' Flora said as she opened the door in
answer to his knock. 'What are you doing here?'

At fourteen, Max was tall for his age and filling
out in all the right places to become a fine, upstanding
and broad-shouldered young man. His ready smile

lit up his warm brown eyes as he said, 'Is Nancy at home, Mrs Weston?'

'Yes, I'll call her. Come in, Max.'

He snatched the cap from his head as he stepped across the threshold.

'We were wondering if she would like to come swimming with us. Dad's taking us, so she'll be quite safe and I'll be sure to keep an eye on her.'

'Where are you going?'

'The baths at Attercliffe. Dad's heard it's a nice pool there.'

'She hasn't got a bathing costume.'

'Jessie's got a spare one. Nancy can borrow that. They're about the same size, so I'm sure it'll fit her.'

Flora smiled to herself. It seemed Max was not to be thwarted and, at his next words, she understood. 'Dad says he hopes to take us to the seaside in the summer. He's trying to organize what he calls a works' outing and we hope you and Mr Weston and Nancy – and Mrs Weston senior too, if she'd like – will come with us. It'd be a grand day out for all of us. It's so sad that my grandma died last year. She'd have loved it.'

Flora thought back to the previous autumn when Evelyn's mother had had a sudden and unexpected fatal heart attack.

'Where were you thinking of going?'

He grinned. 'We're about in the middle of the country, so it depends where they decide to go. East or west.'

Flora was thoughtful. Even though she was an adult now, she'd never been to the seaside and had never seen the sea except in pictures. It would be a lovely day out and she was sure Agnes would enjoy it. Perhaps she might see if Edith and Seffie would join them too.

'Are the workers going to be allowed to take guests as well as family members?'

'I'm not sure, Mrs Weston, but I can ask me dad. Because he works in the offices, he's going to do all the arranging. He says it'll probably be on August Bank Holiday Monday.'

At that moment they heard footsteps on the staircase and Nancy came into the kitchen.

''Lo, Max?'

'Max has come to ask you if you'd like to go to the swimming baths in Attercliffe with them.'

Nancy's eyes widened. 'Ooh, Mam, can I?'

'Of course.'

'Jessie's got a costume you can borrow,' Max put in.

'If you enjoy it,' Flora said, 'and want to go again, I'll get you one of your own.'

Nancy's eyes shone and she clapped her hands. 'When are we going?'

'Saturday afternoon.'

Nancy's face clouded. 'But you go to the football on Saturdays. You never miss.'

'Only when they play at home. We can't afford to go to away matches. So, Dad says, every time there's an away game, he'll take us swimming instead. Besides, the football season's nearly over for this year.'

'Is the pool open in the evenings?' Flora asked.

'I'm not sure but I go to football training three evenings in the week after work.'

Max had recently started as an office boy with the same company where Howard worked, though in a different department, but he was still determined to play football with his friends, even through the summer months. Sheffield United Football Club had been formed at Bramall Lane in March 1889 by the Sheffield United Cricket Club and Howard and Bert had been loyal supporters ever since. Max had been caught up in their enthusiasm.

'So,' he said, turning to Nancy now, 'are you going to come swimming with us?'

'Try to stop me,' she laughed.

Twenty

On the following Saturday afternoon, Nancy crossed the street with a towel and the borrowed swimming costume tucked under her arm. They all walked to the baths; Howard and his six children and Nancy. The two girls skipped along hand in hand, while Max held Warren's hand and Howard carried five-year-old Stanley on his shoulders.

As they neared the large building Howard said to Max and Lee, 'Now, you two, you're the oldest. You must watch out for the younger ones and especially the girls. There'll be a lot of children here, I don't doubt, and I won't be able to keep my eyes on them all the time from the side.'

When they had all changed into their costumes, they met at the side of the pool. Jessie looked about her nervously, a little over-awed by the noise and the thought of plunging into the water.

Nancy took her hand. 'Come on, we'll go down the steps. This is the shallow end and Max is over there, look. He's seen us.'

'Oooh, it's cold,' Jessie said as they went gingerly down the steps into the water.

'Let's get right in,' Nancy shouted above the shrieks of the other bathers. 'It might be better then.'

They bobbed down into the water right up to their necks. 'Yes, it is a bit,' Jessie agreed. 'Lee's coming over.'

'I didn't know he could swim,' Nancy said.

'He can't. Not properly. That's what Dad calls a "doggy paddle".'

Lee reached them and bobbed up and down beside them. 'Come on, then, let's see you swim.'

'I don't know how,' Nancy laughed. 'You'll have to show us.'

Lee stood up. 'Well, first,' he said, with a gleeful grin, 'you have to get used to the water and being able to put your head under. Like this . . .' He caught hold of Nancy and thrust her down into the water. His action was so unexpected that she had no time to take in a deep breath. The water filled her mouth and her nose. She struggled and flailed her arms until suddenly she was pulled upwards out of the water. She spluttered and gasped and hung on to the person who had come to her rescue. Max.

'You all right, Nancy?'

She nodded, still coughing the water from her mouth and drawing in deep breaths.

'Right, you stay here. I'll get that little bugger for this.'

Now Nancy gasped with surprise. She'd never heard any of the Bonsor family swear. Not like that.

She watched as Max swam – really swam – across the pool, following his younger brother until he caught up with him. She saw him grasp Lee by the shoulders and shake him. And then he ducked him like Lee had ducked her. But he did it three times until Howard shouted from the side. 'Stop that, Max.'

Max looked up and shouted back angrily. 'It's what he did to Nancy. See how he likes it.'

Howard beckoned both boys to the side of the pool and squatted down to talk to them. Now Nancy couldn't hear what was being said but, beside her, Jessie giggled nervously. 'It looks like they're both getting a telling off. I'm sure Lee didn't mean to frighten you, Nancy.'

They saw Howard gesture towards them and then the two boys came back, Max swimming and Lee doing his doggy paddle.

'Sorry, Nancy,' Lee said, as they stopped beside the girls and stood up. 'Dad said I could have put you off swimming for life by doing that. I didn't mean to hurt you. I was just having a bit of fun.'

Nancy had quite recovered and said tartly, 'It'd take more than you, Lee Bonsor, to put me off doing something I want to do.' She turned and smiled at Max. 'Will you show us how to swim properly, Max, because it looks as if you know and I think both me an' Jessie would really like to learn?'

'Of course, I will. You help our Jessie, Lee, and I'll show Nancy what to do. And no more funny business. Dad's watching us both like a hawk.'

'What about the others? Aren't you supposed to be looking after them too?'

'They'll be all right. They're splashing around near the side where Dad's standing. Now let's get started. First thing you must do is to learn to float . . .'

The rest of their allotted hour in the pool passed

pleasantly and by the end of it, Nancy felt she was well on the way to being able to swim properly.

'Lee's not frightened of the water, is he, but I think Jessie's still a bit nervous,' Nancy said to Max as they waded towards the side of the pool.

'He'd be a good swimmer if only he would apply himself,' Max said, 'but he's too fond of playing the fool.'

'He's good with Jessie, though.'

'Yes,' Max agreed. 'He is, but he's her twin. And they're very close.' He laughed wryly. 'If either one of them is in trouble at home, you can bet your life they always stick up for one another.'

'It must be lovely to have brothers and sisters,' Nancy said wistfully. 'To be part of a big family.'

Max laughed. 'It is – most of the time, but you're part of ours, Nancy, and always will be. Now, come on, time we were getting out. Dad's beckoning. Our time's up. Mind you dry your hair. We don't want you catching a chill. I've got a spare towel with me if you need one.'

'So did you have a good time?' Flora asked when Nancy arrived home.

'It was great!' Nancy had decided to say nothing about what Lee had done; she was no tell-tale and she didn't want to risk her mother forbidding her to go again.

The afternoon swimming sessions became a regular outing on the Saturdays when Sheffield United were not playing at home. Soon, they could all swim well, though Jessie still struggled a little with her fear of the water. To everyone's surprise, when he decided to put his mind to learning to swim properly, Lee became the best of all of them. He could even beat Max in swimming the length of the pool.

By the time the trip to Blackpool was arranged for the Bank Holiday Monday in August, all of them could swim well enough to be allowed to paddle and bathe in the sea.

Howard had arranged for four charabancs to take all those who wanted to go on the outing. The Bonsor family and the Westons, as well as Edith and Seffie, climbed into the same one and were soon all singing as they rattled up the hill out of the city and headed west towards the coast.

The vehicles drew up on the seafront and Flora gazed open-mouthed at the view. 'Oh Mam, just look at all that water.'

Edith stood beside her. 'And to think just across there somewhere is Ireland. I've never seen the sea before either,' she added softly.

'Haven't you?' Seffie said. 'Then it's high time you took a closer look.' She slipped her arm through Edith's and urged her towards the steps that led down to the sand. Warren and Stanley were already running barefoot along the beach to choose a spot to build their first sandcastle, carrying the buckets and spades Howard had bought.

'Don't go too far away, boys,' Evelyn shouted after them, but they either could not hear her or chose to take no notice.

'I'll go after them,' Max said.

'Don't let them go in the sea on their own, Max,' Evelyn worried. 'I know they've learned to swim, but even so, the sea is a bit different.'

'I won't, Mam. A' you coming, Nancy? Let's show 'em how it's done.'

'You're on,' Nancy said, slipping off her shoes so that they wouldn't be spoiled by the salt in the sand. 'Have we got enough spades? Come on, Jessie.'

They ran across to where the two younger boys were already making half-hearted attempts to build something but it seemed they weren't quite sure how to make a start.

'Aren't Lee and Victor coming?' Nancy asked.

Jessie giggled. 'Lee thinks it's far too childish for a ten-year-old and Victor follows whatever Lee does.'

'That's a shame,' Nancy murmured. She liked it when all the family stayed together.

'Now, first of all,' Max said, taking charge, 'we need to move closer to the sea where the sand is harder. We can't build with this soft, dry sand.' He led them to where the outgoing tide had left the sand wet. 'We draw a big circle the size you want the base of the castle to be and then we all dig a trench and put the sand into the centre of the circle. Like this . . .'

For the next half an hour Max helped them to build a sandcastle, then he sent Nancy and Jessie to look for shells to decorate the sides.

'We've got a castle and a moat round it,' he said, 'but what usually goes in a moat?'

'Water!' Warren shouted and jumped up and down. Nancy smiled at him. He was growing very like his big brother, Max, with dark brown hair and warm

171

brown eyes, while Stanley, the youngest in the family, favoured Lee's colouring with fair hair and bright blue eyes. She held out her hand. 'Right, bring your buckets. We'll go and fetch some water from the sea.'

The next half hour was spent with the five of them running backwards and forwards to the sea to fetch water to pour into the moat. But as fast as they poured it in, it soaked into the sand.

'It won't stay,' Stanley pouted. 'Make it stay, Max.'

Max chuckled. 'We'll have to wait until the tide comes in and make a channel for the sea to run up. Then it will flow into the moat and surround the castle.'

Warren looked towards the sea. To the child, it was some distance away. 'How long will it take to come in?'

'I'm not sure, but watch . . .' Max squatted down beside his brother and pointed, 'watch how each wave comes a little bit nearer to us every time. That means it's coming in now.'

The boy stood watching, fascinated by the waves coming ever closer.

'It won't be long . . .' Max began but at that moment, Lee and Victor ran up.

'Oh, just look at their pretty castle,' Lee said sarcastically as a wicked gleam came into his eyes. 'Aren't you clever?'

He took two strides towards the castle and jumped onto the top of it. Then he kicked the sand aside until the castle was almost flattened.

Stanley began to wail. 'You've spoilt it, Lee.'

Max grabbed Lee's arm and pulled him off the

castle. 'That was mean, Lee. The kids wanted to see the water come round it. You just come with me.'

Lee wriggled to free himself, but Max's grasp was too strong. He marched him up the beach to where their parents and the other adults had now settled themselves on a blanket on the sand.

'Dad, just keep him here, will you?' But as he loosened his grip, Lee pulled away, turned and ran along the beach.

'Lee,' Evelyn called anxiously. 'Come back. You'll get lost.'

'We can only hope,' Max muttered, but not loud enough for anyone else to hear. Unconcerned about his brother, he turned back towards the other children, still standing looking forlornly down at the ruined castle.

'Right, troops, we've just got to rebuild it before the tide gets here. Come on, Stanley, dry those tears and get digging.'

Under Max's instruction, the castle soon took shape again. Nancy and Jessie rescued all the shells, cleaned the sand from them and stuck them back on the sides. The moat was dug again and this time Max said, 'Let's build a bridge with a tunnel for the water to go underneath it.'

'Oh yes, yes,' Warren said, jumping up and down. Then he stopped. 'How?'

Max knelt down and scooped sand into his hands then pressed it into the shape of a bridge in front of two shells that Nancy had placed. 'Look, that's the door into the castle that Nancy's made.'

'But the water can't get through there,' Warren said.

Max pressed the sand forming the bridge down hard, then he scooped out a small tunnel so that the water would be able to flow beneath it.

'There. You'll see.'

'How clever you are, Max,' Nancy murmured, 'I would never have thought of something like that.'

'I came on a school trip here a few years back and I watched the other kids making all sorts of things in the sand. Now,' he went on, 'while we're waiting for the tide to come in, let's build a boat next to it big enough for you all to sit in and when the water comes in, you'll feel you're sailing on the sea. 'It won't last long, but you'll have a few minutes' fun.'

A short distance away the adults sat together watching the children.

'Howard, where's Lee gone? Please go after him. He'll get lost.'

'He'll be all right, Evelyn love. Don't fuss. He'll be back when he's hungry.' He turned to his other son. 'You stay here, Victor. You'd do well not to follow Lee's every move.'

Victor kicked the sand moodily, but he did as he was told.

The other children played in the 'boat' that Max had dug for them and watched the water swirling round the moat and under the bridge. Soon though, the incoming tide swept the castle away, but this time there were no tears; Max had explained what would happen.

Twenty-one

Lee did not come back to his family and when it was time to return to the charabanc for the journey home, he had still not appeared.

'Howard, we can't just leave him here,' Evelyn fretted. 'How will he get home if we go without him?'

'Ought we to inform the police?' Bert suggested. 'Or perhaps one of us should stay here.'

'Just get on board, Evelyn.'

'Oh but, Howard . . . ' But she did as her husband suggested, helping Agnes up the steps and into a seat beside Edith and Seffie. Then she counted the heads of the children, including Nancy, just to be sure that no one else was missing.

Max sidled up to his father. 'Dad,' he muttered, 'I've spotted him. He's hiding behind that kiosk over there.'

'Yes, I've seen him too. Don't look over there. Let's make out we're still anxious. Bert, you get on board.'

'But what about . . .?'

'Don't look round. Max and I have spotted him. He'd hiding over there.'

Bert grinned and climbed aboard, leaving Howard

and Max still glancing anxiously around them as if still looking for the missing member of the family.

'But we ought to tell Mam . . .' Max muttered.

Howard shook his head. 'She'd give it away. She'd go rushing over to him and he'd likely take off again. He'll run across to us when the driver starts the engine. He's a little tyke – we all know that – but he's not stupid. He'll not get left behind. You mark my words. Now, you get on board while I just have a word with the driver. We'll play the little rascal at his own game.'

Just as the engine started, Howard climbed aboard and made as if to close the door. Out of the corner of his eye he saw Lee leave his hiding place and gallop towards them, panic on his face. Howard opened the door again and the boy clambered up the steps.

'Oh, there you are,' he greeted his wayward son with a calmness he had not been feeling for most of the afternoon. 'Had a good day, have you?'

'No, I haven't. I'm hungry.'

Lee marched down the aisle and sat on the back seat to sulk all the way home. Now that her boy was safe, Evelyn ignored him. She knew he had spoiled the younger children's fun and had quite ruined her day by running off. Let him be hungry and thirsty until they got home, she thought. Perhaps it would teach him a lesson. But she doubted it.

The matter was not referred to again, though in years to come it would be remembered as the time Lee ran away.

*

The outing on August Bank Holiday Monday began a regular annual event with the Bonsor and Weston families always going to together. They always went to Blackpool. Although other places were suggested, no one wanted to change.

'We like it there,' everyone agreed.

Lee would wander off on his own but he always promised his mother that he would be sure not to miss the charabanc home. And he never did. As he grew older, left school and started work, they would see him walking along the promenade with his arm round a girl's waist. At the last moment he would appear, leaving the girl waving a tearful goodbye.

'Lee Bonsor's got a girlfriend,' Warren and Stanley would chant from the back seat but Lee would only grin. But as the weeks passed, no girl ever arrived in Sheffield to visit him. No letters came for him, nor did he take days away to visit whoever his 'girlfriend' had been. And every year he would find a different girl to cosy up to for the day. The family shrugged and lost interest.

'It's just Lee having a good time,' Evelyn said indulgently. 'He's not doing any harm.'

'Let's hope not,' Max muttered darkly, but made sure his mother didn't hear.

Max never went off on his own; he stayed with the family, keeping an eye on the younger ones and helping Agnes, Edith and Seffie negotiate the steps and the soft sand.

'I wish we could stay late and go dancing in the Tower ballroom,' Nancy said wistfully.

'I can swim, Nancy, but I can't dance,' Max said

as they walked to where the charabanc waited to take them back to Sheffield. 'I wish I could. I'd love to take you dancing.'

Nancy smiled up at him. 'Maybe one day, Max.'

'You know I can't believe our Nancy's going to be eighteen next week. Where have all the years gone?' Flora said to Evelyn as they sat over their customary morning cup of tea. They were in Flora's home so Agnes had joined them.

Evelyn laughed. 'Well, it must be right, because the twins are eighteen now and they're only a couple of months older than your girl, now, aren't they?'

Flora thought back to the double celebrations the Bonsor family had had for the twins' eighteen birthday.

'I know they're not considered "of age" until they're twenty-one,' Evelyn had said, 'but Howard and me both think eighteen seems somehow significant.'

The Bonsors' terraced house had burst at the seams and guests had spilled out into the street, even though it was January, until all their neighbours were involved.

'We must do the same for Nancy,' Evelyn said, as if reading Flora's mind. 'We don't want her to feel we haven't made the same effort.'

'She's grown into such a pretty girl,' Agnes said. 'With that blond hair and bright blue eyes.'

'She doesn't seem to take after either me or Bert. She's like my sister,' Flora said.

'Will Mary Ellen come back for Nancy's party, do you think?'

Flora shrugged. 'I don't think she wants to come back here at all. Not even for a visit. She came back for my wedding, but I know she felt very unsettled while she was here. She was so frightened our dad would appear. That's why Bert takes us and me mam twice a year to see her. The Clarkes always make us very welcome.'

'Aye well, as long as the lass is happy,' Agnes said. 'That's all we want.'

'She is.'

'She's never had any family, has she?'

Flora hesitated. This was something she hadn't shared even with her mother-in-law or her closest friend. Now Flora sighed and decided to take them into her confidence. She told them what had happened years before and added, 'I don't think she can carry a baby full term. She – she had a miscarriage last summer. And, of course, that's the second that I know of. She may have had more over the years, but she's never said. We only found out because when we visited last August, she was looking quite ill and she was almost *obliged* to tell us the reason.'

There was silence for a few moments while Evelyn, who could bear children like falling off a log, as she often said herself, tried to take in what it must be like not to be able to give birth. 'Poor girl,' she murmured. 'I feel for her.'

'So,' Agnes said after a few more moments, trying to change the subject to a lighter mood, 'what are we going to do for Nancy's birthday?'

Both Nancy and Jessie had been working as shop assistants in Cole's department store in the city since the age of fifteen. Proving their worth, they'd been promoted to work in the ladies' fashion department after a year. They wore smart unforms to work and were well-liked by the other members of staff.

'You're not going to work as buffer girls,' both Flora and Evelyn had declared firmly.

'But you always said you enjoyed it,' Jessie had tried to argue with Evelyn. 'I know they're a rowdy lot, but they've got hearts of gold. That's what you've always said. So why . . .?'

'It's hard work and it's dirty,' Evelyn had explained calmly but there was a hint of steel in her tone. 'Flora and me have talked this over and we're agreed. You're both bright girls. You deserve something better.'

'But . . .'

'No "buts". You'll do as you're told.'

Secretly, Jessie had been quite relieved. She'd seen the groups of buffer girls when they came out into the city streets during their dinner break. They were indeed a merry, raucous bunch who laughed and joked, but woe betide anyone who crossed them. Nancy would have coped; she would have joined in their banter and held her own. Jessie was not as outgoing as her friend – she was quite shy – but she was sweet-natured with pretty brown curls and smooth skin.

'Nancy,' Jessie began as they walked home together after work one evening just before Nancy's birthday in March. 'My mam and your mam are planning a big party for you next week like the one me and Lee had.'

'Yes, I know. You're all coming, aren't you?'

'Of course, but you see, I wondered – I mean, I'd rather like to ask someone from work? I know it's your party, but would you mind?'

'Of course I wouldn't mind. Who is it?' Nancy asked as she pondered which one of their fellow workers Jessie could have become close to.

'It's Andrew Baker.' Jessie's words came out in a rush. 'He works in the stockroom. We've been meeting in our dinner break and sometimes – when you and me haven't been together – he's walked part of the way home with me. I hope you don't mind.' She was gabbling in her nervousness now.

'Mind? Why on earth should I mind? I'm pleased for you. I think I know the lad you mean. He's quite good-looking. Are you walking out with him, then?'

'Not – exactly, but I like him and I think he likes me.'

Nancy laughed. 'Obviously. Do your mam and dad know?'

'Not yet, but I thought your party might be a good time for my family to meet him.'

'That's fine with me, but you know it's not your mam and dad you need to worry about. It's Max's approval you'll have to get!'

Instead of looking surprised as Nancy had expected, Jessie whispered, 'Yes, I know.'

The party was in full flow by the time Andrew arrived. Jessie had been watching out for him but it was Lee who spotted him first.

'Ey up there, pal.' He knew Andrew from seeing him at the football matches. Luckily for Andrew, he was a Sheffield United supporter too. 'Come and meet the family.' He winked at Andrew. 'I'll get you a beer. You might need it, 'specially when you meet our eldest brother. Ah, here's Jessie. Look after him, our Jessie. He looks as if he's going to do a runner any minute.'

'I won't do that,' Andrew declared stoutly, 'but I could use a beer.'

'Come and meet my friend, Nancy, first,' Jessie suggested. 'It's her party after all.'

Jessie took his hand and led him through the throng. Someone had dragged a piano into the street and the player was surrounded by a group of ten or so neighbours all singing lustily.

'Oh hello, Andrew,' Nancy said when they found her. 'I recognize you now, though I didn't know your name. You're very welcome.'

'It's a big party,' Andrew murmured, as Lee returned and thrust a pint into his hand.

'We have to invite all the neighbours,' Lee joked. 'That way, no one will complain about the noise.'

'You're lucky with the weather.' The early-March evening was cold, but fine, and while everyone was muffled in the warmest clothes they possessed, nothing was going to stop their enjoyment.

'Who's this?' A voice spoke behind them making them jump and colour flooded Jessie's face as she turned to face Max.

'It's – um – Andrew from work. You know him, don't you? From football?'

'Yes, I do. At least you support the right team.'

'Of course,' Andrew said and stuck out his right hand. After a moment's hesitation, Max took it. When the two men had shaken hands, the five of them stood in awkward silence until Lee said, 'Come on, I'll introduce you to everyone.' He laughed. 'At least anyone who matters. We'll start with Mam, 'cos I expect you already know me dad and his mate, Bert Weston, from seeing them at matches.'

Their voices faded as they moved away leaving Nancy and Max standing together.

'So,' Max asked softly, 'what's he doing here? Did you invite him?'

Nancy hesitated. She didn't want to betray her friend's confidence and yet, surely the secret would be out after tonight, especially as the young man was now crossing the street to meet Jessie's mother.

'Sort of. I was asked if he could come so I said "yes".' She glanced up at Max.

He was frowning as he asked, 'But why is he going to meet my mam and not yours?'

Nancy sighed. She never told lies and she wasn't about to start now. 'Because it was Jessie who asked me to invite him.'

Max's frown disappeared and he began to smile. 'So he's here to see *Jessie*, not you?'

'That's right. Do you mind?'

'Not a bit,' he said airily. 'Come on,' he added, as he threw a brotherly arm around her shoulders, 'let's go and join in the sing-song.'

Twenty-two

The following Sunday afternoon, Jessie said, 'Mam, I'm going to the park to meet Andrew and before you say owt, Nancy's coming with me.'

Before Evelyn could answer, Max butted in. 'What's that?'

Patiently, Jessie explained. 'I'm meeting Andrew. Mam and Dad have both said they like him and approve of me walking out with him.'

'Mm, all right. But you be careful and mind Nancy stays with you all the time.'

'I'll go with 'em,' Lee said, throwing aside the newspaper in which he had been reading the racing page. 'I'm not doing owt this afternoon. I'll keep me eye on 'em, Max, don't you worry.'

It became a regular outing for the four young people on a Sunday afternoon through the summer months and often they did not return home until after dark. But neither of the parents were worried; Andrew seemed such a nice young man and, of course, they had Lee with them.

But early one morning in July, Flora found Nancy kneeling on her bedroom floor retching into the chamber pot. Flora stood in the doorway, her blood feeling as if it was running ice-cold through her veins, her hand still gripping the doorknob as she watched her daughter. It was as if time had slipped and gone back twenty years. It was how she had found Mary Ellen when the truth of her pregnancy had come out. She hadn't understood it then, but now she did, having experienced morning sickness herself too. And now she was watching another blond-haired, blue-eyed young woman – Mary Ellen's niece – doing exactly the same thing.

'Oh Nancy, no. Not you,' she breathed, as the girl raised her head and wiped her mouth. Tears streamed down Nancy's face.

'I'm so sorry, Mam.'

Flora sat down on the edge of the bed. 'Come here, love.'

Nancy sat beside her and wept against her shoulder. 'He said he'd be careful. He said he wouldn't let anything happen,' she cried. 'He said he loved me. I believed him. I *trusted* him.'

Flora stroked Nancy's hair and tried to think rationally, tried to work out what could be done. Gently, she said, 'But I thought Andrew was coming to see Jessie, not you.'

Nancy raised her tear-streaked face. 'Oh Mam, it's not Andrew.'

Flora stared at her. 'Then – then who?'

'I – I can't tell you.'

'Oh now, come on, Nancy. Whoever it is, do you love him? Do you want to marry him? He must be made to understand his responsibilities. He should stand by you if he's any sort of a man at all.'

Nancy was shaking her head vehemently. 'I can't. I – I daren't say.'

Flora sighed heavily. It was history repeating itself. Flora didn't know to this day who the father of Mary Ellen's child had been, although she had a shrewd idea.

'Nancy, love. Your dad will be upset and worried but he's not the violent sort. He's not going to go round to the young man's house with a shotgun.'

'It's not Dad I'm worried about,' Nancy said in a small voice.

'Then – who?'

Fresh tears flowed as Nancy said, 'It's Max.'

'*Max* is the father?' Now Flora was shocked.

'No – no.' Nancy gripped her mother's arm painfully. 'Max will kill him if he finds out.'

'I don't understand . . .' Flora began and then the truth began to dawn as she visualized the times she had watched the four youngsters walking down the street every Sunday afternoon and often not returning before dark. She had thought them safe – had believed the girls were safe with Andrew and . . .

Flatly, she whispered, 'Oh no! Not – not *Lee*.'

When Nancy did not deny it, Flora groaned. 'I see now what you mean. About Max. He will surely kill him.'

'We can't tell *any* of them, Mam. It would tear their family apart. It would ruin your friendship with Aunty Evelyn and Dad's with Uncle Howard. We just can't.'

'So what do we do when you start to show?'

'I'll have to go away. Like Aunty Mary Ellen did.'

'Let me talk to your dad. We'll work something out together. The three of us. No, it'll have to be the four of us, because your gran will have to know.'

Nancy shuddered in Flora's arms. 'Dad will be so ashamed of me,' she whispered.

'He'll be upset. There's no denying that, but he'll stand by you. He won't throw you out like my father did with Mary Ellen.'

Nancy stayed in her bedroom when her father arrived home until her mother called her to go downstairs. She rushed through the kitchen, not daring to glance in the direction of her grandmother who was making pastry at the table, and into the front room. She was shaking from head to foot, but when she dared to look up, Bert was standing on the hearthrug with his arms wide open to her. With a sob, she rushed into them. 'Oh Dad – Dad. I'm so sorry.'

He held her tightly and stroked her hair. At last, he said, 'Your mother's told me what you've said and I can understand how you feel, but he ought to be told. He ought to be given the chance to do the right thing.'

Nancy pulled back and shook her head violently. 'No, no.'

'Look, love, you ought at least to tell Lee himself. If it's done in the right way, the rest of the family won't be involved, now, will they? It'll all be arranged before they need to be told.'

Nancy was silent for a moment before saying in a whisper, 'All right. I'll tell him on Sunday.'

'And now,' Bert said softly, 'we'd better go and tell your gran.'

Agnes was just as supportive as her parents had been and Nancy sobbed into her lap while her grandmother stroked her hair. 'There, there, me love. These things happen. Just make sure you tell Lee and let's see what happens then, eh?'

On the Sunday afternoon, Flora and Bert watched from the front-room window as Nancy crossed the street to join her friends for their usual walk.

'This has come as a real shock to me, Bert,' Flora murmured, 'I thought I'd brought her up better than this.'

Bert put his arm around his wife's shoulders. 'Don't blame yourself, love. I expect he used the age-old persuasion "show me how much you love me".'

Flora looked up at him. 'You never did.'

Bert laughed softly. 'Oh, I wanted to a million times. I was desperate to make love to you but I loved and respected you too much to even ask, especially after what you'd been through with your sister.'

Flora laid her head against his shoulder as she said huskily, 'You're a good man, Bert Weston.'

As the four youngsters met up and moved away down the street, Flora and Bert could see that three of them were laughing and joking as usual, only one was quiet and withdrawn.

'Do you think he'll stand by her?' Flora asked as the foursome turned a corner and disappeared from their sight.

Bert wrinkled his forehead. 'Hard to say. He's what I call a loveable rogue. I've always liked him, but now . . .'

'Yes, there's always a "but", isn't there, with Lee?'

'Now, if it had been Max . . .'

'Yes, but Max wouldn't have done this in the first

place. I've never known a young man care so much about his family. And he treats Nancy as one of them. Always has done.' Flora sighed. 'Oh well, we'll just have to see what happens.'

'Nancy's right about one thing,' Bert said slowly. 'Whatever Lee decides to do, feathers will fly when Max gets to know.'

When Nancy returned, she was subdued, but her face was no longer ravaged with tears.

'He says we'll get married straight away.'

'Are you sure, love?' Bert asked gently. 'We don't want to force either of you into marriage just because of one mistake. We'll take care of you and bring the baby up as our own. Marriage is for a lifetime in our world, Nancy. And your poor mam knows what a bad marriage can be like.' For a moment, Nancy looked startled and glanced between them.

Bert laughed. 'Oh, not us. Your mam's parents weren't exactly happy, were they?

'That's an understatement if ever there was one,' Flora muttered.

Nancy understood. Although she perhaps didn't know every detail, she knew enough to know that her grandparents' marriage had been a miserable one. She knew how her grandfather had reacted when Mary Ellen had got pregnant. Nancy realized just how lucky she was to have parents who were standing by her. Although she knew she had disappointed and saddened them, there had been no ugly scenes, not even any recriminations. They were just trying to deal with the situation in the best way they knew how.

Even now, her father was wanting to be sure that getting married was the right course for her and even for Lee too.

'I do love him, Dad, and he's – he's the only man I've ever – you know. I don't want you to think I'm a – a . . .'

'No, love. We wouldn't think that,' Bert said hurriedly. 'And I do know how persuasive young fellers can be.'

'He asked us not to go over there. He wants time to tell his family and let them get used to the idea.'

'Aye well, mebbe that's not a bad idea. Let the lad do it in his own time.'

'It's Evelyn's turn to come across here for elevenses in the morning,' Flora said. 'She'll know by then and we can have a chat about it all. You go to work as normal, Nancy, and leave it to us to sort out what's to be done.'

Evelyn did not appear at the usual time for their elevenses.

'I expect she's upset,' Flora said.

Agnes snorted. 'Can't face us, more like.'

Half an hour later, there was a loud banging on the back door and Evelyn rushed in without waiting for it to be answered. Usually, she let herself in with a cheery, 'It's only me.' But not this morning.

'He's gone,' she blurted out. Her hair was wild and uncombed, her eyes red with weeping.

'Oh Evelyn,' Flora hurried to her side, her own troubles forgotten for the moment. Her friend's distress was obvious. 'Whatever's happened? Sit down. Let me get you a drink.'

Gently she led Evelyn to an easy chair by the range. 'What do you mean by "gone"? And who's gone?'

Evelyn lay back in the chair and closed her eyes, holding her hand to her chest. 'Lee,' she whispered. 'He left a note. Says he's gone away to join the navy. Oh Flora, whatever would make him do such a thing? We're such a close family. Oh, I know, we're a bit cramped at times now they're all growing up, but we manage.'

Flora and Agnes exchanged a glance, but Flora gave an imperceptible shake of her head and Agnes answered it with a brief nod, understanding that nothing should be said about Nancy, at least for the moment.

'Here, drink this, love,' Agnes said, pushing a cup of tea into Evelyn's shaking hands.

The two women sat down opposite her and waited until she had drunk half the liquid. 'I just don't understand it.'

I do, Flora thought. He's running away from his responsibilities. That's what. But she said nothing.

Tentatively, she asked, 'Does Jessie know anything? After all, they're twins and they spent a lot of time together, especially their walks on a Sunday.'

'She's as mystified as the rest of us.'

'And – Max?'

Evelyn frowned thoughtfully. 'It's funny, but he doesn't seem that bothered. He just says Lee's a man – well, almost – and that he's old enough to make his own decisions. If that's what he wants to do . . .' Her voice trailed away.

'And his dad? What does Howard say?'

191

'Much the same as Max. We've always agreed that we'd never stand in the way of whatever our children want to do.'

Evelyn stayed until almost dinner time. While they were very fond of her, both Flora and Agnes were impatient for her to be gone; they wanted to discuss what they should do next about Nancy.

Twenty-three

'I've been thinking,' Agnes said, after they'd seen Evelyn crossing the street and knew she was safely out of earshot. 'I have a suggestion, though I'm not sure you'll agree with it.'

'Any ideas are welcome.'

'I wouldn't want you to think I'm interfering.'

'We'd never think that. We always discuss everything as a family. Go on.'

'Let's sit by the range while we have a bite to eat.'

When they were sitting together with a sandwich in front of them – though neither of them felt much like eating – Agnes began, 'There's no need to make hasty decisions. She won't show for a while yet, so, I wondered if you could ask your sister to have her go to live with them until after the baby is born.'

'I could, I suppose,' Flora said slowly, 'although it might be a bit painful for Mary Ellen.'

'Yes, I realize that but I thought she'd want to help. I'm sure she's never forgotten how you helped her.'

Flora shook her head. 'No, she won't have done that, but there's the Clarke family to consider. It's still their farm, although they're both getting rather frail. Jack and Mary Ellen now run the place with a little outside help when they need it.'

'And I thought . . .' Agnes began and then stopped, unsure whether or not she should proceed. 'You see, I have this rather odd idea. It was something Bert said that made me think of it. You might not like it but, well, it would be a way to deal with it all.' Agnes was 'going all round the houses' to get to the point but Flora listened patiently. 'You see,' Agnes went on, 'I don't believe in adoption, at least not by outsiders. T'lass has made a mistake but we'll cope with it as a family and we'll bring the bairn up –' She paused a moment and bit her lip, casting a glance at Flora.

'Go on,' Flora said gently.

'If you and Nancy both went to Mary Ellen's until after the baby is born . . .'

'But that'd be months. Why would I need to stay? I'm sure Mary Ellen will agree to look after Nancy.'

'I know – I know, but I'm suggesting that *you* go too because – because when you come back here you say the baby's yours and you and Bert bring it up as if it really is.'

Flora stared at her and her mouth actually dropped open. 'Mine? But . . .'

'You're still young enough.'

The idea, preposterous though it sounded, began to take shape in Flora's mind. It was possible, of course, but there were other snags. Now she frowned, mulling over the idea. 'So,' she said slowly, thinking aloud, 'if it's mine, why would Nancy need to stay all that time in the country?'

Agnes waved her hand a little impatiently. 'Oh, I haven't worked out all the finer details. We'll think of something.'

The two women were silent, each busy with their thoughts. Ideas flitted in and out of their minds; some to be discarded, others to be considered.

Flora jumped up. 'I'll put the kettle on. I think better with a cup of tea.'

'What if . . .' Agnes began, as Flora placed a cup of tea in front of her mother-in-law and sat down herself, '. . . we tell everyone around here – except your mother, of course –'

Flora pulled a face. 'Yes, I'll have to tell her the truth.'

'We tell them all that Mary Ellen isn't well and you've gone to help out. You've already said that her in-laws are too frail to work on the farm any more.'

'Yes, but why would *Nancy* need to go too? I would certainly go in those circumstances, but I don't think that Nancy would give up her job to go with me, now, would she?'

'She might if we say that she's gone to work on the farm for her aunt and uncle. It sounds as if more than one person would be needed if that actually happened. Jack couldn't work the farm completely on his own, now, could he?'

'No, though they get locals to help out when needed. They already do that at very busy times.'

'No one *here* knows that, now do they?'

'No,' Flora said slowly. 'I suppose not but . . .'

'But – what?'

Flora smiled. 'Actually, "but" nothing. It's a brilliant idea.'

'So now we've got to convince Bert.'

'He might say we should tell the truth. Brave it out.'

'We can't if we don't want to hurt the Bonsors any more than they already have been with Lee just running off like that without a word,' Agnes argued. 'Max would no doubt go looking for him, drag him back by the scuff of his neck and make him marry her. And I'm not sure that would be a good idea for either Lee or Nancy. I don't want to see them forced into marriage just because of one mistake.'

'That is *exactly* what Max would do,' Flora said in a whisper, 'and Howard would probably help him.'

To their surprise, Bert took no persuading. In fact, he was pleased with the idea. 'I suppose when he or she is older, we'll have to tell them the truth and we must do everything legally. I don't want any false information on his or her birth certificate. Nothing like that, but in the meantime, I think it might work. So what are you going to do, Flora? Write to Mary Ellen and ask her?'

'If you can borrow the pony and trap again, I think we should go and see her. I think it needs discussing face to face and Jack will have to agree, of course. I'll write and tell Mary Ellen we'll be visiting next Sunday. I don't like to just turn up without warning.'

'And there's his parents to consider too. Don't forget them.'

'No, I haven't, and there's someone else I must see. My mother.'

Flora went to see Edith the following morning. She talked freely in front of Seffie; the woman was a close friend and would keep their secret.

Edith was saddened to think that the same thing had happened again, but this time the girl would not be cast out. This time she would be treated with kindness and understanding.

Bert and Flora set off on the Sunday morning arriving in time for dinner. Mary Ellen looked well and happy; she was now in charge of the kitchen as Mrs Clarke's legs were swollen and painful and Mr Clarke was suffering badly with arthritis. The old couple were now sleeping downstairs in the front room. But, unsurprisingly, they were both as cheerful and welcoming as ever.

'I don't know what we'd do without Mary Ellen,' Winnie Clarke said, as they finished eating the apple crumble served after a huge roast dinner. 'She's a Godsend to us. Neither Matthew nor I can do much now and all the work is falling very heavily on Jack and Mary Ellen.'

Flora and Bert exchanged a glance, which was seen by Mary Ellen.

'Is there something wrong, you two? We're delighted to see you, of course, but your visit has come "out of the blue", as they say.'

'You tell them, Flora, though I'm not sure we should ask them what we were going to.'

'Please ask anything you want, Bert,' Jack said. 'Would you rather speak to Mary Ellen in private?'

'No, no. It's no secret – well – not from any of you anyway.'

Mary Ellen turned worried eyes on her sister. 'Is it Mam?'

'No, no, she's fine. Happier than she's been for

years. In fact, I think she's probably the happiest she's ever been in her life. No, it's . . .' Flora's gaze found Mary Ellen's worried eyes as she pulled in a deep breath and said, 'It's Nancy.'

There was a long silence in the room as the two sisters stared at each other.

'Oh no!' Mary Ellen whispered at last. 'Not that. Not Nancy.'

Slowly, Flora nodded. 'Who . . .?' Mary Ellen began and then dropped her gaze. 'No, I shouldn't ask that. I'll just say, is there no chance of her marrying whoever?'

'We thought there was,' Bert said. 'It's Lee Bonsor, but after she told him, he's done a bunk. Left a note for his family that he's gone to join the Royal Navy.'

Mary Ellen gasped. 'But – but they're like family to you. They must be devastated.'

'They don't know,' Bert said, 'and we want it left like that. If they found out, it's more than likely they'd find him and force him to marry her and we don't want that for either of them.'

'But – when she starts to show, questions will be asked . . .' Mary Ellen began but Jack put his hand over hers.

'I rather think that's why they've come to see us. Am I right, Bert? So how can we help you?'

On the other side of the table, his parents smiled and nodded too.

There it was again, Flora thought. The unquestioning goodness and kindness of these people was incredible. Tears sprang to her eyes.

Bert outlined the idea that his mother had come

up with. As he spoke, he was aware of the old couple glancing at each other and then the thought came to him. He and Flora had completely forgotten the strong moral values held by the Clarke family. He looked across at the elderly couple as he added, 'I know you will not agree with deception so I'll say now, we would do nothing whatsoever illegal . . .'

As Bert went on, Flora too realized why he was saying things now that they hadn't actually discussed in detail, hadn't even thought of. But she understood at once why they needed to be said.

'We would have the child registered properly – perhaps even baptized here if the vicar was understanding enough. And we plan to tell him or her the truth when they are old enough to understand. It's just that we want to spare Nancy – and the child as it grows – the nasty gossip where we live.'

There was silence in the room until Jack broke it by saying quietly, 'One thing surprises me. I'm wondering why you haven't asked if Mary Ellen and I would be willing to adopt the baby.' He squeezed his wife's hand as he said gently, 'Poor Mary Ellen has suffered a total of three miscarriages and the doctor has said it would be dangerous for us to try again.'

'I'd be willing if Jack is,' Mary Ellen said quietly. 'But we have Jack's mam and dad to consider . . .'

Matthew Clarke laughed. 'Now don't you let us stand in your way, lass. It'd be wonderful to have a bairn about the place again, wouldn't it, Ma?'

'It would, but we'd have to remember that the work would fall even more heavily on Mary Ellen than it does now. Though I think I could help out with a baby . . .' Winnie laughed too. 'At least until it started running about.'

Flora looked unsure but she murmured, 'It's certainly something for us to think about.'

Jack said, as if catching on to Flora's hesitation, 'But we're willing to go along with what you're suggesting if that's what you'd prefer. A final decision can be made later. In all fairness, that decision should involve Nancy.'

Bert nodded. 'Yes, you're right, Jack. That's why we thought of this. To be honest, it was my mother who came up with the idea. I think she thought that it was a way to keep the child with us and yet save Nancy from the embarrassment. And we all know what happens to an illegitimate child when they get to school.'

There was silence around the table. All of them had witnessed the name calling, the shunning of an innocent child because of the circumstances of their birth.

Just before they set off home, Flora had the chance of a private word with her sister. 'I'm so sorry if this revives bad memories for you, but we couldn't think of what else to do except to brazen it out. And then, the Bonsor family would find out.'

'Why are you so intent on saving their feelings? That's what I don't quite understand.'

Flora sighed heavily. 'Perhaps we're wrong, but we're all such good friends. It would break Evelyn's heart if she knew, and as for Max . . .'

'What about Max? He's the eldest, isn't he?'

'Yes. He's such a caring, thoughtful chap – has been right from being a young boy. He looks out for all his family, and Nancy – because she's an only child, I suppose – is always included in their circle. If Max got his hands on Lee at this moment, well, I daren't think what he might do to him. We just don't want to cause trouble in their family.'

'Actually, it is true that I could do with some help,' Mary Ellen said. 'And we can always do with an extra pair of hands about the farm. Most of it's hard work, but there are a few less strenuous jobs both you and Nancy could help with.'

'So we can go there whenever we like,' Flora said, as, back home in Sheffield, the four of them sat around the tea table. 'Mary Ellen said I didn't even need to let them know. She'll make sure everything's ready for us, even if we just turn up.'

'And there's another suggestion for you to consider, Nancy love, though perhaps not yet,' Bert said gently. 'Mary Ellen and Jack are willing to adopt the baby. It seems very unlikely that they will ever have any of their own.'

Nancy stared at her father. 'Really? Oh.' She dropped her gaze and appeared to be deep in thought. 'I suppose that would solve everything. No one need ever know around here.'

'Well, Lee knows,' Agnes reminded her.

'Huh!' Nancy laughed wryly. 'I don't think he's going to tell anyone, now, is he?'

'Don't make a definite decision yet,' Flora said. 'Wait and see how you feel once the baby's born.'

Later in the privacy of their bedroom, Bert said, 'You don't want Mary Ellen to have the child, do you?'

'It's not that, Bert. Not really. Mary Ellen would be a wonderful mother and maybe she deserves the chance to be one, but . . .'

'But?' Bert prompted.

Flora sighed. 'However it's come into the world, that child is going to be our grandchild, Bert. I just don't know if *I* can bear to part with the little mite, never mind what Nancy feels.'

'I understand exactly how you feel love, because I feel much the same.'

They got into bed together and lay down. Bert was snoring gently in seconds but sleep evaded Flora. She lay awake, staring into the darkness, until the early hours of the morning.

Twenty-four

Flora and Evelyn still went to each other's homes for elevenses most days but the visits were not so cheerful now as they had been. Evelyn spent most of the time bemoaning the fact that Lee had gone off without a word and Agnes did not join them so often now.

'I can't sit there, Flora,' she'd said, 'pretending everything's all right when it isn't. I'm beginning to think they ought to be told. I'll stay in me room, when she comes over here, if you don't mind. Make some excuse for me, will you, love?'

Agnes now had the front room as a bed-sitting room. It was an arrangement that worked out well for all of them.

'I just don't understand it,' Evelyn would begin almost before she had sat down. 'Nothing was wrong at home and he was always such a cheerful, happy-go-lucky lad. A bit of a rascal, I know. I'd be the first to admit that, but he wasn't a bad boy, was he, Flora? And he's never said anything about being interested in joining the navy. Something must have happened, but I can't for the life of me think what it can be.'

Oh, something's happened all right, Flora wanted to shout. Your precious son has got my girl pregnant and won't stand up to his responsibilities. That's

203

what's wrong. But she kept silent. She was startled out of her own thoughts by Evelyn saying, 'Has Nancy said anything? Does she know what's wrong?'

Flora jumped, caught off guard. 'I – um – I can ask her, if you like.'

Evelyn sighed. 'I'd've thought our Jessie would know if anyone does, being his twin, but she *says* she doesn't know and, to be fair, she seems as surprised as the rest of us. Anyway, enough about my troubles. You're a good friend to listen to me keep harping on about it. Is Agnes all right? She hasn't had a cuppa with us for several days now.'

Flora took a deep breath. 'She's fine, but I think she'd rather leave us alone to talk about Lee.' Then she went on, deciding in that moment to plant a few ideas in Evelyn's head.

'I have to admit that I'm rather worried about Mary Ellen.'

'You and Bert went to see her last week, didn't you?'

'Yes. Her husband's parents are getting rather frail now and of course all the housework is falling heavily on Mary Ellen. And then there's the farm. Jack's father does very little now either. It's heavy work.'

'Doesn't Jack employ someone to help him?'

'He does at busy times, but the farm's not big enough to support several labourers. So,' she said slowly, and her heart beat a little faster, 'Bert and I were thinking that I should go and help out for a week or two and that . . .' she paused and licked her lips, 'that Nancy should take some time off work and come with me.' She didn't add that Nancy would be taking quite a lot of time off work. That news could filter through gradually.

'What about Bert and his mother?'

'Oh, they'll be fine. Agnes still loves to cook and Bert's not the sort of man who thinks helping out around the house now and again is beneath him.'

'Well, tell them they can always ask me if they need a hand.'

'That's kind of you, Evelyn. I appreciate it.'

Evelyn heaved herself up with a sigh. 'That's what friends are for. I don't know what I'd have done without you these days since Lee went. But Howard says it's high time I pulled myself together and stopped worrying. He's a grown man and we're bound to hear from him sooner or later. Well, I'd best be getting back. It's me day for doing the bedrooms. See you later, m'love.'

As the weeks went by, Nancy grew pale and exhausted and when she came home one evening in August to tell her mother that she had fainted at work, Flora knew the time had come for them to go to stay with Mary Ellen.

'Right,' she said decisively. 'Go into work tomorrow and ask the head of your department if you can have next week off to visit your aunt who lives in the countryside.'

'Just – just a week?'

'Yes. I've thought it all out. When we get there, you can write to her and give in your notice. You can say you've decided to stay in the countryside and help your aunt and uncle on their farm. She doesn't need to know any more than that.'

Nancy nodded slowly. 'Yes, that's a good idea, Mam. I'll do that.'

'We'll go on Sunday, if your dad can get the pony and trap. And now, we'll need to get packing what we need to take.'

On the Saturday night, just as they were finishing tea, there was a knock at the back door. Nancy went to answer it. When she saw who was standing there, her heart began to beat faster. Why had he come? Was he the bearer of bad news or had he heard . . .?

'Max! Whatever are you doing here? Is – is everything all right?'

His warm brown eyes smiled down at her. He was tall, broad-shouldered and strong and he towered over Nancy's slight figure.

'I just came to see you, that's all. Mam says that your aunt isn't well and that you and your mam are leaving tomorrow to stay with her for a week. I'm sorry to hear that, Nancy. Just tell your dad and your gran –'

'Oh Max, come in, do. I'm forgetting me manners.' She opened the door wider, inviting him in, though she was quaking inside. Would he guess the truth? She wondered now if they had been right to keep it from the Bonsor family. At least it would have answered their questions about why Lee had disappeared so suddenly. When she brought Max into the kitchen the other three members of the household stared at him for a moment and then all began to speak at once. Nancy realized that they were as nervous as she was.

'Come and sit down,' Bert said.

'I'll get you a cup of tea,' Flora said and bustled into the scullery while Agnes just said, 'It's nice to see you, Max.'

'I just came to see you,' Max repeated, 'because Mam said Mrs Weston and Nancy are leaving for the country tomorrow. I hope things are better than you fear.'

Nancy almost laughed hysterically. Things couldn't get much worse, she thought, but then she castigated herself for being selfish. Of course they could; there were much worse things that could happen to a family.

'We've had a bit of news,' Max was saying in his deep voice. His gaze was on Nancy as he added, 'We've had a letter from Lee.'

Nancy held her breath and tried to stop the colour rising in her face, but it was impossible.

'He's been in Liverpool and he's signed on a ship sailing to New York. He'll be at sea now.' Max smiled grimly. 'He posted the letter just before he sailed so that it wouldn't reach us until he was safely away. I expect he thought I'd go after him.' His gaze held Nancy's as he added softly, 'Which I would have done.'

Bert cleared his throat self-consciously. 'We wish him well – safe passage and all that.' Then his voice faded away and he avoided meeting Max's gaze. There was now an awkward silence in the room until both Flora and Agnes spoke together trying to fill the gap.

'I expect your mother's relieved to know where he

is,' Agnes began, while Flora said, 'If you'll excuse me, Max, I've still got a lot to do before tomorrow morning.'

'I'm sorry, I shouldn't have intruded,' Max said, beginning to stand up.

'No, no, finish your tea and have a chat with Bert. Nancy, I need your help upstairs.'

The two women left and Agnes went into her bed-sitting room, leaving the two men alone.

'Mr Weston,' Max began quietly, 'please tell me if Lee going has upset Nancy. She doesn't look quite her cheerful self. I know they must have been good friends, always going out on Sunday afternoons with Jessie and her young man. I wondered if they'd – well – grown close.'

Bert couldn't look the earnest young man in the eyes. He cleared his throat nervously. 'Don't you worry about Nancy, Max. She's fine. We'll look after her.'

Bert felt Max staring at him as if he was trying to read what actually lay behind his words. After a moment's silence between them, Max nodded. 'I just hope he hasn't hurt her in any way, because if he has, I'll break his bloody neck when I catch up with him.'

In that moment, Bert knew that they had been right not to tell the Bonsor family the truth. All hell could have broken loose.

The welcome that awaited them at Dale Farm could not have been warmer. The farmhouse was big enough for Flora and Nancy to have a bedroom each upstairs.

'We've turned the front parlour into a bed-sitting room for Jack's mam and dad. They both find the stairs very difficult now and it's so much easier for me looking after them too.'

'We've done that at home for Bert's ma,' Flora said. 'She can still get up and down the stairs but as we've only two bedrooms upstairs, it was the sensible thing to do. She's quite happy with the arrangement. In fact, it was she who suggested it.'

When dinner was finished and Bert had said a fond farewell to his wife and daughter and set off back to the city, Flora said, 'Now, Mary Ellen, you must tell us what you want us to do to help both in the house and on the farm.'

Her sister's eyes twinkled as she laughed. 'Oh, you can be sure we will. I think Jack's got a few nice easy jobs outside lined up for Nancy. Nothing too strenuous, obviously, but if she can do them, it frees him up to do other things. We thought perhaps she'd like to be in charge of the hens. Jack will show her how to feed them and collect the eggs. But he'll still be responsible for locking them up every night. He doesn't want to put that burden on Nancy, because if Mr Fox got into the hen house, we'd likely lose the lot. Oh, and we wouldn't expect her to muck 'em out. That's a heavy job. There's a young school lad comes on a Saturday and that's his job when it's needed. And she can take the baskets of food and drink out to the men when they're working in the fields. That'd be a help and not too heavy for her. We're coming to the end of harvest time but there's still a lot of work to do even though we don't grow a lot of crops. We're mainly livestock.'

'I suppose the hillsides are very difficult to grow

crops on,' Nancy said. 'Is that why you have so many sheep and cattle on the grassland on the hills?'

'Partly. The ground is also very stony. You can soon break a plough.'

'And what about me?' Flora asked. 'What can I do?'

'If you could help me about the house, Flora, that'd be grand. There's always such a lot to do and that will release me to do a bit more outside to help Jack.' Mary Ellen smiled and put her arms around her sister. 'Oh Flora, despite the reason, it is so good to have you both here.'

'And it's good to see you so happy, Mary Ellen. You really love it here, don't you?'

'I do,' Mary Ellen said simply.

The household settled down well together. Nancy did not attend church with them on Sundays, but Flora joined her sister and brother-in-law. Mr and Mrs Clarke went occasionally, being driven there in the pony and trap by their son, while Flora and Mary Ellen walked the mile or so to the church.

'Hello, love,' Iris Beckett greeted Flora one Sunday. 'I remember you from years back. You're young Mrs Clarke's sister, aren't you?'

Flora smiled. 'Fancy you remembering, Mrs Beckett, after all this time. How are you?'

'Aye well, it wasn't a time you'd forget easily, was it? And I'm very well, thank you.' She laughed. 'I'm still bringing babies into the world.'

Mary Ellen appeared at Flora's elbow and drew both her sister and Mrs Beckett to one side, a short distance from the rest of the congregation leaving the church. In a low voice she said, 'We will need your expert services again in a few months' time, Mrs Beckett.'

Iris's face clouded. 'Oh Mrs Clarke, is it wise for you to –'

Mary Ellen smiled sadly and shook her head. 'No, no, it isn't me, Mrs Beckett.' She glanced at Flora, who took up the conversation. 'It's my daughter, Mrs Beckett. We've come to stay with my sister while . . .'

But Iris Beckett was not easily shocked. She had seen it all, even in this small village. She sighed. 'Ah, I understand. I'm sorry to hear it, but I'll do all I can to help the lass. It would be a good idea – if it's all right with you – for me to see her a couple of times leading up to her confinement. I shall be able to make sure everything is going the way it should.'

'I'd be very grateful, Mrs Beckett,' Flora said and Mary Ellen nodded her agreement.

'Mrs Beckett often comes to see the old folk,' Mary Ellen said. 'She's wonderful when it comes to treating my mother-in-law's bad legs.'

'Oh, so you do a lot more than deliver babies,' Flora said.

Iris nodded and said modestly, 'I help out wherever I can.' She patted Flora's hand. 'I'll pop in and see your girl sometime this week. Word will get around, I'm afraid, but I assure you it won't be from me. I never gossip about my patients.'

As they climbed into the pony and trap – there'd been just the three of them attending church – Mary Ellen said, 'She's right. She's very discreet, but word will get around the village, probably from Ned, the young lad who helps out on a Saturday.'

'Ah well,' Flora sighed. 'It can't be helped.'

'But at least the gossip won't be malicious,' Mary Ellen said. 'I can promise you that.'

Jack flicked the reins and they bowled home.

Twenty-five

Just as Flora, Mary Ellen and Jack were returning to the farm from church, back at home, Max was knocking on the back door of the Westons' house.

'Hello, Max.' Agnes greeted him with a smile when she opened the door. 'Come away in. He's fixing a shelf for me in the pantry that's looking a bit unsafe. Bert!' – she raised her voice – 'Max is here.'

Bert came into the kitchen. 'That's got that fixed nice and sturdy, Ma. Nowt'll come crashing down now. Ey up, Max, sit yarsen down. Everything all right?'

'Aye. Mam's settled down a bit about Lee now she knows where he is and what he's doing, though none of us can understand why he went so suddenly. If he'd been on about going to sea, we could have understood it, but he's never said a word about being interested in that life.'

'You're in luck. Ma's just fetched some beer.' Bert avoided meeting Max's honest gaze as he poured two glasses for them.

'If you'll excuse me, Max,' Agnes said, 'I've got the dinner to get ready. You two sit and have a chin wag.' She disappeared into the scullery to peel vegetables.

'Is your mam managing all right?' Max asked. 'It

213

must be quite hard for her at her age without your wife and Nancy to help her.'

'Oh, Ma's as fit as a butcher's dog,' Bert said, 'and I keep an eye on her if she starts to look a bit tired.' He chuckled. 'I'm not too proud to turn my hand to a bit of housework if it's needed.'

There was a short silence before Max said, 'And how are Mrs Weston and Nancy? Is Mrs Weston's sister improving?'

Bert sighed inwardly. It was difficult; when one told even the smallest lie it always seemed to escalate until you had to tell more and more to cover up the first untruth. Neatly, Bert avoided answering the question about Mary Ellen's health directly.

'They're getting on well. Jack's parents aren't able to do anything now, so I understand there's a lot of work about the house and the farm too. It's just coming to the end of harvest time now, so there'll be plenty of work still needs doing.' He forced a laugh. 'I only wish I could go with them.'

'Are you visiting them, because if you are, I'd like to come with you?'

'Oh – er – I hadn't really thought about doing that,' Bert stuttered, completely thrown. He avoided meeting Max's honest eyes. 'I suppose I keep – um – hoping they'll come home soon.'

'Yes, of course,' Max murmured, but Bert was sure he could detect a note of doubt in the younger man's voice. This deception was getting harder by the day to keep up.

They talked a while longer about Rowleys, where they both worked.

'I was pleased that both our Jessie and Nancy got nice jobs in town,' Max said, 'but I don't reckon they'll keep Nancy's job open for her indefinitely. Jessie says that the head of their department has had a letter from Nancy saying she'll be staying away for quite a while.'

'No, she realizes that, but she loves it in the country. I think she'll take her chances of picking up a job somewhere when she comes back, even if it's not at the same place.'

'I'm sure she'd get a very good reference. Jessie says she was very popular with the staff and customers alike,' Max murmured and then, after a short pause, he asked, 'She will come back, though, won't she, Mr Weston?'

Bert forced a laugh that even to his own ears sounded hollow. 'Oh yes, she'll come back, Max, but I can't tell you when.'

Obliged to believe what Bert was telling him, Max stood up and held out his hand. 'Give them my best wishes when you write and, don't forget, if you go to visit, I'd really like to come with you.'

After the young man had left the house, Agnes came and sat with her son for a few moments. She could see he was troubled and, as he explained what Max had said, Agnes could see the reason for his concern.

She chewed her lip for a moment before saying thoughtfully, 'Perhaps we should do something to spread the word that it is Flora who is having a baby. You should write to them, Bert, and suggest it. We can then say you've had a letter from Flora saying she's found out she's with child.'

215

Bert sighed heavily. 'I'm beginning to wish we'd never started this deception.'

'It's to save Nancy's good name,' she reminded him bluntly. 'There aren't many Jack Clarkes out there, son.'

Bert sighed heavily. 'You're right, Ma, I know you are. I'll write to Flora tonight.'

Flora wrote back by return:

> *Mary Ellen, Nancy and I have discussed this and we think it's a very good idea of your mother's. If you could have a quiet word with Howard and Evelyn, at least they'll be prepared when we do return home. If word gets out down the street so much the better. Only my mam and Seffie will know the truth, but they live far enough away not to be put in an awkward position by having to answer questions. As regards Max coming with you to visit us, that's a lot more difficult. I suspect it's Nancy he wants to see and that's impossible. We wouldn't be able to hide it now. So, sadly, it looks as if you won't be able to come to see us either.*

That same evening, Bert rehearsed what he was going to say and then crossed the road diagonally to the Bonsors' home. Evelyn opened the door. Bert thought she looked so much better than the last time he had seen her. Evelyn still had elevenses with Agnes once or twice a week but not every day as she had done when Flora had been at home. But then, of course, Bert was always at work and he had not seen her recently.

'Hello, Bert. Haven't seen you for a while. Come in, come in. Howard and Max are in the kitchen toasting their toes by the fire. I'll find you all a beer.' She paused before turning away towards the scullery. 'Nothing wrong, is there?'

'Not exactly wrong, no, but I have to admit I've – we've – had a bit of a shock.'

She led the way into the kitchen. 'Howard, Max, Bert's here. He's got summat he wants to tell us.'

Max stood up and offered his chair to Bert while both he and his mother stood waiting. Evelyn was going nowhere until she'd heard what Bert had to say.

'We've had a bit of a surprise – well, a shock, really. Soon after they got to Mary Ellen's Flora started to feel – well – not exactly ill but not quite her usual robust self.' Now came the hard bit – the deliberate lie. 'She's – she's found out she's expecting a bairn.'

There was a stunned silence in the room. No one moved or spoke for several seconds and then Evelyn, still staring at Bert, sank into a chair near the table. Max remained standing, but he was frowning.

Evelyn was the first to break the silence. 'But – but she shouldn't. It might be dangerous.'

'I know,' Bert whispered, hanging his head so that he didn't have to meet their eyes.

'Is she coming back home? To be nearer a doctor or even a hospital? I mean, she had such a lot of trouble giving birth to Nancy. She ought to have the best care possible on hand.'

'I – don't think she'll come back here. There's a very good woman in the village who helped Mary Ellen through her trouble. I think Flora's happy to rely on her.'

They were all still staring at him. Bert felt disconcerted. Max's gaze particularly unsettled him. Only Evelyn seemed to have accepted the situation, odd though it must sound.

'You tell her from me that when she comes home, we'll do everything we can to help her. I'll go across tomorrow morning to see your mam.'

Max spoke at last. 'What about Nancy? Is she coming home soon?'

Bert shook his head. 'I don't think so. She'll stay there to help out now that Flora won't be able to do as much to help Mary Ellen.'

'Is Mary Ellen improving?' Evelyn asked. 'She was the reason they went there in the first place, wasn't she?'

Bert gave a short laugh. 'Flora didn't say. I think this has been such a shock, it's driven everything else from her mind.'

'I think we'd better find you something a bit stronger than a beer, Bert,' Evelyn laughed.

When Bert had left after an hour, Max sat down in the chair by the hearth again. 'I don't know about you two, but I don't believe a word of it.'

'What? What d'you mean, Max?' Evelyn asked.

'Exactly what I say. I think he's telling us a pack of lies.'

'Why? Why would he do that?'

Max's face was bleak as he said, 'Because I don't think it's his wife who is expecting, I think it's –' He hesitated, unwilling to say the name. He swallowed painfully and his voice was husky as he whispered, 'Nancy.'

'*Nancy!*' Evelyn's mouth dropped open as she gaped at him. 'But – but she's never had a proper boyfriend. She only goes out with Jessie to chaperone her and –' Her voice faded away as realization hit her. 'Oh no! No! Not – not that!' Evelyn covered her face with hands that trembled.

'I don't know what you're on about.' Mystified, Howard glanced between his wife and his son.

Max sighed and his voice was heavy with sadness as he said, 'Nancy went out every Sunday afternoon with Jessie and Andrew, didn't she?'

Howard nodded. 'Yes, that's right. I mean, he seems a nice enough lad, but we didn't know him at first and we thought it better that someone should go with them. So what are you saying? That Andrew has transferred his affections to Nancy?'

'No, that's not what I'm saying, Dad. Not at all, else Jessie would be upset. But just think, who else went with them almost every weekend?'

Howard stared at Max before he too, echoing his wife's exclamation, said, 'Oh no! Not – not our *Lee*.'

Max's voice was grim now. 'Think about it. Why did he run off so suddenly without a word to any of us? Nancy must have told him and he panicked because, for one thing, he knew I'd give him "what for" when I found out.'

Evelyn slowly dropped her hands from her face

and met Max's angry gaze. 'Why? Why would you want to have a fight with him?'

When Max didn't answer her at once, Howard, catching on at last, said softly, 'Because he's in love with the lass himself. Is that right, son?'

Hoarsely, Max said, 'For as long as I can remember, Dad. Of course at first, she was like another little sister to me. I loved her just the same as I loved Jessie. It wasn't until – until she started going out with Lee every Sunday that I realized I felt more for her than brotherly affection. A helluva lot more.'

'So why didn't you say something to her?' Howard asked. 'Why didn't you start courting her? She's old enough now.'

Max sighed heavily. 'Because I could see that it was Lee she – she seemed to prefer. And she must be in love with him to – to have –' His voice broke and he could say no more. Evelyn squeezed his hand and Howard touched his shoulder, but neither of them could think of anything to say to comfort him.

To see her eldest son – her eldest child – the one who was always so kind, so loving and caring, hurting so much almost broke Evelyn's heart.

Suddenly, galvanized into action, she jumped up. 'Let's talk to Jessie.'

'Do you think we should, Mam? Perhaps we should keep this between the three of us for the moment. I mean, I don't *know* that I'm right.'

'I think we should talk to Jessie but we must impress upon her that she must not speak to anyone about it. Not even Andrew.'

'All right, then,' Max agreed reluctantly.

'I'll call her down.'

Moments later, Jessie appeared looking a little apprehensive.

'It's all right, Jessie love,' Howard said at once, stretching out his arm towards her in an invitation to sit beside him. 'You're not in trouble. We just want to talk to you. But first we must have your solemn promise that you will speak to no one about this, not even Andrew. Do you understand?'

Jessie nodded, but she still looked anxious. She couldn't think what on earth this could be about.

'When the four of you went out on Sunday afternoons,' Howard asked her gently, 'did you ever sort of – pair off? You know, you and Andrew and Nancy and Lee?'

Colour flooded Jessie's face and she twisted her fingers together nervously. Before she could answer, Max said, 'We're not accusing you of doing anything wrong, Jessie . . .'

'I haven't! I swear I haven't. We cuddle and kiss a bit but nothing more. I promise.' Now tears spilled from her eyes as she looked at her mother. 'Mam, I'm a good girl. I wouldn't . . .'

'You're not the reason we're asking, love,' Evelyn said. 'It's about Nancy and – and Lee.'

Jessie stared at her and then glanced at both Max and Howard. 'Why? Do you think that's why Lee's gone off? That it's something to do with Nancy?'

Evelyn bit her lip but nodded.

'But – but Nancy's a good girl. She wouldn't. We talk about things like that. Just girl talk, just between ourselves, you know. And Nancy always said her mam

221

had drilled it into her never to let a boy touch her – like *that*. She – she told me about her aunt and all the trouble it caused. And besides, Lee would never –' Her voice faded away uncertainly. Now she wasn't too sure.

'Did they ever go off on their own, Jessie?' Max asked softly.

Jessie's eyes widened as she was forced to admit in a reluctant whisper, 'Yes, yes, they did. But –' Now she stopped. She couldn't say for definite what the pair might have got up to; she hadn't been there. She could only say with certainty that she and Andrew had done nothing that her mam would say was wrong.

'Why – why are you asking me?'

Evelyn explained about Bert's visit and then Max chipped in. 'When I went to see him the other evening, I said that if he visited them, I'd like to go with him. He seemed very reluctant and then a few days later, we get this story.'

'And you think it's Nancy that's – that's . . .'

Evelyn nodded.

Jessie was thoughtful for a few minutes before saying slowly, 'That last Sunday we went out together before Lee left on the Monday, they did go off together and when they came back there was – there was something different. I thought at the time they must have had a row and then when he disappeared the next day, well, I thought she must have called it off, you know. Because I had seen them growing closer over the weeks. They used to walk hand in hand and then sometimes Lee would put his arm around her waist and – and one time, I saw them kissing. But I never thought . . .' Her voice trailed away and she hung her head as if she carried some of the burden of the guilt too.

Sensitive to her daughter's feelings, Evelyn put her arm about her and said, 'It's not your fault, Jessie. None of it is.'

'It's Lee's fault,' Max said harshly. 'It's all his fault.'

'Not entirely,' Evelyn snapped. 'It takes two, Max. Nancy must bear some of the responsibility too. I'm not the sort of mother who thinks her children can do no wrong and we all know Lee's a little devil, but he's not the sort to force a girl against her will.'

Max's jaw tensed and his eyes glittered. 'But Nancy bears all the shame while he scarpers and gets off scot-free.'

'Not entirely,' Howard said. 'Either he can't ever come home again or he'll have to face the music some time.'

'Aye.' Max got up suddenly and made for the door. 'And I'll be waiting for him if and when he dares to show his face. You can count on that.'

Twenty-six

Back in his own home, Bert sat near the range opposite his mother. 'That was the most difficult hour I
think I've ever had in me life, Ma.'

'D'you think they believed you?'

'Not for a minute. I did me best, but they're not
daft. They'll put two and two together and come up
with the right answer. 'Specially Max.'

'Mebbe they'll go along with it to save their own
faces.'

'They might, but Flora's wish to save them the grief
hasn't worked, I'm afraid.'

'So are you going to write to Flora and tell her
that they might as well come home?'

'I'll tell her what I think has happened with the
Bonsors but they never said anything to me and I don't
think they will. Besides, there's the rest of the neighbourhood to think about. If we can still stop the gossip
about Nancy, it would be something, wouldn't it?'

'True,' Agnes said. 'So you think they're best stopping where they are and then, when the bairn's born,
a decision will be made as to whether Mary Ellen
adopts it or it comes home to us as Flora's. Because
I'll tell you summat now, Bert, I'll not have me
great-grandchild adopted by strangers.'

'No, I agree with you there, Ma.' A small smile curved his mouth. 'I must admit, I'm not happy about how it's happened, but it might be very nice to have a little 'un about the place again.'

'Well, son, we'll just wait and see what the next few months bring.'

Now that he thought he'd guessed the truth, Max realized that he'd put Bert in a very awkward position, so one evening when they walked down the street together on their way home from work, Max said, 'If you go to see Mrs Weston and Nancy, I won't come with you but please give them both my best regards and – and tell them we'll all do whatever we can to help when they do come home.'

Bert's voice was a little shaky as he said, 'Thank you, Max. I'll be sure to give them your message.'

Towards the end of November Bert decided that he really should make a trip into the countryside to see his family. Agnes declined to go with him, as did Edith.

'I'll see them when they get home,' she said. 'Just so long as I know everything is all right.'

'I'll come and see you next week,' Bert promised, 'to let you know how everything is.'

When Bert climbed down from the pony and trap he'd borrowed once again, he was surprised to see that only Nancy came out of the back door of the farmhouse to greet him. He sighed deeply as she came towards him, though he plastered a smile on his face and held out his arms towards her. There was no mistaking now that she was with child. But she was blooming; there was a healthy pink tinge to her cheeks he'd never seen before.

'They've all gone to church, even the old couple,' Nancy said as she hugged him. 'They love the services leading up to Christmas.'

'How are they keeping?'

'Not too bad really. Neither of them are good on their feet now though.'

'And your mam?'

'She's missing you – and Gran too, of course – but she's enjoying a little holiday in the countryside.' She paused and then asked tentatively, 'And how's everyone at home? How's Jessie and – and all the Bonsor family? Do they know? Have – have they guessed?'

'Not that I know of,' Bert was able to say. He didn't tell her that he suspected they might have guessed the truth. 'Though there was a sticky moment when Max wanted to come with me to visit you.'

Nancy's mouth fell open. 'Max did? Oh dear. How did you stop him?'

Bert shrugged. 'I didn't. He just decided himself he wouldn't come.' Changing the subject deftly, he said, 'I hardly need to ask how you are. You look really well.'

'It's the country air. This life isn't for me, Dad, but I can see how Aunty Mary Ellen loves it here.'

'Next time I come I must bring your Grandma Edith. It's a while since she's seen Mary Ellen. Now, while I turn the pony loose in the paddock, go and get the kettle on the hob. I'm parched.'

When the family returned from church, Flora

hugged Bert hard. 'Oh, how I've missed you,' she whispered.

'And me you,' he whispered back. 'She's looking well though. I'm sure we've done the right thing.'

Then Flora plied him with questions about how life was in the city, ending, 'And do you think the Bonsors have guessed?'

Now he could be a little more truthful with his wife. 'To be honest, love, I really don't know.'

'Ah well, no doubt we'll see when we get home.'

'Is there any more talk of Mary Ellen and Jack adopting the baby?'

'No and it'll be up to Nancy to decide once it's born. I'm not going to force her to give it up unless she really wants to.'

'I agree, but it would be a good solution.'

Flora bit her lip. 'But now we've told folks that it's mine, wouldn't that look a bit odd?'

'Yeah, I see what you mean.' He sighed. 'Oh dear. What seemed like a good idea at the time is starting to cause us problems we'd never thought of.'

'Let's not worry about it now.' Flora hugged him again. 'I've a bit of news. Mary Ellen, Jack and his parents too have all said you and Ma must come here for Christmas.'

'What kind people they are,' Bert said, his voice suddenly a little shaky. 'I'm sure I can answer for both of us. Tell them, we'd be delighted.'

'What about the Bonsors? We always team up with them at Christmas.'

It had long been a tradition that the two families celebrated together. One year they would be at Flora's for Christmas Day, with Boxing Day spent at Evelyn's and Howard's house, the following year the days would be reversed.

'Aye well, it's going to be a very different Christmas for all of us.'

'D'you know, Mrs Weston,' Evelyn said, 'I really haven't the heart for Christmas this year. What with our Lee gone and now Flora and Nancy staying in the countryside . . . You and Bert must come to us for both days this year.'

'That's very kind of you, Evelyn, but we've received an invitation to go to the farm for Christmas. I hope you understand.'

'Of course I do, but it won't be the same without you all.'

'It wouldn't be anyway,' Agnes said gently. 'With Flora and Nancy not here.'

Evelyn sighed. 'How are they, by the way?' She watched closely as Agnes, now refusing to meet her gaze, said carefully, 'Blooming, from what Bert says.'

'Is Flora really all right?' Evelyn asked, playing along with the story the Westons were telling everyone. 'She's a bit old for starting a second family. And she had a lot of trouble giving birth to Nancy, didn't she?'

'I think it's what the old wives call a "change baby".' Agnes said, trying to add credence to the story they had concocted.

'Ah yes, I've heard of that before.' Evelyn smiled wryly. 'And they also say that when you've had a large family, you can go on conceiving quite late.' She laughed. 'I'd better watch mesen, then, hadn't I?'

Agnes smiled weakly.

'Well, I'd best be getting on,' Evelyn said, heaving herself up out of the chair. 'That mountain of washing sitting near me copper won't sort itself out. Ta-ra for now, Mrs Weston.'

Agnes watched her neighbour leave, wishing, not for the first time, that she'd not come up with the idea. It would have been so nice to have been able to talk to another woman about their troubles. And there was no one closer to her family than Evelyn Bonsor. But, she asked herself, if they did learn the truth would the friendship ever be the same again between the two families? It was a question she could not answer. But one thing remained uppermost in her mind. It was all to save Nancy's reputation. She must cling to that thought.

Despite their troubles, the Weston family had a wonderful Christmas at the farm. The welcome they received was as warm as it could be; nothing was too much trouble for Mary Ellen and Jack. Even Winnie insisted on helping to prepare the vegetables for Christmas dinner. And Mary Ellen was thoughtful enough to ask her mother-in-law's advice about the cooking of the goose.

'I forget the timings from year to year,' she told Flora, with a huge wink that told her sister she did nothing of the sort, but Mary Ellen's kindly nature wanted Winnie to feel she still had a say in the work-ings of the farmhouse kitchen. 'And as for making the Christmas puddings, well, I'd be lost without her help.'

Overhearing, just as Mary Ellen had intended, from

her chair near the range, Winnie beamed. She'd not been put out to grass just yet. Despite her physical frailties, her mind was still as sharp as ever.

'Now, we all go to midnight Mass on Christmas Eve,' Winnie said when Bert and Agnes had settled in and they were all seated around the huge kitchen table. 'I hope you'll all come along with us, even you, Nancy. No, don't be shy. Word's got around now, thanks to our Saturday lad, who couldn't wait to spread a bit of gossip. But they're a kindly lot, our villagers. No one will say anything nasty to you. At least,' she added firmly, 'not in my hearing, or in Matthew's, they won't.'

So on Christmas Eve the whole household attended the church service. Nancy kept her gaze lowered, though she was aware of one or two curious glances from the other parishioners. As they were leaving, the vicar stood in the porch to shake everyone's hand. He held Nancy's for a moment longer than was strictly necessary and, leaning towards her, murmured, 'If you need anything, my dear, don't be afraid to let me know.'

For the first time since she had arrived at the church, Nancy raised her head and looked up into his face. He was smiling down at her with not a trace of disapproval in his expression. Tears filled her eyes. 'You're – very kind,' she whispered. 'Thank you.'

He gave her hand a little squeeze and then let go, nodding as he did so. 'Don't forget now.' And then he was turning to greet Flora and to shake her hand too.

When they got back to the farmhouse, Mary Ellen bustled about the kitchen making everyone a hot drink before they all went to bed.

'The vicar was so kind,' Nancy said.

'He's a good man,' Matthew said. 'He's been here about twenty years. I think he'll stay here until he retires now.'

'I hope so,' Winnie said. 'We've never had a better one. He never criticises. He's just there to help his flock in whatever way he can. Don't be afraid to see him, if you need to, Nancy. Right, I'm taking my hot milk to bed with me. Good night all and Happy Christmas.'

It had been a perfect three days' holiday, but on the day after Boxing Day, Bert and Agnes had to go back to the city.

Bert held Flora tightly. 'You will let me know the moment anything happens with Nancy, won't you?'

'Of course I will, Bert. Do you really need to ask me that?'

Bert looked shamefaced for a moment. 'No, I don't, really. It's just that it's so hard being away from you both and not knowing what's happening.'

'I know, but I'll keep writing every week and I'll certainly write the minute there's any news. And you will keep my mother informed, won't you?'

'Of course.'

He kissed her soundly and then climbed up into the trap to sit beside Agnes who was ready and waiting, warmly wrapped in blankets against the late December weather.

'Safe journey,' Flora shouted after them as Bert turned the trap and they headed for the road back to the city.

Twenty-seven

Early on a cold, rainy morning in February, Nancy knocked on the door of the bedroom where her mother was sleeping.

'Mam,' she whispered urgently. When there was no response, she went into the room and touched her mother's shoulder. Flora woke at once.

'What is it? What's the matter?'

'I – I think the baby must be coming. I've had a back ache for a couple of days, but now I've got pains low down in my groin.'

Flora scrambled out of bed and reached for her clothes. 'Let's get you back to bed, but first I must find something to protect the mattress.'

'It's already on. Mrs Beckett said to put it on a couple of weeks before she thought I'd be due. Just in case me waters broke.'

'They haven't broken, have they?'

'Not yet.'

Flora dressed hurriedly and followed Nancy into her bedroom. Seeing that she was safely back in bed, Flora said, 'I'll go down and stir the range fire into life. It won't be long before Mary Ellen and Jack are up and I'll ask him to fetch Mrs Beckett.'

At that moment a contraction struck and Nancy

let out a cry before she could stifle it. As it subsided, she said, 'Oh, I'm sorry. I don't want to disturb anyone else this early.'

'They won't mind. It's nearly their normal getting-up time, anyway. Will you be all right if I go downstairs?'

'Yes, yes, I'll be fine but don't be away too long, will you? I don't want to have to shout for you. That would wake everyone.'

But only a few minutes after Flora had reached the kitchen, Mary Ellen appeared. 'We heard Nancy shout out. Is it coming?'

'Yes, we think so.'

'I'll get Jack up. He said I was to tell him if he was needed to fetch Mrs Beckett.'

'Thank you. I think it would be for the best.'

The next few hours were a flurry of activity. The whole household was soon awake and aware that Nancy had gone into labour. Iris Beckett arrived with her calming presence and entered the bedroom with her words of wisdom and advice. The rest of the family tried to continue with the day-to-day chores, but it was difficult for them to concentrate; their ears were tuned to the noises coming from upstairs. Even Jack kept returning to the house more often than usual to see if there was any news. As it turned out, they didn't have long to wait. Despite her youth and the fact that this was her first child, Nancy gave birth surprising quickly and easily.

'It's a boy!' Iris announced triumphantly as she dealt expertly with the umbilical cord, wrapped the squealing infant in a warm towel and handed him to his grandmother while she dealt with the mother's afterbirth. 'And he's got a good pair of lungs on him,' she laughed.

Flora cradled the little boy in her arms, smiling down at him. Any feeling of shame at the circumstances of his arrival disappeared in that moment. What was it she'd heard someone say years ago? 'They bring the love with them.' Well, this little chap certainly had. She didn't think she could bear to leave him with Mary Ellen. She just prayed that Nancy would feel the same.

Iris completed all that had to be done and declared that everything was as it should be with both mother and baby.

'I'll be off, then,' she said, 'but I'll be back tomorrow to check on them both.'

'Thank you so much, Mrs Beckett. You've been wonderful,' Flora said, as she laid the baby in her daughter's arms and Iris slipped quietly out of the room. Tears ran down Nancy's face, but they were tears of joy, no longer of shame or regret.

'Oh Mam,' she said shakily. 'He's beautiful, isn't he?' She stroked the baby boy's downy fair hair as she whispered, 'I can't bear to leave him with Aunty Mary Ellen. Will she mind terribly?'

'I think she'll understand but we should let her come up to see him.'

Nancy nodded.

'Have you got a name for him?'

Nancy hesitated. 'I've been thinking about that. If he wouldn't mind, I'd like to call him after Dad. Robert, but he'd be known as Robbie? Do you think that'd be all right?'

'I'm sure he'll be thrilled and if we are taking him home and making out he's mine, then it's most appropriate.'

At that moment there was a tap on the bedroom door and Mary Ellen came in. 'May I see him?'

She stepped closer to the bed and as she looked down at the infant, tears filled her eyes.

'Oh Aunty . . .' Nancy began, but Mary Ellen interrupted. 'Don't say anything, Nancy love. He's where he belongs. I can see that. You should take him home and confound the gossips. Hold your head up high and be proud of your son, but always know that you both have a home here if you should need it. Jack and I have both agreed on that.'

Now it was Nancy who shed tears. 'Oh Aunty, thank you. But are you . . .?'

'I'm fine,' Mary Ellen said, brushing away her tears with a smile. 'We'd gladly have taken him if you'd – if you hadn't wanted him, but I can see in your face that you love him already.'

'Oh, I do, I do.'

'And so do I,' Flora said softly.

Later, when she was able to snatch a few moments alone with her sister, Flora asked, 'Be honest with me, Mary Ellen. Are you dreadfully upset?'

'Not really. I always thought that once Nancy held her baby in her arms, she wouldn't be able to part with him. She's lucky that you and Bert aren't forcing her to give him up. Many poor mothers are and spend a lifetime of longing and wondering. I – I often wonder what would have become of me if my baby had lived.'

'I think you'd still be right where you are. The

Clarkes wouldn't have turned their backs on you – or your baby. Besides, Jack was already in love with you, wasn't he?'

Mary Ellen's eyes softened and she smiled. 'He's a wonderful man. One of the best. I've been very lucky.' She glanced at Flora. 'Is there really no chance that Lee Bonsor will marry her?'

Flora's mouth tightened. 'No, and to be honest, I'm not sure I'd want him to now. I don't want her tied to a man who obviously doesn't love her enough to do the honourable thing.'

'So you're going to go home when she's well enough and say he's yours, are you?'

'That's the plan.'

'I wish you well, but to be honest, I doubt it's going to work.'

'We'll see,' was all Flora could say.

In the second week of March, one month after the child had been born, Bert travelled in the borrowed pony and trap to fetch his wife, his daughter and his new grandson home, though he had to keep reminding himself that the little boy was to be known as his son. He had already spread the word up and down the street and among his closest co-workers at the factory. He'd had to stand a lot of ribbing from the men, but he was by no means the oldest father among them. One of the knife-grinders in the factory had fathered nine children, his youngest being born when he was in his early fifties and his wife forty-five. By the time Bert had told his neighbours and workmates and listened to the teasing, when his family arrived home, he almost believed that little Robbie was indeed his.

Nancy had breastfed the baby for three weeks and then Mrs Beckett, who had been let into the secret of what they planned to do, helped Nancy learn how to bottle feed him. The days following when she stopped feeding him herself were painful but, gradually, her milk flow eased and, thankfully, Robbie took to the bottle.

It was a tearful goodbye on the morning they left. Even Winnie Clarke shed a tear. 'It's been grand to have you. You must visit us whenever you can, Flora.'

Not much had been said about the planned deception in front of the Clarkes; Winnie didn't approve, but she was wise enough to hold her tongue.

They arrived home in time for Flora to cook tea for all the family while Nancy laid the baby in his great-grandmother's arms. Agnes looked down at the bright eyes gazing up at her and smiled. 'He's a bonny little chap, isn't he? Yer dad's been busy making a cradle and I've been knitting quite a few baby clothes once we knew it was a boy. They're all in your bedroom, Nancy.'

'They should be in ours, Ma,' Flora put in as she moved between the scullery and the kitchen table. 'He's mine, don't forget. We've got to play it out. And Nancy will be going back to work. I'm not sure they'll have her back at the store after all this time away, but she'll soon find something else.'

'Bert's been busy telling everyone he'll have to get used to sleepless nights again,' Agnes murmured.

Flora laughed. 'If Bert's anything like he was when

Nancy was a bairn, he'll never stir even when t'little 'un cries to be fed in the night. But it's something men have to get used to. I bet Howard Bonsor didn't have a full night's sleep for years when his brood were young. How are they all, by the way?'

There was a silence until Agnes said, 'I don't think they believed Bert, but I'll tell you one thing: you'd better be ready for Evelyn. She'll be across in the morning to see the bairn for herself.'

Agnes was right. As the clock on the mantelpiece struck eleven, Evelyn knocked on the back door and walked straight in as she always had done.

'Now then, Flora love. You're looking well, I must say.'

'I was luckier this time, Evelyn, than when I had Nancy. No trouble at all.'

'Where is she?'

'Who?'

'Nancy.'

'Oh, she's gone into town to see about her old job.'

'Will they take her back, d'you think? Jessie's been trying to sound out the head of their department, but she's very tight-lipped. Evidently, she didn't like the way that Nancy went on holiday and then wrote a letter giving notice. Anyway, where's this bairn of yours, Flora? I want a hold of the little chap.'

'He's in the front room with Ma.' Flora laughed, a little nervously. 'She seems to have taken charge of him.'

Flora led the way to the room that was Agnes's bed-sitting room. She tapped on the door and opened it. 'Robbie has a visitor, Ma.'

'Come in, Evelyn,' Agnes called. 'He's been asleep but he's just stirring. You can hold him if you want.'

'I certainly do,' Evelyn said. There was a strange edge to her tone, which made Flora and Agnes glance at one another.

Gently, Evelyn picked the baby up from the sofa. 'Now then, little feller, come to your' – she paused for the briefest moment before finishing – 'Aunty Evelyn.'

She smiled down at him as he rested in the crook of her arm and gazed up at her. She touched his cheek tenderly. 'There, there, little man,' she whispered. The baby waved his arm and Evelyn put her forefinger into his tiny hand. His fingers curled around it.

'He's got a good grip,' she murmured.

'And he's got a good pair of lungs on him when he gets going,' Agnes laughed.

'Are you feeding him yourself, Flora?' Evelyn asked, without taking her gaze from the baby.

There was the slightest hesitation before Flora said, 'No. I hadn't enough milk so he's on the bottle, but he's taken to it well.'

'He certainly seems to be thriving,' Evelyn murmured. 'He's a fair weight.'

She laid him back on the sofa and straightened up. She glanced between Flora and Agnes, unsure whether or not to say what she wanted to say in front of the older woman. She didn't want to upset her. As the baby began to whimper, Flora hurried to prepare a bottle for him and Evelyn sat down to chat to Agnes until she returned. Their conversation was stilted. Neither seemed to know what to say to the other and both of them were relieved when Flora came back. Agnes held out her hand for the bottle. 'I'll see to him. You go and have a cuppa and a chat with Evelyn.'

Back in the kitchen and sitting at the table with two cups of tea in front of them, Evelyn said quietly, 'Flora, we've been friends for a long time now, haven't we?'

Flora's heart felt as if it missed a beat but she managed to answer calmly, though she was wondering exactly what Evelyn was leading up to. 'We have. Ever since we worked together as buffer girls and even more so after Bert and I were married and I came to live here in the same street.'

'And we've seen our children grow up together, watched over them through all the ups and downs of their childhood, helped each other out when needed, haven't we?'

Flora nodded, but avoided meeting Evelyn's clear gaze.

'So why,' Evelyn asked softly and with a note of sadness in her tone, 'could you not trust me? That baby in there . . .' she flung her arm out towards the front room and now there was a note of barely concealed anger in her voice – 'is no more yours than it is mine.'

Flora's hands began to tremble but still she did not look up to meet Evelyn's eyes nor answer her.

'He's Nancy's, isn't he? And if I'm not very much mistaken, our Lee is the father.'

Tears flooded down Flora's cheeks, giving Evelyn her answer without a word needing to be spoken.

Evelyn wanted to move towards her friend, to put her arms around her, but first she had to know why Flora – indeed all the Weston family – had lied to her and her family.

'We didn't dare to tell you. We knew it would tear your family apart and we – we were so afraid what Max might do to Lee when he found out. And then we thought this was a way of saving Nancy from the shame too if everyone believed that he was mine . . .'

Evelyn listened in stunned silence until Flora's voice faded away and she seemed to be waiting for the storm of Evelyn's anger to flood over her. But it didn't come.

'But – if he'd known, Lee would have married her.'

Heartsore at having to disillusion his fond mother, Flora whispered, 'He did know. Nancy told him the night before – before he went away.' Now she raised her tear-streaked face to meet Evelyn's shocked gaze. 'So do you see why we didn't want to tell you? Max would have gone after him and either had a fight with him or dragged him back to force him to marry her. And we didn't want that. Not for either of them. Marriage is hard enough without being pushed into it if it's not what you really want. I saw that with my own parents. We didn't want that for Nancy – or for Lee, if it comes to that.'

Evelyn blinked, still unable to take in what Flora was telling her. 'He ran away *because* of what Nancy told him?'

Flora nodded. 'It must have been that. There was no other reason, was there?'

Evelyn shook her head and then, after a long pause,

added haltingly, 'So you mean – you mean you've done all this to save *us*?'

'Partly, yes, but mainly to save Nancy from the shame that would follow her for the rest of her life. And, of course, for the boy as he grows up. You know how bastard children are treated when they get out into the big, wide world.' Now she faced Evelyn as she pleaded with her. 'Will you and your family keep our secret? Please, Evelyn.'

'Of course, but . . .'

'But – what?'

'Does Nancy still want to marry Lee?'

'To be honest, I'm not really sure how she feels about him now. But, like I said before, Bert and me don't want a shotgun wedding. We don't want either of them to live in an unhappy marriage for the rest of their lives.'

Evelyn nodded. 'I agree with you, but I'm still having a job getting my head round it all.' She pulled herself up from her chair. 'I'll have to be going, Flora, and I'll tell the family tonight, though what Max will do, I daren't think. Now, come here and give me a hug.'

Twenty-eight

That evening, as the Bonsor family finished their tea, and made as if to leave the table, Evelyn said, 'I'd like you all to stay for a minute. I have something to tell you and I must impress upon all of you that this is to be kept secret. You must tell no one.'

'You're not pregnant again, Mam, are you, like Mrs Weston?' Warren, always the joker in the family, piped up.

Evelyn didn't smile but fixed him with a steely gaze. 'No, Warren, I am not, but this is serious, so I'd be glad if you'd treat it as such. And you, Stanley, you do understand what I'm saying, don't you? You must tell no one outside this house about what I'm going to say.'

Stanley, a serious thirteen-year-old, nodded.

Evelyn glanced at Max. At family mealtimes, they all sat in the same place. Howard was at one end of the table, with Evelyn at the other. Next to her on one side was Max, beside him was Jessie, and then there had always been Lee, but his place was empty now. The three youngest boys sat on the opposite side of the table. Now all eyes were turned towards their mother – all except Max, who sat with his head down, his gaze on the empty plate in front of him.

Evelyn guessed he knew what she was going to say. She took a deep breath. 'It wasn't Mrs Weston who was expecting a baby, it was Nancy.'

The three younger boys gaped at her but had the sense to say nothing. One glance at their eldest brother was enough to silence any one of them.

'And' – Evelyn took another deep breath – 'our Lee is the father.'

Jessie began to cry quietly and Max put his arm around her shoulders but still, he said nothing.

'Is that why he ran off?' Warren dared to ask.

'I – expect so.' Now Evelyn glanced down the table at her husband as she explained further, telling them everything that Flora had said.

'The idea of passing the child off as hers was mainly to save Nancy from the shame and embarrassment, but also to save us the heartache about Lee.' She glanced briefly to her left to look at the still figure of her firstborn. 'And also, they were very much afraid of what Max might do.'

Slowly, Max raised his head and met his mother's steady gaze. He smiled grimly. 'They were right to be afraid if I'd caught up with him then. But now' – he shrugged – 'I'm still angry with him, mainly because he's run off and not faced up to his responsibilities, but . . .' he paused before saying slowly – 'perhaps the Westons are right not to want to force them into marriage.' He glanced round the table. 'And we must all do what Mam is asking. Not a word to anyone outside this house.'

It was obvious that the younger members of the family were more in awe of their older brother than of their mother or father. The three boys nodded vigorously and Jessie leaned against his shoulder, still weeping.

'It's my fault, isn't it? If I hadn't wanted to go out walking with Andrew, Nancy and Lee would never have – have . . .'

Max squeezed her shoulders. 'It's not your fault, silly. I'll go across shortly and reassure them.' He did not tell his family that it was really Nancy he wanted to see. He needed to see for himself that she wasn't heartbroken. If she was, despite what he had said to his family, nothing would stop him giving Lee the hiding of his life when he caught up with him.

Half an hour later, Max knocked on the back door of the Westons' home. It was Nancy who opened it and they stood staring at each other for a long moment until the colour rose in Nancy's face and she dropped her gaze.

'Whatever must you think of me, Max?'

He stepped into the scullery and closed the door behind him. Then he stood close to her, towering over her. He took her cold hands into his strong, warm ones. 'I don't think any differently of you now than I always have, Nancy.' Now was not the time, he decided, to tell her how very much he loved her; always had and always would. Instead, he said, 'I am just so sorry that Lee has hurt you the way he has. I have to ask you. Are you – are you heartbroken? Are you still in love with him?'

Nancy raised her head slowly to meet his concerned

gaze. Her answer surprised her as much as it did Max.

'I was distraught at first because I – I thought I was in love with him. I truly thought he loved me too and that we'd get married. He – he said he would when I told him about the baby but then the next day, he was gone and I knew then that all his sweet promises had meant nothing. And I – I think that killed whatever I felt for him. So, no, although he has hurt me deeply, I'm not heartbroken over Lee, but I am so, so sorry for the trouble I've caused my family and yours too.' Before he could answer, she added, 'But there's one thing I'll never be sorry about and that's the baby. He's a little darling and I love him dearly, so I don't want him growing up with the burden of being illegitimate and thinking he's not wanted. And it's a cruel world out there when other kids find out he hasn't got a father. You know the sort of names he'll be called. That's what I'm most sorry about. Not for myself, but for him.'

'We'll look out for him,' Max promised her softly. 'We'll all watch over him. And now, may I see him?'

Max stood over the cradle looking down at the child sleeping there. How he wished the boy was his, but then, he would never have treated Nancy in the way his brother had done. Standing beside him, Nancy was wishing exactly the same thing; if only . . .

Once the shock for both families had subsided, they bonded together as a unit to protect one of their own. They had always been the closest of friends, but now they were like one family. And if anyone else in their community had their doubts about who the baby's mother really was, not one of them was foolish enough to comment. Bert and Howard were formidable enough, but Max was another matter. No one wanted to cross the normally gentle giant, who was known to leap to the defence of any member of his own family and that of the Westons too. For once, the gossips were silent. 'It's their business,' they all decided. 'Besides, we've more serious things to think about now, haven't we?'

During the time Flora and Nancy had been away from home and the Bonsors had been worrying about Lee and his sudden departure, the rest of the country had been made painfully aware of the unrest in Europe. After the assassination of Archduke Ferdinand, the heir to the Austro-Hungarian throne, and his wife in Sarajevo at the end of June, that anxiety intensified. And by the end of July, even the two families who had been so wrapped up in their own concerns, could not fail to be caught up in the fear of a coming war.

Evelyn, who now came across to Flora's home every morning, was especially anxious.

'If this country gets involved in a war, the navy will be in the thick of it, won't it?'

Guessing her mind was on Lee, Flora said, 'Try not to worry. Surely our government won't be stupid enough to let us get involved in a war that is nothing to do with us?'

'Howard seems to think we will be. He says the talk at work is about nothing else. And all the young fellers are eager to volunteer. I just hope –'

But at that moment, Agnes came into the kitchen

carrying the baby and interrupted whatever she had been going to say. 'I think he's hungry, Flora. He never stops eating, this one.'

'Oh please, can I feed him?' Evelyn said and held out her arms to her grandson. The three women chatted while the baby guzzled noisily.

'How's Nancy?' Evelyn asked, but her gaze was on the child in her arms.

'She's to start back at the store next week,' Flora said. 'She only heard yesterday, so she's not had time to tell Jessie. The head of department has been very good about it.'

Evelyn's head shot up. 'She doesn't know, does she?'

'Heavens, no. I mean she's been good taking her back when she'd been away for so long. Evidently, some other girl has left suddenly so there was a vacancy and she – the department head – was pleased to be able to let Nancy have her old job back. She won't need any training, you see.'

'Did anyone question *why* she'd been away in the country so long?'

'Not that she's said.'

'There's been tittle-tattle in the street about you having a baby so late in life, but no one's actually said anything about him being Nancy's.' Evelyn smiled. 'I think you've got away with it, Flora love.' She paused and then asked quietly, 'Are you ever going to tell him the truth? Robbie, I mean.'

'Oh yes. We decided that from the start. As soon as he's old enough to understand, we shall tell him. He has a right to know the truth, but we shall impress upon him that it must be a secret both for his own sake and for Nancy's. We had his birth certificate all done legally too, though Lee's name doesn't appear on it. You can't put the father's name down unless he's there to agree.'

'And he wasn't,' Evelyn murmured and in her tone there was what sounded like a note of apology. With her head still bowed over Robbie, she added, 'What will happen when Lee comes home, though?'

Agnes chipped in. 'We'll face that at the time, Evelyn. We bear him no ill will. It takes two and Nancy must bear some of the blame too because never, for a moment, have we thought that Lee forced himself on her. She must have been willing.'

'Thank you,' Evelyn said huskily. 'It means a great deal to me to hear you say that.' She paused and then, haltingly, added, 'I am so very sorry for the trouble he has brought on Nancy – on you all. We thought we had brought our sons up to be better than that.'

It became a morning ritual that Evelyn should come across the street and, if the baby needed feeding, she was only too happy to oblige. The three women formed an even stronger bond as the threat of war came even closer – and was finally declared on 4 August.

Twenty-nine

'Mam,' Max said one evening after tea when his younger siblings had left the room, 'I need to talk to you and Dad.'

It was towards the end of August and the war was already three weeks old. Untouched by the talk of war, the three youngest Bonsor boys had gone to the park to play football while Jessie met up with Andrew. Extracting a solemn promise from her that she would never let things go too far, they now allowed her to meet him unchaperoned.

'Mam, I promise you he's a gentleman,' Jessie had said during a heart-to-heart with her mother. 'He never even asks to do more than kiss and cuddle me. That's all right, isn't it?'

'Yes,' Evelyn had said. 'Just mind it doesn't get out of hand, that's all.'

'I won't.' She'd paused and then added hesitantly, 'There's one thing, though, Mam. He's talking about volunteering. And – and if he does, he wants us to get married first. Would you let us?'

Evelyn had stared at her. She'd known this moment was coming, but not quite so soon. 'I – we'd have to talk to your father about that. That would be a big step and I wouldn't want either of you to rush into marriage just because he's going to war.' She bit her lip against saying more, but Jessie, blushing a little, forestalled her by saying, 'He wants to know – to know what it's like to be married before he goes. And he also said it'd give him something to make sure he comes back – something to live for. But he says he thinks he should go and fight for his country. He says there's talk among the young fellers at work that if they don't go, they're cowards.'

Evelyn's heart had felt as if the life was being squeezed out of it. All her boys would hear the talk, even her youngest, Stanley, who'd only just turned fourteen and started work. They'd all be fired up by the fevered patriotism that was sweeping the whole country according to what Howard had told her. 'I'll talk to your dad,' was all Evelyn had been able to promise her daughter.

And now, here was Max, wanting to have a serious talk with his parents. With a sinking heart, Evelyn realized it could only be about one thing.

'You must know,' he began, 'that there's a lot of talk at work about volunteering. There's been a series of lectures on the war at the Victoria Hall. There's another on Tuesday evening. There are strong rumours that a Sheffield City Battalion might be formed.' He paused and then added quietly, 'I intend to go along.'

Neither Evelyn nor Howard spoke; they just allowed Max to continue at his own pace.

Bluntly, he went on, 'When we came out of work today, there was a group of women standing near the gates handing out white feathers. A girl – she can't have been more than fifteen or sixteen – handed one to me.'

'I've heard about that,' Howard murmured. 'It's called the Order of the White Feather. It's some sort of organization where women are supposed to encourage the fit and able young men in their families to volunteer instead of being – what they are calling – a coward.' He met his son's gaze steadily. 'But don't you be pushed into volunteering because of something ridiculous like that, Max. If – if you feel you really should go for your own conscience, then that's a different matter, but not because some girl who's far too young to understand what she's doing, shames you into going.'

Evelyn, who was not the sort of woman who wept easily now wiped tears from her eyes. 'Oh Max, whatever is going to happen to us all? I'd better tell you both something else too. Andrew is thinking of volunteering and if he does, he wants to marry Jessie before he goes.'

Father and son glanced at each other. Howard sighed deeply. 'Well, I can understand that and I suppose I wouldn't mind, but there's always the chance he'll leave her with child and then not come back. We'd have to face up to that happening and be prepared to help her.'

Max was silent. How he wished he could ask Nancy to marry him. How he wanted her to be able to hold her head up high as a married woman, but that matter had been dealt with and was out of his hands. As far as all their neighbours knew, little Robbie was Flora's child. It amazed him how everyone had seemed, on the face of it at least, to accept the fact, although he guessed that maybe in the privacy of their own homes, doubts were expressed. More likely, he thought, with all the anxiety of this war, gossip about a young girl having a child out of wedlock now seemed unimportant.

Evelyn's touch on his arm brought his thoughts back to the present. 'I don't want you to go, Max,' she said huskily, 'but you're a grown man and must make your own decisions. Do you – do you think Lee will already be involved in some way?'

Father and son glanced at each other. 'You'd better tell her, Max. It's not our way in this family to keep things from each other.'

Evelyn's eyes were suddenly wide with fear. 'What? Tell me what? You've heard something about – about Lee?'

'No, no, Mam . . .' Max took hold of her hand. 'It's just that we know now that Lee is in the Royal Navy, don't we?'

Evelyn nodded. 'What have you heard, Max? Tell me.'

'Nothing about Lee specifically, though I do wish we knew what ship he might be on.'

'Why?'

Max sighed and then said, 'There was a report in the newspaper a couple of weeks back that the Royal Navy had suffered its first loss. A ship called the *Amphion* struck a mine off the Thames Estuary and sank.'

'Were many of the crew lost?' Evelyn whispered.

'Over one hundred and thirty.'

'Of course, we don't know if Lee was on that ship,' Howard said, trying to reassure Evelyn. 'He most probably wasn't, but what we have to face, love, is that wherever he is, he will now be involved in the war.'

'I just wish he'd come home or at least let us know where he is.' She glanced at Max. 'We could sort it all out reasonably now, couldn't we? About Nancy, I mean?'

Max smiled wryly. 'I expect so. I would still have words with him, but I don't feel like battering him to a pulp like I did at first.'

'Nancy's all right now, isn't she?' Howard said. 'And Robbie's a grand little chap. He's still our grandson and your nephew, when all's done and said.'

Max's face was grim now. 'Aye, well, it's not all said as far as I'm concerned. He shouldn't have got the poor lass into trouble – any lass, if it comes to that. You've brought us all up to be better than that.'

'We thought we had,' Howard murmured.

'Just make sure the three young 'uns understand what trouble it can cause,' Max said softly.

'I will,' Howard declared.

'So,' Evelyn asked sadly, bringing them back to the original conversation. 'Have you decided to volunteer?'

'Not definitely. I'll go and listen to what's being said at this lecture first and then I'll make up my mind.'

'Just don't get carried away on a tide of fanatical patriotism,' Howard said, 'because if what I hear is right, that's what happens at these recruitment rallies.'

Now Max grinned. 'Come with me, Dad. You can hold me back if I start to get over enthusiastic. I won't be going until after we finish work.'

Howard chuckled. 'What if it's me that gets eager?'

'Don't you dare,' Evelyn said. 'Else you'll have me to reckon with, ne'er mind Lord Kitchener and his call for one hundred thousand volunteers.'

Father and son exchanged a smile. 'That's me told, then,' Howard laughed.

'Seriously, Dad, at the moment I understand it's for men of between nineteen and thirty-eight, but they must fit the army's regulations as to height and chest measurement and general fitness too. But don't forget, that factories in Sheffield will probably soon start producing war machinery and equipment. You'll be far more useful here.'

'Aye, but I'm only an office worker, aren't I? I'm not actually helping to make anything useful.'

'No big company can operate without its office workers. It'd be chaos.'

Howard nodded and sighed heavily. 'I expect you're right, but life's going to change, isn't it? Nothing's ever going to be quite the same again.'

'No, Dad, I'm afraid it isn't.'

Bert joined Howard and Max at the lecture. The three men listened intently to the speaker who explained the reasons the war in Europe had come about and how, because of various long-held alliances between different countries, Britain had felt obliged to become involved. As the audience filed out, Howard said, 'What did he say about the formation of a city battalion? I couldn't quite hear the last bit because of all the cheering.'

'They expect to receive formal approval from the War Office any day and that volunteers can begin enrolling at the Town Hall tomorrow afternoon,' Max said.

'But they're only asking for white-collar workers, aren't they? Professional men like lawyers, clerks and the like. I did catch that bit. Why don't they want the ordinary working man in the street?'

'I expect they will eventually, but the idea of forming a city battalion has come from university personnel. Perhaps that's why.'

'And there's maybe another reason,' Bert put in. 'The ordinary man in the street, as you call him, Howard, will be far more useful in the factories making armaments and ammunition, 'specially in Sheffield.'

'I think you've got a point there, Mr Weston,' Max agreed solemnly.

'So, Max, have you made up your mind?'

'Not quite, Dad.'

As they reached the street where they lived, Bert put his hand on Max's shoulder. 'Think very carefully, lad, that's all I ask. I have to say that I admire all the young men's patriotism we saw tonight, but I'm afraid many of them are getting caught up in the fever of it all. Just be sure that whatever decision you come to is made rationally with a cool head. And, for what it's worth, you'll have my backing whatever you decide.'

'Thank you, Mr Weston. That means a lot to me.'

*

There was one person Max would have liked to talk to, but he couldn't. If he spoke to Nancy and she begged him not to go, he knew his resolve would waver. No, he decided, this was a decision that only he and he alone could make.

He left work early the following afternoon, having told his superior what he was going to do. Mr Peterson, who was in charge of the office, was reaching retirement age. 'I can understand, my boy, but don't do anything hasty. I have already put your name forward to take over as office manager when I retire. War is a cruel and bloody business. Make no mistake. I lost my son – my only son – in the Boer War and my wife never got over it. She died five years ago; I believe of a broken heart. And another thing, I don't agree with the idea that men who live in the same place, or who work together, should go to war together, should serve together. Oh, I can understand that the authorities think the camaraderie will ensure loyalty and possibly courage, but just think, Max, if a whole company is wiped out at once, just think of the tragedy that will cause back home. Whole streets of friends and neighbours, relatives even, all mourning at the same time. So, Max, think very carefully before you take an action that you will not be able to reverse.'

'I will, Mr Peterson,' Max promised him solemnly.

Max walked to the Town Hall, his back straight, his arms swinging. He was almost marching as if in readiness for what was about to come. He joined the queue waiting to go into the building. There was a festive air, almost a carnival atmosphere. Young men were laughing and joking as if they were on an annual outing to Blackpool. As he thought back to the many times his family and the Westons had enjoyed their day trips to the seaside, Max felt a twinge of sadness. That would not be happening this year, nor possibly for a few years to come. Little Robbie might be three or four years old before he felt the warm sand between his toes and the coldness of the sea water, before he could learn how to build a sand castle . . .

'Get a move on, mate.' Max felt a prod in his back. 'You're holding up Kitchener's soldiers. Not having second thoughts, a' yer?'

Max turned and smiled at the young man behind him. 'No, I was just thinking, that's all.'

'Not a good idea, that, mate. Just let's get in there and sign on. Then we can't change our minds.'

Max didn't bother to argue. He rather feared the young man hadn't given serious thought to what he was about to do. Still, it was no business of his except . . . He was suddenly curious.

'D'you mind me asking what you do for a living?'

The young man grinned. 'I'm a journalist. I work for the *Sheffield Daily Telegraph*, so I'll be able to write pieces and send them back home for the paper. That's what my editor hopes anyway.'

The queue shuffled forward and before long, Max found himself at the front and signing the declaration form.

'You'll get a postcard in a week or so's time,' he was told, 'telling you where to go for a medical and so on.'

The man raised his voice. 'Next.'

*

The promised postcard arrived six days later telling Max to report to the Corn Exchange on the Thursday.

'I'll come with you after work,' Howard said. 'Just to the door, mind. I don't want to embarrass you.'

'You wouldn't, Dad, but I'd be glad of your company.'

On the appointed day, as they walked from their places of work, Howard and Max met up and made their way to Sheaf Street and the Corn Exchange. As they rounded the corner, they stopped in amazement.

'Well, I'll be . . .' Howard began. 'Look at 'em all. There's hundreds queuing up. You're going to be here all night, son.'

'You go home, Dad –' The words were scarcely out of his mouth before Max stopped speaking. He was staring at the entrance to the building. 'Oh no!' he whispered hoarsely.

'What?' Howard said. 'What's the matter?' His glance followed the line of Max's gaze and he muttered the same words as his son.

They moved as one towards the young man emerging from the building.

'Victor,' Max spoke before his father, 'what the hell are you doing here?'

Victor was grinning widely. 'I've enlisted in the Sheffield City Battalion. Me and me mates – there's four of us – we're all going together and they say we'll stay together. We'll be able to look out for each other.'

'You're not old enough. The age is nineteen. You're only seventeen. We'll go in and tell them . . .'

Victor's grin faded. 'Don't shame me, Max, there's

a good chap. I've taken the King's Shilling. All four of us are the same age and as long as we passed the medical – which we all have – we're in! They never asked us our age.'

Howard and Max looked at each other again. 'He's right, Max,' Howard said sadly. 'We can't undo what's been done, though what your mother is going to say, I don't know.'

Victor puffed out his chest. 'She'll be proud of me, that's what. Besides, with a name like mine, I've got to go, haven't I?'

Max sighed. 'Let's just hope they're right in what they're saying. That it'll all be over by Christmas. Maybe you won't get anywhere near the front line.'

'Anyway, what are you two doing here? Did you come looking for me?'

'No,' Max said quietly. 'I'm enlisting.'

Victor frowned. 'Oh, so it's all right for you to go, but not me, eh?'

'I'm older. I'm the age they want and if the war does go on for any length of time, they'd be calling me up anyway. This way at least I can join my home city battalion.'

Victor thought for a moment and then nodded. 'Yes, I can see that.' He paused and then looked at his father. 'I hope you're not thinking of going, Dad.'

Howard shook his head. 'No, I won't be volunteering to join the army, but I do intend to do some sort of war work here in the city.' He put his hand on Max's shoulder. 'On you go, then, lad. Me and Victor will go home and face yer mam. I dread to think what she's going to say.'

While Victor and his father headed home, Max went through the various procedures. First, he faced a doctor for a medical and was pronounced fit. After that, he sat patiently while a clerk filled in all his details and, finally, he received the King's Shilling.

He emerged from the Corn Exchange feeling a little dazed, but not for a moment did he regret his decision to enlist.

Thirty

Evelyn was surprisingly calm about the news; not only was her eldest son volunteering, but also her third son. At only seventeen, Victor had taken the oath and would be going too.

'I'd like to stop them going, love,' she said to her husband. 'You know I would, but I can't. If they're getting handed white feathers and being branded as cowards, then' – she shrugged – 'who are we to stop them? Before this is all over, there'll be many sorrowing mothers throughout the whole nation, not just in this city. We're powerless, Howard. We're being stripped of our rights as parents. We have no control over what they do now, not even before they come of age. If the authorities aren't even making the effort to stick to the rules, what can we do?'

'Very little, love, but at least we can make sure that Warren and Stanley don't go.'

'Warren's just turned sixteen and you know how headstrong he can be.'

'He's far too young. Surely . . .'

Evelyn shrugged. 'You said they didn't even ask Victor his age. And Warren's a big lad for sixteen.'

'Well, Stanley was only fourteen last month. He'll be safe enough.'

'But if it goes on for several years and his brothers have all gone to war by then, he won't want to be left behind . . .' Her voice trailed away with the heavy weight of sadness and tears trickled down her cheeks. 'All my baby boys could end up going to war.'

Howard put his arms around her and held her close, but he could think of no words to comfort her. After a few moments, Evelyn bravely dried her tears and forced a smile. 'Where is Victor, the little scallywag?'

'He's outside. He was afraid to face you.'

Now Evelyn actually laughed. 'Not afraid to face German bullets, eh, but daren't face his mam.'

Despite their worries, Howard chuckled. 'It's always been you they're more frightened of than me.'

'Or Max. Max always had them at a word.'

'You're right there. It was Max he was worried about when we met him coming out of the Corn Exchange.'

As Howard called Victor into the kitchen, Evelyn wagged her finger at him. 'You're a bad lad to go before you need to, but' – she crossed the space between them and hugged him hard – 'I'm proud of you even so.'

'Oh Mam,' Victor hugged her in return, 'at least me an' Max'll be going together. That'll be good, won't it? We can look out for each other.'

'Mind you do,' Evelyn said, as she turned away to hide fresh tears she couldn't stop. 'I'm just going across the road to see Flora. I won't be long.'

She hurried out of the back door, crossed the road and went round to the back door of her friend's house, where she knocked and went straight in. Flora was busy at the kitchen table with a pile of mending in front of her, while Agnes sat near the range with the baby on her lap.

Looking up, Flora at once saw her friend's tears. Quickly, she stood up and guided Evelyn to the chair near the range opposite Agnes.

'What's the matter, love? What's happened?'

'It's Max and Victor. They've both volunteered. At least, Victor has. Max was still queuing to get into the Corn Exchange when Howard and Victor left him.'

'Victor! But he's not old enough.'

Evelyn shrugged helplessly. 'Seems they're not too fussy about knowing their age. He wasn't even asked.'

Flora pulled a chair out from under the table and sat close to her friend, holding her hand. 'I have to say I'm not surprised to hear Max has enlisted, but Victor. Now that has shocked me.'

'Max was handed a white feather as he left work the other day,' Evelyn whispered.

'That's dreadful. What do these women think they're doing?'

'Encouraging their menfolk to be heroes.'

Flora bit back the ready retort that sprang to her lips. She wanted to say, aye, dead ones, but that would have been cruel.

The baby gurgled happily, drawing the attention of all three women and reminding them all of Lee.

'And I don't even know where he is,' Evelyn murmured. 'I expect he'll be involved too, sooner or later, if he isn't already.'

'Can you find out where he is? He ought to come home and see you, Evelyn, 'specially now this war's on. We're not going to demand that he marries Nancy. Not now. Everyone around here seems to have accepted that Robbie is mine.' Flora gave a wry chuckle. 'At least to my face. What they say behind my back might be another matter.'

'Nowt's been said to me,' Evelyn said, 'but then everyone knows how close we are. I expect they daren't say owt in my hearing because they know I'd tell you. And they'd get a mouthful from me into the bargain.'

Evelyn stayed with her friends for an hour. At last, she rose reluctantly. 'I'd best get the supper. It won't do itself and there's still mouths to feed. I'll have to go shopping tomorrow, though I dread going out now. The women either have drawn faces or they're beaming with delight. In both cases, it's because their menfolk have volunteered.' She shook her head sorrowfully. 'I just don't understand it, Flora. Why do we have to have wars at all? Why can't the world live in peace? Life is hard enough without fighting each other.'

'It's all to do with power, isn't it? Or one country wanting something another country's got. Though I'll be hanged if I know what this one's about. I'm with you, Evelyn, but sadly women don't have charge of the world. I reckon it'd be a better place if they did.'

'If all these men keep joining up,' Agnes said wisely, 'women will be needed to do all sorts of jobs they've never done before. You mark my words.'

*

That same evening, Max crossed the road to see Nancy. As he always did, he picked up Robbie and rocked him in his arms. 'He's growing fast, isn't he?'

With unshed tears in her eyes, Nancy said, 'Mam's told me you've joined up. Oh Max, why? Why did you do that?'

'If this war goes on for any length of time –'

'But it won't. They say it'll all be over by Christmas.'

Soberly, Max went on, 'But if it isn't, then I'd be called up soon enough and just sent anywhere they want me. This way, at least I get to go with my fellow Sheffielders.' He sighed. 'Even my younger brother, as it turns out.'

Nancy nodded. 'Yes, I was sorry to hear that too. I'm surprised they took him.'

Max laughed wryly. 'I'm not. He's a strapping lad. All of us Bonsor boys are. He'd soon have been getting handed a white feather like me.'

Nancy gasped. This she hadn't known. 'Oh, that's awful.' She paused and then asked softly, 'Oh Max, that wasn't what made you go, was it?'

'No, Nancy, it wasn't, but, maybe, if I'm honest, it tipped the balance. I was thinking about it, but I had to look at it from an outsider's view and –'

'You saw a big, fit man who looked like a shirker.'

Max sighed and nodded. 'Yes, I did. And, like I said, because I'm going of my own accord, I've been able to join the Sheffield City Battalion that's being formed. I won't be pushed just anywhere.'

'I can understand that,' she murmured, 'but it doesn't make me any happier about you going to war.'

Robbie had fallen asleep in his uncle's arms and Max looked down at him with a tender expression on his face.

'Dad's going to try to find out where Lee is,' he said softly. 'If he does, do you –?'

He hadn't finished speaking before Nancy shook her head and said vehemently, 'No, I don't.'

Max looked up at her and chuckled. 'You don't know what I was going to say.'

'Yes, I do. You were going to ask me if I wanted him brought back to marry me.'

'Well, yes, as a matter of fact, I was.'

'Then my answer is, no, I don't. I don't want any man to be forced into marrying me. If he'd wanted to, he wouldn't have run away, would he? I made a mistake, Max, a bad one that will probably spoil the rest of my life. Men don't like damaged goods, do they? But that's for me to bear. All I want is for Robbie not to have to bear the stigma of being a little bastard and my wonderful parents have done their best to prevent that happening. But he'll have to know one day. The truth is on his birth certificate.' She smiled wryly. 'Even we daren't break the law by filling in an official document with false information. And the vicar in the village where Aunty Mary Ellen lives was so kind and understanding. We had a small, private christening just before we left.'

'You should tell Robbie yourself when he's old enough to understand. Don't let him find out accidentally.'

'Yes, I plan to do that.' She sighed heavily but continued bravely, 'So, if your dad can find Lee and get word to him, tell him it's safe for him to come home. My dad's not waiting with a shotgun.' She faced Max's steady gaze. 'It took two of us, Max. We're both to blame. But I will admit to you that your brother has hurt me. It will probably be a long time before I can trust a man again. He declared his love for me, promised he wouldn't hurt me and I believed him, but I shouldn't have. That was my naivety.' She laughed wryly. 'I wonder now if he said the same sweet nothings to all those girls he used to meet every year at Blackpool. What promises did he make to them and never keep?' She sighed deeply. 'But, like I say, I don't want Lee to stay away from his family because of me so, if you can get word to him, tell him to come home, even if it's only for a visit. For his mother's sake if no one else's.'

Max nodded but could find no words to say. He still wasn't sure what he would do if Lee did come home. He was still burning with rage at what his brother had done to Nancy. But her next words gave him hope that she was rising above the hurt Lee had inflicted.

'But there's one thing I'll never regret,' she was saying, 'and he's lying in your arms. Even if the whole world finds out the truth, I'm not sorry about Robbie and I never will be.'

Howard didn't have to make enquiries about Lee. Only a day after Max and Victor had volunteered, a telegram arrived telling his parents that the ship, *HMS Pathfinder*, on which he had been serving, had been sunk on 5 September and that Ordinary Seaman Lee Bonsor had been posted as missing.

Evelyn, who was normally strong and resolute, wept bitter tears against Howard's shoulder. 'If it hadn't been for *her*, he would never have gone.'

'Now, now, Evelyn love,' he said, holding her close even though his own heart felt as if it might break. 'That's not like you. Nancy's not to blame.'

'She should have said "no". It's the girl who should say "no", and don't you dare tell me he forced her, because Lee wouldn't do that.'

'No, that's not what I'm saying. I wouldn't dream of saying any such thing.' He was about to add, 'But you know how charming and persuasive he could be', but he thought better of it and bit back the words. No grieving mother wants to hear a word said against her son at that moment, not even the truth.

Her voice muffled against his shoulder, she said, 'I'm sorry. You're right. I shouldn't have said that about Nancy. Don't tell anyone, Howard, please.'

''Course I won't, love.' His arms tightened around her. 'I'll go across and tell them so you don't have to.'

Evelyn straightened up and wiped her eyes. 'No, no, I'll go, but however are we going to tell his brothers and sister?'

'Leave that to me.'

Evelyn didn't admit it – not even to Howard – but she wanted to see Nancy's reaction to the dreadful news. When she was once again in control of her own emotions, Evelyn crossed the road.

'Come in, Evelyn love,' Flora called out cheerfully. 'What brings you back? We only saw you this morning.' As she turned, Flora saw Evelyn's tear-ravaged face. 'Oh, my love, what's happened?' She held out her arms and Evelyn went into them.

'Is Nancy here?'

'Yes, she's not at work this afternoon. She's upstairs with the baby.'

'Call her down, will you, Flora?'

Sensing that something serious had happened, Flora called to Nancy from the bottom of the stairs. Moments, later, the girl appeared. As soon as she saw Evelyn's face, she stood still, just staring at her. 'It's Lee, isn't it?'

Evelyn nodded.

'What's happened?'

'We've had a telegram. The ship he was on has been sunk and he's – he's missing.'

Agnes, hearing the voices, appeared from her room. The older woman guessed at once that there had been bad news. 'I'll make tea for us all,' she said and disappeared into the scullery.

Nancy met Evelyn's eyes as she said huskily, 'You blame me, don't you? But for me, he wouldn't have gone.'

'No, no, of course not,' Evelyn said hurriedly, a little too quickly to be convincing.

'Aunty Evelyn, I can see it in your eyes. You don't need to deny it, because I blame myself too.'

'Nancy –' Flora began, but Nancy held up her hand to stop whatever her mother had been about to say.

'Mam, it's to be expected. The truth is that Lee wouldn't have run away to sea if I hadn't got pregnant. But I want you to know, Aunty Evelyn, that Lee made his own choices.'

Evelyn nodded. 'I know. That's what my head tells me, but –'

'But your heart tells you to blame me,' Nancy said softly. 'All mothers take their child's side, as I am sure I will one day for Robbie.'

Evelyn's voice was full of tears then as she murmured, 'We do have his son, don't we? I suppose, in a funny way, I should be thankful for that.'

'You said the telegram said "missing"?' Flora said tentatively, trying to draw Evelyn away from her bitterness towards Nancy. Nancy was her daughter and Flora would always support her and defend her, but she was honest enough to admit, though only to herself, that in Evelyn's position, she would have felt just the same.

In answer to Flora's question, Evelyn nodded.

'Then – then there is hope.'

'I suppose so,' Evelyn said flatly, but the tone of her voice told her listeners that she couldn't even summon up the courage to hope.

Thirty-one

'Have you heard, we've to report at the Norfolk Barracks on Monday for the first parade?' Max told Victor.

'They're not hanging about, are they?'

'No, they're not,' Max said soberly. Despite his initial anger at Victor being foolish enough to volunteer when he had no need to do so, he was secretly quite glad to have his brother by his side. 'Have you been following the progress of the war in the papers?'

'Yes, I have, but I see them at work. I didn't want Mam and Dad to see me reading them. Mind you,' Victor gave a swift grin, 'I don't suppose it would matter now I've joined up.'

The brothers went to the barracks together and were fortunate to be able to stay together. There was a lot of sorting out to be done. It wasn't an easy task to form all the volunteers into companies.

Max and Victor were assigned to D Company alongside the reporter on the local newspaper whom Max had met in the queue when signing on.

'Hello again,' the cheerful, red-haired, freckle-faced young man said and shook Max's hand vigorously. 'My name's Sam Norton. Pleased to see you again.'

*

'Then we all lined up,' Max told Nancy that evening when he crossed the road to see her and to tell her about his day and the other men he'd met. 'And were inspected by a colonel. After that, there were speeches from various dignitaries. They gave stirring addresses, I have to admit, but warned us that the road ahead will be hard. Most of us haven't had any sort of military training before so it will be tough. We've to report back there tomorrow but I think the drill will be carried out elsewhere.'

'Are you going to live at the barracks?'

'No, it's not big enough.' Max laughed. 'There're about nine hundred men who've been accepted. We're to live at home for the time being until they can find us a suitable camp.'

Nancy smiled. 'That's good. At least we'll have you at home for a bit longer.' She paused and whispered, 'I don't suppose there's been any news of Lee, has there?'

Max shook his head. 'No. Mam's very upset, naturally, and me and Victor haven't made it any easier for her by volunteering. But, like I've tried to tell her, we'd have been called up soon enough anyway. At least, I would.' He was silent for a moment before saying, 'Well, I'll have to be going. I have to get my beauty sleep before reporting for more drill tomorrow. At the moment I feel as if every muscle in my body is aching.'

Nancy pulled a face. 'Poor you.'

'I'll see you again tomorrow night.'

'Of course. The neighbours have decided to meet up in the street after tea, if it's fine, of course, to exchange news and read the newspapers. We're going to buy two or three between us – our local ones and maybe a national one too – and pass them round.'

'So that's what you were all doing when I got home tonight. I did wonder. I was a bit worried there had been some more bad news.'

Nancy sighed. 'Sadly, I think there will be before all this is over, but at least we can all support each other.'

'It's a good idea. About the newspapers, I mean.'

'I was reading tonight in our local paper about a big battle near the river Marne,' Nancy told him. 'It sounds as if our side is winning, but it's difficult to know the truth, isn't it?'

'One of the local journalists is in our company. I think, once we get out there, he'll certainly be sending back the facts.' He laughed. 'I'll try to stay mates with him so that I'm the first with the news. Anyway, I must go. I'll see you tomorrow night.'

The following evening was fine and quite warm for mid-September. The Bonsor family strolled into the street and were soon joined by other neighbours, Flora and Nancy among them. Max and Victor had not yet arrived home.

'D'you know they're drilling them for about six hours a day?' Evelyn said. 'Our lads are shattered by the time they get home. All they want is a bite to eat and their bed.'

'It's nice they're still at home for the time being though, isn't it?'

Evelyn nodded, not trusting herself to speak and

Flora realized she was thinking of Lee. Boldly she asked, 'No more news, I take it?'

Evelyn shook her head. 'If only I could hear, Flora. Even if – even if it's bad news it'd be better than this awful not knowing.'

A short distance away, Howard and Bert were talking to another neighbour, Paul Gadsby, who lived next door to the Bonsors.

'So sorry to hear about your lad,' Paul said to Howard. Paul also worked with him and had been one of the first to offer his condolences when the news had circulated that Lee had been posted missing. The report of the sinking of the ship had been in the newspaper two days after it had happened, but Lee's name had not been among the brief list of casualties at that time. But then the telegram had arrived and soon the whole street had heard the news.

'Aye, it's a bad business. And Max and Victor will be off too soon enough.'

'I know it's selfish,' Paul said, 'but I can't help being thankful our two lads are far too young.'

'I don't blame you, pal. I'm glad Warren and Stanley are an' all.'

'How old's Warren now?'

'Sixteen.'

'Then you want to keep your eye on him. I heard there's a lad in the next street who volunteered at sixteen and they took him.'

'Never! Don't let my missus hear that, will you?'

Paul shrugged. 'She won't hear it from me, but . . .'

Dusk was falling and mothers sent their small children to bed, but still the menfolk and some of the women and unmarried girls lingered, talking in low voices, taking comfort in the company. Flora had gone indoors to see to the baby and she and Agnes watched from the front-room window. Flora rocked Robbie in her arms as she saw Nancy talking to two girls from further down the street.

'I'm glad we've done what we have,' Flora murmured to her mother-in-law as she nodded towards Nancy. 'She wouldn't be out there now, talking and mixing with the neighbours, if they knew.'

'It was all we could do really,' Agnes agreed.

As they stood together in silence, they saw the three girls nudge each other. One pointed up the street and, as Flora's glance followed the same direction, she gasped. 'Oh my!'

A young sailor was walking jauntily down the street, his kit bag slung over his shoulder.

As others in the street became aware of the new arrival, there was a sudden stillness as everyone stared at the approaching figure. And then Evelyn picked up her skirts and began to run towards him.

'Nancy's coming in,' Flora murmured, as the two women still stood together watching what was happening in the street.

'Does she look all right?'

'A bit white.'

'She's not gone to him, has she?'

'Sensible of her not to, really. All the tongues would be wagging if she did.'

'Thank the good Lord he's come back. He's obviously been given leave because of what happened. Do you think he'll come across to see her?'

Flora shrugged. 'Who's to say? Only time will tell on that one.'

'All I hope is that no one in his family tries to make him offer to marry her.'

'You mean Max, don't you? I reckon she'd refuse anyway. It's all nicely sorted out and probably best all round.' Flora glanced down at the baby in her arms and smiled. 'Isn't it, my little one?'

Robbie waved his tiny hands. 'Look,' Flora said, 'he's smiling.'

'Wind,' Agnes said sagely and turned away to greet Nancy as she came in the back door and sat down in a chair at the table.

'That's a surprise,' Agnes said, as she set the kettle on the hob. 'But a nice one. I'm glad the lad survived. I don't wish him any harm.'

'No, Gran, neither do I,' Nancy said quietly. 'I just hope –'

She stopped but Agnes nodded. 'Yer mam and me have just said the same thing.'

Nancy met her gaze. 'You don't know what I was going to say.'

Agnes smiled. 'Oh, I think I do. You were going to say that you hope no one will try to make the pair of you get married.'

Nancy stared at her for a moment and then nodded. 'I was, yes.'

'No one in this house will, I can promise you that,'

Flora said, 'but I can't answer for the Bonsors, especially not for Max.'

'Are you going to see him?' Agnes asked bluntly as was her way.

Nancy knew she now meant Lee. 'Yes, I'll go across tomorrow if he doesn't come here first.'

'They might go as far as that. Making him come to see you, I mean.'

Nancy nodded.

There was a mixed reception in the Bonsor household for Lee. Evelyn couldn't hide her joy at her boy being safe. Howard, though naturally thankful that his son was alive, couldn't quite dispel the disappointment he still felt in him. Warren, however, greeted him with a grin as he shook his brother's hand in welcome. 'It's good to see you, but I'll warn you, you're in trouble.'

Lee pulled a face. 'I'm sure I am. Where is he?' No one was in any doubt that he meant Max and there was no hiding the fact that it was his elder brother he was most afraid of meeting.

'Him and Victor have both joined the Sheffield City Battalion that's just been formed,' Warren told him. 'They're training at Bramall Lane, but at the moment they come home every night. There's not enough accommodation for all of them at the barracks.'

'*Victor*? He'd not old enough. Why ever did you let him volunteer, Dad?'

'I couldn't stop him. He'd signed on before I knew about it.'

As they all sat down together while Evelyn hurriedly

made a meal for him, the frostiness thawed a little and, led by an inquisitive Stanley, they listened to Lee's story of how he came to be sitting here with them, alive and well while many of his shipmates had perished.

'It was terrifying,' Lee said. 'We were just off the Firth of Forth. It was about four o'clock, tea time and we had no warning until almost the last moment before a massive explosion.'

'What caused it?' Howard asked.

'I'm not sure. Some say we hit a mine, others think we were torpedoed amidships but whatever it was I think it must have ignited the ammunitions store because there was a huge explosion and the ship was on fire in minutes. I was knocked to the deck and there was debris flying everywhere. We tried to man the boats but they'd been too badly damaged so then we heaved anything that could float overboard. When the order came "every man for himself", I dived into the sea.' Lee glanced at his father. 'I was never more grateful that you insisted on us all going to the swimming baths every other week and learning to swim properly, Dad. It saved my life.'

'It was Max more than me, to be fair,' Howard murmured. 'He was always the protective big brother.'

There was a slight pause before Stanley piped up again. 'So what happened then?'

Lee didn't speak again for a moment and his face darkened as he whispered, 'The scariest moment was not when the ship was hit or when I was in the water. It was when I'd swum as fast as I could to get away and I turned back to see the ship with its stern in the air, about a hundred feet up and – and it began to fall over towards me. Then I was scared. I felt I'd escaped serious injury only to be hit as it keeled over. But I was lucky. It missed me but I had to swim for me life again because I was afraid of being pulled under the water by the suction as she went down. There was another explosion that caused huge waves that threw me all over the place. I managed to hang on to a piece of wreckage that kept me afloat until help arrived. The sinking had been seen from the shore and it wasn't long before a lifeboat and several other boats and ships came to help.'

'The report in our paper said only about fifty or sixty survived out of a crew of two hundred and sixty,' Howard said.

Lee nodded. 'That's what I heard, but I'm not sure if those figures are accurate. It was just sheer chaos.'

'Then you were lucky,' Howard said soberly. 'Very lucky.'

Lee forced a weak smile. 'Well, you know what they say, Dad. The devil looks after his own.' He pulled himself up slowly and met his mother's gaze. 'I am so sorry for the grief I've caused you.' Now his tone was serious and sincere. 'You must be very disappointed in me. And now I'd better go and make my peace – if I can – with the Westons.'

No one else spoke or even moved as Lee left the house and crossed the road.

Thirty-two

'I'm pleased to see you safe and sound, Lee,' Agnes said at once when she opened the front door to his knock.

'Thank you, Mrs Weston. I 'preciate that more than you could know.' He stood a moment in awkward silence before blurting out. 'I – I've come to see Nancy. I've been given a second chance at life and now I ought to do the right thing by her.'

Agnes opened the door wider, silently inviting him to step inside. As she closed the door she said, 'She's in the backyard taking in the washing. You'll have a bit of privacy there.'

As he stepped out of the back door, he saw her pulling tiny blue garments from the line. He felt as if his heart turned over. He must have a baby boy – a son. Then she turned and saw him and for a long moment they stood staring at each other. Slowly, she came towards him, but her expression was unreadable. She stopped about two feet away from him and then, to his amazement, she smiled. 'I'm so glad you're safe, Lee. Welcome home.'

He grinned awkwardly and shifted uncomfortably from one foot to the other. 'Nance, I – I've come to ask you to marry me. I want to do the right thing by you. I'm so very sorry I ran away. That was wrong of me. I've got quite a long leave because of what happened with the ship and everything. I'm sure we could get something organized before I have to go back . . .'

'Lee,' Nancy said softly, 'answer me one thing truthfully. Are you in love with me?'

'Of course I love you, Nancy. You're like another sister to me –' He stopped and stared at her. Nancy was shaking her head.

'Not good enough, Lee.'

'What – what do you mean? That I'm not good enough for you?'

'No – no, I don't mean that. Of course I don't. But to get married, two people should be so madly in love that they can't bear to live the rest of their lives without one another. Is that how you feel about me, Lee?'

He hesitated for a fraction too long and Nancy had her answer. But she was still smiling, even though there were unshed tears in her eyes. She had too much pride to beg him to marry her. If he didn't love her enough to *want* to marry her, they would face a lifetime of unhappiness and regret if they did get married. Instead, in a kind of absolution, she said, 'Lee, we were carried away that night on a tide of – well, I don't quite know what – but we both were very foolish. I've put it behind me now, and thanks to my understanding parents, Robbie is being brought up as theirs and as my little brother. The gossips in the street might think otherwise, but they can't prove it.'

'What – what about his birth certificate?'

'That was all done legally. It's my name on that as his mother – his unmarried mother – because the registrar – who was very kind and understanding, I might add – explained that to have the father's name added, he had to be present to give his agreement and, of course, you weren't there. But we plan to tell Robbie the truth when he's old enough to understand.'

Lee hung his head and shuffled his feet. 'Are you sure, Nance? Really sure?'

'Lee – please be truthful. You don't want to marry me, do you?'

With his gaze still on the ground, Lee shook his head.

'That's settled, then. Now, do you want to see your son?'

Slowly, he raised his head. 'Oh Nance, can I?' There was such longing in his voice that Nancy would not have had the heart to refuse him, even if she had wanted to.

'Of course, you can.' She tucked her arm through his and led him back into the house.

'Now, don't get any ideas, Mam,' she said cheerfully as they entered the kitchen. 'There's not going to be a shotgun wedding or any kind of wedding, but Lee does want to see his son.'

If Flora felt any disappointment that her daughter was not going to be made an honest woman, as the saying went, then she showed no sign of it. As she'd always said, marriage was hard enough anyway and if the love wasn't there to begin with, it was unlikely to succeed. Flora forced a smile and handed the baby into Lee's arms.

'Fortunately – if we're to carry on with the deception – he's not a bit like you,' Agnes said tartly. 'If he resembles anyone, he reminds me of Bert as a baby.'

'That's good,' Lee murmured, his eyes still on his son. He was drinking in the sight of him, committing every tiny feature to memory.

'We're having a studio photograph taken of him this week,' Nancy said softly. 'I'll let you have one before you go back, if you like.'

Lee nodded. 'I'd like that.'

Agnes sniffed. She hadn't taken the news that there was to be no wedding quite as well as Flora. Although it had been she who had mooted the idea first of passing off the child as being Flora's, now that the father was back, she wasn't so sure that the suggestion had been a good one. She'd already heard that there'd been some gossip in the street and that the remark, 'If you believe that bairn is Flora Weston's, then you'll believe anything' had been bandied about.

Lee left the house a little later. One hurdle had been surmounted, but there was still Max to face. He doubted that encounter would go quite as well.

Lee was waiting in the street for Max at the time their mother said he and Victor might be coming home. Lee didn't want a fall-out between the two brothers in front of their mother, but then neither did he want a brawl in the street. If Max wanted fisticuffs, then perhaps they'd better go to the local boxing club or even to the park. But one way or another, he wanted the confrontation over and done with. He saw his brothers round the corner at the end of the street and march towards him, both with their arms swinging as if they were still drilling. As he drew closer, Lee could see that both his brothers had broadened even more than he remembered. They even seemed to have grown taller and certainly both had filled out. Although Lee had done so too from all the drill he'd been doing, he would never reach Max's level of stature and fitness.

Max came to a halt about three feet in front of Lee. They stared at each other for several moments, Lee standing on the balls of his feet ready for flight.

Victor mumbled. 'Glad to see you back safely, Lee, but I'll leave the two of you to it.' And, brave soldier though he was, he scuttled inside the house and closed the door firmly behind him.

'So,' Max said at last. 'Have you come back to do the decent thing and marry the girl you've shamed?'

'I've suggested it, but we've agreed it's not the right thing for us.'

Max was totally unprepared for the tidal wave of relief that swept through him, making his heart race and his whole body break out in a sweat. Even though he had admitted to himself that he loved Nancy, he'd always been adamant that Lee should stand by his responsibilities and marry her. It was all he'd thought about since finding out about her pregnancy. If his brother hadn't run away, he would have made sure that he'd done just that in spite of what it would have cost him personally. He'd wanted whatever was best for Nancy. He still did and even though he wanted Nancy for himself, Max had to ask himself the question: would she want him? Despite what she'd said, was she still in love with Lee? Like picking at a scab, Max could not let the matter drop.

'Do you really not want to do the honourable thing? I mean, if you don't survive the war, at least she'd have your pension to help bring up your son. You might not be so lucky next time.'

'Leave it, Max, will you? The way things have been dealt with is for the best.'

After a few moments' silence, during which time Max struggled with his inner feelings, he said, 'Very well, then. But I still think you should have stood by her.'

'And subjected us both to a lifetime of misery,' Lee retorted, 'just because of one mistake? It was only the one time, Max, when we'd both had too much to drink. I swear to you.'

This too was a revelation Max hadn't expected. He'd imagined them making love over weeks and months, torturing himself with the images in his mind's eye. But now, if Lee was telling him the truth, and he'd no reason to believe that he wasn't, it had been a one-off – a drunken fumble in the darkness that had gone too far. He acknowledged that perhaps love, real love, had had nothing to do with it. But still, there was the inescapable knowledge that his rapscallion of a brother had got a girl into trouble; a disgrace that could have ruined her whole life if her family hadn't rallied around her to hide the truth. And there was still the niggling doubt that even if Lee didn't love Nancy, perhaps she still loved him.

They'd been standing in the street for some time and now it was dark.

'We'd better go in,' Max said, stiffly, still unable to bring himself to hug his brother, even though he was thankful to see him still alive and surprisingly well after what must have been an ordeal. He hadn't heard the details like the rest of the family, but he guessed enough to know that it was a miracle that Lee had come back to them.

'I thought you'd want to give me a good hiding,' Lee said gruffly as they turned toward the ginnel, the alleyway leading between their home and their neighbour's to their backyard.

'I did. Part of me still does, but it wouldn't serve any purpose now and it would upset Mam.' Max paused with his hand on the door handle and turned to say, 'But don't let it happen again with another girl. Next time, her father might not be so understanding and you might find yourself facing the wrong end of a shotgun.'

'I reckon both of us are going to be doing that anyway,' Lee said grimly, 'but for a different reason.'

To that Max had no answer. But there was one thing he knew he still had to do. He needed to hear it from Nancy's own lips that what Lee was saying was true; that she really had refused his offer of marriage. He could no longer trust his brother's word completely nor could he shake off the feeling that what she had told him before was just her putting a brave face on the situation.

Thirty-three

Because of the naval disaster, Lee had been given a week's leave but then he had to return to Liverpool to join a new ship. On the evening of the day Lee left, Max crossed the road after he'd returned from training to see Nancy.

'She's upstairs putting the baby down,' Agnes told him as she welcomed him into the kitchen. 'Flora's with them too.' She smiled. 'They do it together. I'm not sure who's the most besotted with him.'

Max nodded and said haltingly, 'He's a grand little chap. I just wish . . .' He stopped, afraid he would say too much in front of this wise and all-seeing woman. He would only have to say one word too many in front of Agnes Weston for her to guess his true feelings for Nancy.

'His coming into the world wasn't the way we would have wanted it,' she went on, 'but now he's here, we all love him dearly and best of all, Nancy is able to get on with her life without the stigma of being an unmarried mother.' She paused and when Max didn't say anything, she added, 'Lee went back this morning, didn't he?'

Max nodded.

'Ah well, may the good Lord keep him safe. I

don't wish the lad any harm. I hope you know that, Max.'

'I do.'

'And what about you and Victor? I was shocked to hear he'd been accepted, though not surprised that he'd volunteered. He's a big, strapping lad who'd soon have been given white feathers despite him really being too young.'

'We're still in training at the moment, Mrs Weston. I think they're trying to find a camp for us to go to, but it seems to be taking a while.'

'Now, maybe you can explain something to me, Max. I read in the newspaper that Paris has been saved from falling into the enemy's hands by some sort of plan. I don't understand what that means.'

'Have you heard about the Schlieffen Plan?'

Agnes frowned. 'Yes, yes, that was it.'

'It was a German plan to capture Paris by going through Belgium in an unexpected surprise attack on the French. They thought they could reach Paris in a matter of weeks. It was their invasion of Belgium which brought us into the conflict. We've got a journalist from the *Sheffield Daily Telegraph* in our Company and I've made friends with him.' Max grinned. 'I have to admit to you, Mrs Weston, that I have an ulterior motive. I want to get to know the news and he seems able to get it before the rest of us. His connections with the newspaper, I suppose. But, he is a decent sort of feller anyway. He has explained a lot of the background to the war which I didn't understand. Evidently, we had a decades-old treaty with Belgium that guaranteed their neutrality, so we were obliged to honour our agreement and that also brought the whole of the British Empire into the conflict.'

'I did read that America had declared its neutrality.'

Max wrinkled his forehead. 'Can't blame them, I suppose. It's a European conflict.'

'But we won't have their might on our side.'

'True, but don't forget Germany declared war on Russia at the end of July, so, by default, they'll be on the same side as us. We retreated from the first major battle at Mons, but we seem to be faring a little better at the moment and have held the line on the River Marne. The Germans have withdrawn to the River Aisne and started to dig trenches. Protected by barbed wire, they're trying to deter any frontal attack from our side.'

'Oh Max,' Agnes shook her head sadly, 'it just seems a lot of silliness to me that will result in a huge loss of life on both sides.'

'You're right, but what can we do? We can't just let a country invade another and do nothing, can we?'

'No,' she said sadly. 'You're right, of course. But . . .' Whatever she had been going to say next was cut short as the door from the stairs opened and Nancy and Flora came in.

'I thought I heard voices,' Nancy said. 'How are you, Max? How's training going?'

He grinned. 'They're getting us whipped into shape gradually. We can now line up in fours without half of us ending up facing the wrong way.'

'You're looking very fit,' Flora remarked.

Max chuckled. 'That'll be all the drill and the cross country runs.'

There was an awkward silence before Agnes said, 'Come on, Flora, we'll go into my room and leave the young ones to have a chat. Bert's gone to the pub, I suspect with your dad, Max, so he won't be back for a while. They'll be poring over the newspaper in the bar there. So, Nancy, you see if you can find a beer for Max.'

The two older women disappeared into the front room while, once she had poured him a beer, Nancy and Max sat down on either side of the kitchen table.

Max launched straight into what he had come to say. 'Nancy, Lee told me he'd asked you to marry him but you'd both agreed that it wasn't right for either of you. Is that correct?'

'Yes, it is, Max.'

'But are you just saying that because you think he doesn't really want to marry you?'

'No, Max, I'm not, I promise you. Like I said before, it's not right for either of us. I love Lee, I always will . . .'

Her words were like a knife in his chest but the pain lessened a little as she added, 'But like the brother he's always been to me. I know now that it's not the sort of love that I should feel for the man I marry.'

How he wanted to say more, to push her to say more, but now was not the time and especially when she went on, 'Please, Max, don't let's speak of this again. I want to put it behind me and move on with my life.'

Max took a deep breath. 'If you're sure that's what you really want?'

'I am. Very sure. So,' she went on, swiftly changing the subject, 'are you still marching up and down all day long?'

Max smiled. 'Drill will continue, of course, but we're starting to do other things now. We're learning how to dig trenches in Norfolk Park.'

Nancy's mouth dropped open. 'Never! I bet the park keepers don't like that.'

'They don't, and the Bramall Lane groundsmen aren't too happy either. We're doing a lot of our training there. You can guess what hundreds of marching feet has done to their pitch. But, as everyone keeps saying, there is a war on and sacrifices have to be made.'

'What's a bit of turf besides men's lives?' Nancy murmured.

'Exactly. Anyway, I'll be off now.'

'No news yet about moving to a camp somewhere?' Nancy asked as she saw him out.

'Nothing yet. I expect we'll hear something soon now. But rumour has it that we should at least be getting some more rifles soon. 'Night, Nancy. See you again tomorrow night.'

Every day they expected to hear that a camp had been found for them, after which there would be no more homecoming every night. It wasn't until October when the whole battalion went on a route march that Max arrived home the same evening footsore and weary to tell Nancy, 'We ended up at Redmires.'

'Near the reservoirs?'

'That's right. That's where our camp is being constructed.'

'So it's not too far away from the city, then, is it? You should be able to get home quite often.'

'I'm hoping so.'

It was early December when the camp was finally ready for the battalion to move in. Strangely, Nancy felt more bereft when Max finally had to leave home than she had done when Lee had deserted her. Max came across to say goodbye to her the evening before they were due to leave. He nursed his nephew until Flora took the baby upstairs to put him to bed.

'My word, he's growing fast,' Max said, his glance following Flora as she left the room. 'He looks as if he'll be trying to walk soon.'

'He crawls everywhere and moves like lightning and he's already trying to pull himself up on the furniture.'

'Have you got a picture you can spare?' Max asked. He knew about the photographs which Nancy had had taken. He'd seen the one she'd given Lee of Robbie lying on a shawl in a photographer's studio.

Nancy jumped up. 'I'll show you all the ones I've got left and you can choose whichever one you want.' She went to a small bureau which stood against the wall in the kitchen and then returned to hand him seven photographs. There were three of the baby on his own, one with Flora nursing him and two of Nancy holding him.

'May I have one of these?' he asked, pointing a

little tentatively to one of the photographs of both Nancy and Robbie.

'Of course you can, and can I have one of you when you get your proper uniform? And Victor too. After all, we've all been good friends for years, haven't we?'

'Of course. What about – Lee?'

'He's promised to send one to me when he gets his uniform for his new ship, though he tells me it won't reveal the name of the ship. Very hush-hush, isn't it?' She laughed. 'I want to have a little row of you on my dressing table. The Bonsor Boys.'

Max glanced down at the photo in his hand. He would carry it everywhere with him and pray that it kept him safe. It would be his talisman. But, he wondered, how many of 'The Bonsor Boys', as Nancy had christened them, would eventually go to war and how many would come back?

'At least you and Victor are going together,' Nancy said, interrupting his thoughts as she valiantly tried to hold back the tears. 'You will write to me, won't you, wherever you are?'

'Of course, if you want me to. But, like you said, we're not far away, at least for a while, and I think we'll be able get home quite often.'

'I just want to know you're safe and – and I'd like you to write letters just to me that I don't have to share with anyone else. I know you'll be writing regularly to your mam and she will most likely share them with us, but – but that's not the same.'

'All right.' His heart lifted a little at her words but he kept the conversation light. 'It'll be nice to have plenty of letters from home.'

'I'm sure you'll have lots. All your family and friends will write to you.'

Max pulled a face. 'Most of my friends and work colleagues of the right age have volunteered too. We're all going together. The authorities are promising that we will stay together as much as possible. I've heard it said that there are several pals' battalions, as they're calling them, throughout the country. It all stems from Lord Kitchener's appeal for volunteers.' He paused and then said, 'I'm sorry, I must go. Mam's putting on a special tea for us all tonight.' He would have liked to have invited her to join them, but he knew his mother was counting on it being just family.

'You're not going out in this lot, surely,' Flora protested the following morning when Nancy put on her hat and coat and picked up her sturdy umbrella. 'It's siling down.'

'I'm going to wave Max off,' Nancy said stubbornly in a tone that brooked no argument. 'They're marching out the city about dinner time and I've got the time off work especially.'

'He'll not see you in all the crowd and if they're marching – which they will be – he won't be able to look around him and he definitely won't be able to wave.'

'He'll know I'm there because I promised to go.'

'Maybe she should go, Flora love,' Agnes put in quietly, 'especially if she promised.' She turned to Nancy. 'I don't often argue with your mam, but I'm just thinking ahead. If he gets sent abroad – and he will eventually – you don't want it on your conscience that you didn't wave him off. Just wrap up against the rain and come straight home afterwards. And I want your promise on that.'

'Oh, I will, Gran.'

An hour later, Nancy was standing with the rest of the people lining the route the soldiers were taking out of the city. She had crossed the road to ask Evelyn if she was coming but their mother had shaken her head. 'I can't bear to see them both go, Nancy. They understand. We said our goodbyes here this morning.'

Evelyn's face was bleak and Nancy put her arms around her. 'Then I'll wave them off for all of us.'

'He thinks they'll be home quite often – at least while they're still at Redmires.'

'Let's hope so, but today is something special when they're all leaving together and the city is so proud of its very own battalion.'

'I've got such mixed feelings, Nancy, I don't mind telling you. One minute I'm bursting with pride, the next, I'm actually shaking with fear that they – they won't come back at all.'

Nancy hugged her even harder.

'Just mind you wrap up warm,' Evelyn murmured, still taking care of everyone despite the ache in her heart. 'Max wouldn't want you catching a chill.'

'They're coming, they're coming!' shouted the woman standing beside her among the crowds lining the streets. 'Where's my boy? I can't see my boy.'

Nancy scanned the rows of marching soldiers as they passed by, searching, searching . . . and then she saw Max with Victor beside him. Both of them were taller than some of the others around them and were easy to spot. But they were marching, keeping in step and looking straight ahead. Nancy waved anyway – just in case. And then as they drew level with her, she was sure she saw a smile on both their faces. Somehow, she thought, they've seen me. They know I'm here.

'Good luck!' she shouted with the rest of the crowd. 'God speed.'

When the lines of soldiers had marched past, the crowd dispersed and hurried home. Nancy, too, went straight home as she had promised her grandmother. There she found Agnes and Flora had prepared the tin bath in front of the fire in the range.

'No arguments,' Agnes said, as she filled it with hot water from the boiler. 'Strip off all those wet clothes and in you get.'

'But . . .' Nancy began, but there was no disobeying her grandmother in that mood, so meekly she got into the warm water.

'Did you see them?' Flora asked.

'Yes.' Nancy's voice was a little shaky. 'They were marching side by side, their heads high. It – it was quite touching to see all those wonderful young men marching off together.'

Agnes and Flora exchanged a glance. Though they said nothing in front of Nancy, as they'd waited for her return, they'd both voiced the thought that the young men, who were marching out of the city so bravely today, would one day be sent to the Front and many of them would never return. They could only pray – among all the other mothers in the city and indeed throughout the nation – that their boys would come back safely. But even then, both women knew it was a vain hope.

'Three of Evelyn's boys gone now,' Agnes had murmured. The unspoken words had lain between mother and daughter-in-law. Surely it was too much to hope that all three would return unharmed?

Thirty-four

'You wouldn't believe how empty the house seems, Flora,' Evelyn said as she stirred her tea the morning after Max and Victor had gone to the newly built camp and were no longer returning home every evening. 'I've still got three of 'em at home, I know, but it's so quiet without the others. And I don't know if any of them will be able to get leave at Christmas.'

'They must have been the ones making all the noise, then,' Flora laughed, trying to rally her friend.

Evelyn smiled weakly. 'I just wish I knew where Lee was. I know the other two won't be far away for a while, but . . .'

Flora sighed. 'Even if you did know, love, it could be different the very next day. You only really know where they are at the time they're writing to you.'

Evelyn laughed wryly. 'Not even then, if I'm honest. They're not allowed to say. I expect he'll be back at sea somewhere by now. Although the other two are still in training, at least they're not far away. Max thought they might be able to get home now and then.'

'It's a dirty business, isn't it? War. Learning how to kill other lads of their own age,' Flora said softly.

'Each one is some poor mother's son, whichever side they're on.'

Lee wrote to Nancy sporadically, just to ask after Robbie, but Max wrote every week, even though he was still only a few miles away. Nancy replied faithfully, as they had promised each other, and sometimes he arrived home unexpectedly before his letter even reached her.

'Victor and I got a forty-eight-hour pass,' he told Nancy when he arrived home only a fortnight after they'd moved to the camp at Redmires, 'and over a weekend too.' He chuckled. 'Some of the lads sneak out of the camp and walk the five miles back home without asking permission. They've found a hole in the wall where they can get back in without the sentry noticing, but it's risky. I'd rather do it above board and wait to be granted proper leave. But I suppose for those with girlfriends or the ones who are feeling a bit homesick, it's a temptation.'

They were walking to the park on the Saturday afternoon, with Nancy pushing a sleeping Robbie in the pram.

'I'd've thought you'd have gone to the football this afternoon. They're playing Bolton Wanderers, aren't they?'

'Dad and the three boys have gone, but I'd rather see you.'

'But you might not have many more chances until the war is over. Dad was saying there's already talk that after this season, all matches might be cancelled for the remainder of the war.'

'It'd probably be sensible. Attendance figures have

300

already dropped since last season. I suppose a lot of the lads who used to go have joined up.'

Nancy sighed. 'Besides, I'm not sure it's a good idea for you to be seen with me and the baby. Folks'll get the wrong idea and gossip will start.'

'Quite frankly, Nancy, I couldn't care less. Let them think what they want to.'

They walked in silence for some moments before Nancy said, 'Do you think you'll get home again for Christmas? It's less than a week away now so it doesn't look like the war's going to be over by then like they said.'

'I doubt it, now we've had this weekend, but I'll get home again as soon as I can.' He paused and then added, 'I'm sorry to say it, Nancy, but I think this war's going to go on a lot longer. Years, even. Are you following the news?'

Nancy nodded. 'I read what we now call "the street papers" when it's our turn to have them, though by the time we do they're sometimes two or three days old. We're getting a national newspaper now as well as the local ones. Maybe you can explain something to me, Max. We've been reading about something they're calling the "race to the sea". Do you know what it means?'

'I do now actually. I think I've told you before that Victor and I have become friends with a lad who was a reporter for the *Sheffield Daily Telegraph*. He still is, I suppose, in a way. Sam Norton. He's a bright spark – a laugh a minute. He keeps everyone's spirits up and, of course, he's the first with any news. He's like a ferret for finding out what's going on. He was telling us that the battle of the Marne in September was a good victory for us but after that the Germans halted their retreat at the Aisne and decided to try to seize ports on the English Channel to cut off supply routes between Britain and France. So, of course, our side wanted that stopped. The two sides began sort of leap-frogging each other to move towards the North Sea, so it became known as the "race to the sea".'

'What happened?'

'A battle near the Belgian town of Ypres halted their progress and both sides dug in. I think both armies could be there for some time.'

'It was frightening to read earlier this week about the enemy warships shelling towns on the east coast of Britain. Scarborough was one, wasn't it?'

Max nodded. 'It's very worrying to think that civilians are now being targeted. Seventeen people were killed in Scarborough alone and many more injured. And there's another concern now.'

'What?'

'We may be subject to Zeppelin attacks and they could be anywhere in the country. Even here.'

'Oh!' Nancy was startled. 'Yes, I suppose you're right. I hadn't thought about that. But would we be a target for them? Wouldn't they go for places that –' She stopped and her eyes widened.

'You were going to say "places that produce armaments and ammunition", weren't you?'

'I was,' she whispered. 'And, of course, we do now, don't we?'

Solemnly, Max nodded. 'But there'll be another

outcome. Rather an ironic one, as Sam said, such attacks will "encourage further recruitment".'

Nancy sighed. 'Yes, that's sad, but I'm sure it's true.'

They walked in silence for a while until she asked, 'What's it like in the camp?'

Max gave a wry laugh. 'Pretty basic, to be honest. It's bitterly cold and we're having to quarry stone from nearby to make a lot of the roads and paths throughout the camp. There's a lot of grumbling, but at least the heavy work will build up our fitness. We're digging ditches and clearing an area to be used as a parade ground.'

'What's the food like?'

Max pulled a face. 'Pretty dire at the moment, but we're hoping the cooks will improve. Despite all this, though, and perhaps surprisingly, morale is very high. Friendships are already being made that I'm sure will see us through the worst of times. Of course, Victor and I have each other and there are other brothers and a lot of pals from their places of work or clubs they belong to who've joined up together.'

As they reached the street where they both lived, Max said, 'We have to go back tomorrow evening, but I'll come to see you before we leave.'

'I think Mam and me are taking Robbie to see Grandma Halliday tomorrow afternoon, but we'll be back about five. Is that all right?'

'Perfect. We don't have to leave until seven. I'll see you then.' He reached down into the pram and tickled Robbie's cheek.

'Ta-ra, little man. Si'thi' again tomorrow.'

*

The following afternoon, Flora and Nancy walked to where Edith lived with Seffie.

'Oh, how lovely to see you,' Edith said as she opened the door. 'Do come in, but you'll have to excuse the mess. We've got a huge order for making the temporary uniforms for the battalion. We're working flat out, even today. On a Sunday,' Edith sounded scandalized at her own admission. 'And that's unheard of in this house, but we have no choice and Seffie says it's a case of "the better the day, the better the deed". Come in, come in. Sit down, if you can find a space.'

The room was filled with blue material and half-finished garments in all sizes. Seffie waved to them from behind her sewing machine, but never paused in her work.

'Take a break, Edith dear, and talk to your family,' she said generously.

'Why are they blue?' Flora asked as she sat down and took Robbie onto her knee.

Edith pulled a face. 'I don't think our boys are going to like it, but there's a shortage of khaki material. We'll get it eventually but, for now, this is what we've got to use. Now, let me hold my great-grandson while you tell me all the news.'

They stayed for an hour and as they walked home, Flora said, 'You know, Nancy, I've never seen my mother looking so happy.'

'She's safe, earning her own living, and has a nice place to live with a good friend. After all she's been through, it's no more than she deserves. And we go to see her regularly.'

304

'I think she misses Mary Ellen.'

'Dad takes you and her to see Aunty quite often. I mean, your sister could come here if she wanted.'

'It's more difficult for her to leave the farm now the old folks are getting less mobile. She certainly couldn't stay away for any length of time. Besides, I don't think she's too keen on coming back to the city, not even for a visit.'

'I was quite surprised that she wasn't more upset when we decided to keep Robbie.'

'She was very sensible about it,' Flora said. 'She told me she deliberately didn't set her heart on it, because she thought that once you'd held him, you wouldn't be able to let him go. Not even to her. Now, here we are, home again. You give Robbie his bath and his tea and I'll see to ours.'

But when they entered the house, it was to find that Agnes had already started the tea. The table was laid and pans were bubbling on the hob.

'I thought I'd make a start,' Agnes greeted them. 'I didn't know quite what time you'd be back and I know Max is coming over tonight to say ta-ra before he goes back later this evening. Now, tell me, how was your mother, Flora?'

'Very well. I was just saying to Nancy as we walked home, I don't think I've ever seen her so happy and contented.'

'Being rushed off their feet with orders must suit her. Her and Miss Kendall are so busy,' Nancy laughed as she picked Robbie up to undress him for his bath. 'They're making uniforms for the City Battalion. Blue ones.'

When Agnes looked puzzled, Flora explained. 'They'll get proper uniforms eventually, probably before they're sent overseas.'

There was a sudden silence in the kitchen as the war – the real war – came suddenly closer.

Thirty-five

The first Christmas of the war was difficult for everyone. The men from Redmires got leave in turn, priority being given by mutual agreement among themselves to those who had young children at home. On Christmas Eve, Nancy received a letter from Max.

We're both sorry not to be coming home for Christmas, but we want to be fair to the lads who have children. We shall so miss being with you all, but several of us are trying to make some sort of a celebration for those still here. Victor and I have helped to decorate our hut to give it a bit of a festive feeling and we've been told that on Christmas Day our dinner will be served to us by the officers. Evidently, it's a tradition. We've also heard that we're to be provided with a YMCA hut. That should be a great addition to camp life. It'll have a canteen, space to hold church services if needed, and quiet spaces for the lads to write letters. It's also to have a post office, which I am guessing will be very busy! I must close now, but wish you and all your family the happiest of Christmases despite the strange times we're living in.

The Westons again spent Christmas in Derbyshire with the Clarke family, but it was a rather subdued one. Matthew and Winnie Clarke were failing in health and were not their usual ebullient selves. Flora, Nancy and Agnes helped Mary Ellen as much as they could and Howard worked outside with Jack, but it was with a sense of relief on both sides when they returned home on 27 December.

Max and Victor managed to get leave together the following week and were able to celebrate the New Year with their family and friends, though 'celebrate' was perhaps not quite the right word. No one knew what the next year would bring or who would still be there to see it. Would the war be over by then? No one had the answer. Not even the politicians.

Towards the end of January, news of the first air raid on Britain was reported in the newspapers. Howard knocked on the door of the Westons' home.

'It's a bit cold to be standing in the street now,' he said as he stepped inside. 'So we're passing it round among our immediate neighbours. I thought I'd come across and share the latest news with you, Bert. It's not good, I'm afraid.'

'Sit down, Howard. Beer?'

'That'd be nice. Thanks.' As he sat down near the range, Howard asked, 'How's babby? Haven't seen him lately. I bet he's growing.'

'He's grand,' Bert said with a fond smile. 'He'll be walking any day now, I reckon.'

'Really?'

'He's almost a year old and Flora reckons he's

forward for his age anyway. He's trying to say a few words too.'

As Bert placed a tankard of beer next to him, Howard handed the newspaper to him and jabbed his finger at one of the articles. 'Read that. It's getting a bit too close for my liking. It's one thing for our lads to have to go to fight – I'm afraid we have to accept that – but it's quite another for women and children to be targeted.'

Bert read the piece and then looked up. 'Zeppelins? That's those big airship things, isn't it? By what it says here, they can carry bombs.'

Howard nodded solemnly. 'So it seems. They've dropped them on several coastal towns in Norfolk, particularly Yarmouth. Three people were killed there. A twenty-six-year-old woman, whose husband had recently been lost in France and a small boy of four were killed at King's Lynn. And see what I mean about women and children? It's not right, is that.'

'No, it isn't,' Bert agreed grimly.

'The weather was foggy and rainy so even though the airship was shot at,' Howard went on, 'it escaped.'

Only a few days later, early in February, Howard crossed the road again. This time he was waving the newspaper excitedly. 'Our warships have sunk a big German battle cruiser in the North Sea. I'd bet my last shilling it was preparing to bombard the coast, like they did at Scarborough last year, only our lads got to it first and sank it. Three other German cruisers fled and got away, but we've given them a bloody nose, Bert. We've shown 'em we're not just sitting ducks.'

'You know what they'll start doing next, don't you?'

Howard frowned. 'What?'

'They'll start targeting supply ships bringing us food. They'll try to ruin our economy as well as starve us into submission.'

Howard smirked. 'They can try, but they'll have the Royal Navy to contend with.'

Both men smiled, thinking of Lee, but neither mentioned his name.

'So,' Howard went on, 'do we know what's happening on land? I haven't seen anything about any big battles going on recently.'

'I think both sides have dug in since the "race to the sea" the papers were talking about, but I expect it will all start up once the weather improves.'

'We'll just have to pray that the winter lasts longer than usual, then,' Howard said in a vague attempt at humour but it fell rather flat as they thought about the appalling conditions the men on both sides must be living in.

By March, it was Jessie who burst into the Westons' home waving the newspaper, her eyes shining with excitement. 'They're calling for women to sign up for war work. The government is setting up a Register of Women for War Service. That's something me an' Nancy could do.'

'Now, now, Jessie, calm down and tell us slowly,' Flora said, while Agnes merely smiled at the young girl's enthusiasm.

But Jessie was anything but calm. 'I want to do

something to help the war. Now three of my brothers have gone, I feel so useless sitting at home doing nothing. And I'm dreading the day when Andrew will go because I know he will have to eventually.'

'You're needed at the store and you do a lot to help your mam . . .' Flora began.

'She doesn't need me so much now there's half of us gone.'

'But what about your job?'

Jessie ignored her. 'And Mrs Pankhurst's all for it, she says.'

'The woman who leads the suffragettes?'

'Yes, and –' Jessie started to say.

'I won't let Nancy get mixed up with that lot. Smashing windows and chaining themselves to railings indeed,' Flora said. 'The very idea. And I'm surprised if your mother agrees with all that.'

'She doesn't.' Jessie chuckled mischievously and then paused to let Flora go on thinking that's what she and Nancy were planning to do. But Agnes had caught the naughty glint in the girl's eyes.

'I think women are far more likely to *earn* the right to vote by helping their country in its hour of need,' Agnes put in mildly. 'And I'm sure there's plenty of things you could do that your mother, and Nancy's too, would approve of.'

'It says here women are needed in industry and agriculture and more than anything else, in armaments. Making shells, for one thing.'

'Perhaps you could both go out to Mary Ellen's and help on the farm there,' Flora said. 'I wouldn't mind Nancy doing that.'

'What wouldn't you mind Nancy doing?' the girl herself asked as she appeared in the doorway.

'Jessie's come across with the newspaper that's saying the government is asking women to sign on to do war work. What has your mother said to this, Jessie? Have you actually told her?'

'Not yet, but I'll talk to her and Dad tonight. I'm sure they'll agree to me registering. Oh, please say you'll let Nancy sign up too.'

Nancy took the paper out of Jessie's hands and read the piece for herself. She frowned. 'I think we should be careful. I'll write and ask Max what he thinks.'

'Max? Why would you want to ask Max?' Jessie said.

Flora and Agnes glanced at each other but said nothing.

'Because when he signed on for the City Battalion, it was partly because he didn't want to wait to be called up and sent just anywhere. He wanted to be able to choose where he went and, in a way, who he went with.'

'Oh, yes. I see what you mean. If we just sign up, we'll get sent anywhere they want us to go and we won't have any say.'

'Exactly.'

'So what shall we do?'

'Make some enquiries first about what sort of jobs are going and apply for something we like the look of.'

'Yes, I suppose you're right.' Jessie looked deflated.

Nancy touched her arm. 'But you're absolutely

right. We should do something. Working at a department store is hardly helping the war effort, now, is it? But it's just a matter of finding something we might like and' – now it was Nancy who grinned impishly – 'something our parents will approve of.'

Jessie wagged her forefinger in Nancy's face playfully. 'And Max. Don't forget Max must approve.'

But Nancy was quite serious when she said, 'Yes – yes, he must.'

After lengthy discussions between the two sets of parents, the girls began making enquiries. Over the next few weeks and months, they asked around and kept their eyes on the local press.

'Don't say anything at work,' Nancy said. 'I don't think the head of our department would be too pleased to hear we're thinking of leaving, even if it is to do war work.'

'Audrey says she's applying to work in munitions,' Jessie said. 'She says the money's ever so good.'

'Dad says that'd be filthy work and quite dangerous.'

'No offence to your aunty, but I don't fancy being stuck in the countryside. I don't really want to leave the city.'

Nancy sighed. 'Neither do I, but if they were desperate, I'd probably have to go anyway to help out. They were very good to me.'

'Have they said they're struggling?'

Nancy shook her head. 'No. To be honest, I think they'll be all right. There should be plenty of villagers willing to help out when needed. They did have a

Saturday lad . . .' She stopped suddenly and then added slowly, 'Mind you, he might have gone to war by now.'

'Can't you get an exemption if you work on the land? There's something called a reserved occupation, isn't there?' Teasing her friend, Jessie added, 'You ought to ask Max. He'll know.'

Not realizing that Jessie was pulling her leg, Nancy said quite seriously, 'Yes, I will, next time I write.'

Max's weekly letters were always a mixture of humorous tales of life in the camp but tempered by serious news of the war.

We had a football match last week with the Sherwood Foresters' boys. Need I tell you that we won handsomely and this week there's to be a sports' day. We expect to do well, considering our normal training is pretty tough. The war news isn't so good, though, I'm afraid. There's a battle going on near Ypres in Belgium for a piece of ground they're calling Hill 60. It must be important. And, in a way, there's even worse news. Sam has told us that the enemy have started using a despicable weapon. Chlorine gas. It chokes and blinds. I hope we never use it, but I expect we will. I suppose we have to fight like with like but I abhor anything like that . . .

As regards you and Jessie finding war work, I think it's a great idea, but please choose wisely.

Through April and into the early summer months the bad news from the war front kept coming. The campaign in Gallipoli was not going particularly well for the Allies, but at the end of April, there was great excitement in the city for all Sheffield United supporters. Their team had reached the final of the FA Cup.

'The match is to be at Old Trafford,' Howard told Bert.

'It's usually in London, isn't it? That's a surprise, especially since we're playing against Chelsea.'

'I've heard it's to avoid the capital all together.'

'Because of the war, I suppose.'

'Isn't everything?' Howard said wryly. 'They're even calling it the "Khaki Cup Final". I expect that's because the stands are likely to be filled with lads in uniform.'

'Just so long as we win, eh?' Bert said and Howard knew he meant both the game and the war.

'Amen to that,' Howard murmured and the two friends exchanged a look of understanding.

They were unable to go to the match, but their hopes were realized when their team beat Chelsea three nil. It was a good note for the city to end the season on because all future league and cup competitions were then cancelled while the country was at war.

Thirty-six

At the beginning of May, came the appalling news of the sinking of the *Lusitania*, a Cunard liner carrying almost two thousand people of which over eleven hundred were lost. It had been torpedoed without warning by a German submarine.

'There were Americans on board,' Howard told Bert. 'D'you think it might bring America into the war?'

'I couldn't say, but what it will do is make them even more sympathetic towards our cause.'

Bert sighed. 'Yes, I suppose it's too much to expect them to come into a war which is predominantly European.'

Howard laughed wryly. 'You can always hope. We could do with their might.'

'Have the girls got any nearer finding some sort of war work?'

Howard shook his head. 'Not that I've heard, but then I don't always get to know until it's been decided. But Evelyn knows what's going on, I would think. I leave it to her.'

'Aye, Flora and my mother usually have the last word.'

Both men chuckled together, but it was all said

with the warmth of love they both had for their families.

Two days after they'd heard of the sinking of the *Lusitania*, Nancy received the news from Max that she'd been dreading.

Rumour has it that we'll be leaving soon, but I'm sure we'll get some leave before we go.

Both Max and Victor arrived home on the Monday evening.

'We've only got until early Wednesday, as we leave on Thursday,' Max told Nancy. 'An advance party leave tomorrow for Cannock Chase but me an' Victor are going on Thursday with the rest of the battalion. It'll be early, but you can come and wave us off, that's if the weather's good.'

'I'll come whatever the weather, though I don't expect you'll see me in the crowd.'

Max chuckled. 'I spotted you last time. So did Victor, even though we weren't supposed to be looking.'

'I'll try to be somewhere near the Town Hall.'

'Will you come out with me tomorrow night? Your mam wouldn't mind, would she?'

'I'd love to and no, Mam won't mind. Do you like opera?'

Max wrinkled his forehead. 'I've never seen one. Why?'

'There's one on at the Lyceum tomorrow night. It's called *Lily of Killarney*. Do you fancy it?'

Max chuckled. 'It'd be an experience. Let's go.'

*

As they left the theatre the following evening, Max took her arm as they crossed the street in the darkness. 'So what did you think?'

'In a funny way, I enjoyed it. I couldn't always understand what they were singing about, but somehow I managed to follow the storyline – I think.'

'I know just what you mean. The music was wonderful and that baritone had a marvellous voice.'

'If I'm honest, though, I think I would rather have seen a play that I could really follow.'

'Me too. Next time I'm on leave, eh?'

'I'll hold you to that. It'll be something to look forward to.'

When they reached Nancy's home, she said, 'Thank you for a lovely evening, Max, and I promise I'll be there on Thursday morning.'

Then she stood on tiptoe and kissed his cheek. 'Please take care of yourself,' she whispered and then hurried away before her tears should fall.

Nancy was up very early on the day Max and Victor were due to leave.

'What about work?' Flora said. 'You'll be in trouble if you're late.'

'Actually, I don't think we will. Mrs Davenport's own son is in the City Battalion and I'm sure she's going to be there to see him off. I really don't think anyone will find fault with us and besides, Max said the first train leaves at about half past eight and he'll be on that. Jessie and me can still get to work before nine.'

Flora said no more. She couldn't blame both girls

for wanting to see the Bonsor boys off. She was wise enough to realize that they might never see them again though she didn't voice her fears.

They were there in time to see the battalion form up outside the Town Hall, after they'd marched through the streets lined with relatives and accompanied by marching bands.

'There's thousands here,' Jessie said in awe. 'Fancy all these folks turning out to see them off.'

'It's a big day for the battalion and for the city,' Nancy said, her voice a mixture of pride and trepidation.

They listened while the Lord Mayor made a farewell speech and cheered with everyone as their boys marched away towards the station. Jessie had tears running down her face. 'I couldn't see them. Could you?'

'No. Let's just hope they saw us.'

'They'd know we were here.'

'Yes, and we must write to them straight away. Max gave me an address last night.'

As the marching line of soldiers disappeared, the two girls turned and hurried to the department store.

'I saw Mrs Davenport in the crowd,' Jessie said. 'Let's just make sure we're at work before her. She can hardly say anything then, can she?'

'I don't think she will anyway. Poor woman must be feeling dreadful. He's her only son. Her only child, I think. And she's on her own. Her husband died two years ago, so she's only an empty house to go home to tonight.'

'I know she's strict, but she's always fair,' Jessie said. 'I quite like her.'

'She's only doing her job. You and me never cause her any problems, but one or two of the other girls do. They take advantage if they think they can get away with it.'

'Let's watch out for her, then.'

The two girls agreed that, without making it obvious, they would do what they could to help their head of department.

That evening Nancy sat down to write to Max. She told him everything that had happened that day from seeing the soldiers standing in line outside the Town Hall to watching them march away and how sorry they'd both been not to be able to spot him and Victor among the throng. She even told him about her feelings for their superior at work and how she and Jessie planned to help the woman whenever they could:

> *. . . without making it too obvious, of course. We don't want to be seen as a couple of boot-lickers, but we feel so sorry for her being left entirely on her own. Please stay safe, Max, and let me know when you get settled . . .*

'Is Nancy at home?'

Just over a month after the battalion had left, Jessie stood at the back door of the Westons' home holding a newspaper.

'Yes, she's just helping with the ironing. Come in, love.' As Jessie stepped inside, Flora asked worriedly, 'What have you got there? I hope it's not bad news.'

'No, no, Aunty Flora. Far from it. It's a copy of

the *Sheffield Independent* and I think there's something in it that Nancy and me could do to help the
war effort. That's if you and Uncle Bert will let her.'

Flora chuckled, relieved for the moment that there
was no distressing news in the paper. Casualties were
reported regularly, sometimes with photographs, and
Flora was becoming afraid to open the pages in case
she saw someone she knew.

'If she wants to do something, Jessie love, Nancy
will do it. You should know her better than that by
now.'

Jessie smiled as she followed Flora into the kitchen
where Nancy was standing at the table. The blanket
used as a base was spread on the table and two flat
irons, heated alternately, were standing on the hob.
As she picked one up, Nancy turned to greet her
friend. She too frowned when she saw the newspaper
in Jessie's hands.

'It's all right,' Jessie said swiftly. 'There's nowt
wrong.'

Now Nancy's expression relaxed too.

'There's a piece in the paper here saying that they
want women to take the place of postmen who've
enlisted. They've already got at least six working and
they want more for the central districts of the city.'

'You mean actually delivering the post, not just
sorting it at the office?'

'No, proper postmen. Well, postwomen, I expect
they'll be called. What d'you think, Nancy?'

Nancy set the iron back on the hob and took the
newspaper from Jessie's hands to read the piece for
herself.

'There's just one thing you ought to think about,' Flora put in softly. 'You might be asked to deliver telegrams sometimes, if a telegraph boy isn't available.'

Both girls looked up at her, their eyes widening. Then they looked at each other.

'Yes, we would, wouldn't we?' Nancy said. 'Could you do that, Jessie?'

Jessie bit her lip but nodded resolutely. 'Yes, I think I could. I'd be thinking about the poor souls receiving it, rather than myself.'

'That's a very good way to look at it, love.' Flora nodded her approval of their courageous attitude. After all, they'd only both just turned twenty earlier in the year, Flora thought. It wouldn't be an easy thing for young girls to do.

'What about your jobs at the store?'

Nancy and Jessie exchanged a glance. 'We like it there, Aunty Flora,' Jessie said, 'but we both want to do something that would actually help the war effort.'

'What does your dad think?' Nancy asked.

'He thinks it's a good idea for me to try it, at least, though he's a bit doubtful about the early morning starts, especially when it'll still be dark in winter.'

Nancy turned towards her mother. 'Do you think Dad will agree?'

'You can only ask him, love.'

'Now, it's funny you should bring this up, Nancy,' Bert said as the family sat around the tea table later. 'I saw that piece in the paper myself and wondered if it might be something that would suit you.' He smiled at her. 'I know how keen you are to help with the war effort and I'd sooner you did something like that than go into a munitions factory. Necessary though they are, they're not the healthiest of places to be, from what I've heard. So by all means go along and see what you can find out. Are you and Jessie planning to go together?'

Nancy nodded. 'As long as her dad agrees too.'

'I expect you'll be given proper uniforms,' Agnes said. 'I think a uniform would give you some sort of protection if you decide to join.'

'Protection? What do you mean, Gran?'

Agnes wriggled her shoulders. 'Young girls out at all hours would need the – the status of a uniform to show that they're on official business.'

Nancy blinked and then said, 'Oh – oh yes, I see what you mean.'

After their initial enquiries and two rounds of interviews, both girls were each offered the new position of postwoman and, early in July, they were tramping the streets delivering mail. They couldn't, of course, work together, but often they could meet up to cycle home. Both Bert and Howard had provided their daughters with second-hand bicycles to make life a little easier for them.

'You'll have done plenty of walking by the end of your shift,' Howard teased. 'You'll be glad of a sit down, even if it's only on a bicycle saddle.'

Nancy wrote gleefully to Max: *Jessie and me are working as postwomen now. We're doing our bit to help win the war.* She went on to tell him about the streets she visited on her rounds: *The worst bit is delivering telegrams. Mam warned me it would be hard. But it didn't prepare me for the shock on people's faces when you hand them the envelope, because everyone recognizes what it is now before they even open it. Not many open it in front of me, so I don't get to know what's in it.*

Max wrote back by return: *Do be careful, Nancy, there can be some strange folk about early in the morning when all the men are going to work. Have you got a uniform to wear?*

Not yet, Nancy answered in her next letter, *but we are to get one eventually, they say. Please don't worry about us. You're quite right, there are a lot of men going to work when we're doing the first delivery, but I take comfort in the fact that there's so many about that if anything untoward were to happen, I'm sure there'd be someone to come to my rescue. And don't tell anyone this, because I don't know if we're supposed to have one, but your dad has given both me and Jessie a whistle. It looks suspiciously like a police whistle, but I'm not asking where or how he got it. I'm just thankful to have it.*

At the beginning of August, Max wrote to say: *We've moved again. We've come to a camp at Ripon for musketry training . . . Goodness knows when we'll get any leave, even though we're not that far away from home now.*

In September, he told Nancy: *We had a wonderful concert last night to celebrate the formation of the battalion. Who'd have thought we'd still be in this country, still training, a whole year later. But the War Office must have their reasons, I suppose, for keeping us kicking our heels. Most of the lads want to see some action now.*

Thirty-seven

A fortnight later, the battalion were on the move again, this time to Salisbury Plain.

We're here for final training before being sent to the Front, Max wrote.

Nancy's heart sank but she said nothing to her mother; Max would tell his family in his own good time. As the days passed, it seemed she had been right. All Flora said at the tea table was, 'Evelyn tells me that Max and Victor have gone to a camp somewhere in the Salisbury district. More training, I expect.'

Nancy felt her mother's gaze rest on her for a moment but Nancy averted her gaze. She didn't want to tell lies, but she would not reveal what Max told her. She knew now that his letters to her were for her alone. She felt a warm glow to think that he trusted her so much.

Flora, however, was astute enough to guess that Max could unburden himself to Nancy in a way that he could not to his family, especially his mother, and she was also wise enough not to ask her daughter awkward questions. She was just glad, for his sake, that Max had someone with whom he could share his worries. She also knew her daughter was strong enough to deal with whatever he told her.

In November, in a carefully worded letter that only Nancy would now understand because of what he'd written earlier, Max said, *Well, it looks as if the lads might soon get their wish.*

She sat on the side of her bed holding his letter. So they must have had orders for going to the Front. The days passed and she heard nothing more until there was a knock at their back door late one Thursday evening at the beginning of December.

'Now, who on earth can that be at this time?' Flora began to grumble and then stopped, her eyes widening fearfully. Someone at the door late at night could only mean one thing: bad news. Her fingers fluttered to her lips as she gazed at Bert with wide eyes. 'You – you go, Bert. I – I can't.'

'I'll go,' Nancy said quietly and got up before her father could rise from his chair.

She opened it to see the shape of a tall, broad man standing there. 'Max, oh Max. Whatever are you doing here? Come in, come in.'

He moved into the kitchen 'I'm sorry to call so late, Mrs Weston, but I only got home an hour ago and I have to go back tomorrow.'

Flora flung her arms around him and hugged him hard. She was so relieved to see him standing there, but still . . . she drew back and looked up into his face. 'Why are you here? Is – is there bad news?'

'No, not really. It's just that we were given orders for going abroad and then they were cancelled, so we've been given a short leave. Half the battalion today and tomorrow and the rest on the following two days. But I think we shall shortly be sent somewhere, though we don't know where yet. So I thought I'd come home, even if it is only for a flying visit. But I'll go. I'll see you in the morning . . .'

'No, no, sit down. Stay for a while now. Bert and Nancy will have to go to work tomorrow. They won't have a chance to see you. Besides, you should spend that time with your mother. What about Victor? Is he here too?'

'No, he's coming when I get back.'

They all sat with Max until almost midnight; even Agnes could not be persuaded to go to bed. They wanted to spend as long as possible with him. Max had been so much a part of their lives, not one of them could bear to let him go.

At last, Agnes stood up. 'Well, I'll really have to go to my bed though I am loath to say goodbye to you, Max. Come here, give an old lady a hug.'

Max obliged and then hugged Flora too and shook Bert's hand firmly. As Agnes went to her room and her parents went upstairs, Nancy met his gaze. Suddenly she felt tears prickle her eyes. Ever since this terrible war had started, she had remained strong and steadfastly supported the menfolk who had enlisted, but now at this moment of parting with the young man who had been her friend and protector for as long as she could remember, her resolve crumbled.

'Oh Max, I don't want you to go.'

He put his arms around her and held her close as she wept against his shoulder.

'Nancy, please don't cry,' he whispered. 'It'll be the undoing of me. And I have to go. You know I do.'

She lifted her head and looked up at him, but she did not pull away from the circle of his arms. 'Promise me you'll come back safely, won't you?'

'I'll do my very best. You can be sure of that.'

'And watch out for Victor,' she added, almost as an afterthought but the sentiment was keenly felt none the less. 'How are your mum and dad taking it?'

Max grimaced. 'Stoically, I think is the right word. Families are just as brave – if not more so, in a way – than us soldiers. We've got a job to do. All they can do is sit and wait.'

'And worry,' Nancy murmured.

'Now I must go and you must go to bed. You have to be up early in the morning, don't you?'

Nancy nodded. 'Yes, and I'm sorry, because I think by the time I get home after my shift, you'll have gone.'

For a moment, fresh tears welled in her eyes, but she brushed them away impatiently now. Tears were not what a soldier going to war wanted to see. She made a valiant effort and smiled through them.

'That's better.' Gently he kissed her forehead, gave her a final hug, turned and was through the door and into the night before she had realized he had gone. She stood a moment gazing at the closed door and then turned and went upstairs to bed.

When they met in the street as dawn filtered over the rooftops to cycle to work together, Nancy noticed that Jessie's eyes were as red as her own. Max was a huge figure in their lives and both their families would miss him dreadfully.

'Come on,' Nancy said, as she began to pedal harder. 'We've a job to do and we know just how much all these letters we deliver mean to folk.'

'Just so long as there are no telegrams today,' Jessie said, as she strove to keep up with her friend. 'I couldn't bear it. Not today.'

Victor arrived home the next evening. He too came across the road to see the Westons. He was as ebullient as ever. He picked Nancy up and swung her round. He was not quite as tall or as broad-shouldered as Max had become, but he was just as good-looking. In fact, as all the local girls agreed, all the Bonsor boys were a handsome lot.

'We don't reckon we're going to the Western Front,' he told them all as he sat at the kitchen table. It looked like being another late night for the Westons, but they didn't mind. They didn't want to feel a terrible guilt if any of the boys didn't come back. While they shied away from such pessimistic thoughts, the daily casualty lists told them a different story. Facts had to be faced.

'At least not yet,' Victor went on. 'There's a rumour going around the camp that a whole load of tropical kit has been delivered. Now, that doesn't sound like France in the depths of winter, does it?'

'No, it doesn't,' Bert said. 'I wonder where you can possibly be going.'

'Nobody's saying but I'm not going to grumble if it's somewhere nice and warm.'

As he left a little later, he kissed the women's cheeks and shook Bert's hand. Nancy saw him to the door.

He turned, looked down at her and said softly, 'Keep writing to old Max, won't you, Nancy? He loves to get your letters. His face lights up when there's one from you.'

'Of course, I will. I'll write every week. Now, you take care, Victor, and come home safely.'

'I'll do my best,' he said, echoing his brother's words.

On the same day, which also happened to be the shortest day of the year, that Max and Victor left Britain on a ship bound for warmer climes, Nancy was thankful to have the whistle nestling in her pocket. The morning was dark and cold and as she came to the last house on her route, there was a figure loitering in the shadows. She popped the letters through the letterbox but when she turned round, she saw that the man had moved and was now barring her way back down the short path and out of the gate.

Nancy stood her ground, her fingers touching the whistle in her pocket and hoping that perhaps the man who lived in the house behind her would emerge on his way to work. But the door remained obstinately shut and no light appeared in any of the windows. Then she remembered; the letters she delivered to this address were only ever to a Miss Brown. There was no one else living here.

'We meet at last,' the man still standing in front of her said softly.

Nancy's fingers were trembling now, but she still gripped the whistle firmly. In a voice as steady as she could muster, she said, 'Let me pass.'

'There's no need to be so snappy. It's high time we were introduced.' There was a pause while neither of them spoke. 'So,' he said slowly at last, 'you're the next little trollop in the family to have a bastard, a'yer?'

Even in the half-light of early morning, Nancy felt the colour flood her face. She had guessed there would have been gossip in their own street, but how did a complete stranger, living some distance away, know about her? She didn't answer him; she didn't know what to say.

His humourless laugh came out of the darkness. 'You don't know who I am, do you?'

'No, I don't, so let me pass,' she said again, tightening her grip on the whistle. She was about to draw it from her pocket, when he said harshly, 'I'm your grandfather. I live on this street and I've been watching you delivering the post. It took me a while to realize who you were but I knew you reminded me of someone. You're very like your aunt and it seems not only in looks. I made it my business to find out what had been happening. Trying to pass your little bastard off as your mother's? D'you really expect folk to swallow that?'

Nancy lifted her head higher. She was no longer afraid. 'You're a fine one to talk. I know how you treated my grandma, even setting fire to her house after you'd run off with your floozy.'

'Now, that's slander, that is,' he said, stepping closer and wagging his finger in her face.

Nancy grinned. 'I don't think so when you've been in prison for it and I notice you're not denying it, either. So, *Grandad*, are you going to let me pass or do I have to bring my self-defence training into use?'

For a brief moment, he seemed unsure, then he laughed. 'Think a slip of a girl like you could tackle a man?'

Although he could not see her, Nancy's eyes narrowed. 'Would you like to give it a try – *Grandad*?'

'Feisty piece, aren't you?' Patrick sneered, but there was grudging admiration in his tone. He liked a woman with a bit of spirit. Edith had always been quiet and whatever spark she might have had in the early days of their marriage, he had destroyed it soon enough. After years of her kow-towing to him, he had become bored of her and had begun his affair with Lily. When the light of his life – Mary Ellen – had gone, there was nothing at home for him to stay for and so, he had left. Life with Lily was tempestuous, but it was exciting. There was never a dull moment with Lily. Now it was he who was frightened she would leave him or turn him out. It was she who rented the house they lived in. It was her name on the rent book, not his. But she had stood by him through his trouble with the law and they were still together.

The morning was growing lighter as he held Nancy there. He didn't touch her, but he still barred her escape. Now up close he could see that she resembled Mary Ellen even more than he had thought. And in turn, Nancy too reminded him of his beloved mother.

With a sigh, he capitulated. 'Look, I don't want to fall out with you, lass. I'm heartsore that you got yourself in the family way . . .'

'Robbie is my little brother,' Nancy said, with such conviction that Patrick almost believed her.

'Aye, well, if that's the way you want to play it . . .'

'It's the way it is,' she said with such firmness that brooked no further argument. To her surprise, he moved aside. 'I'll let you go, but I'll see you again.'

Nancy marched past him, her head held high. When she reached the street and he was no longer a threat, she turned back to say pertly, 'Not if I see you first. Bye, *Grandad.*'

She walked quickly away, breathing more easily with every step she took. But her hand was still on the whistle in her pocket.

'You'll never guess who I bumped into today,' Nancy said as the family sat around the tea table. There was one good thing about starting work early in the day; it gave her a chance to get home and help her mother and grandmother get the tea ready for when Bert came home. And it was a nice family time when they sat together telling one another about their day. And best of all, little Robbie was now able to sit in his high chair alongside them.

'Oh, who was that, love?' Flora said, piling mashed potato onto Bert's plate.

'Your father, Mam.'

The spoon clattered onto his plate, scattering potato in all directions. Flora turned wide, fearful eyes on her daughter. 'Oh Nancy, no.'

Calmly, Bert scraped up the mess and took the tureen from his wife's shaking hands. 'Sit down, love, while she tells us what happened.'

'Did he – did he . . .?' Flora couldn't go on. While she had stood up to him in defence of her sister all those years ago, she had no wish to see him back in their lives; lives which she and Bert had fought so hard to protect. She was also fearful for her mother. Would he try to hurt her again?

'He didn't touch me, Mam, I promise you, but he did trap me in someone's tiny front garden so I was forced to speak to him.' She shrugged. 'In a way, I was glad it was him. If it had been a stranger – well . . .' She said no more, but they all understood.

'Did you know who he was?' Bert asked.

Nancy shook her head. 'Not at first. It was still hardly light and I wouldn't have known him anyway until he told me who he was.'

'How – how did he know you?'

'He said he'd seen me early one morning and realized that I reminded him of Mary Ellen. So he asked around and found out who I was.'

Flora sighed. 'Yes, I can see why. You're very like her.'

Nancy bit her lip. 'He also said he knew that I'd followed in her footsteps in another way too.'

Flora gasped. 'He – he knows?'

'I denied it, of course, but I don't think he believed me.'

'How did he find you?' Bert asked.

'Evidently, I've been delivering in the street where he now lives. He said he'd been watching me for a while.'

'You'll have to leave – give it up . . .' Flora began.

'Mam, there is no way he's going to frighten me

into giving up a job I really like. Well, most of the time I love it, except when I have to deliver sad telegrams.' She sighed. 'But even that has to be done.'

'Oh Bert, what . . .?'

Bert put his hand over Flora's. 'Don't worry, love. I don't think for a minute he'll hurt her. And she's got her whistle.'

Nancy chuckled. 'Yes, he never saw it – I didn't need to use it – but I had my hand on it in my pocket the whole time I was talking to him.' She laughed louder now. 'And I told him I've been learning self-defence.'

'And have you?'

'A bit, yes. All the postwomen got together and decided we should go once a week to a chap who's willing to teach us. That's where me and Jessie have been going every Friday evening.'

'That's a really good idea, love,' Bert said. 'I'm glad – and relieved – to hear it.'

'And I thought you were going to the cinema,' Agnes put in quietly. She turned to face her granddaughter. 'I'm proud of you, lass.'

Nancy turned pink with delight. After all the trouble she had brought on her family, her grandmother could still say that she was proud of her.

Thirty-eight

'They've completed the withdrawal from Gallipoli, then,' Bert said, as he showed Howard the piece in the newspaper just before Christmas. 'There've been huge losses there so I expect everyone was relieved to hear they're leaving, but it's so sad that it will no doubt go down in history as a failure for us.'

'Sensible, though, to withdraw and not to continue with further loss of life, I'd have said.'

'True, and they'll be needed elsewhere, if what this piece says is right. Another big attack is expected from the Germans who are trying to get to Calais.'

That same week, Nancy had received two letters from Max. In the last one, he wrote:

You may not hear from me for a couple of weeks or so as we'll be travelling. Sorry I can't be more specific than that but you know how it is. I will still write every week and post them to you when we get there, though how long letters will take to reach you, I can't guess.

Nancy knew they were going to somewhere hot and neither Max nor Victor had been on a ship before. She wondered if they would be good sailors and how they would deal with the very different climate. She wrote every week, hoping that Max would receive her letters eventually, most likely all in one bundle.

The Westons were to spend Christmas at home this year. Mary Ellen had written to say that although they would love the family to come again, Mr Clarke was very ill and was having to be nursed round the clock.

I don't know what we'd do without Mrs Beckett's help. She is a Godsend.

So Flora and Agnes invited the depleted Bonsor family to spend Christmas Day with them.

'Then you must all come to us on Boxing Day,' Evelyn insisted. 'It'll be very different, but we'll just have to make the best of it.'

At the beginning of January, 1916, both families received three letters from Max all at the same time though written on different days. Evelyn also had a short one from Victor, who was the first to admit that he was 'no letter writer'.

'He's like Lee in that,' Evelyn said. 'Thank goodness for Max. He writes such long newsy letters.'

In the letter to Nancy, which had the earliest date, he put:

We had quite a good Christmas considering we are away from all those we love. We had a church service on deck but not much else as we were passing through a dangerous area. However, we celebrated properly a day or so later with a concert. This voyage is a bit odd

*at times – we seem to keep going over the
same area – but we are not allowed to ask
questions, of course . . .*

In his next letter, dated 29 December, Max wrote:

*I have no idea when you'll receive this but
we've stopped at an island and although none
of us except the big wigs are allowed ashore,
the locals row out in small boats to sell things
to us. We even got some English newspapers.
The trip's not too bad though several of us
(including me and Victor) suffered seasickness
at the start during some nasty storms. When
it's calmer, it's quite enjoyable, though there
are still parades and drills on deck. We don't
seem to be able to get out of that! The food is
quite good (better than at . . .)*

Here the word had been heavily scored out by the
censor, but Nancy guessed he'd put Redmires.

*. . . It's much warmer now. The weather is
calmer and we are able to play sports on deck,
though I am guessing it will get much hotter
very soon. We should be arriving in port in a
couple of days' time so I will post my letters
then . . .*

'Dad, I'm pretty sure I know where they've gone.
When Max was home, we worked out a code, hoping
it would get past the censor. He said he'd write a

sentence where each word began with the letter of the place they were. And read on, look, he's written "Every girl you pick to", so I think it's Egypt.'

Bert frowned. 'But that sentence doesn't make any sense. Surely the censor would have questioned it.'

'No, no, you don't understand. It's buried within a paragraph. He was saying that a lot of the lads, who haven't got girlfriends back home, would like to have someone to exchange letters with. We'd arranged that the word that would tell me he was starting the coded sentence would be *so*. I was then to write out the first letter of the words that followed until I had a place name. Other words would perhaps follow to make a proper sentence, but they don't matter. I could ignore them.'

'Ah,' Bert said now. 'Actually, I think you could be right because rumours at work think they've gone to protect the Suez Canal. In that case, I'm guessing they'll be based at somewhere like Port Said.'

Nancy frowned. 'But why? Why is the canal important?'

'Because it allows British communications with East Africa, India and Asia. Otherwise, ships would have to travel all the way around Africa. Have a look at your old school atlas and you'll probably understand then.'

In the middle of January, Max wrote:

I received four of your letters together and some from Mother and Jessie too. What's this I hear from Jessie about a man stopping you on your postal round?

340

Nancy grimaced when she read his words so she wrote back at once to reassure him: *It was a bit scary at first, I must admit, but it turned out to be my grandfather.*

She went on to tell him how Patrick had watched her delivering letters on the street where he lived and had worked out who she was. She was always truthful with Max, so she told him too how Patrick seemed to know that Robbie was hers and not Flora's. To her surprise, Max's reply was philosophical.

Never mind about that. The little feller's part of the family now. Mine as well as yours. By the way, did you get the Christmas presents I left with Mam for you and your family?

Letters arrived irregularly from Lee but only to ask how Robbie was. He didn't write to his family very often either, much to Evelyn's disgust.

'You'd think he'd be able to write to us a bit more often, wouldn't you?' she'd say to Flora and Agnes as they sat over their elevenses. 'Max writes every week without fail and even Victor about once a fortnight. Have done ever since they left home.'

Flora would sigh. 'Trouble is, you never know where Lee is. Being a sailor, he'll be moving on all the time and at sea most of the time, won't he?' She would glance at Evelyn to see if she was in the mood to take a joke. Then she'd chuckle. 'But then, you never did know where he was, even when he was a nipper.'

At that, Evelyn would smile wryly and, not for the

first time, was thankful that, after all the trouble between the two families, they could still joke and laugh together.

'Just be thankful that the other two do let you know how they are at the moment. They might not always be able to tell you exactly *where* they are, but most of the time we can have a good guess. At least Nancy, Bert and Howard seem to be able to. Despite Lee having been the first to go through real danger, I reckon he's safer at sea than those two are going to be when they eventually get to where the real fighting is and they're bound to be sent there sooner or later.'

Evelyn had shuddered. 'I know. And you're right. Let's just hope they stay in Egypt as long as possible.'

Since Max and Victor had sailed to a distant country and they were all sure that Lee was somewhere out at sea, Nancy crossed the road to visit the Bonsor family more frequently, often taking Robbie with her. After all, he was Evelyn's grandson too. Jessie and she not only still worked together, they were still the best of friends. When Jessie wasn't seeing Andrew, the two young women spent their leisure time together, though there didn't seem to be much of that these days.

The day came, inevitably, when a tearful Jessie opened the door to Nancy's knock. 'I haven't brought Robbie today,' Nancy began, 'He's asleep – Oh, Jessie, whatever's the matter?' Her heart felt as if it had skipped a beat and then began to hammer. 'Is it . . .? Have you had bad news?'

'No, no, nothing like that. It's Andrew. He's finally made up his mind. He's going.'

'Joined up, you mean?'

Jessie nodded and rested her face against her friend's shoulder. Nancy put her arms around her.

'Oh Nancy, I do love him and I'll miss him so much. And if – if anything happens to him, I don't know what I'll do.'

'We all have to be brave,' Nancy murmured. 'Just think how your mam must feel. Three of her boys are going to be in the fighting, if they aren't already.'

'I know. She's so strong,' Jessie said through her tears. 'I don't know how she's coping with it all.'

Nancy was thoughtful for a moment before saying, 'I thought you and Andrew were hoping to get married before he had to go?'

Jessie nodded. 'My mam and dad have agreed, but his mam won't.'

'Ah. I see.' Nancy paused and then asked, 'Why?'

Jessie shrugged. 'I'm not sure she likes me all that much.'

'Oh Jessie, I'm sure that can't be true.'

Jessie sighed and drew back, wiping the tears from her face and trying to be brave. 'I have to admit, though I wouldn't say it to anyone else and certainly not to my family, but I trust you, Nancy.' She bit her lip before bursting out, 'He's a bit of a mummy's boy.'

'Really? Well, I wouldn't have guessed. But if he's joined up – she can't be happy about that.'

'She isn't. She threw one of her fits.'

'She has fits?'

Jessie smiled wryly. 'In a child, you'd call it a temper tantrum.'

'Oh my!' Nancy had never come across anything like that in a grown woman. 'Is there – I mean, has he got a father?'

'He left years ago, when Andrew was small.'

'That's hard for her, then. I've heard how it was for my grandma when her husband left her, though in her case I think she's been a lot happier since he went.'

'Have you seen your grandfather again?'

'Occasionally, but he's not causing me any trouble. I've told Mam and Dad all about it but not my grandma. I haven't said anything to her.'

'How is she, by the way?'

'The happiest she's ever been, my mam says. She and Miss Kendall are busier than ever. They're making bespoke uniforms for officers now.' Nancy paused and then added, 'But to get back to what you were saying about Andrew and his mother. Did she try to stop him going?'

'Oh yes. She even went to the recruiting centre where he'd volunteered to try to persuade them to rescind his enlistment. But of course, there was no chance of that.'

'Has he got into the City Battalion?'

Jessie shook her head. 'No, he joined the Sherwood Foresters. He went all the way to Newark, hoping his mother wouldn't find out. But she did. Heaven knows how.'

'Has he gone yet?'

'No, he's leaving next week, I think.'

'He won't get sent overseas yet, Jessie,' Nancy tried to comfort her. 'Look how long it's taken Max and Victor to be trained.'

'There is that, Nancy. You're right. Maybe it will all be over before Andrew has to go abroad.'

One morning in late January, Evelyn sat down heavily on the chair in Flora's kitchen.

'I've given three of my lads already to this nonsense,' she said flatly, 'And now another one's determined to go.'

Flora stared at her, open-mouthed. 'Not Warren, surely? He's far too young.'

'He's seventeen. He'll be eighteen this August.'

'Oh my, so he is. With all this nonsense going on, I've lost track of how time is passing. I can't believe that little Robbie will be two next month.'

'The war's been going on almost eighteen months now. You forget, don't you? You just sort of – sort of deal with each day as it comes. Pray that a telegram doesn't arrive. Pray that their names don't appear in the casualty lists. I'm so tired of it all, Flora, I don't mind admitting to you. And now this.' Evelyn seemed defeated. It wasn't like her, but Flora understood. It was their children's generation which was having to deal with this war and there was nothing they – their parents – could do to prevent it.

'Have the City Battalion accepted him?'

Evelyn shook her head. 'He's not got the right job, working in the factory. The city's for white-collar workers. That's why Max and Victor got in, but Warren's so determined to go, I think he'll join the

Barnsley Pals or the Accrington Pals or even the Sherwoods, like Andrew.'

'Yes, Nancy told me about Jessie's young man,' Flora said, setting a hot cup of strong, sweetened tea in front of her friend. 'Maybe they'll be more thorough about age.'

Evelyn sighed. 'I doubt it.' She paused and then added quietly, 'And then there's Stanley.'

'Oh now, you can't be worried about him, Evelyn, surely. He's only fifteen.'

'If the war goes on for another year or two, which Howard thinks it will, then Stanley will go too.'

To that, even Flora had no answer.

Thirty-nine

Early in 1916, letters began to arrive from Max regularly again. He still couldn't say exactly where they were, but Nancy knew they were not near the main fighting. But even in an area like the Suez Canal, a place that needed protection because of the war, Max and Victor might still be in danger.

At the end of January, she wrote to Max:

You'll be pleased to know that there's no more need for the Order of the White Feather brigade; conscription has been brought in for unmarried men between the ages of eighteen and forty-one. Has your mother told you that Warren is itching to enlist and, of course, by August this year, he will be old enough? Thank goodness Stanley is only fifteen.

But Max was not so optimistic about his youngest brother. *Stanley will be sixteen later this year,* he wrote back, *and he will not want to be the only one left at home. He's a big lad like all us Bonsor boys. They'd take him like a shot, believe me.*

As they cycled home together one cold February

347

day, Nancy said, 'Jessie, what's happening with Warren now?'

'He's being very secretive. Mam's worried to death about him and worse still, Stanley is catching on. You know he's always idolized all his older brothers, especially Max. He's always looked up to him and, given half a chance, would copy anything he does. And now that the one nearest to him in age is almost old enough to go, well, I just don't know what Stanley might do. I know he's not old enough yet but he's . . .' She paused for a moment, anxious not to hurt her dear friend, but decided the best way was to carry on normally. 'He's very like Lee in a lot of ways. He's a little rascal. If Warren does go, then Stanley will likely run away and join up and once he's done that . . .'

Jessie needed to say no more; Nancy knew exactly what she meant. There was nothing that could be done. Andrew's mother had proved that. Once someone had signed up – and, it seemed, whatever their age – it was a done deed.

They cycled in silence for a while until Jessie said in a small voice, 'I had to deliver two telegrams today and one of the women opened hers before I got away. She came rushing out of her house to meet me. It was almost as if she knew. It must have been bad news, because she fell to her knees in the road and began to wail. I didn't know what to do, Nancy, but luckily two of her neighbours came out, helped her up and took her inside. It was awful. If my poor mam ever gets a telegram like that . . .'

'I'm just so glad we don't deliver in our own street.'

'One of the other postwomen told me that she thinks our supervisor organizes the rounds on purpose so that no one delivers to their own neighbours.'

'You know, that's very thoughtful of him. By the way, have you heard from Andrew?'

'Yes, he writes every week – just like Max does.'

'Do you know where he is?'

Jessie shook her head. 'No, he's not allowed to say. I keep trying to find out where the Sherwoods are, but it's not easy.'

'What about his mother? Have you been to see her?'

Jessie gave an unladylike snort. 'I went round once but she more or less showed me the door. She blames me for him going.'

'Why on earth is she doing that?'

Jessie shrugged. 'I think she thinks I was one of these girlfriends who told their young man to volunteer to prove they weren't cowards. Do you remember the poster early in the war of two women and a little boy watching soldiers marching off?'

'I do. The one that said "Women of Britain say – GO!"?'

'Yes, that one. Well, she thinks that's what I did. But I didn't, Nancy. In fact –' Jessie bit her lip as if she was reluctant to admit such a thing. 'I – I tried to stop him.'

'I don't blame you,' Nancy said firmly. 'I'd have stopped M . . .' – she cleared her throat and altered what she had been going to say – 'your brothers going, if I could have done.'

'I know you would,' Jessie whispered. 'And so would I.'

As they turned into the end of the street where they both lived, Jessie said, 'Dad will bring the newspaper across tonight. He does the rounds of the neighbours while it's too cold and wet to gather in the street.' She gave a wide yawn. 'I won't come with him. I'm so tired, Nancy. I'll be having an early night. I'll see you at the crack of dawn tomorrow.'

Nancy laughed and pedalled towards her own home, calling back over her shoulder, 'Cheer up, Jessie. It'll be March next week. Spring's almost here.'

Jessie's voice echoed back to her, 'Can't come soon enough for me.'

Nancy could understand Jessie's longing for warmer weather; their early morning rounds in the bitter cold had given them both painful chilblains, but what her dear friend had perhaps not thought about was that with the better weather throughout Europe, the war would escalate again. No doubt somewhere in darkened underground rooms politicians and war chiefs on both sides were already plotting offensives that would cost thousands of lives and probably for little gain for anyone.

And still they were demanding more men to go to war, even young men who were no more than boys; boys like Warren Bonsor and his younger brother, Stanley.

Howard arrived at the Westons' home after tea. Almost before he had sat down, he said, 'I don't like the look of what's happening on the Western Front, Bert.' He passed the newspaper across the hearth.

'There's a piece in here about the Germans launching

an offensive against the French front line to the north of a place called Verdun, wherever that is.'

Bert reached up to a shelf at the side of his chair. 'Let's have a look at the map. I bought this so we can follow where the lads might be.'

'Our lads aren't there yet, though, are they? In France, I mean. Not from what Max is hinting in his letters. I think they're still in Egypt.'

'True. Nancy says much the same, but think on, Howard, if these offensives continue, they'll likely be sent to the Front sooner rather than later.'

Howard sighed and murmured, 'That's what I'm afraid of.'

The two men pored over the map.

'This is really interesting, Bert. We never did much geography at school. At least, not about other countries. I've heard the names, of course, but I didn't know where they were.'

'I know what you mean, but just look at this, Howard. Look how big Germany is. What on earth do they want to invade other countries for? Why can't we all live in peace, that's what I'd like to know?'

'Wouldn't we all?' Howard said wryly.

'There's Verdun,' Bert said jabbing at the map. 'North-east France.'

'It's not really near the border with Germany though, is it? Does that mean the Germans have got that far into France?'

'It must do.'

'D'you think our lads will get sent there?' Howard asked worriedly.

'I expect they could be sent anywhere where rein-forcements are needed.'

Over the coming days and weeks, the two men followed the news avidly, still thankful that, as far as they knew, their two army lads were not involved. But then came the news that the two families had dreaded. Max wrote to both his own family and Nancy with similar news.

We are leaving where we've been since New Year and if you remember what I said when I was last on leave, well, I think the lads are getting their wish at last. But let me tell you straight away that we're not going to where the biggest battle is taking place at the moment, so do try not to worry.

So, Nancy thought, he's not going to Verdun. Thank goodness for that. In his letter to her, he added:

Jessie wrote to me last week and said how she hated delivering the telegrams. I expect that's the worst part of your job as they usually contain some sort of bad news. I hope you haven't had any more frights on your early morning rounds. Have you seen him again?

Nancy had not seen Patrick since that time, but iron-ically, the day after she received Max's letter, her grandfather waylaid her in the street again. Now the early mornings were a little lighter, she recognized him straight away but she was no longer afraid. There were other early morning risers in the street, either going to work or returning home after a night shift. And, besides, she still had the whistle in her pocket.

'Hello, there,' Patrick said affably. 'I was hoping I'd see you again.'

'Really,' Nancy said. 'I don't think we have very much to say to one another, do you?'

'Aw now, don't be like that. I just wanted to ask about your grandma? Is she all right?'

Nancy gave a short, humourless laugh. 'Oh, has the famous Lily turned you out and you're looking for a way back? Well, let me tell you here and now, there isn't one, so don't even think about it.'

'Nah, me and Lil are fine and dandy.' He paused and then blurted out, 'How's your aunty, Mary Ellen? Is she all right?'

'Why would you want to know that? You turned her out when she most needed help. You didn't care what happened to her then, so why would you want to know now?'

Patrick glowered at her. 'Where's your grandma living? I'd like to see her – tell her I'm sorry . . .'

Nancy laughed aloud, the sound echoing down the street. 'You really expect me to believe you after everything you did? Well, I don't. And as for where she's living? Timbuctoo, if she's any sense. Now, if you'll excuse me, I've more letters to deliver.'

As she made to stride past him, Patrick caught her arm in a vice-like grip. 'Clever little madam, aren't you? Well, you ain't seen the last of me, not by a long chalk. So don't think you have. And the Bonsor boys are no longer around to come running to your rescue.'

Nancy twisted her arm out of his grasp and thrust her face close to his. 'You don't frighten me, mister, so stay out of my way.' With that parting shot, she marched away, but when she turned the corner out of his sight, she leaned against the nearest wall for a few moments. Despite her bravado, she was trembling from head to foot.

When she had calmed down and carried on with her deliveries, she realized that the words that had upset her the most were not about her grandmother or her aunt, but he had reminded her, brutally, that Max, her friend and protector, was no longer here.

When she arrived home later that day, Flora, perceptive as always, asked, 'You all right, Nancy love?'

'I think so, Mam, but I ran into Grandad again this morning and – and he wasn't very nice.'

'He didn't hurt you, did he?'

'He grabbed my arm, that's all, but it was more what he said than what he did that has – disturbed me.'

She related all that had passed between her and Patrick.

'We'll tell your dad and Uncle Howard tonight. Howard will be across for their nightly chat about the war. Anyone would think the pair of them were directing its progress,' she added fondly.

'I only wish they were,' Agnes, who had been listening to their conversation, said. 'It'd soon be over if we had chaps like Bert and Howard in charge.

Now, about Patrick Halliday. We'll tell Bert and Howard, like your mam says, but do you think we should tell the police? He has no right to accost a young woman in the street, let alone someone who is going about her work for His Majesty's Royal Mail. But he's right about one thing,' she added with a chuckle.

Nancy and Flora glanced at each other, mystified. 'What's that, Gran?'

'If the Bonsor boys *were* still here, Max would be out patrolling the streets with you to make sure you were safe.'

The thought made tears spring to Nancy's eyes, but all Flora said was, 'We'll see what Bert and Howard think.'

As they had expected, Bert and Howard were horrified to think that Patrick Halliday was still bothering Nancy.

'Have a word with your supervisor. He's a decent chap. He might change your routes,' Bert suggested.

'We could suggest that Jessie swaps with Nancy. Patrick's no reason to –'

'No, I don't want that, Uncle Howard. He knows Jessie – knows she's a Bonsor. And I don't want the supervisor to think I'm not up to the job. We're still having self-defence lessons,' she added grimly, 'and I'll use it if I have to.' Then she grinned. 'Besides, Dad, don't forget I always carry the whistle Uncle Howard gave us both and I certainly wouldn't hesitate to use mine. There are a lot of fellers on their way to work or home when I'm delivering. I'm sure several would come running. And, if it makes you feel better, I've got to know one or two of the coppers whose beat is on my round. I'm sure they'd answer the sound of a whistle.'

'We'll let it rest for now,' Bert decided, 'but if he turns up again, I'll have a word with him myself.'

'What does still worry me, though,' Nancy said slowly, 'is why he was asking where Grandma is living. Why, after all these years, does he want to know that?'

Flora gave a very unladylike snort. 'Whatever the reason, he'll be up to no good. I'd better see her and warn her.'

'Just mind you're not followed. I wouldn't put anything past that bastard.'

Bert rarely resorted to bad language and so his use of it only accentuated his anxiety.

'It's good of you to come, Flora. It's always lovely to see you,' Edith said the following afternoon. 'But please don't worry about me. Seffie has such good neighbours on both sides – big burly men who actually quite enjoy a bit of fisticuffs if given an excuse. They're both ex boxers who used to do bare-knuckle fighting in their younger days. Patrick would be no match for either of them, I promise you.' She leaned closer and lowered her voice. 'I think Harry who lives next door that way' – she indicated to the left with her thumb – 'is a bit sweet on Seffie. He'd do anything for her and we're very safety conscious ever since we had that bit of trouble with your father years ago. There's enough locks and bolts on our doors to keep the army out. Now, tell me how everyone is and when are you bringing my great-grandson to see me again?'

They spent a very pleasant afternoon, chatting about the family and Flora left promising that Bert would take them both to see Mary Ellen as soon as he could. They'd both recently received a letter from her telling them that Mr Clarke had sadly passed away.

It was what they call 'a happy release', Mary Ellen had written. *He was suffering so much that none of us could wish it to go on any longer. My mother-in-law is very strong and though we shall all miss him, Jack and I will try to follow her example. The one good thing is that all the village folk have rallied round to help us on the farm and, in turn, we are able to help them with the food shortages.*

Forty

In May, Bert said, 'Howard, did you see in the paper that they're planning to extend conscription to include married men?'

'Aye, I did see it. But we're both too old, aren't we?'

Bert laughed. 'We are and until this moment I've never been happy about growing old, but I'm thanking my lucky stars now.'

'You're not tempted to volunteer, then?'

Bert shook his head. 'No, I'm not and, to be honest with you, I'm not even bothered if anyone thinks I'm a coward.'

'I know you're not that,' Howard declared stoutly. 'Besides, we're giving quite enough of our fine young men without decimating the older generation too. Someone's got to keep things running back home.'

'Aye, well, let's face it, the women of this country aren't doing a bad job now, are they? Our daughters included.'

'You're right. The country would have ground to a halt by now if they and many more like them hadn't stepped up. I reckon Mrs Pankhurst's lot will have earned the right to vote once this is all over.'

There was silence between them for a moment

before Howard said, 'So where do you think my lads are, then?'

'I'm only guessing, of course, but from what Max has said in his letters to you and to Nancy, I don't think they've gone to Verdun . . .'

'That's the French's battle, isn't it?'

'Primarily, yes.' Bert nodded. 'But the allies have to support them.'

'So what's your guess?'

'I reckon the Brits are going to start something else to take the focus away from Verdun.'

'Reading between the lines, it sounds as if Verdun is a bloodbath. You think we'll start something to draw the enemy away from there?'

'It's what I'd do if I was in command of the British Army,' Bert said. 'Somehow the French have got to be helped. It would be foolish for us just to send more and more troops to the same area. We need to start something somewhere else to weaken the German focus on Verdun. Force them to divert their troops.'

Both Howard and Bert were intelligent, deep-thinking men. They might not have had the chance of a higher academic education after the elementary schooling they'd both received, but they were blessed with common sense in abundance.

Howard sighed heavily. 'I know, you're right, but I can't help thinking that if they do that, my lads will more than likely be in the thick of it.'

'I'm afraid I have to agree,' Bert said sadly.

'I've got a bit of news,' Howard said on another visit to see Bert. Now that the weather was improving, the evening gatherings among the neighbours in the street had resumed, but if the weather was bad, Howard and Bert still visited each other. 'The son of one of the chaps at work has been sent home injured. He's in hospital down south, but Bob and his missus went to see him at the weekend. He'll be all right, they say, but it looks like the end of the war for him. He might have to have his left leg amputated.'

'Poor lad,' Bert murmured.

'He's in good hands, his father said, so they're hopeful. But his son was able to tell them things that don't appear in the newspapers. He was with the Sheffield City Battalion and they were in Egypt guarding the Suez Canal, as we guessed, but they've been in France for some time now and they've taken over a stretch of the front line opposite a village called Serre. They're at a place called Colincamps.'

'Let's have a look at the map,' Bert said, eagerly. Perhaps now they might know where Max and Victor really were.

He spread the map on the table and they both bent over it.

'There,' Bert jabbed his finger on the map, 'there it is. There's Serre and Colincamps is to the west. It's near the northern end of the River Somme, by the look of it.'

'Look, Ypres in Belgium isn't that far away either,' Howard said quietly. 'There's already been two big battles there. We've read about them in the papers, haven't we?'

Howard grimaced. 'Yes, I remember. So it looks like our lads are really going to be involved, Bert. What shall we tell the women?'

'The truth, Howard. There's no point in hiding anything . . .'

'And just what were you thinking of hiding, Dad?'

'Oh Nancy, love. I didn't hear you come in.'

'No, you and Uncle Howard are too busy with your heads bent over that map. So, come on, what have you found out?'

The two men glanced at each other and then, with a sigh, Howard repeated what he'd heard from the wounded soldier's father.

Nancy nodded. 'From Max's most recent letter, I gleaned that they had moved and that they were heading for where the action is. It was bound to happen sooner or later.' Her fingers touched the name of the place where Howard believed his sons might be. It was fanciful, she knew, and Nancy wasn't usually given to flights of fancy. She was a down-to-earth practical girl, but in that brief moment she imagined she could touch Max with her silent prayers.

Aloud, all she said was, 'Don't keep anything from us. We can handle the truth. All of us. It's the not knowing that's the hardest to bear.'

'We won't, Nancy,' Howard promised.

It was only two days after this conversation between her father and Howard, that Nancy received a letter from Max.

Margaret Dickinson

*I can tell you this, but I don't want to worry
Mam and Dad. We're on the move and going
to the Front. I can't tell you where, of course,
but if you're following the progress of the war,
you might have a good idea. We don't spend
the whole time in the Front trenches. There's a
sort of rotation; a few days at the very front,
then a few days in the support trenches and
then perhaps in the communication trenches
and then right back behind the lines for rest.
So it's not as bad as you might think.*

She wrote back at once, asking him to tell her more
about life in the trenches, exhorting him to take care
of himself and ending her letter as she always did,
Please write back as soon as you can . . .

But it was several days before Max's reply reached
her and as she read it, she understood why.

*We have been in the front line and, of course,
the time we do have to spend in the trenches
is pretty dismal. Apart from the constant
danger from snipers and shelling, and, when
it's raining, the mud we have to contend with,
the rats (cheeky little beggars that even snuggle
up to you under your armpits when you're
asleep) and the never-ending company of lice
which are the very devil to get rid of, it's actually not that bad. Unless there's some action
(which common sense tells me we shouldn't
really wish for) life is pretty boring actually,
though I'm sure no one back home would*

believe that. The days consist of 'stand to' half an hour before daylight just in case the Hun decides this is the morning he will launch an attack. The best part of this is that we get a rum ration. Then, half an hour after daylight, we stand down and have breakfast. After that we wash and clean our clothes as best we can and our weapons, which is probably more important than keeping ourselves clean! Dinner is at midday, after which is rest time when we can write letters or play card games. After tea, we stand to again half an hour before dusk until half an hour after dusk. Then we work all night with some periodic rests: patrols, digging, putting up barbed wire and fetching stores. The longer we stay in one position, the better the trenches become with dugouts to sleep in and better protection from their artillery. We even managed to get some planking for the floor of the trenches called 'duckboards'. Of course, as you can guess, this is the boring bit, but if the enemy, or our side, decides to have a 'party', then it's a whole different scenario.

Nancy wrote back at once and told him she found his letters very interesting and asking him to tell her more and especially what the food was like.

It's not too bad actually, Max wrote back in his next letter. *We get daily rations of meat, bread, vegetables, cheese, jam, tea, sugar and even, would you believe, rum and tobacco. But we all fall on the parcels from home like a pack of wolves though the good thing about being in the City Battalion is that everyone shares their parcels. So keep them coming, Nancy. Oh, and by the way, please can you ask your gran if she'd kindly knit me and Victor some more socks. The last lot she sent were a Godsend . . .*

The next day, when Nancy returned home after her postal round, she found Flora and Agnes sitting across the kitchen table from each other, just staring into the distance.

Nancy glanced between them, her heart missing a beat in fear. 'What is it? What's happened, because I can see there's something?'

Slowly, Flora turned her head. 'They've gone.'

Ironically, she knew there'd been a telegram that morning to someone in their street, because her colleague who was on this round had told her so. Now, Nancy feared the worst. She clutched at the back of the chair to steady herself and whispered huskily, 'Who? Who've gone? Not – not Max and Victor?'

'No, no, love,' Flora said, swiftly rousing herself as she saw her apathy was causing Nancy to jump to the wrong conclusion. 'Evelyn came across earlier. It's Warren and Stanley. They've both been to Barnsley and enlisted there. In the Barnsley Pals.'

Nancy sat down heavily in the nearest chair. 'Oh no, the stupid, stupid pair. I'll give 'em what for when I catch up with them. Have they no sense?' she railed. 'Can't they see the pain the others going have already caused their mam and dad?' She knew there was nothing that could be done to stop them. Not now, but she'd give them the sharp edge of her tongue when she saw them.

'They both hero-worship Max,' Agnes said. 'They'll do anything he does.'

'You can't blame Max,' Nancy said sharply. 'He'd've had to go eventually and, like he said, by volunteering he could go with the City Battalion. But Warren and Stanley, they're just being foolish and selfish.'

Agnes gave a huge sigh and levered herself up. 'Well, it's done now and there's nowt Evelyn or Howard can do about it, though I'm sure they'd love to try.'

'No, there isn't, but I'm going to have my say. In fact, I'll go across right now . . .'

'Oh Nancy,' Flora began, 'I don't think you should . . .' But Nancy had gone, flying out of the door and across the street.

She burst in the back door of the Bonsors' home without even bothering to knock. 'Where are they, Aunty Evelyn? I'll bang their silly heads together.'

Evelyn straightened up as she took a pie out of the oven and laid it on the kitchen table. Her face was creased with sadness and anxiety but there was also a look of calm resignation. 'Don't upset yourself, Nancy love. It was bound to happen sooner or later. Those two weren't going to stay safely at home while their three brothers got all the glory.'

'Mam and Gran are blaming Max. They say the boys worship him and will do whatever he does.'

Evelyn shrugged. 'They've got a point, I suppose, but it's not Max's fault. He'd have been called up by now even if he hadn't volunteered.' She paused and then said, 'Sit down, love, and have a cup of tea with me. I think we deserve one and Howard won't be in for his tea for half an hour or so. Now, tell me about your job? Are you enjoying it? Jessie certainly is, except when there's a telegram to deliver.'

'Yes, that's not good but it has to be done. We're also starting to see the casualties that have come back home because their injuries are too bad to allow them back into the fighting. We see some dreadful sights now. There's one poor guy living in one of the streets where I deliver – funnily enough the same one where my grandfather waits for me – well, I see this chap now and again. He shuffles along but all the time he's shaking from head to foot.'

'That sounds like what the papers are calling "shell shock". At least it's starting to be recognized as a proper diagnosis. At the very beginning of the war, rumour was that there were some soldiers shot at dawn because the officers thought it was cowardice.'

Nancy gaped at her open-mouthed. 'That's dreadful. There's no way that poor soldier I see is play acting. He's a poor, broken thing who'll probably never fully recover.'

'This war is a terrible business,' Evelyn murmured. She was silent for a few moments then, thinking back to what Nancy had just said. She added, 'Your mam told me about your grandad waylaying you now and again? You want to be careful with that one, Nancy.'

They chatted for half an hour until Nancy felt she should leave and let the family have their tea, so it wasn't until later in the evening that she caught up with the two miscreants. Fortunately for them, her temper had subsided a little by then, but she was still very angry with them.

'What on earth did you think you were doing? Isn't it bad enough for your mam and dad that three of their boys have already gone?'

The two boys looked shamefaced. They both loved Nancy – had done ever since they'd been little. They didn't like making her angry.

'We can't be the only ones not doing our bit, Nancy.'

'But you'd no need to go yet. Either of you. You've been very silly and I'm very cross with you.'

The two boys hung their heads.

'Oh, come here, the pair of you.' She pulled them to her and hugged them hard. 'Just make sure you both take care of yourselves and each other.'

'We will, Nancy. We promise. Besides, we won't be going yet. We've all that training to do first. It might all be over before we actually have to go.'

There was a catch in her voice as she said, ''Course it might.' But she knew better.

Forty-one

In June, just after Warren and Stanley had left home to go to training camp, Max wrote to Nancy:

Thanks for the newspaper cutting of the photo of you and all your postwomen colleagues. You all look very smart and I can pick out you and Jessie standing together in the back row. I especially like the hats – very fetching. There is an air of excitement and anticipation among the lads. We all feel that something big is being planned and we're sure we're to be a part of it. The shelling from our side has been going on for days and we're guessing it's an opening salvo for a big push . . .

It seemed that the censor had not bothered to cut anything from Max's letter; the sound of the bombardment along the Somme could be heard for miles. It was no secret. There was no letter from Max the following week or the week after that. And then, a few days later, early in July, Nancy, her family and the Bonsors read in the newspaper of the huge offensive along the River Somme.

Howard, and this time Evelyn and Jessie too, came

368

across the road to the Westons' house. It was easier this way because of little Robbie being in bed. Flora and Agnes bustled about getting drinks for everyone, but they were still listening to the conversation and didn't like what they were hearing.

'The seven-day bombardment from the Allies didn't work,' Howard said. 'The Germans had been in that position long enough to dig down so deep that our shells couldn't touch them and when, on the sound of the whistle, our lads went "over the top", as they call it, on 1 July, the Germans were ready for them. The allies were mown down in their thousands. It was carnage.'

Nancy's heart began to beat rapidly. 'Have you – have you heard from either Max or Victor?'

Howard shook his head. 'Not for over three weeks now.'

'Victor doesn't write very often,' Evelyn said, and her voice trembled, 'but Max writes as regular as clockwork. Every week.'

'Yes,' Nancy whispered, 'to me too and I haven't heard either.'

There was silence in the room as the family members glanced anxiously at one another.

The news, when it came at last, was not what they wanted to hear. Max wrote to both his parents and to Nancy at the same time.

I am heartbroken to have to tell you that we
have lost our dear Victor. You may already
have had a telegram and know the awful news.
It happened on the first day – 1 July – when

369

*our battalion suffered five hundred casualties,
killed, wounded or missing. It was a disaster
and those of us left have been taken out of the
line now. After the shelling and the gunfire
finally stopped, several of us went out into no
man's land, bringing in the wounded and
searching for relatives or friends. I was out
there all night looking for him and it wasn't
until dawn started to break and I was forced
to go back towards our trenches that I stum-
bled across him lying in a shell hole. There
was nothing I could do except carry him back.
I will see that he is buried properly. It will be
somewhere near where we are. Near . . .*

But whatever he had written had been heavily scored
out by the censor. Nancy held the paper up to the
light and was sure she could see that the word that
they had tried to obliterate was five letters and began
with an 'S'. So, she thought, perhaps her father and
Uncle Howard had been right in their assumption.
Their boys had been near a place called Serre at the
northern end of the Somme.

With tears flooding down her face, Flora put her
arms around Evelyn, who seemed, to everyone's
surprise, strangely calm.

'It was bound to happen,' she said, in a flat,
emotionless tone. 'You can't send five sons to war
and not expect to lose at least one of them.'

'Pray God there'll be no more,' Agnes said quietly.

'We must be prepared,' Evelyn went on, seeming
to be the bravest of them all. And yet they all knew

her heart must be breaking. 'Max is still out there and now Warren and Stanley will go very soon, especially if they've lost so many men. And as for Lee . . .'

'Have you heard from him lately?' Nancy asked.

Evelyn shook her head. 'But then I don't expect to. He's not good at writing and being at sea must make it difficult for the mail to get here.' She paused and then whispered, 'Poor Max. He's on his own out there now.'

No one reminded her that he was anything but 'on his own' but they knew what she meant. He had lost his beloved brother, who had been at his side since the day they had volunteered.

In the days following the beginning of the offensive on the Somme, pictures of Sheffield men who had been killed, wounded or had been posted as missing began to appear in the local press. The two families scoured the newspapers every day, searching, always searching, for a name or a face they knew and yet dreading to find it.

'That's Mrs Doughty's son,' Flora said, in the second week of August as she pointed at the picture in the evening paper of a young soldier. 'She helps her husband run a stall on the market. I see her almost every week when I go shopping. How awful. He's been killed.'

'That's the first time you've seen someone you know listed in the paper, isn't it, Mam?' Nancy said.

Flora nodded. 'But I know several telegrams have been received up and down the street.'

Nancy sighed. 'It's the same on my deliveries and

on Jessie's round too. There are more and more arriving every day now. And' – her voice shook as she added – 'and I haven't heard from Max again since he told us about Victor.'

'No,' Flora said sadly, 'Neither has Evelyn.'

At the end of August, Nancy said, 'Dad, there's a film been made of the battle of the Somme. It's being shown at the Coliseum. Me an' Jessie are going. Do you and Uncle Howard want to come?'

'I'll ask him, but it might be a bit raw for him.'

'Well, I'm certainly not going,' Flora said firmly. 'I might see someone I recognize and I don't want to.'

'That's why half the folk in the city *will* go, love. Just to see if they can spot someone they know.'

Flora shuddered. 'Well, you can ask Howard, but I don't think Evelyn will want to go.'

To everyone's surprise, Evelyn insisted on going to see the film. 'I want to see for myself what my boys are going through.'

'Don't try to stop her,' Howard said fondly. 'She's always had a mind of her own. You know that.'

'Then I will come too, to support her,' Flora declared. 'You'll be all right looking after Robbie for an evening, won't you, Ma? I'll get him ready for bed before we go.'

Robbie was a lively two-and-a-half-year-old now, with sandy-coloured hair and hazel eyes like his grandfather and a cheeky smile that melted everyone's heart.

'Of course. We'll be fine. Little chap's no trouble.'

'We'll go to the earliest showing so that we're not too late back. It starts just before seven.'

It was a harrowing experience for them all, indeed for everyone watching the flickering pictures. The Sheffield City Battalion was not featured and so no one in the pictures was recognized by those watching, but they could all imagine that in some parts of the country loved ones would have been seen.

They walked home in silence and congregated in the Westons' home.

'I'll make us a drink. Do you fellers want a beer?' Flora said, as she took off her hat and coat. When they were all seated in the kitchen, Agnes asked, 'Was it very terrible?'

'It wasn't good to watch, Ma,' Bert said. 'But I'm glad I've seen it. I don't know about the rest of you.'

They all agreed.

'They played stirring patriotic music to accompany the film but that didn't lessen the impact of the pictures.'

'Tell me about it?' Agnes asked.

So, in turn, they described what they had seen, each filling in the bits they could remember.

'Every so often there was a written piece to explain what we were going to see,' Bert explained to Agnes. 'It started by telling us that preparations were being made before the offensive began. Evidently, our side shelled the enemy lines for seven days solid, hoping to obliterate their trenches.'

'Just like Max said,' Nancy murmured.

'And then we saw platoons of soldiers moving up to the front line the evening before the attack,' Howard added. 'They'd got horses, motorcycles, and horse-and-carts, and I'm sure I saw some donkeys.

And then there were covered lorries delivering munitions to the dumps.'

'What I couldn't believe was the sight of the French peasants still working in the fields,' Nancy said, 'and yet they must have known a big battle was going to start any time. The night before it was due to start, a general addressed the troops, but it didn't tell us what he said.'

'And there was a church service that night too with a proper vicar in his white surplice,' Jessie said.

'I think they call them padres in the services,' Bert murmured.

'Did you see those huge round bombs they were firing from the trench mortars to smash the enemy barbed wire?' Howard said.

'Oh yes, the writing said they called them "plum puddings".'

'I couldn't believe it when they showed us the men eating a meal in camp the night before.'

'I noticed a lot of the men were smoking,' Flora said. 'We must be sure to send cigarettes in the next parcel.'

'They were laughing and joking as if they hadn't got a care in the world.' Nancy shook her head sadly. 'But probably the next day most of them would have been killed or wounded. It must have been awful at roll call the next day.'

'Maybe that's why they formed the pals' battalions, so that there'd be the camaraderie at such a time,' Agnes said. 'They'd all help each other.' Although she hadn't wanted to go to see the film – she'd been quite content to look after her great-grandson – she couldn't help wanting to hear about it all now. 'So what happened on the morning of the attack? Did they show that too?'

'It began at about seven-thirty,' Bert said. 'The whistle went and the soldiers climbed up and over the parapets of the trenches. They call it "going over the top".'

'One soldier didn't even make it out of the trench,' Nancy said quietly. 'He fell face downwards on the bank.'

'Like the papers said, the seven-day bombardment hadn't worked and our lads were just mown down,' Howard said. 'Some got as far as a shell hole in no man's land, but then came under heavy fire.'

Evelyn spoke for the first time. 'I expect it was a shell hole like that where Max found Victor that night.'

'There must have been some sort of – I don't know – understanding that both sides could go out at night to pick up the wounded.'

'Did you see them doing that?' Agnes asked.

Bert nodded. 'The stretcher bearers must have been overwhelmed.'

'But all those who hadn't been wounded – like Max – would join in, looking for their friends and helping to carry the casualties back, wouldn't they?'

'It said . . .' Nancy licked her lips, not knowing if what she was going to say would be well-received. 'It said they picked up wounded German soldiers too and brought them back to our lines. Piggy-backing them when they hadn't got enough stretchers.'

'They'd be treated, of course,' Bert said, 'but they'd be prisoners of war then.'

Howard sighed and shook his head almost in disbelief. 'Yes, it was strange to see them helping each other even though only hours before they'd been trying to kill one another. Our soldiers were handing them drinks and cigarettes and then inspecting their papers and making notes.'

'Do you think that would be so that the authorities could let the other side know who'd been taken prisoner?'

'I expect so, Gran,' Nancy said. 'It looked as if the wounded were attended to pretty quickly. I think the first-aid post must have been quite near the front line.'

'That's comforting to know,' Agnes murmured.

'There were some awful sights,' Nancy went on. 'Men advancing over ground where the dead still lay and everywhere was just being laid waste. A whole village had been obliterated and trees were just bare stumps. It'll take years for the land to recover.'

'But the soldiers still looked happy,' Jessie said, almost in disbelief. 'They were smiling and waving at the camera.'

'Especially when the mail arrived,' Nancy added, smiling.

'Yes, it obviously means a lot to them. We must keep writing every week. I know how happy it makes me to receive one of Andrew's letters.'

Nancy nodded but could not trust herself to speak now. There was still no word from Max. Now she had seen the conditions of life at the Front, she was even more worried for his safety.

Forty-two

As the days went by more telegrams were received by their neighbours and throughout the city as the soldiers of the City Battalion were reported wounded or killed.

'I know it sounds a wonderful idea for friends and neighbours to go to war together, to fight side by side,' Howard said, 'to support and encourage each other, but did anyone stop to think what would happen when they went into battle and were killed or maimed at the same time?'

'I don't think they can have,' Bert said. 'It's what Ma said early on in the war when the idea was first suggested.'

'Your mother's a wise woman, Bert.'

'We've lost so many, the whole city's in mourning. I bet there's hardly a street that's untouched in one way or another. It's what Nancy and her fellow post-women think and they should know.'

'And we're not the only city,' Howard added. 'There are so many places that have sent pals' battalions. Barnsley, Accrington, Hull, Grimsby . . .'

'And think of all the little villages. There must be some in the country where they've only got old men and young boys left.'

'You'd think so, wouldn't you?' Howard stood up. 'I'd best be getting home. I don't want to leave Evelyn too long when I do have the chance to be with her.'

'How's she bearing up? I thought it was incredibly brave of her to come with us to watch that film.'

'Stoic, I think the word is. She's not even crying.'

Bert sighed. 'I've heard my mother say some things are too deep for tears. Maybe this is one of them.'

Howard nodded, shook his friend's hand and left without speaking, the lump in his throat preventing him from uttering another word.

Nancy pushed her last delivery of the morning through a letterbox and turned towards the top of the street. There weren't many folk about this morning. The September day was cold and wet, but shuffling towards her was the wounded soldier she had told her family about; the one whom they thought must have what was being called shell shock.

As she neared him, she said gently, 'Good morning.'

He stopped and glanced up at her, warily at first, but then a small smile stretched his thin lips. He nodded, but whether it was in greeting or the perpetual shaking causing it, she couldn't be sure. His mouth moved as if he were trying to speak, but no sound came out. She smiled at him as he shuffled past her and continued down the road towards his home. She watched him go a short distance and then she turned away to walk back up the street.

'Oh no,' she breathed as she saw who was standing at the top of the road, obviously waiting for her. She fingered the whistle in her pocket, took a deep breath and marched towards him. As she neared him, he stood, arms akimbo, as if to bar her path.

'Morning, Grandad. No time to stop for a chat today . . .'

He grabbed her arm in a vicious grip. 'You'll listen to me, girl. Now, tell me where your grandma is, or else . . .'

'Let go! You're hurting me.'

'I'll hurt you, you little trollop.'

Nancy wriggled, but could not free herself from his grasp.

'Ah, so now where are all your clever self-defence moves, eh?'

Struggling was serving no purpose, so Nancy's fingers tightened on the whistle. Before Patrick realized what she was doing, she drew it from her pocket, put it between her lips and blew as hard as she could. The shrill sound echoed through the early morning air.

'You little –' Patrick began. His grip loosened and she pulled herself free. She stepped away from him but before she could take flight and put distance between them, she heard a blood-curdling cry from behind her and turned to see the injured solder charging towards them both as if he was carrying a rifle with a fixed bayonet. He headed straight for Patrick, cannoned into him and knocked him to the ground. Then he stood over him while he made the motion of stabbing his foe repeatedly with the bayonet he believed he was carrying. Nancy watched in horror.

'Stop, stop!' she cried, but the man didn't heed her.

She heard more footsteps and turned to see two policemen running towards them.

'It's all right, miss. You stand back. We'll deal with this.'

Nancy was only too relieved to do as they said. They hauled the soldier away and helped Patrick to stand.

'He's a bloody maniac,' Patrick spluttered. 'He should be locked up.'

'I'm not sure yet who should be locked up, sir. Now, if you'll just calm down, we'll take some statements.'

'I'm not giving no statement . . .'

'You'll do as you're asked, sir, or we'll take you to the station.'

At that moment, two more officers arrived.

'Hello, Nancy, love,' one of them, who Nancy knew to be called Ralph, greeted her. The street was on his regular beat and he and Nancy had often exchanged a word of greeting. 'Been causing trouble, have you?' he teased her, but without waiting for an answer he turned to the soldier, his tone gentle. 'Now, Tom, did the whistle bring back bad memories for you? Thought you were going over the top again, did yer? Don't worry, lad, that's all over for you. Now, let's get you back home where your lovely missus can look after you.'

'Oi, aren't you going to arrest him?' Patrick shouted.

One of the officers, who'd been first on the scene, glared at him. 'Like I said, sir, I'm not sure yet who should be arrested, if anyone, but I intend to find out.'

'I'll see Tom down the street to number eleven,'

Ralph said, 'while you sort this lot out? I know where to find him, if needs be.'

'Righto,' the first policeman said and then turned to Nancy. 'Now, lass, what's been going on?'

Nancy took a deep breath and glanced at Patrick. She didn't like telling tales on a member of her family and yet . . . She thought quickly and smiled at the policeman. 'This is my grandfather, but he's estranged from our family. He left home to live with – someone else, before I was even born. He found out I was delivering the mail on this street and has been waiting for me.'

'I only wanted to get to know my granddaughter,' Patrick said in a whining voice. 'Is that so very wrong, officer?'

'Not if that's all it was, no, but we know you, Patrick Halliday, so don't think you can pull the wool over our eyes. If we hear this lass has had any more bother from you, we'll run you in. Understood?'

'Yes, officer.' Patrick pretended meekness, but the gleam in his eyes told a different story.

They parted company and Nancy hurried back to the sorting office. She was about to ask her supervisor if she could change her delivery routes, when he forestalled her by saying, 'Nancy, sorry to ask you this, but I need to change your route. I've two off sick and one looks like being off for a while. I've got someone else who'd be able to cover your usual route. Do you mind?'

If he could have seen the relief flooding through her, her supervisor would have had his answer. 'Of course not,' she said brightly. 'When do I start?'

'Tomorrow, I'm afraid. You'd be really helping me out, Nancy love.'

'Do I report at the same time?'

'Half an hour earlier, if you can. You've further to go to get to the area.'

'I'll be here.'

That evening, Nancy told her parents and grandmother about the incident.

'Right,' Bert said decisively, 'it's high time I paid your father a visit, Flora. I'm not letting this go on any longer. I don't like him waylaying Nancy and I can't think what his motive for wanting to find your mother can be.'

'Get Howard to go with you.'

'I would, but I don't like to ask him with all the trouble he's got.'

'Bert, he'd be upset if you didn't ask him, now, wouldn't he?' Flora said. 'Just tell him what's happened and that you're going to pay my father a visit and see if he offers to go with you.'

Howard didn't hesitate when Bert told him he needed to see Patrick Halliday. 'Then I'm coming with you,' he said at once. 'It's high time this business was stopped.'

As they walked together, Bert told him about the incident with the whistle and the wounded soldier.

Howard nodded soberly. 'I expect they've been trained that hard that it was an automatic reaction even though he'd been so badly affected. It would just galvanize him into action. Poor feller. Ah, is this the street?'

'Yes, down here on the left, if I remember right, but it's been a few years since we were last here.'

'I wonder why on earth he's asking about Edith? I don't like the sound of it, Bert.'

'Neither do I,' Bert said grimly, as they approached the door to knock. 'But I'm hoping we're about to find out.'

Lily opened the door. She had altered a little in the intervening years. She had put on weight and her hair was not quite so bright. 'Well, well, well, and to what do we owe this pleasure?'

'We've come to see Mr Halliday,' Bert said.

Lily raised her eyebrows. 'Then you'd best come in.'

She left the door open for them to enter and led the way into the kitchen. 'You've got visitors, Patrick.'

He was sitting near the range and got up as soon as the two men entered the room. 'Now, look, I don't want no trouble. I just wanted to know where Edith is living, that's all. There was no need for the silly little cow to blow her whistle and get the law.'

'You manhandled her,' Bert snapped. 'I won't have you touching our Nancy. You hear me? And why do you want to know where your wife is after all this time?'

Patrick glanced briefly towards Lily. 'Because I want a divorce, that's why.'

Lily's mouth dropped open and she stared at him for a moment before crossing the room to put her arms around his neck and plant a kiss on his cheek. 'Oh Patrick.'

'No sloppy stuff, Lil,' he muttered, embarrassed at her display of affection.

'Then why didn't you just say that to Nancy instead of scaring the girl half to death?' Howard said, not prepared to let Patrick off so lightly. He glanced at Bert before adding, 'Besides, I'm not so sure I believe you. Why now? Why after all this time? A divorce can be very expensive for the likes of us.'

Patrick shuffled his feet. 'Lil's stuck by me through thick and thin and she deserves a ring on her finger, that's why, an' I've been saving up for years.'

The two young men stared at Lil, wondering why on earth she had indeed stood by him. Perhaps, as the years took their toll, Patrick Halliday was her last chance, her only chance.

'Well, I hope you know what you're doing, Lil,' Bert said.

'I do, and thanks for your concern. I 'preciate it.' Then she gave a saucy smirk. 'But I know how to handle him.'

As they turned to leave, Patrick said, 'So you'll see Edith for me, will you?'

'Certainly,' Bert said. 'We'd be glad to.'

As they walked home, Howard said, 'He says he's been saving up for years, but has he got a job now? Since he came out of prison?'

'I heard he's working as a cellarman and general dogsbody at the pub down the road from us. Where Lily still works. He couldn't get his old job back as foreman at Rowleys. The men would no longer have respected him, for one thing.'

'Ah, I didn't know that. It's not a place I go now.'

'Me neither.' The two men grinned at each other.
'Still, there's one thing,' Bert added.
'What's that?'
'Flora's mam will be finally – and legally – free of him.'

Forty-three

Nancy woke with a start. It was still the middle of the night, or rather early morning, she guessed, but something had disturbed her sleep. She listened and then she heard it. A low, continuous drone. She threw back the covers and felt for her dressing gown. As she opened her bedroom door, her father was halfway down the stairs.

'Help your mother with Robbie and get downstairs quickly. I'll wake Ma.'

'What is it, Dad?'

'I reckon it's a Zepp raid. I must warn Howard . . .'

By the time Bert had returned from across the road, the rest of his family, including a sleepy Robbie, had gathered in the kitchen. 'Howard says we're to go across there. They turned their cellar into a bedroom for the boys. We'll all be more comfortable there. Flora, bring extra blankets and candles. Nancy, get anything you might need for Robbie ready. Ma, put your warmest clothes on. And be as quick as you can, all of you.'

Ten minutes later, they were hurrying across the road, Bert carrying a sleepy Robbie. Howard was waiting for them and ushered them down the steps into the cellar.

'It's sounding rather close now and I've heard bombs dropping,' he said. 'I reckon they're falling on Burngreave.'

'Oh no,' Jessie said. 'That's on my rounds.'

They settled down, sitting on the two single beds and on the floor on rugs and blankets. 'You all right, Mrs Weston?' Howard asked Agnes. 'Sorry it's a bit of a squash.'

'I'm fine, thanks. Don't you worry about me. It's good of you to shelter us. How many bombs d'you think have dropped already?'

'To be honest, I haven't been counting.'

'Stanley would have been counting if he'd been here,' Evelyn murmured. 'He loved anything to do with sums.'

'There've been a few,' Bert muttered, glancing worriedly up at the ceiling. He hoped the house wouldn't get a direct hit because even being in the cellar wouldn't save them if it did.

Howard was still listening intently. 'I think it's moving away.'

The falling bombs did indeed sound to be further away now.

'Perhaps we could –' Flora began, but Bert said sharply, 'You stay right where you are. It might come back again.'

They waited until there had been no more sounds for half an hour.

'Me and Bert will go out and see if it's safe for you all to come out,' Howard said. 'Stay here until we come back.'

They were only gone for ten minutes before

Howard returned to say that it seemed all right. 'There's a lot of smoke over Burngreave way, but there's no damage in our street.'

'Oh dear,' Jessie said as she climbed up into the early morning light. 'I hope there's been no fatalities. Nancy, we'd better get going. We're late already.'

'I'll just have a quick wash and get into my uniform. I'll see you in about ten minutes.'

'Do be careful, girls,' Flora warned, ''specially you, Jessie, if you're going anywhere near where the bombs have fallen.'

Jessie kissed her cheek. 'I will, Aunty Flora. Don't worry. I expect our supervisor will give us instructions.'

When the girls returned home after their shift, they were both in tears.

'Oh Mam, it was awful,' Nancy said shakily. 'We still had to go to the streets where the bombs had fallen. Rescuers were digging in the rubble and we saw them pulling people out. Some were still alive, but – but there were dead bodies, Mam. Even little children. It was heartbreaking. And to think poor Max and all our other boys have to see that sort of thing every day.'

Later that week, Bert came home with the news that there had been twenty-eight people who had died as a result of the bombing that September night and several more who had been injured.

'Most of them are to be buried in Burngreave cemetery,' he said. 'One of the chaps who works in our factory lost his life. I shall go to his funeral if I can find out when it is.'

Nancy wrote to Max at once; she was afraid he would hear reports of the bombing of their city.

'That Sam Norton he's pally with will no doubt hear,' she said to Flora. 'I must let him know we're all right.'

Christmas 1916 was a subdued affair. The whole city, indeed the whole nation, were in mourning after the colossal losses of the Somme offensive. The Bonsors and the Westons spent the day together, but even though Warren and Stanley came home on a forty-eight-hours' leave, the families were further disheartened when Warren told them that they were likely to be sent to France in the New Year. They'd been lucky enough to get leave over Christmas but everyone realized without the words being spoken that it could be their last one before being sent overseas.

'We'll write,' they both said. 'We promise.'

'The house feels *really* empty now,' Evelyn said as the families gathered on New Year's Eve. 'Me, Bert and Jessie are rattling around in it with all the lads gone now. And one who will never come back. My poor Victor. Oh Flora, I've always tried to be so strong for everyone but – but this is killing me. And now my two babies will be going. When is it all going to end?'

'Oh Evelyn, I only wish I knew,' Flora said, putting her arms around her friend and holding her close.

David Lloyd George became Prime Minister in December 1916 and as if the last few years hadn't been bad enough, the dawn of 1917 seemed to threaten even more tumultuous events.

'I don't envy him his job,' Bert said. 'He's got a lot to deal with.'

'Rumours at work have it that there was a lot of skulduggery among the politicians to get rid of Asquith.'

'I wouldn't doubt it for a minute, but they say that Lloyd George will pursue the war much more vigorously than it has been.'

'Mm,' Howard mused. 'Not sure whether that'd be a good thing or not.'

'It might bring it to an end more quickly.'

'Aye, but at what cost to our lads, eh? Answer me that.'

But Bert had no answer. Instead, he said, 'There's a lot of unrest in Russia. I wouldn't be surprised at them pulling out of the war.'

'We'd be in big trouble if they did. They're our mightiest ally at present,' Howard grimaced. 'If only America would come into the war, we'd be all right then.'

'Do you think they ever will?'

Howard shrugged. 'I really don't know.'

There was worse news to come from Russia. In March, the Tsar abdicated after months of internal turmoil. The Russian offensive on the German front had cost a vast number of casualties and the people were clamouring for peace, but their voices went unheeded. There was starvation through the country and revolution seemed inevitable.

'How dreadful,' Evelyn said when she heard. 'The war is bad enough without having civil unrest too.'

'We've got unrest here at home too,' Howard said.

'In Ireland. I don't know how all that is going to end either.'

In April, Howard got his wish when America entered the war but at the same time, they heard that the City Battalion was engaged in a battle at a place called Vimy Ridge where the Canadians were heavily involved.

Max had written faithfully every week, but suddenly his letters ceased. No one – not even Nancy – had a letter from him for over a month.

The missing letters from Max arrived all at once, on the same day and on the same delivery; four for Evelyn and six for Nancy.

I haven't received any letters from you for three weeks, Max wrote, *but the mail has been dreadful just recently. No one seems to know why. I hope you are all well and that there haven't been any more Zeppelin raids.*

Nancy wrote back at once: *We haven't been getting your letters either and we have all been so desperately worried, especially since Warren and Stanley both write regularly now and we've been getting theirs. We are all so relieved to hear from you . . .*

Max's next letter was full of concern for his two younger brothers: *Have you any idea where they are? I wish they'd been able to join the Sheffield Battalion. I could have kept an eye on them . . .*

In June, the newspapers reported that the first Americans had landed in France to a rapturous welcome.

'Better late than never, I suppose,' Howard said, with a wry laugh.

'Actually, I don't blame them,' Bert countered. 'Why get drawn into a war if you don't have to? I just wish our country hadn't been tied up in alliances and obliged to get involved.'

Bert and Howard often had a debate. It never got heated and they never fell out, but neither held back on voicing their opinions which were sometimes not quite the same.

'I'm not sure the motive was as altruistic – I think I've got the right word – as it sounds on the surface,' Howard said.

'How do you mean?'

'Well, going to help another country. Just think about it. Look at your map for a start.'

Bert frowned, then shrugged his shoulders and reached for the map from the shelf. When he'd spread it on the table, he said, 'So?'

'If the Kaiser overran the whole of France, then just look how close he'd be to Britain. Just a hop across the Channel – a mere twenty miles or so. And do you really think he'd have stopped there? The south coast of England would look very enticing to a power-hungry man like him. Don't forget too, that he is cousin to our King. He was Queen Victoria's grandson too, just the same relationship to her as George V. Wilhelm might even think – no, believe – that he has a right to rule Britain.'

'Mm, I see what you mean,' Bert murmured, looking at the tiny stretch of water on the map between Dover and Calais. 'So much for happy families, then?'

'Exactly. It's a pity they can't settle their differences another way. An old-fashioned duel or something, without having to involve millions of innocent young men.'

'Mind you, there is a bit of good news closer to home,' Bert said with a grin. 'Flora's mam has got her divorce. You should have seen her face when she came round to show us the papers. "I'm free," she said. "I'm really free at last."'

'Now that is good news. I'm very pleased for her.'

Far from anything being settled, the war news was even graver by August. A battle had begun near Ypres, the third that the city had suffered.

'Is Max there, Nancy? Has he said anything to you?' Evelyn asked. 'He never tells us where he is at the time. Sometimes he'll tell us afterwards, but not always even then. Doesn't want us to worry, I suppose. Doesn't he realize we're *constantly* anxious?'

Nancy bit her lip. Max never said outright where he was when there was a battle raging, but he did occasionally give Nancy a hint. Aloud she said, 'Oh Aunty Evelyn, he's not allowed to say where they are at the time. He can tell us afterwards, like the newspapers do, but everything has to be kept so secret before they launch an offensive to try to surprise the enemy, I suppose.'

'Not much of a surprise, I'd have thought,' Evelyn said bitterly, 'when they're lined up opposite each other in their trenches. Still, I do understand what you're saying, Nancy, m'love. But let me know if he gives you any hints, won't you?' Nancy felt Evelyn's shrewd glance rest on her for a moment and wondered if she guessed that Max often told Nancy more than he told his parents. 'He doesn't seem to realize,' Evelyn added, 'that the not knowing is harder to bear than knowing where he is, even if he's in a dangerous area.'

The next time Nancy wrote to Max, she told him what had passed between her and his mother.

I really think they'd rather know the truth. Both your parents are strong. Your mam and mine are always scouring the casualty lists and searching for pictures of local lads to see if they know anyone. And sadly, they find them. Two of your school friends were reported killed last week, your mam told us, and they're not the first. I learned a saying at school when we had to read Macbeth. *'Present fears are less than horrible imaginings'. I think it's very true and especially in this case. We read all sorts in the paper about the battles that are taking place – too much probably – and imagine you're there. And the ironic thing is, you're probably not!*

In his reply, Max teased her, trying to keep the tone of his letter light: *Fancy you quoting Shakespeare. So education wasn't wasted on you, then.*

Writing back, she ribbed him in return: *Nor on you, it seems, because I didn't say it was Shakespeare!*

Max still didn't tell either of them exactly where he was, but news came from Warren that he and Stanley were both heading for the Front.

Forty-four

'Have you seen the reports in the papers?' Howard said, as he threw a copy of one of the previous day's national newspapers onto the table in the Westons' kitchen with a gesture of disgust. 'The conditions near Ypres are appalling. Evidently, the city is in ruins and now the weather is atrocious. They've had double the average rainfall and the battlefield is a quagmire. And look at this photograph Max has sent us. His pal Sam something – the journalist on our *Telegraph* – took it, but he let Max have a copy to send to us. It's a picture of seven men – seven, mind you – carrying a wounded comrade on a stretcher and they're knee deep in mud. And do you know when it was taken?'

Bert shook his head.

'The first of August. You'd think it was November by the weather, wouldn't you? This war is getting ridiculous. That battle is going to go on for months in those conditions. How can either side move forward? If that's where Warren and Stanley are now, then God help them.'

Howard sat down opposite Bert and dropped his head into his hands, his anger draining away but leaving a terrible fear for all his sons. There was nothing his friend could think of to say to comfort him. And to make matters worse through the weeks of September, there were no letters from Max. And then, late one Saturday at the beginning of October, there was a soft knock on the back door of the Westons' home. Normally because of getting up early to do her postal round, Nancy would have been in bed, but on Saturday nights she stayed up a little longer.

A tall, broad figure, blocking out the moonlight, stood there. She recognized him at once.

'Oh,' she breathed. 'Max!' She stepped towards him, put her arms around his waist and rested her face against his chest. 'You're safe.' His arms came around her and he held her close and rested his cheek against her hair. He didn't speak; he couldn't. He just held her, savouring the moment. How he wanted to pour out all his feelings for her, tell her everything that was in his heart. But he couldn't. The time was not right. There was a war to win and he was still a part of it.

At last, they drew apart and Nancy tried to pull him inside but he resisted. 'No . . .' His voice sounded raspy, quite unlike his normal rich tones. 'I won't come in tonight, but I just wanted to let you know I am home on leave for two weeks. I'll see you tomorrow.' He leaned forward to kiss her forehead and then he was gone.

Slowly, Nancy closed the door and went back into the kitchen in a daze.

'Who was that at the door?' Flora asked.

'Oh so, I didn't dream it, then?' Nancy said.

'Whatever do you mean? Who was it?'

'It was Max.'

'Max!' Her parents exclaimed together.

Bert struggled out of his chair, 'Then tell him to come in. I know it's late, but he must come in.'

'He's gone. He says he'll see us tomorrow. He's got two weeks' leave so there's plenty of time.'

Her words were hollow; there was never enough time for her to be with Max. She knew now that she wanted him beside her always.

He came across the road about mid-morning the following day. Flora welcomed him with open arms, Agnes hugged him and Bert shook his hand vigorously.

'We're so glad to see you,' Flora said. 'We haven't been getting your letters again just recently.'

'No; Mam said.'

'What's the matter with your voice?' Bert asked.

Max tried to clear his throat but it made little difference.

'Have you had a bad cold?' Flora asked in a concerned tone. 'It's hardly surprising with all that wet weather we've read about in the papers.'

Max shook his head. 'No, no. The battalion have been in action at Vimy Ridge . . .'

'Oh, I heard about that,' Bert said. 'That's where the Canadians were. In April, wasn't it?'

Max nodded. 'But we've been back there more recently and we got gassed.'

'*Gassed?*' his four listeners repeated in horror.

'Oh Max, no,' Nancy whispered, but there was a note of hope in her voice as she added, 'So are you home for good? Are you out of the war?'

Max shook his head. ''Fraid not. I've been given a fortnight's leave, but I have to see a military doctor here and then, if he pronounces me fit enough, which he will, I must return.'

'Isn't there any way . . .?' Flora began but Max shook his head.

'There are rumours,' he said, 'that the Sheffield City Battalion is to be disbanded before long. We've lost so many men that we've been seriously weakened and the heart has gone out of the battalion. Though those of us who are left fight on bravely and never shirk our duty, the character and camaraderie is not the same now as when we started. I think we'll be transferred to another battalion, possibly the Barnsley Pals. I shall certainly try for that if I can. I want to be with my brothers. I'd like to try to keep my eye on them.' He smiled ruefully. 'Mind you, I'm not even sure what battalion they're with now. They'll still be with the York and Lancaster Regiment, but sometimes lads get moved to another battalion where they're needed.'

'You shouldn't take on so much responsibility, Max,' Bert said gently. 'I know you felt Victor's death keenly, but you shouldn't blame yourself.'

'My head tells me that, Mr Weston, but my heart tells me differently. If only I'd been with him . . .'

Despite his ordeal, Max was surprisingly well in himself and over the next ten days, he and Nancy spent every evening together and some of the early mornings too, for Max insisted on accompanying her on her rounds.

'You really ought to be resting while you're home, not tramping the streets with me.'

'Nancy love, it's a joy to be back home, walking the streets of our city and away from the constant sound of shelling. And,' he added, greatly daring, 'I want to spend time with you. One day – but it won't be for a while, I'm afraid – I want to make good my promise to take you dancing in Blackpool.'

Playfully, trying to lighten the sadness of their imminent parting, Nancy tapped his chest and said, 'I shall keep you to that promise.' But she could not hold back the fear for long. 'I wish you could stay at home for good. You've done your bit – more than your bit – surely.'

'I want to see it through, Nancy. I want to know that we have won and have saved our beautiful country from invasion. Despite the huge loss of life, the morale is still quite good. We all know we have to win. We just have to. And I know your father's right when he said I shouldn't feel responsible for my brothers, but I just want to be with them if I can. Perhaps we could see this thing through and all come home together.'

Max's wish was thwarted in the cruellest of ways. Three days before he was due to return to duty, two telegrams arrived at once. Luckily, he was at home with his mother when she received them. He found Evelyn sitting at the kitchen table, just staring down at them in her hands. She hadn't even opened them.

Max squatted down in front of her. 'Come on,

Mam, let's see what they say. It might not be – the worst.'

'It is. I know it is. And there's two. That must mean it's both of them.'

Max eased the envelopes from her fingers and tore them open. First one and then the other informed their parents that both Warren and Stanley had died on the same day, 9 October.

And still, Evelyn did not cry.

Max ran across the road to fetch Flora to stay with his mother while he went to the office where his father worked to ask him to come home. By evening the two families were together in the Bonsors' house. Only Agnes had stayed behind to put Robbie to bed.

'There'll be a letter following from their commanding officer, but when I get back' – even Max, big and brave and strong as he was, was having difficulty in holding back the tears – 'I'll find out more and let you know.'

'I want to know where they're buried,' Evelyn said quietly. 'One day, I'll go to see them. And Victor too.'

'Of course, Mam,' was all Max said, but later, as he lingered in the street with Nancy, he said, 'I should have been there. I should have been with them – looking after them.'

'Dear Max, you couldn't have done anything. You couldn't have saved them. And if you had been there . . .' she hesitated a moment and her voice was shaking as she added, 'you'd probably be lying beside them now.'

Max was quiet for a moment before he said, 'I hope they have been able to bury them properly. So many are without a known grave or they're buried as an unknown soldier because they had no identification on them and no one knew who they were.'

'That's dreadfully sad. Find out what you can, Max, and please, please take care of yourself.'

'Yes, I will. Poor Mam has lost three of her sons now. She doesn't need to lose any more.'

'It's more than that. You're – you're her firstborn. You're very special . . .' She touched his cheek. 'To all of us.'

He held her hand against his cheek for a long moment, then leaned forward and kissed her forehead. Without another word, he turned and crossed the road. She watched him go, her heart heavy with sadness at the grief he and the rest of his family were feeling. She and the rest of her family mourned alongside them.

Nancy looked for him the following morning, but he was not waiting in the road for her. She was not surprised; his parents needed him so it was not until she returned at the end of her shift that she heard Max had already left.

'He wanted to get back to find out what actually happened to his brothers,' Howard told them. 'He's promised to write as soon as he can. He said to say "goodbye" to all of you.'

Nancy nodded, not trusting herself to speak for the huge lump in her throat. She was more terrified than ever now that something would happen to Max too. And of Lee, there was still only spasmodic news.

*

Max's letters to his parents and a separate one to Nancy arrived the following week.

> . . . *They were killed together, fighting shoulder to shoulder and, for once, it is true to say that they died instantly and did not suffer. So many relatives are told this when it's not true, but I promise you I have asked so many questions and do believe what I'm being told. They are to be buried side by side in a cemetery not far from where they fell. It's called Tyne Cot.*

Forty-five

The Third Battle of Ypres in which Warren and Stanley had fallen went on until the beginning of November. The conditions in which the battle had been fought had been appalling. Many had died, not from an enemy bullet or exploding shell, but from falling into the mud.

The Bonsors and the Westons met over Christmas again but no one felt like merrymaking.

'We thought you might have gone to see Mary Ellen this year,' Evelyn said, forcing a smile when she and Flora met on the morning of the 27th for elevenses in the Bonsors' home after the menfolk and Jessie and Nancy had all gone back to work. 'We weren't very good company, I'm afraid.'

'Oh Evelyn, we wouldn't have left you at a time like this.'

For a moment Evelyn's face crumpled at Flora's kind words, but then she took a deep breath and forced a smile. 'You're good friends. The very best.'

'And we're family now, don't forget.'

'I don't and I also never forget how you tried to protect our family at that time.'

Flora waved her hand dismissively. 'It's all worked out for the best.' She paused for a moment before

403

saying, 'Have you heard from Lee? Does he – does he know about Warren and Stanley?'

'Yes, we have,' Evelyn said. 'We had a letter just before Christmas. He'd received our letters, but he'd been at sea for a while. He was ashore when he wrote although I expect he's back aboard a ship somewhere now. Has Nancy heard from him?'

'He sent a little toy for Robbie for Christmas,' Flora said. 'And a little sailor suit. It fits perfectly. It was – very good of him.'

They sat in silence until Flora said, 'I really must go. I can't leave Ma on her own too long with Robbie. He's a lovable little boy, but he's so mischievous. He's into everything.'

'Just like his father,' Evelyn murmured. 'I can't believe he'll be four in February. We must have a little party for him, Flora. He shouldn't suffer just because of the grief we're feeling. He's too young to understand.'

'He's a bright child and forward for his age. I was wondering if it would be a good idea to see if the school will take him in September. It'd be a bit early, I know, but it might be worth asking. They can only say "no". I'll talk it over with Bert and perhaps you and Howard could consider it. He plays out with the two little boys from down the street but it's such a job keeping him occupied when the weather's bad.'

'It's good of you to involve us,' Evelyn said.

'He's your grandchild as much as ours. It's only fair.'

'By rights, it's Lee who should be involved.'

Flora sighed, but all she said was, 'Ah well.'

*

A letter from Max to Nancy early in the New Year of 1918 told her that he was to be attached to the Barnsley Pals. As he had forecast, the Sheffield City Battalion was being disbanded. *It's a shame we couldn't see it through to the end as a battalion but I can see the reason for it. It's ironic, isn't it, that this is where I wanted to be with Warren and Stanley, but I'm too late?*

Nancy shuddered as she read his final words. How poignant they were. She felt deeply for him.

Howard and Bert still met every night at one or other of their houses to peruse the newspapers and to look at the map.

'Have you heard?' Howard said, almost before he had stepped across the threshold of Bert's home one evening in March. 'Russia has signed a peace treaty, but the papers are saying it's the most humiliating capitulation in history.'

Bert took the paper from his friend's hands and read the piece for himself. 'My God! They don't want much, do they?' he said sarcastically. 'They're demanding lands, about half its industry and nearly all the coal mines. This will anger the Allies, but Russia has got so much unrest in their country, I suppose they haven't much choice when they're in the middle of a revolution.'

'But you know what this will do, Bert, don't you? It'll release a lot of soldiers from the Russian front that will now be turned on us.'

'I hadn't thought of that, but you're right. Have you heard what's happened to the Russian royal family?'

'No more since it was in the papers last autumn that they'd been sent to Siberia.'

'Poor devils,' Bert muttered.

A few days later, Jessie came running across the street. She burst in through the back door of the Westons' home, beaming and waving a letter. 'He's coming home. He's been wounded but not too badly, though he'll be out of the war. He won't have to go back.'

Nancy's heart felt as if it had skipped a beat and tears of thankfulness ran down her face. 'Oh, thank God,' she whispered, but at Jessie's next words her joy was shattered.

'He says we'll be married as soon as he's well enough. He's not going to let his mother stand in our way any longer.'

'Andrew? Your – your letter's from Andrew?'

Jessie stared at her and then colour flooded her face. 'Oh Nancy, I'm so sorry. You – you thought I meant Max, didn't you?'

Nancy forced a smile. 'For a moment, yes, I did.'

Jessie started to apologize again, but Nancy hugged her and said, 'I'm so pleased for you, darling Jessie. I'm glad he's safe.'

'Max will come home too. I know he will. This war can't go on much longer, surely.'

But Jessie's words were said more in hope than certainty and the news was no better for the Allies through March and into April. As Howard had predicted, with a significant number of its troops released from the Eastern Front, the German Army now turned its full fury on the Western Front.

On 9 April, Germany launched a Spring Offensive with the Battle of Lys near Armentieres mainly against the British.

'You know what I think they're trying to do,' Bert said.

'Well, overrun us, but what in particular?'

'Get control of the Channel ports that supply our army with everything it needs; food, equipment, everything. They'll try to starve us into defeat.'

At the end of May, the enemy began another Spring Offensive, this time against the French.

'Now they're trying to split the British and French forces before the American troops arrive in greater numbers,' was Bert's opinion.

'Yes, but have you seen that the Americans have won their first major action?'

'I did,' Howard said. 'A bit of good news for a change, but the rest of it looks like a disaster to me. We could be going to lose this war, you know.'

'Never,' Bert said stoutly.

Letters came spasmodically from Max now, several arriving at once and then two or three weeks would pass before another batch arrived. Nancy wrote faithfully every week but she had no idea whether they reached him until in one of his letters he said: *I hadn't heard from you for three weeks and then four letters arrived together. I expect it is much the same at your end. I'm sorry I can't tell you where I am, but keep reading the newspapers . . .*

'That must be a hint to tell us that he's in the thick of it,' Nancy said when, during an evening in early

June, she sat with her father and Howard reading the newspapers and scouring the map. 'Where do you think that might be, Dad?'

'I've got a newspaper dated the third of June,' Howard said. 'I know that's two days' old, but I don't think the news will have changed much since then. There's a piece in here from a special correspondent in Paris who says that the battle is not diminishing and, although it's intense and bitter, the French reinforcements are beginning to make themselves felt.'

'But where is this battle exactly?' Nancy asked.

'It says here that their Front – that'll mean the French – forms a salient . . .' He glanced up. 'What's a salient?'

There was silence from the other two until Nancy jumped up and reached for a dictionary.

'In military terms it's a bulge that projects into enemy territory,' Nancy said.

'Ah, right,' Howard said and then went on, 'he says their Front now forms a salient into enemy lines from Montdidier and Noyon to Villers Cotterets, Soissons and Chateau Thierry.' Howard glanced up again. 'Who's Ludendorff?'

'The general in charge of the German forces, I think. Why?'

'This journalist thinks he's trying to push back against this salient so that he can create a base to launch his attack on Paris.'

'How far are they from Paris?'

Bert tried to measure it on the map. 'About eighty miles, I reckon.'

'That's quite a long way in battle terms. I mean,

some battles have been over a few yards of ground. Let's hope he doesn't make it.'

'I just wish we knew exactly where Max is,' Howard murmured.

'Can we find out where the Barnsley Pals are now?' Nancy asked.

Howard wrinkled his forehead. 'We could try, I suppose.'

Soon, Howard was saying, 'I don't know how the Germans are managing to fight on such a long front. The papers reckon it's over three hundred miles. You'd think their army would be weakened, wouldn't you?'

All Bert could say was: 'They're able because they're not having to keep the Russians at bay any more so now they can concentrate solely on France.'

But just as the Germans seemed to have everything going their way, their attempt to seize railway lines was foiled by the French. During four days in July a battle, known as the Battle of Soissons, was fought between the French, with British and American assistance, and the German armies. The objective was to cut off the supply routes for the German forces, thus forcing the Germans onto the defensive. They gradually began to withdraw and when, early in August, the Allies went into action near Amiens, the resistance collapsed. General Ludendorff, the papers reported, was heard to say that 8 August was a 'black day for Germany'.

'They can't hold out for much longer, surely,' Bert said as they read at the end of September that the

Allies were sweeping all before them along the whole of the Western Front.

'You'd think not, but they're a stubborn lot,' Howard said, his mind still on why they had, after several weeks, still heard nothing from Max. 'Evelyn is convinced he's been killed,' he confided in Bert, 'and is one of the thousands who are missing and will probably never be identified.'

'Don't give up hope, Howard. You haven't heard anything officially, have you?'

'No, but it must be chaos out there.'

'Just wait, Howard.'

Forty-six

On a warm evening in September, when several of the neighbours had congregated in the street, Bert asked Howard, 'Have you heard from Max yet?'

'No, we haven't. We're both worried sick. What about Nancy? I presume she hasn't heard either or else she would have let us know?'

'I'm sure she would, but let's ask her. She's upstairs.'

'Don't disturb her, Bert, if she's in bed. She has to get up very early every morning, doesn't she?'

'I'll just creep up and see if she's still awake.'

Moments later, he returned with Nancy following him in her dressing gown.

'I really shouldn't come out here not properly dressed,' she chuckled. 'Gran will tell me off.' But still she crossed the street towards Howard.

'Have you heard from Max?' she asked at once.

He shook his head. 'No, that's what I wanted to ask you.'

'No, I haven't heard for several weeks now,' she said, the fear growing like a living thing in the pit of her stomach. 'And he's written faithfully right through the war. Oh, I know letters used to be late

411

arriving sometimes and then we'd get a batch together, but they were dated every week. He – he never missed writing even if they were delayed reaching us.'

'Then maybe that's what's happening again now,' Bert put in reasonably. 'Perhaps you'll both get a stack of them together.'

She knew her father was right, but somehow, this time, his words failed to comfort her and as the weeks went by without any news from Max, her anxiety grew. She tried to hide it from her family and from the Bonsors too, but she knew that they were just as worried as she was.

While the whole country dared to begin to hope that the end of the war might be in sight, the Bonsor and Weston families were still worried sick. As the weeks had lengthened into months, still neither of them had heard from Max.

'He's gone, I know he has.' Evelyn would not be comforted and, although she too was eaten up with anxiety, Nancy still clung to the hope that somewhere Max was still alive.

At the beginning of October, Howard almost ran across the road, waving the local newspaper. 'The Germans have asked for an armistice so that peace negotiations can begin.'

Word soon spread and the neighbours gathered in the street, chatting excitedly. 'It'll end soon now,' they all agreed. 'It must.'

Only Evelyn stood alone in the window of her front room, looking out on the excited crowd.

'It's not over yet,' she whispered to herself.

With cruel irony after the moments of joyous euphoria and hope, the very next morning the postwoman on their street approached the Bonsor house with her heart beating fast. In her hand she held a telegram and this was not the first one she had delivered here. She remembered that last year there had been two to this address in the same delivery. Later, she had found out that two brothers had been killed fighting side by side. And now, here was another. She knocked on the front door and her knees trembled as she waited. She wasn't usually so nervous – this was something they'd all had to get used to when they'd signed up to deliver the city's mail – but this was different. Jessie Bonsor was a fellow postwoman and Nancy, too, lived just across the street. She jumped when the door opened and for a moment she stared into the calm face in front of her. Silently, she handed over the telegram and hurried away before she could hear the woman break into wails of anguish. But Evelyn merely stepped out into the street, pulled the door shut behind her and crossed the street to her friend's house.

She walked slowly in through the back door and sat at the kitchen table. Flora came in from the scullery, drying her hands on a towel to see Evelyn sitting quietly there, her arms resting on the table, the still-unopened telegram between her fingers.

'Oh Evelyn, no,' Flora whispered, sinking into a

chair. The two women stared at each other. 'What – what does it say?'

'I – I haven't opened it yet, but I know what it says. Flora. I know only too well what it says.'

'No, you don't,' Flora said firmly. 'Do you want me to open it?'

Evelyn nodded and passed it across the table. Flora tore it open and read it swiftly. She looked up. 'It's Max, but it says he's missing, Evelyn. Missing. Not killed or even wounded, but missing. Here, see for yourself.'

Her movements slow, as if in a trance, Evelyn reached out and took back the piece of paper. *Deeply regret to inform you that Pte Max Bonsor of the 13th Battalion Yorks and Lancaster Regiment has been posted missing. The Army Council express their sympathy.*

Before either woman could move, the back door rattled and Nancy came into the kitchen.

'Hello, Aunty Evelyn, what are . . .?' She stopped as she saw the telegram on the table. The colour drained from her face and her eyes rolled. Before Flora could reach her, Nancy slipped to the floor. She came round to see her mother bending over her and holding smelling salts under her nose. She coughed and tried to sit up.

'Lie there for a minute, love,' Flora said.

After a few moments, both Flora and Evelyn helped Nancy to her feet and guided her to a chair near the range. 'What – what . . .?'

'Just sit still.'

'What's happened?'

'It's Max,' Evelyn said in a flat, monotone voice. 'He's been posted missing.'

Nancy leaned her head against the chair and tears ran down her cheeks. 'Oh no, no. Not Max. Please, not Max.'

The days following the dreadful news were long and lonely. There was nothing to look forward to now; nothing to hope for. Nancy dragged herself to work every day, determined not to be destroyed by the same news that a great many households in the city had already received. Life would never be the same for any of them but somehow, they had to carry on. Somehow, they must go on living even if only for the children.

Robbie, Nancy thought, clinging to her son's name like a lifeline. I must carry on for Robbie's sake. But if only . . . She pushed the thought aside. She mustn't let that thought keep coming into her head. But it refused to be denied. If only Robbie had been Max's son. But the little boy still had the same familial blood in his veins, she told herself, and Max had been very fond of him. She'd watched him often, ever since Robbie had been tiny, holding him, playing with him. He'd been more of a father to him than ever Lee had been or ever would be. He'd already said in one of his letters that when all 'this nonsense' was over he looked forward to taking his nephew on a trip to the seaside and showing him how to build a sandcastle. It would have been Max who taught him to swim, to ride a bike; Max, who would have played footie in the street with him and taken him to his first football match. But now, none of that would ever happen. Max would never take her dancing and, at that thought, the tears would flow.

Evelyn had been right. Negotiations to end the conflict dragged on for another month because reparations, which the winning side demanded must be paid by the losing side, could not be agreed upon. The war wasn't finally over until a date in November had been decided upon. The eleventh hour of the eleventh day of the eleventh month. And then it was really over and there were riotous celebrations throughout the country and yet, in many streets, there was no revelry. Too many loved ones would never come back. Too many names would be inscribed on the memorials already being planned.

On a cold and wet November Saturday afternoon, Nancy turned into her street at the end of her morning shift. The days since the telegram had arrived at the Bonsors' home had been filled with despair for them all.

Hearing excited voices, she looked up to see several of the neighbours congregating in the street, especially outside the Bonsors' home. She quickened her foot-steps as she spotted her mother and father talking to Howard and Evelyn. Agnes was there too, holding tightly on to Robbie's hand, though he was wriggling to be let free to run about.

'What is it? What's happening?' Nancy asked.

'We don't know exactly,' Bert said, 'but there's an air of – I don't know – expectation somehow. There's a rumour that a train has arrived loaded with soldiers returning from France.'

'Wouldn't we have heard if – if . . .' Nancy's voice trailed away as she spotted a group of soldiers turning into their street. One or two peeled away from the rest as they reached their own homes, leaving just two still marching down the slope towards where the group of neighbours waited. One was a soldier – tall and broad – dressed in the khaki uniform, the other was dressed in naval uniform, his cap set at a jaunty angle.

'Oh! *Oh!*' Nancy breathed. She dropped her bag to the ground and threw off her postwoman's hat and then she was running, flying up the street, her arms outstretched.

The two men stopped and waited until she launched herself against one of them.

'Oh Max, you're safe! My darling Max. Don't ever leave me again. Promise me you'll never go away again.'

And then he was burying his face against her hair and hugging her so tightly that he almost squeezed the breath from her. 'Nancy, oh Nancy, my love.'

Lee watched them with a wistful smile, realizing in that moment just what he had lost. Then he gave a little nod and turned to carry on alone towards his waiting family.

Flora and Evelyn stood with their arms linked. So many emotions were coursing through both women. Joy and relief that the war was finally over and yet such deep sadness for all those who would not return.

'We must build a better world,' Evelyn murmured,

smiling through her tears. 'As a tribute to all those who have given their lives.'

But Flora didn't seem to be listening. 'She's – she's gone to *Max.*'

Evelyn nodded. 'I'm glad. He's been in love with her for years.'

'How – how do you know?'

'Because he told us.'

'*Did* he? Then – then why didn't he . . .?'

'Because he thought she wanted Lee.'

Flora's gaze went back to the young couple, who were still hugging and kissing as if they'd never stop. They were oblivious to their loving families waiting for them.

A broad smile spread across Flora's face. 'Well, that's all right then. Nancy's come to her senses at last.'

'Thank goodness,' Evelyn murmured.

The two women smiled at each other and then turned to walk up the street together to greet the two young men who had come home safely.

ACKNOWLEDGEMENTS

My love and grateful thanks to Helen Lawton and Pauline Griggs for reading and advising on the first draft. Your comments are always so very helpful.

My special thanks to my fantastic agent, Darley Anderson, who is always at the end of the phone for advice and encouragement. I wouldn't be where I am today without the wonderful support and help of you and your team.

And then, of course, there is the marvellous team at Pan Macmillan, headed by my new publisher, Lucy Brem. Thank you to each and every one of you for all the work you do.

As always, this is a work of fiction; the characters and plotline are all created from my imagination and any resemblance to real people is coincidental. However, I do like to get my background facts correct and a lot of research is always necessary. Several sources are used, but I must pay tribute to two wonderful books that have been so helpful with information on the Sheffield City Battalion in the Great War: *Sheffield City Battalion: The 12th (Service) Battalion York and Lancaster Regiment* by Ralph

Gibson and Paul Oldfield (Pen and Sword Military, 2010); *The First and the Last of the Sheffield City Battalion* by John Cornwell (Pen and Sword Military, 2019).